W9-CKR-126

Seducing Harry

Seducing Harry

An Epicurean Affair

Judith Marks-White

Ballantine Books
New York

Seducing Harry is a work of fiction.
Names, characters, places,
and incidents are the products of the
author's imagination or are used fictitiously.
Any resemblance to actual events, locales,
or persons, living or dead,
is entirely coincidental.

A Ballantine Books Trade Paperback Original

Copyright © 2006 by Judith Marks-White

All rights reserved.

Published in the United States by
Ballantine Books, an imprint of
The Random House Publishing Group,
a division of Random House, Inc.,
New York.

BALLANTINE and colophon are registered
trademarks of Random House, Inc.

LIBRARY OF CONGRESS CATALOGING-IN-PUBLICATION DATA

Marks-White, Judith.
Seducing Harry : an epicurean affair / by
Judith Marks-White.
p. cm.
ISBN 0-345-49238-2
1. Middle aged women—Fiction. 2. Married women—
Fiction. 3. Women journalists—Fiction. 4. Women
humorists—Fiction. 5. Suburban life—Fiction.
6. Gourmets—Fiction. 7. Adultery—Fiction. I. Title.

PS3613.A7659S43 2006
813'.6—dc22

Printed in the United States of America

www.ballantinebooks.com

2 4 6 8 9 7 5 3 1

Book design by Mercedes Everett

For Elizabeth,
The loveliest of daughters

"Why does man kill?
He kills for food. And not only food,
frequently there must be a beverage."

—Woody Allen

Acknowledgments

A novel is the sum total of the characters who inhabit its pages. Similarly, the people who inspire those characters are influential, each in their own way, for bringing a book to life. They entertain us with a turn of a phrase, a surprise twist, a dollop of humor, as they move the plot along the literary landscape en route to its conclusion.

To those whose help and inspiration made *Seducing Harry: An Epicurean Affair* possible, I offer my thanks.

My husband, Mark, for his unconditional love and support.

My daughter, Elizabeth, and my grandchildren, Andrew and Caroline Dent, the precious gems of my life, and Dad, Noel Dent.

The Myers clan: Judi, Aimee, and Erin, with special thanks to Roberta ("Robbie") Myers for her enthusiasm and encouragement.

My first family: Brian Rosenfeld, David Rosenfeld, Penny Rosenfeld Morris, and Lisa Lenihan.

Wendy Sherman, agent extraordinaire, for her infinite patience, brilliant instincts, and confidence in me, who brought *Harry* into the world and delivered him into the capable hands of:

Allison Dickens, my editor at Random House/Ballantine, whose microscopic eyes and "sense and sensibility" helped whip *Harry* into shape. Editorial Associates, Ingrid Powell and Becca Shapiro for their attention to the smallest details and for being part of this exciting ride.

Ann Chernow, my reader and best friend whose built-in radar detector guided me with gentle firmness through the entire process and to whom I am indebted for more reasons than can ever be counted.

June Walker Rogers, who never stopped reminding me I had a book to write.

Alice Moskowitz, for all the things you are.

Claire Hooten and David Myers, my East Hampton relatives who are a constant source of inspiration and joy.

Joseph B. O'Connell, M.D. of Westport, CT, my medical guru, whose knowledge I passed on to *Harry.*

Baker Graphics, Inc. of Westport, CT, who kept it all together.

Isabel Rose and Julie Riven for their wonderful quotes.

To all the members of my cheering section, the bright lights of my life, I offer my heartfelt thanks: Patricia Knutson and Ronald Knutson, Dr. Harold Jonas Goldfarb, Sandra Goldfarb, Judy Teichberg, Ira Teichberg, Martin West, Carole Teperow-Goldberg, Dr. Jerry Goldberg, Alina Rodescu-Pitchon, Leslie Orofino, Susan Hopper, Lynn Bernstein, Joan Stone, Lesley Rubinger, Muriel Goldberger, Dr. Barri Hammer, Mark Goad and the gang at "V" for keeping my water glass filled and table #10 available, Creagh Connors, Jane Hammerslough, Prill Boyle, Susan Hopper, Joan Gray, Michael "Spike" Fritchman, Barbara Ivler, Howard Munce, Stan Mack, Susan Champlin, Annie Taylor, Betsy Beach, and our favorite girl, Annabelle. Charles Manuel, Tom Orofino, Michael Castagna, Lucy Ullman, Rhoda Berke, Cynthia Wallace, Debra Sue Selden, Melissa Pordy-Lefkowitz, Andree Brooks and Sylvia Kronick and Murray Kronick.

The *Westport News* and most especially B. V. "Dexter" Brooks, Kevin J. Lally and Editor-in-Chief, Will Rowlands.

To my students and colleagues at Norwalk Community College, with a big hug to Gary Carlson and Linda Dempsey.

And to those great men who came before *Harry,* who live on in my heart forever: Benjamin D. Katz, Mort Rosenfeld, and Burt "Whitey" Chernow.

Menu

"The Seaport Gazette"

COLUMNS

PART ONE

Appetizer

(Whetting the Appetite)

1

"The road to good intentions is paved with hell."
—Variation on Samuel Johnson quote

Cocktails at Five

The minute I met Éclaire I wanted to bump her off. There was something about her that exuded what I detest most in a woman: perfection. She had that sleek, well-pampered look that came from years of self-indulgence. Then there was her husband, Harry, who just happened to be the leading plastic surgeon on the upper East Side—a husband who, when he wasn't removing fat from the thighs of the rich and famous, was salivating over a rack of lamb or a crème brûlée in a restaurant that was Zagat-approved and lived up to his culinary standards. No wonder Éclaire was a vision of loveliness. Harry left no laugh line untouched, no wrinkle un-Botoxed. Éclaire was a walking advertisement of Harry the Miracle Maker's masterpieces.

But I digress. Before Harry came along I was moving at my usual clip, married to Parker Harding, living in our house in the burbs, and conducting a nonorgasmic sex life that guaranteed a large dose of ennui would kick in as soon as we hit the sheets. It wasn't that Parker wasn't a good man. God knows he provided me with a lifestyle that bordered on extravagant. I was free to indulge myself on all levels. Parker asked no questions. He wanted me to be happy, and if happy meant my blowing a wad of money on incidentals, he was more than willing to comply. One might say I had it made: During daylight hours I wrote my humor columns for our local paper, *The Seaport Gazette,* which paid me a pittance for trying to evoke a laugh from thirty thousand of Seaport, Connecticut's finest residents.

Each week, I sat at my picture window, looking out on our three acres of lush lawn, composing satirical essays on any subject that happened to move me at the time. If Parker and I argued, if my twenty-year-old daughter, Eliza, drove me to distraction, if a conversation with a friend seemed particularly amusing, it showed up in my column the following week. I had free rein to toy with other people's lives as I deemed fit, and while I usually tried not to overstep the bounds, I would stop at little to be perceived as a droll and witty writer. And so, when I was asked by my editor, Gillian, on a bright, sunny day in May, to cover a story on vegetables, I was puzzled.

"Coco, we want to do a piece on La Chaîne des Rôtisseurs," she said. "And you're the perfect person to do it. Our focus is vegetarian."

"I'm a humorist," I said. "Vegetables aren't funny."

"Make them funny," she said. "Your assignment is to do dinner and mingle with some of the finest diners on the east coast, many of whom will be present at the Chaîne banquet on Friday evening at the Briarwood Club in Greenwich. You might want to brush up on its history."

Clearly, there was no arguing with her, so all week I buried myself in research. After all, if I was going to be hobnobbing with the culinary greats, I had better know what I was talking about.

La Chaîne des Rôtisseurs is an international gastronomic society founded in Paris in 1950. It is devoted to promoting fine dining and preserving the camaraderie and pleasures of the table. The Chaîne is based on the traditions and practices of the old French royal guild of meat roasters, whose written history has been traced back to the year 1248. Today, the society has members in more than one hundred countries around the world. In the United States, there are nearly one hundred and fifty "bailliages" (English "bailiwick") headed by a "bailli" ("bailiff") and other officers who plan the individual chapter's activities. Each bailliage holds one gala event each year to celebrate the induction of new members, who receive a distinctive ribbon worn at all Chaîne gatherings. The Briarwood Club was the perfect place to host such an event: It not only boasted outstanding cuisine, but a view of Long Island Sound to die for.

The following Friday afternoon, I slipped on my favorite tobacco silk pantsuit, got into my Range Rover, and with notebook in tow, I headed toward Briarwood and my first Chaîne dinner. As I tooled down the Merritt Parkway I asked myself the big question I had been mulling over all day: How could I take the subject of veggies and turn it into a laugh riot? Of all the assignments Gillian had thrust upon me, this was the worst.

"Handle it any way you want," she had said. "The idea is to bring vegetables to the forefront and give them a lot of press. The Chaîne is doing an all-vegetable banquet, proving that one can dine eloquently and well without being carnivorous."

I recalled the 1920s Carl Rose cartoon from the *New Yorker* with a mother and small daughter sitting at the table, eyeing a plate of vegetables. In E. B. White's caption, the mother said, "It's broccoli dear," to which the child replied: "I say it's spinach and I say the hell with it."

If a vegetable-based cartoon was good enough for the *New Yorker*, I guessed I could equally follow suit with an article on the same subject.

High on a hill, a winding road led me to the clubhouse just as the sun was setting. The valet greeted me at the main portico where I deposited my car and watched as he whisked it away to an area filled with BMWs, Mercedeses, Lexuses, and a lone Ferrari. My little Range Rover was in good company. Adjusting my clothes and giving a shake of my wild, silver mane, I went over to a small table on the side to register. A well-coiffed and pretty blond matron greeted me with a set of perfectly laminated teeth.

"So you're Coco, the one from the paper," she shrieked. "I simply adore journalists."

The writing was on the wall: This was going to be the evening from hell.

I immediately grabbed my name tag with "Seaport Gazette" emblazoned in bold letters and slapped it across my chest to alert the gaggle of gourmands that anything they said could be used against them. And then, without missing a beat, I turned around to scope out the bar. A nice glass of Chardonnay would take the edge off what could be a disastrous night ahead. The room was filled with men in tuxedos, all of whom resembled penguins bobbing around and nodding at one another.

"I don't think this is what you want to be drinking." A hand reached over, removing my glass and replacing it with a Sapphire martini.

I looked up at yet another penguin in full regalia. Around his neck was the distinctive medallion hanging on a ribbon, bearing the coat of arms of the Confrérie, signifying membership into La Chaîne.

"I'm Harry Troutman." He extended a hand, holding mine longer than protocol required. "And you must be Coco."

"Yes," I said, staring back into a pair of eyes that held me momentarily captive. "I'm from the *Seaport Gazette*."

"I know all about you," Harry said, "and I've been looking forward to meeting you all day. I'm hosting this Chaîne banquet. Welcome to our inner sanctum of fine dining."

I took a sip of the blue martini, feeling an immediate flush of warmth penetrate my throat. In the distance, a lean and lanky figure emerged, moving closer as Harry and I exchanged pleasantries.

"And here she is." Harry welcomed the gorgeous creature that descended upon us. "This is my wife, Éclaire."

My immediate impression of Éclaire was that she was put together like a magnificent ice sculpture, except, unlike ice, Éclaire never melted.

I studied her, noting first her name, deliciously reminiscent of French pastry. Then my eyes moved in with telescopic accuracy on her face, her body, and the designer dress she wore that cost more than my two recent root canals. She was the epitome of perfection, a well-chiseled work of art sculpted by the hands of her husband—the very same hands that only moments ago rested in mine.

His name echoed in the back of my mind until it became clear who Harry Troutman was and why that name was so familiar. *New York Magazine,* the ultimate Bible on the Best Doctors in New York, had touted him as one of the finest plastic surgeons in Manhattan.

Éclaire peered out from her striking blue orbs, which, like Days of the Week underpants, I would come to learn, were interchanged daily. Éclaire didn't stop with matching shoes and bag. Tonight, she had obviously chosen her colored lenses with great precision to coordinate with her cobalt blue designer cocktail ensemble. It was obvious that her hair was styled by Charles of the Beautiful, her body toned by her personal trainer. Her nails were recently manicured into ten painted stilettos and with a voice that sounded very Five Towns, Long Island, she offered a limp wrist.

"I'm Claire," she said with a nonchalance that bordered on aloofness. "But Harry insists on calling me Éclaire. As you might have gathered, he's into food."

Looking at Harry, it was hardly obvious how much food and wine ruled his life. He was just under six feet two and looked fit from his daily workouts at the gym. He had an aliveness about him that, from the get-go, made me melt. His searing brown eyes danced, as he looked me over, checking out, I imagined, every flaw on my face. He had a square jaw and his straight black hair was styled casually, barely touching the collar of his Ralph Lauren suit jacket. Halfway through my martini, which I was ordinarily unaccustomed to drinking, I felt relaxed and uninhibited, taking in the charm that Harry draped over me like my pumpkin-colored pashmina shawl.

I can say with utmost certainty that I had never fallen so fast and furiously for a man as I did that night at the Briarwood Club. The minute Harry and I exchanged hellos, I was hooked. In between the first course of braised artichokes in a tangerine sauce, and a chilled gazpacho with a dollop of crème fraîche, I was in extreme lust with Dr. Harry Troutman and nothing or no one, not my husband, Parker, or the lovely Éclaire, would keep my emotions at bay. But I was here to write an article, and mixing work with pleasure was a dangerous combination.

Harry had made sure that I would be seated next to him during dinner. He was my Chaîne coach, asking me to interrupt with questions whenever the mood struck. I placed my napkin on my lap, and with pen poised, I began waxing eloquent on the allure of the artichoke, scribbling notes along the way.

The artichoke, I reminisced, can fool unsuspecting souls. I recalled my first married dinner party when our cleaning lady, who was filling in that evening as server, had removed all the leaves on the artichokes, so that when our guests moved in from cocktails to dinner, all that remained on their plates were large, unadulterated, naked hearts.

"What happened to the leaves, Lucille?" I asked in amazement.

"Oh Missy," she explained, "everyone always plucks those leaves so I thought I would save them the trouble. I threw them in the garbage."

I told Harry, who was on my left, the story and he guffawed out loud, revealing a set of pearly whites that were lined up in perfect symmetry in his mouth.

Tonight's artichokes were a different story. Each one was perfectly snipped and sat atop an emerald green glass plate, blending in with the artichokes themselves. Tiny crystal bowls were off to the left, receptacles for the tangerine sauce in which to give each leaf a delicate dip before scraping it between the teeth and consuming the pulp. I watched Harry eat. He pried loose a leaf, and nonchalantly whisked it through the sauce, coating it ever-so-slightly before raising it from bowl to lips. His movements were deliberate, but subtle, almost as though he weren't eating at all, so that the artichoke became an appendage to our conversation.

Éclaire, who sat on Harry's left, was another story. She poked at the vegetable as though she was pulling apart a dead animal's innards. I might be mistaken, but I believe she even winced.

"The last time I ate one of these," she said, "I pricked my palate. My dentist told me to stay away from sharp legumes. They can be very dangerous. I hate food you have to work at."

I suddenly imagined Harry and Éclaire in bed, Éclaire trying her best to gingerly give her husband a blow job, but being ever so careful lest, with one false move, Harry's seminal fluid might, in Monica Lewinsky style, soil her 450-thread count percale sheets. My guess was she never swallowed—that was a definite no-no for a woman as well put together as Éclaire. If she was having difficulty maneuvering an artichoke, how could she handle something as messy as sex? Perhaps I could write about that for the *Seaport Gazette*.

2

"My mom is very possessive. She calls me up and says:
'You weren't home last night. Is something going on?' I said,
'Yeah, Mom, I'm cheating on you with another mother.'"
—Heidi Joyce

My Mother, the Siren

The Chaîne des Rôtisseurs is as fastidious about its wines as it is about its food. It has a society within the society: l'Ordre Mondial des Gourmets Dégustateurs, for those who have a special knowledge of, or interest in, wine and spirits. Members of this inside group organize special events, including trips to wine-producing regions around the world, many of which Harry and Éclaire had visited. Harry had gone to great lengths to select only the finest wines for tonight's dinner. As the evening progressed, the wine flowed, starting with a light sauvignon blanc from New Zealand during the first and second course, which blended nicely with the slightly tart gazpacho. Harry was in charge of it all. He regaled me with stories of their adventures to some of the best resorts in the world and I was lapping it all up with the same gusto with which Harry consumed each delicacy that lay before us.

A zucchini and leek mousse was presented to us in a light dill sauce. This delighted Éclaire who, after grappling with her artichoke, could now partake of more user-friendly food. As Harry and I chatted away, occasionally pausing to draw her into the conversation, I scribbled away voraciously in my little notebook, noting key words that I would later work into my article.

And then, from nowhere and with relevance to nothing, Éclaire suddenly blurted out, "Did you know that marriage can make you fat?"

I stopped midway between my mouthfuls of mousse.

"Really?" I said.

"Yes, a recent study in a leading women's magazine has confirmed that one's weight is contingent upon the number of years one is married. The longer couples are married, the fatter they become. Isn't that amazing?"

"Uh, yes," I said, but what was even more amazing was Éclaire's six-carat emerald-cut diamond ring, which nearly blinded me as she gestured to emphasize her point. I reached over for a sip of Pellegrino. There was no doubt: Harry's magical hands kept his wife happy. Clearly, being a "cutting-edge" plastic surgeon meant keeping his trophy wife in perfect working order with the finest clothes money could buy and accessories that had Harry Winston written all over them.

Parker certainly kept me in style, too, but unlike Éclaire, I had never been one to worry about being fat or having wrinkles. I used the latest creams and walked three miles every day, but I wasn't visiting my plastic surgeon every month or sporting giant sparkles on my fingers.

The rest of the evening went off without a hitch. Altogether there were seven courses, each one cooked to perfection—a cornucopia of vegetarian delights ranging from cabbage stuffed with eggplant and calabaza puree to grilled shiitake mushrooms in a wild herb sauce that tasted mildly like meat. The dinner was punctuated by a fresh Mista salad with an avalanche of pine nuts and warm goat cheese. Scattered about were a few dandelion greens that gave it a slight bite. By the time we got to intermezzo, a key lime sorbet, Harry had actually turned his attention away from the food and was now ingesting my each and every word, as though they were cultured pearls of wisdom.

"So, how did you get to be Coco?" Harry asked. "It can't be your real name?"

Dare I tell him that my mother, a woman who was as eccentric as she was original, had actually chosen that name because of her passion for chocolate? While other children were named for deceased or cherished family members, I was being honored for her four favorite and essential food groups: milk chocolate, dark chocolate, white chocolate, and cocoa.

"Your mother must be an interesting woman," Harry said.

He has no idea. A few years ago, I had devoted an entire column to my mother, Yvonne.

The Seaport Gazette

MY MOTHER, THE SIREN

My mother had flair. She had style. My dad affectionately called her "The Siren" long before I understood what the word even meant. That's because she dressed in black. To her, black was chic. Black was correct. Black was sensual.

"You can never go wrong with the little black dress," she had drummed into my head.

Little did she know that some of my "wrongest" moments happened during a few of my black periods. At age twenty, I leaned over a table in a dimly lit Manhattan bistro and stared into the eyes of a handsome cad who plied me with wine and ordered dinner in perfect French. That's because I looked alluring in my black dress—the very one my mother made me buy at Saks because she had said, "It's very slimming."

Slimming though it was, the dress was to die for. That cad took one look at the plunging neckline with a hint of cleavage and spilled his burgundy all over himself. Yes, men couldn't contain themselves. I turned heads in that dress. I was perceived as mysterious and provocatively wicked. Like my mother, I, too, was fast becoming a Siren.

Her wardrobe consisted of an array of black clothes, all divine and respectively seductive. The only time she deviated from her "noir chic" was at my wedding when she wore emerald green and broke her ankle tripping over a pat of butter that had fallen from her roll. As she was carried off on a stretcher, champagne in one hand, her green gown trailing behind her, her words reverberated through the Grand Ballroom of the hotel.

"I should have worn my black Balenciaga."

After that, her fashion statement consisted of only black suits and dresses adorned simply and elegantly with a string of pearls or a diamond brooch. I recently met a childhood friend who remarked:

"Whenever I remember your mom, black comes to mind."

How could it be any other way? While other mothers wore flowered housedresses, my mother served me breakfasts in her black silk robe. When I came home from school, she was baking cookies in a black-and-white checkered apron. When we dined out, she wore an appropriately black dinner dress and kissed me good night in her black nightie. Her dresser drawers spilled over with black lingerie and black nylon stockings. Let's face it, the woman had a monochromatic wardrobe that defied imagination.

In summers, she bathed in black swimsuits. On vacations to tropical islands, while other women wore dresses in muted pastels, she sat poolside, nibbling canapés and looking engaging in black linen. Her look, dark though it was, seemed more genteel than somber, and though I always felt that I had a mother who was strangely different, others considered her unique and ahead of her time.

It wasn't unusual then that my road to adulthood was paved with an array of black dresses: long-sleeved, short-sleeved, cap-sleeved, sleeveless, and haltered. When Vogue *and* Bazaar *introduced their spring fashions in bold prints exploding in color, Mom and I walked away from shopping expeditions with yet another black dress. I was the only girl to wear black to my senior prom.*

My mother thought that black spoke volumes—a back-

drop from which the personality could emerge and not be overshadowed by clothes that screamed, "Look at me!" In black, I could be completely myself. I learned to understand that black looked good on everyone. Blondes in black were captivating. Brunettes were sultry. African-Americans in black reeked of animal magnetism. When my redheaded friend Paula wore black, her hair cascading down her back, every man in the room took notice.

"It must be her hair," her boyfriend, Jim, remarked.

"Trust me, it's the dress," I said. "Black is beautiful."

With that in mind, I regularly rummage through my closet deciding which of my thirty-two black ensembles I should wear. My choices are endless.

"A black dress can change a woman's life," she said, as I wiggled my adolescent body into a formfitting sheath that made me feel both beguiling and naughty. It was a time when life was fraught with exciting possibilities at every turn and black helped it along. Now, years later, the little black dress doesn't seem quite as magical as it did when I stood on the rim of adulthood ready to take on the world.

But to my mother, black was always sensational and in her understated, charismatic way, she was a Siren. And so, I tried following in her footsteps.

"Wearing black makes me want to dance," she once said.

Now, I slip into a black bodysuit and black skirt, toss my hair over my shoulder, and I'm out the door. My mother taught me well. Let the dance begin!

Harry was fascinated. "But, I see that this evening you've chosen to wear brown. What would your mother say?"

We laughed frequently that night and by the time dessert arrived and a lovely ice wine was served, I felt I had known Harry longer than a few hours. There is a strange comfort one often feels at first meetings. After the initial charge of introduction and small talk is over, one settles in to that easy place where pretense is shed and the confines of congeniality are replaced with genuine interest in wanting to know the other person. I didn't want the evening to end. I was certain Harry felt the same, for when I went to retrieve my napkin that had fallen from my lap, his hand suddenly reached under the table and found mine. I felt the blood rush to my cheeks. My first inclination was to turn toward Éclaire and see if she had noticed. But as I would later come to learn, she registered little emotion over anything. While Harry's hand moved playfully around my fingers, Éclaire was applying Chanel gloss to her full, collagen-laced lips, oblivious of anyone but herself.

"If you'll excuse me," she said, "I think I'll use the Little Girl's Room."

Harry released my hand and rose from his chair on cue, the perfect attentive husband. "Hurry back, darling," he said.

I was amazed by how Harry was clearly the great charmer of all time. He could seduce a woman in full view of his wife and get away with it. Or else Éclaire was more of a bimbo than I thought. Thinking about it, though, I realized that Harry dealt with women every day and knew exactly how they worked. I could tell that he prided himself on being not just the good doctor who could morph a woman from frump to fabulous, but he possessed the one quality they couldn't resist: He listened. I knew that I had entered dangerous turf and should know better than to succumb to a man like Harry, but by the time I had eaten my poached pear in a brandy sauce and sipped a glass of champagne served with a basket of strawberries dipped in dark chocolate, Harry had touched the most erogenous zone in my body: my brain.

While Éclaire was freshening up, Harry reached into his pocket and retrieved a business card. It was simple, white, elegant. Engraved was the name Harry B. Troutman, MD, and his phone number. No extraneous verbiage. Understated and classy all the way, like the man himself.

"You might have some questions you'll need to ask," he said, handing over the card.

"Questions?" I tried sounding cool, detached.

"About tonight," he said. "For your article. Call my office and we'll make an appointment to talk. I'm sure you'll want some more information on the Chaîne."

Harry and Éclaire walked me to my car. Éclaire offered a weak handshake while Harry kept watch for his SLK 350 Mercedes Roadster with the vanity license plate: NIP IT. By 10:30, I was behind the seat of my car heading back to Seaport and my husband, Parker, who would be waiting up to hear all about my evening with the inhabitants of Food City.

"Meet any interesting people?" he would ask.

"You know how these things are," I'd tell him. "Just another assignment with a different slant."

I also knew that with one phone call to Harry, my life could change in a heartbeat.

That night I lay in bed and decided to leave well enough alone. It had been a nice evening where I collected some good material. There were no questions I couldn't address myself or check on the Internet. Under no circumstances would I call Dr. Harry Troutman. Then I fell asleep in a champagne glow.

I rose early to a clear, sunny Saturday morning. Parker had already left to play golf at the Seaport Country Club. I rubbed the sleep from my eyes and in that moment between semiconsciousness and full awareness, I rewound the prior evening's tape in my head. There was Harry, as big as life, running around my mind. I could recount little snippets of the Chaîne evening, but it all seemed muddled. All I could think of were Harry's hands, slipping beneath the white linen tablecloth, seeking mine. I should have untangled my fingers then, alerting him to the fact that this was inappropriate behavior and I wasn't buying into it. Instead, I had squeezed back in acknowledgment, letting him know, in no uncertain terms, that I found him attractive. In that split second, I had crossed over from *Seaport Gazette* writer to interested party who was willing to fall prey to his charms, even with his wife sitting only several inches away. Harry obviously "played dirty" and I had signaled back that I was a willing participant.

3

"The end depends upon the beginning."
—*The Emperor's Club*

From Soup to Nuts

Once upon a time I, Coco Plotnick Hollander Harding, was a nice girl and only child of Dr. Sam DDS and Yvonne Plotnick. I grew up in South Orange, New Jersey, in the '50s, went to all the right schools, dated boys who were preapproved by my parents and had been handed a Tiffany lifestyle. This was Yvonne's word. Yvonne used "Tiffany" as her measuring rod for everything fabulous.

"Darling, I love your hair. You must be going to a Tiffany stylist." Or,

"Coco, you *will* go to Smith. It's the Tiffany of all colleges." Or,

"Sam, sweetheart, of course you should raise your rates. After all, you're the Tiffany of dentists."

She and Sam had also selected my first husband, Mitchell Hollander, after my father witnessed Mitch's root canal work.

"This kid is the wizard of roots," my father announced to my mother one morning when I was home for summer vacation after completing my sophomore year in college.

"He's a gardener, Sam?"

"No, an endodontist and a Yale man with a practice in my medical building."

I could see my mother's wheels turning as we ate our breakfast.

"Maybe Coco should meet him," she told my father, while I sat there as though invisible.

"No, I wouldn't like to meet him thank you," I said.

"What's wrong with meeting a nice Jewish boy who happens to be available, darling?"

"Maybe he's not available."

"He happens to be," my father chimed in.

"You see, sweetheart, he just hasn't met the right girl."

My mother removed a wad of dough from a bagel, massaged some lox spread into its shell with her Grand Baroque patterned butter knife, and handed it to my father.

"Such opportunities don't present themselves every day, Coco. I smell possibility here. This is a rising star, dentally speaking. An eligible bachelor."

"Then you date him, Mother."

"Don't be fresh to your mother," Sam chimed in.

"I can find my own men," I said.

"Not a Jewish-endodontist-who-is-on-his-way-up, you can't," Yvonne barked back without missing a beat.

And so it came to pass, that I, Coco Plotnick, did meet the Wizard of Roots, Mitchell Howard Hollander, got engaged in my senior year, and married the summer following my graduation from Smith. My daughter, Eliza, was born two years later. My parents couldn't have orchestrated it better.

My father's dental work paid for our wedding: gold inlays were the fuel for my wedding dress, the extractions paid for the reception, and bridgework took care of the down payment on an apartment in Manhattan, near to Mitch's new endodontic practice on Park Avenue and 87th Street. My parents may have been pains in the asses, but they were generous pains in the asses. My wedding took place at the St. Regis Roof. Yvonne insisted that Dom Perignon flow freely all night.

"New York State champagne is as good as French," Sam said. "Nobody will know the difference."

"Do I tell you how to fix teeth, Sam angel?" Yvonne said over sirloin steaks at The Palm.

Some of my family's finest conversations took place in the best restaurants in New York.

And I, with a pear-shaped three-carat rock on my finger was caught up in the fanfare, never stopping to realize that Mitch and I had absolutely nothing in common except that we both had teeth and Mitch never stopped talking about them.

"It's all so je ne sais quoi," my mother cooed the night of our wedding.

That "je ne sais quoi" had cost my father, Sam Plotnick, DDS, nearly $150,000.

And it didn't stop there. My mother had a heavy hand in decorating our little pad. A week after we arrived home from our honeymoon to France, Yvonne brought in Rose Harris, the most prestigious interior designer in the tristate area, to "take a little look-see."

"Puce!" Rose Harris said, standing in the foyer. "Definitely puce with a touch of burnt sienna."

"I was thinking something more along the lines of blues and greens," I said.

"Earth tones, sweetheart," Rose said. "Trust me, I've been in the business for more than thirty years. The new in color is puce. Blues and greens are passé."

"Rose has an eye," my mother said. "Not every bride is so fortunate as to have a Rose Harris decorate their apartment."

"Mitch and I can do our own decorating."

"What?" my mother said, "and deprive your father of the thrill of getting you started in life?"

"Mitch makes good money. We don't need help."

"This isn't help, it's an investment," my mother said. "When Rose Harris gets through with it, you'll be able to sell this apartment for three times what you paid for it."

It was crystal clear: Unless my parents were controlling my life they weren't happy.

"Mitch hates puce," I said.

My mother put on her serious face, and with lips pursed, she lowered her eyes and cleared her throat. "Coco, you need to establish your boundaries now. In a year it will be too late. Let Mitchell handle teeth. When it comes to your home, you should have the final word."

"Did you know that puce was the new in color?" I asked Mitch that evening.

"I refuse to have diarrhea walls," he said.

"Fine," Rose Harris said the following week, "I'm flexible. We'll go an entirely different route: black and red with a touch of white to soften the edges."

"I love it," Yvonne shouted.

"It's very Stendahl," Mitch's mother, Estelle Hollander, squealed, even though she didn't know what the hell she was talking about.

"It's so you, Coco," Rose Harris said and several thousands of dollars later, we began married life with a red lacquered headboard, a black leather and chrome chair, a salt-and-pepper Rya rug, a black enamel refrigerator, a white couch, and a Lucite coffee table on which lay random books with red, white, and black vinyl covers.

Six months later, I was pregnant with my daughter, Eliza, and five years later, Mitch and I divorced due to irreconcilable boredom.

When I told my parents, they went ballistic.

"You should have gone with the puce," my mother said, soulfully. "Living in a black apartment is depressing. It's bound to destroy any marriage."

"Mother, it wasn't our color scheme that did it," I said.

"Sexual incompatibility?" she whispered. "Because there are people you can go and talk to."

"If I knew it would come to this," Sam broke in, "you could have gotten married at the Park Avenue Synagogue instead of the St. Regis."

Then, to make her feel better, Sam bought my mother a bottle of Shalimar at Saks and took us all out to lunch at the Promenade Café where she and I discussed my marriage ad infinitum and my father watched the skaters do figure eights at the Rockefeller Center ice skating rink.

~

Once divorced, I never looked back. Eliza and I stayed in our "Stendahl" apartment for a few more years, which was redecorated by me instead of Rose Harris. Mitchell took the red-and-black furniture to his new bachelor-cum-daddy pad, and I replaced it with soft taupes, grays, and a hint of terra cotta. Rose would have approved.

While Mitchell may not have been the model husband, he was a great father. He agreed to pay for Eliza's private school, summer camp, college education, and all expenses that guaranteed Eliza would live a life befitting the child of an endodontist extraordinaire. As my mother predicted, Mitch became a shining star in the dental world. He gained quite a reputation, so much so that when the cousin of a friend of Barbra Streisand had a toothache, he was sent to Mitch who removed his nerve without so much as a whimper from the cousin.

One night I awakened at 3 A.M. with a throbbing ache in my upper left jaw. The next morning, I was sitting in Mitch's mauve leather state-of-the-art dental chair being injected with a shot of Novocain that could have numbed an elephant. Within minutes, he put me out of my misery. It was the first and only time that Mitchell and I had bonded in any sort of meaningful way.

As for my career, for the next twelve years, I made my way as a freelance writer, submitting pieces to major magazines and writing for the kids' publications, known in the trade as "Kiddy Litter." Eliza went off to Wellesley in the fall of 1995, leaving me unmarried and dating an assortment of men who made "singlehood" a desirable state, despite Sam and Yvonne's concern that I would die an old maid.

"I can't die an old maid," I told them. "That term only applies to women who have never been married. I just haven't met Mr. Right."

"How about Mr. Maybe?" Yvonne kept prodding.

I heaved a sigh and wrote down in my scribble book: "Meeting Mr. Maybe," an article that I didn't know, then, would eventually launch me as the *Seaport Gazette*'s humor columnist.

Yvonne drove me periodically crazy, but also provided me with great column fodder I would use for years to come.

~

It was a time of endings and new beginnings.

I had turned forty-five. My father, Sam, retired, and he and my mother sold their home in New Jersey and moved to Boca Raton. Mitch got involved with Maxine, his new receptionist/nurse/secretary/lover who had the IQ of a gnat, but made up for it in body proportion. On a scale from one to ten, ten being knockout, Maxine was an eleven. Mitch had obviously hired Maxine based on physical attributes, not intellect. But then, Mitch was always somewhat shallow.

Eliza met Maxine before I did when the three of them had brunch at Sarabeth's one Saturday over her Thanksgiving vacation. Later, she came bursting through the door with a detailed accounting.

"She's very bosomy," Eliza said, slamming the door of our apartment.

"You're kidding," I said.

All these years, Mitch had said he was a leg man. I had taken special pains to keep my legs in shape: waxing, toning, and spritzing with special emollients. I wore the proper shoes to emphasize my calves. I had toe cleavage to die for from weekly pedicures at

Elizabeth Arden, only to find out he was marrying a girl with boobs. I went through my list of questions about Mitch's recent acquisition.

"I want all the gory details," I said. "What about her face?"

"Long," Eliza said, "like a horse, but a pretty horse."

"Hair?"

"Blond and straight, down to her butt."

"Butt?"

"High and hard. She wore Marc Jacobs jeans that really fit, Jimmy Choo black boots, and a Prada bag."

"Personality?"

"She giggles."

"Giggles?"

"All through brunch, every time Dad said anything, she'd laugh. You know that high-pitched, jittery laugh that borders on fake. She was trying to impress Dad."

"How?"

"Pretending to be interested in his stuff."

"Like?"

"Like when Dad started talking teeth, she got all excited."

"How?"

"'Oh, Liza,' she said. 'Your dad is such a genius with mouths.' It's E-liza, I told her. 'Yes, well . . . EEEEliza, as I was saying, yesterday a woman came in with her poodle and your dad was brilliant. She felt absolutely no pain.'"

"A poodle? Your dad did a root canal on a poodle?"

"That's what I was wondering," Eliza said. "When I asked them, she and Dad laughed so hard, they couldn't control themselves. Everybody at Sarabeth's stared. I'm telling you, Mom, the woman is a ditz."

"A ditz with big boobs," I said. "I always knew your father was lying when he said he didn't care that I had small breasts. He told me, 'Your breasts are fine, Coco: Good and plenty and just right for me.'"

"Yeah," said Eliza, "that's why you're home writing an article on a Saturday afternoon, and he's hanging with a Dolly Parton look-alike."

That afternoon, Eliza and I went to the movies where I stuffed my face with two boxes of Good & Plenty and an extra-large tub of buttered popcorn.

4

"One should keep his words both soft and tender,
because tomorrow he may have to eat them."
—Unknown

A Light Bite

One Thursday night after I had come home from yet another date-from-hell, there was a message on my answering machine from my best friend and former college chum, Annie, who lived in Seaport with her husband, Saul, and her cat, Winston, who kept her company now that her two grown sons were out of the house. The cat, close to sixteen, had more energy than Saul did.

"Call me back tonight," Annie said. "I have some news."

With Annie one never knew if the news was good or bad. It was always a surprise. A few months ago she had phoned with the latest headline.

"What's up?" I asked.

"I had a mammogram today," Annie said. "They saw something."

"What kind of something?"

"I don't know. Something that wasn't there before."

"So why do you sound so cheery?"

"Who's cheery? I'm freaking out," she said.

It turned out to be breast calcification. From that day on, Annie never touched calcium again, except for an occasional pint of Ben & Jerry's, which she said didn't count because it melted.

Tonight I wasn't sure if I would be dealing with a catastrophic illness or winning the lottery.

"There's someone I want you to meet," Annie said when I called her back.

"I dunno," I said, "the last one you fixed me up with was a major disappointment."

"I can't understand why. Eddie Schenker was very eligible. Successful, rich, and he loves to travel."

"He's a loser," I said. "When he took me out to dinner, he flossed his teeth."

"So he's into good hygiene. What's so terrible?"

"At the table?" I said. "In full view of everyone?"

"Parker is different. He's very refined. A definite catch. Besides his house in Seaport, which is spectacular, he has an apartment in the city and a house in the Berkshires. You could do Tanglewood any time you'd like."

"If he's such a catch why is he still available?"

"His wife died six months ago. He just started seeing people. I think you'd like him."

I had to agree: A widower sounded more appealing than a man who spent the entire evening complaining about how much his divorce had cost him. A grieving man was decidedly better than an angry one.

"And what does this Parker do?"

"His grandfather owned a set of clubs, one in Connecticut and one on Long Island."

"Golf clubs?"

"Yes, literally: the Seaport Club here and the fancy Greenwood Club in Great Neck. I'm talking old money here, Coco. The grandfather, Myles Harding, a liberal goy, started allowing Jews into the clubs back in the 1950s. Parker took over when gramps croaked. If you and Parker got together, you would have automatic membership."

"Aren't you rushing things? We haven't even had our first date. And anyway, I'm hardly the club type."

"It's just dinner," Annie said.

"Okay, you can give him my number, but tell him to do his teeth before we go out."

Within an hour, the phone rang. It was Parker.

"Excuse me for phoning so late," he apologized, "but Annie said you're a night owl."

The night table clock said 11:25. I was just nodding off to sleep.

"Hi," I said, trying to muster up some perkiness. "Nice of you to call."

"Annie tells me you're a writer."

"Yes."

"Writers are a very interesting breed."

The American Kennel Club immediately popped into my mind. Why was it that everyone found writers so interesting? And why did they feel compelled to always ask the same questions? The list went as follows:

1. Would I have seen anything you've written?
2. Where do you get your ideas?
3. What are you working on?
4. How long does it take to knock out a piece?
5. Do you actually make a living from your writing?

And these were just for starters. The last thing I needed was a "résumé" evening where I regaled my date with inside trade talk while he sat there like a wide-eyed puppy lapping it all up.

"How about dinner?" Parker asked.

"Maybe drinks," I retorted.

"That way," Parker said, laughing, "if I'm a total dud, you can break away early? I understand, Coco."

I laughed, nervously. Parker was on to me from the start. Even better, he wasn't rattled by my obviously transparent dating rituals.

"We'll have drinks and then a light bite," he said. "We won't call it dinner."

"Sounds good to me," I said, and I meant it.

We chatted for a while as Parker gave me an abbreviated overview of his life. He had studied electrical engineering at Princeton and worked for a company in Massachusetts until he inherited and took over gramp's country clubs, which were now thriving successes. He had been happily married for thirty-seven years to his wife, Joan, with whom he had sired two sons, Hudson, thirty, and Clark, twenty-five, both living on the west coast. Joan died of breast cancer six months ago and Parker's world suddenly fell apart. His voice was steady and slow as he spoke, and he seemed refreshingly unpretentious. I felt comfortable.

The fact that I lived in Manhattan and Parker in Connecticut wasn't a problem. He was in the city several times a week and not wanting to make the hour drive back to Seaport after theater or concerts, he stayed in his East End Avenue apartment. Often, he drove out to Great Neck to play golf and tennis at Rolling Hills. He had fired two maître d's in the same year because of attitude problems. Parker didn't waste time with employees who couldn't deliver the goods. He was decisive and went after what he wanted.

"Are you free on Saturday evening?" he asked.

"This Saturday?"

"Yes, are you available?"

He had caught me off guard. Here it was Thursday. If I agreed to meet Parker on Saturday night, he might think I was hard up for dates. On the other hand, my own daughter had long ago given up playing these games, so who was I to play hard to get at forty-five? I bit the bullet and gave it to him straight.

"Yes, I am free Saturday night," I said with a modicum of bravado.

"I'll pick you up at seven o'clock," Parker said. "I'll make a reservation for 'a bite' at Le Refuge."

Some bite. Le Refuge just happened to be one of my favorite French restaurants on 82nd Street. Its unassuming warmth made it the perfect spot for a first date. Parker had definite style. By the time I got off the phone, twenty minutes later, I was already looking forward to Saturday night.

5

"I am a typical New Yorker. I don't own a car.
I don't own a house. The only thing I own of
value is my Monday night table at Rao's.
I know what's important."
—The late Dick Schaap

Something to Chew On

At 6:45 sharp, Parker met me in the lobby of my building. He was dressed for a night befitting the unrelenting heat of early July; a seersucker jacket over gray pants, a shirt and tie and tasseled loafers gave him that casual but well-put-together look I liked. His handshake was firm and he grinned shyly when he met me, extending a hand that bore his family crest ring and a Rolex watch. He had a gentleness about him that eased me into the first few awkward moments of introduction.

As we taxied over to Le Refuge, we chatted away as though we had known each other longer than only a few minutes. The taxi swerved slightly. I fell against Parker's shoulder, catching a whiff of his Armani aftershave. Outside, the sun was starting to set and splashed an orange and magenta glow over the buildings along Park Avenue. Summer in New York has always been intoxicating. The heat of the city forces many New Yorkers to vacate their apartments and find solace in rented homes in the suburbs. Tonight, the city seemed less frenetic with so many people out of the way. A hazy glow enveloped us as we entered the restaurant and were seated at a small table on the side.

Parker ordered a gin gimlet and I, a Perrier with lime, as I felt parched from the heat. I would forgo the wine until dinner. Our waiter, sensing we wanted to be alone and not deal with intrusion, kept his distance, appearing only to recite the specials of the evening and occasionally inquiring if we needed anything.

"She's all I need," Parker said, reaching for my hand.

It was at that moment I knew I had Parker eating out of that very hand. By the time we reached dessert, he was practically drooling all over my black georgette silk Eileen Fisher dress.

I phoned Annie after Parker dropped me off at my apartment at eleven.

"So?" Annie said.

"So!" I said. "He's not the usual nightmare."

"Does that mean you'll see him again?"

"We're going to the ballet tomorrow afternoon," I said.

For the next six months, Parker and I dined our way through some of the best restaurants in New York. Having no desire to date other people, we began seeing each other exclusively. Parker, twelve years my senior, turned fifty-seven at the end of January. We celebrated his birthday with a small dinner party at my apartment where I cooked an all-Indian meal, Parker's favorite cuisine. His sister, Bridgette, a divorcée who lived in Greenwich, and who pronounced her name: "Bridge-ette" with emphasis on the "ette" met me for the first time, and was remotely cordial. After all, I was a Jew and she needed time to evaluate the situation.

"My brother is a gem," Bridgette said, "but I'm sure you already know that."

"He's the best thing since white bread and mayonnaise," I wanted to say, but instead, I smiled sweetly, agreeing that the sun rose and set where Parker was concerned.

"And his late wife, Joan, now she was a treasure."

"I'm sure she's irreplaceable," I bantered back.

In some inexplicable way, Bridgette reminded me of a WASP version of my mother.

As for Eliza, I had passed a major obstacle. Even she, who was critical of most of the men I had dated, approved of our relationship in her own convoluted way.

"He's less weird than most," she said. "And he's obviously crazy about you."

There was only one drawback: the sex. For Parker, bells rang. For me, they occasionally chimed. For all his charm, good-naturedness, and adoration, Parker was not the sexual giant I had hoped he'd become. He assured me that he and his late wife, Joan, had enjoyed a functional sexual relationship, and while "functional" was respectable, when it came to sex, I preferred mine smoldering hot and passionate.

"So he's got a lazy libido," Annie said, when I shared with her the missing piece of our romantic puzzle. "Give it time."

"The man's pushing sixty," I said. "Trust me, unlike wine, sex doesn't improve with age. Next stop is Viagra Valley."

"He makes up for it by being rich and successful."

"If you think I'm marrying a man because he has a fat bank account, forget it," I said.

"Honey," Annie said, "there's nothing wrong with trading a little nookie for a comfortable lifestyle."

I grappled with this for a while. Then I decided to go back to see my therapist, Dr. Irwin Finkelman, and toss around the sex issue in the comfort of his Central Park West office. While Dr. Finkelman wasn't exactly the most animated of shrinks, he had the best collection of bow ties I had ever seen, and a view overlooking Central Park that I found strangely comforting. He personified the perfect shrink image and was right out of central casting.

Once, in his waiting room, I had scanned his bookshelves and discovered that he had the entire collection of Agatha Christie. When I mentioned that, he told me his favorites were the ones featuring Hercule Poirot. No surprise, as Finkelman himself resembled Poirot in that he was a tidy, rotund man with a head that was rounded like a perfectly shaped egg, he was no more than five feet four inches tall, and sported a mustache that looked as though he waxed it with black shoe polish. At times, he even took to quoting lines from Christie's books.

"What brings you back to see me?" Dr. Finkelman inquired that day.

Dare I tell him that I liked sitting in his air-conditioned office on hot summer afternoons? That venting my life was an indulgence I found as satisfying as other women did their manicures and massages? Nice bow tie, I wanted to say. Instead, I got right down to business. "I met a man," I said, "and it's pretty serious."

Finkelman heaved a sigh, digging his pinky deep into his right ear and retrieving a ball of yellow wax that he studied in the ray of the late afternoon sunlight.

"I see . . . yes, well . . . that's nice, Coco," he said. "Tell me about him."

"He's successful. He's rich. He's caring. He loves me," I said.

"Notice the order of importance," Dr. Finkelman said, "in which you describe this man."

I had to hand it to him: Finkelman zeroed right in.

"And what about your intimate life?"

"You mean the sex?"

Dr. Finkelman's lip began twitching as it always did when the issue of sex came up.

"It's tepid," I said.

"I see," Finkelman said.

Once, in the middle of my divorce from Mitch when I was seeing Dr. Finkelman, I spent an entire forty-five-minute session counting his "I sees," which came to eleven. For that I dished out two hundred bucks a week?

"I do love Parker," I said, "but shouldn't it concern me that the sex isn't hot?"

Finkelman's lip twitched so badly, he paused to wipe his mouth with a white handkerchief and then downed a full glass of water, poured from a cut glass pitcher that sat on the table next to his 1970s frayed leather Eames chair.

"Hot?" he asked, toying with his wedding band.

"Passionate," I said. "Parker's lovemaking isn't passionate. It's predictable."

"I see."

Actually, he didn't. Finkelman didn't quite get why "predictable" was a problem.

"Isn't it comforting to know that you can count on Parker to be consistent?"

"Actually, I like spontaneity in bed."

Finkelman shifted. "Yes, well . . . uh . . . playfulness is nice, but sex between a mature man and woman is often less heated and more loving."

"Why not both?"

"Coco, I think you might be sublimating sex for something else that is lacking in your life. We need to explore some of those issues."

It was at times like this, I wondered why Finkelman was my shrink of choice. Perhaps a younger, more compassionate therapist, maybe a woman, was the person I should be seeing. Yet Finkelman came highly recommended and did ask probing questions that gave me pause long after the sessions were over.

"What worries me," I said, trying to sound lucid, "is that I care very much for Parker. We have fun together and his devotion, though a bit boring at times, is the very thing I admire. Yet, he is a bit anal and his feng shui is driving me nuts."

"Anal?"

Finkelman didn't like me dropping psychiatric buzz words that infringed on his area of expertise.

"You know, methodical. He's a neat freak. He lines things up."

"Lines things up?"

"Shoes. All his black shoes are neatly lined up together, followed by his brown shoes, saddle shoes, athletic shoes, and then there are his suits, his sports jackets, and his goddamn ties."

"What about the ties?"

"They're all color coordinated: solids with solids, stripes with stripes, paisleys with paisleys."

"I see," Finkelman said, adjusting his paisley bow tie. "I see."

Our session abruptly ran out of time just as I was waxing eloquent over how anal Parker was in bed.

"We'll pick up on this at our next session, Coco," Finkelman said.

Session Interruptus. I figured there was only so much Finkelman could handle in one afternoon.

I was meeting Parker at the Stanhope, where he sat outside, sipping his usual gin gimlet and waiting for me to join him. I plunked myself down and ordered an iced tea.

"So, how's old Finkelman?" Parker asked. "Have you solved the problems of the world?"

He should only know that for the past forty-five minutes I had been dissecting every nuance of our sex life.

"Finkelman's as crazy as ever," I said. "He still twitches every time I bring up X-rated topics."

"Like what?" Parker's interest was piqued.

"Like anything sexual."

"Do you often talk sex with Finkelman?"

"When it's relevant," I said.

No matter how much any man in my life supported my seeing a therapist, none of them could handle the thought of having our lovemaking dissected. The exception had been Mitch, who was so egomaniacal that the idea of having his lofty cock up for discussion was enough to give him an erection.

"Let's face it, honey," I told Parker. "There's not a shrink in the world who isn't curious about his or her patient's sex life."

"So, what did you say?"

"The truth, that everything's great in that department."

"Damn straight," Parker said. Then he ordered another gin gimlet, sat back, and watched as tourists strolled by the Stanhope, cameras poised and ready to capture a New York Kodak moment. I had learned my lesson long ago: The less I told Parker about my sessions, the better off our relationship would be. And the better I made him feel about our lovemaking, the more his sexual prowess might heat up.

~

I continued seeing Finkelman. Every Thursday at 4 P.M. I spilled my guts and we analyzed why Parker Harding the Second was such a good catch. Finkelman and I put in more hours talking about my sex life than Parker and I actually "did it." I don't know if I was finding answers, but Finkelman seemed to be getting something for his troubles. At one point, I believe he got excited, because after four consecutive "I sees" in the middle of a discussion of the "Big O," he started sweating profusely and asked if I minded if he turned up the AC. Once, when I got on the subject of oral sex, he actually needed to leave the room. When he returned a few minutes later, he seemed quite flushed and was twitching more than usual.

"I'll make up the four minutes," he assured me.

Talk about anal.

Parker and I flew to California in early August so I could meet his sons, Hudson and Clark, who lived in the San Francisco Bay area. Unlike Eliza, who critiqued every move I made, they received me with open arms. Whether or not they liked me, or were simply relieved to know their father had a companion, I wasn't sure, but Parker said that when he and Hudson went out for a morning game of tennis, his son had told him that we were a match made in heaven.

"They think you're the best thing that's happened to me since Joan died."

"I like them, too," I said.

Hudson's wife, Susan, and two daughters were a joy to be with. Clark, the more subdued of the two, was brilliant and sweet. We spent the week sightseeing and becoming familiar with one another. When it was time to pack up and leave, I realized I would actually miss them.

"You must come to New York," I told them, "and I want you to meet Eliza."

Hudson, a physics professor at San Francisco State, promised that during his Christmas vacation he would try and bring the family to New York. Clark, an architect and eligible bachelor, worked for a prominent San Francisco firm, and came to New York several times a year to visit Parker. He, too, assured us he would see us the next time he was in town.

"His kids are great," I told Finkelman upon my return. "We all got along so well."

"That's one problem out of the way," Finkelman said, wiping his glasses with the corner of his trusty handkerchief. "Now, let's get back to the sex."

6

"When my fiancé proposed it was very romantic. He turned off the TV. Well, he muted it. During the commercial."
—Wendy Liebman

The Icing on the Cake

How I ever got involved with a WASP from Connecticut borders on the absurd. From the beginning, my parents had groomed me for men from "the tribe": Jewish men who were once Bar Mitzvah boys. Men who were programmed by their Jewish mothers to become doctors or lawyers. Boys whose peckers were circumcised at birth. Not a WASP from Connecticut. And what a WASP he was. Parker oozed WASP through every pore. He dressed WASP. He spoke WASP. He personified all things WASP. But, underneath that WASP exterior was a full-fledged mensch, so much so that when Sam and Yvonne came to New York to take a gander at my significant other, despite all they had raised me to be, and in spite of themselves, they fell head over heels in love with Parker.

"So you approve," I asked my parents, "even though he's not Jewish?"

"Well, nobody's perfect," my father said.

"At your age, Coco, all the good Jews are taken," Yvonne said.

And so, on Saturday afternoon, Parker and I escorted my parents to Seaport Country Club where Parker and Sam played nine holes while my mother and I sat under an umbrella on the patio, sipping chilled glasses of mint iced tea.

"This is a very nice club, darling," she said. "Very liberal."

By that she meant that it was a mixed membership club, where Jews and non-Jews congregated together. The one ingredient they all shared was money. Women (the WASPs) in Lilly Pulitzers, hobnobbed with women (the Jews) slinging their Louis Vuittons over their shoulders and wearing Stuart Weitzman pastel-colored sandals with their knee-length sundresses. At Seaport Country Club, life was picture postcard perfect: Birds chirped, the grass was profusely green. Couples in golf carts waved to each other, balls smacked against tennis rackets on Har-Tru courts, while the less athletic sat by the Olympic-sized pool, streaked with zinc sunblock and reading the hottest novels of the week.

A while later, Sam and Parker joined us for lunch. For the next hour my parents watched as Parker held my hand and stroked my hair, punctuating our conversation with endearments, signifying that I was the end-all and be-all in his life.

"You know I'm crazy about your daughter," Parker announced over steak sandwiches for the men and spinach salads for the women.

Yvonne lowered her eyes demurely as though she were the one who was being wooed. "I can see that," she said.

"Enough of that," Sam interrupted my mother's euphoria. "This guy plays one hell of a game of golf."

Lunch consisted of greasing each other's egos ad nauseum. By the time we left the club, we were all encased in a saccharine glow so sickeningly sweet I could have gone into insulin shock right there in the parking lot.

A month later, during dinner at Daniel, Parker proposed marriage. Over a coffee praline bombe, he handed over a velvet box from Tiffany in which a sapphire and diamond ring stared up, just begging me to fall into a deep swoon. As rings went, this was, as Sam would say, "nothing to sneeze at." Then, in front of the entire restaurant, Parker got down on one knee and proposed marriage. And there, with dust on his Ermenegildo Zegna pant leg, I agreed to become the wife of Parker Harding the Second.

The first one I wanted to tell was Eliza, who was fast asleep in her room even though it was eleven o'clock in the morning. She mumbled a few incoherent congratulatory grunts and fell back asleep. Then we called Hudson and Clark, who said they weren't surprised, and, finally, Sam and Yvonne.

"Oh darling," my mother shrieked into the phone, practically going into cardiac arrest, "let me tell your father."

Sam immediately picked up the other phone and offered his mazel tovs.

"Did he give you a ring?" Yvonne predictably followed.

"Not just a ring . . . a *ring.* A sapphire with diamond baguettes on each side."

"It's new, right?" she whispered into the phone.

"What are you talking about, Mother?"

"Sometimes, a widower likes to pass his dead wife's ring on to the new wife."

"For God's sake, don't act crazy. It's not a one-size-fits-all. Of course, it's new. And, it happens to be drop-dead gorgeous."

"It sounds like the Tiffany of all rings," Yvonne chirped.

"As a matter of fact, it is," I said.

I saved my phone call to Annie for last so I could be interrogated without interruption. Parker had gone out to do some errands, leaving me alone for a few hours.

"I knew it," she said. "I just knew this was coming, and let me say, you made the right choice . . . you did say 'yes'?"

"Of course, I said yes."

"I mean, with the sex thing and all, I wasn't sure if that was an issue."

"Only when we're in bed," I quipped. "No, Parker is a prize. A little Viagra, a little instruction manual, and we'll work out the kinks."

When Parker returned, we called our gallery of friends, all of whom wished us the very best. Then we called his sister, Bridgette.

"Bridgey," Parker said, "I have some good news."

There was a deafening silence for a few seconds during which I imagined Bridgette putting down her drink and lighting a cigarette so she could better absorb this crucial piece of information. Hearing only Parker's side of the conversation, I surmised the worst.

"No, it's not too soon. Yes, the boys are delighted. Yes, of course I gave her a ring. No, I wasn't drunk."

"She sounds thrilled." I shot Parker a look.

All of us have to answer to a higher power. Parker's highest power was his sister. Then he handed me the phone.

"So, you snagged my little brother," Bridgette said, inhaling so deeply I could practically hear the tar and nicotine entering her lungs. If she kept it up, her ciggies might eventually lead her to an early grave and make our married life more manageable.

"We kind of snagged each other," I said. I needed to be on my toes at all times where Bridgette was concerned.

"Of course you did, darling. I hope you're not planning to have one of those humongous weddings. They can be so déclassé."

Her voice had "My Big, Fat, Jewish Wedding" written all over it.

"Parker and I haven't even gotten that far," I said. "We just became engaged."

"Well, that makes sense," Bridgette said, "no sense rushing into anything until you're sure."

"Believe me, we're sure," I said, handing back the phone to Parker.

I retreated to the bathroom where, in Mary Martin *South Pacific* style, I tried to wash Bridgette out of my hair.

It had all happened so fast. I knew I had made the right decision, but there were still unresolved issues. And then there was Dr. Finkelman to contend with. I burst in to my session on Thursday, flapping my left hand in his face.

"I see," he said. "I assume that means you're betrothed."

"Yes, Parker proposed and I said yes."

"Aren't we rushing things a bit?"

"No, we're not. I'm not in my twenties; I know what I'm doing."

"Do I detect defensiveness?" Finkelman asked.

"No, downright hostility. Why don't you trust me to ever make the right decisions about my own life?"

I parroted the same words I used on my mother throughout my adolescence.

"Your anger is very transparent, Coco," Finkelman said. "You're doing a lot of displacing. Perhaps, we should use the session to discuss this. You sound angry."

Instead, I used the session to tell Finkelman I didn't need to waste my money on anger management. What I wanted to discuss was my pending marriage and all the minutiae that went along with it.

"This is not a cram course in marriage 101," Finkelman retorted. "We can cover the main areas of your concerns and deal with each of them one by one."

"I'm not exactly sure," I said.

"Free-associate."

I sat there looking out over Central Park, trying my damnedest to focus and give Finkelman what he wanted, which was to allow him to emulate Siggy Freud whenever possible.

"Just say the first word that comes to mind," he said, his notepad resting on his lap, his Mont Blanc ready to take dictation on my subconscious ramblings.

"Sex," I said. "Sex. Sex. Sex."

And so for the final remaining time, I went at it with a vengeance, giving Finkelman the thrill of a lifetime as I explained in graphic detail why Parker couldn't bring me to orgasm and why I felt that just might mean trouble.

"Trouble?"

"Like the elephant in the living room. You know it's there even though nobody wants to address it."

Finkelman suddenly stopped jotting and became momentarily

human. "Coco, I'm sure that Parker is a fine man and I'm happy that you are able to be open to a new relationship after being bruised from your last. I'm merely saying that there is no reason to be jumping off the high board into the marriage pool when there is no urgency. After all, your biological clock has just about stopped ticking. You need to work through some matters that will enable you to ultimately make sense of your life and move on from there."

I stared back at Finkelman, who made perfect sense. Then I got up, walked out of his office, and went home. That same evening Parker and I set a wedding date.

7

"Marriage changes passion . . . suddenly
you're in bed with a relative."
—Unknown

The Whole Enchilada

We decided a winter wedding was preferable to any other time of the year. I envisioned a snowfall. I envisioned little twinkling lights. And of course, in keeping with Yvonne, I envisioned black.

"Have you gone bonkers, Mom?" Eliza came to a screeching halt when I told her that white was so ordinary, so conventional.

"A bride who wears black is a bride who defies tradition—who dares to be herself. Your grandmother thinks it's a great idea."

"Yvonne is from another planet. Why can't you go the beige route? Something ecru."

"I'm not an egg," I said. "Eggshells are ecru."

"What about gray?"

"What? And look like a ballistic missile?"

And, finally, my daughter counterattacked with the coup de grâce.

"Mother, if you wear black, I'll die."

"Well then," I said, "I'll be perfectly dressed for the occasion."

It was now August. Eliza was heading back to Wellesley in a few weeks to begin her senior year. As happy as she was about Parker and my engagement, she was still loyal to Mitch, and didn't want to get more than peripherally involved this time around. After we decided on a December date, Parker and I began discussing geography.

"We don't need two New York apartments," Parker said. "Would you consider giving up yours and moving to Seaport full-time?"

The burbs? Was he mad? Why, it was like moving to the opposite end of the earth.

"We still have my East End Avenue place," he said, "and then there's the house in Lenox for weekend retreats. Really, Coco, I think you'd find that living in Seaport could be an exciting adventure."

"Let me mull it over," I said.

~

"I feel like I'm taking a step backward," I told Annie.

"Seaport is a happening place," she said, "and we'd be able to see each other all the time."

Annie was a successful artist who showed extensively both in Connecticut and New York. One of her pieces even hung in MoMA and she was forever presenting her work in group shows. Seaport was her oasis for the solitude she needed to do her art.

I was used to the noise of the city: taxi horns, sirens, the cacophony of street sounds that lulled me to sleep and provided the perfect backdrop for stirring my creative juices. When I was working on an article I would sit at my desk, the windows flung open, and bring the city to me. Going to the suburbs seemed the antithesis of all that. I imagined being transported into a world of green lawns stretching for miles, mild-mannered folks instead of cranky New Yorkers, garbled voices over garden fences, a lazy cat, half asleep in a ray of sunlight. If I were lucky, the clank of a garbage truck or screech of an SUV would be the only occasional reminders that real life actually existed. I feared I would miss the everyday drama of life in the Big Apple.

Conversely, Seaport was only an hour from Manhattan and did attract a diverse group of interesting people. Aside from being a bedroom community for daily commuters who made back and forth runs on Metro North from home to office, there was a large segment of Seaport who, like Annie, lived and worked here. Artists, writers, playwrights, architects, small business owners—those seeking creative outlets found the town inspiring. It boasted a community theater and the Seaport Country Playhouse, often home to Broadway-bound plays. For those who insisted on legitimate New York theater, museums, concerts, and the like, a car or train ride had them on the streets of New York in an hour.

But the biggest draw for me was the beach with a panoramic view that spanned miles. Seaport was on Long Island Sound and the drive from Parker's house to the water was under seven minutes. All summer, when Eliza and I were staying in Seaport, we did our morning walk, stopping for our bagels and coffee at the corner café just around the beach walk bend. Parker had his golf, I had my walks, and we would meet up later at the club for lunch. When Eliza was staying with us, she often joined us, but most of her summer was spent in our New York apartment or off with her friends at their summer homes in the Hamptons or on Martha's Vineyard. As she moved into adulthood, I felt the subtle winds of change tweak at our relationship. Another year of college and she would be on her own to pursue a career in psychology, then going on for a masters and the obligatory Ph.D. Because we were so close, cutting the ties that bound us, mother to daughter, would not be an easy transition. My engagement to Parker softened our separation. Eliza was comforted by the fact that once she was gone, there was a man who would pick up the slack. She didn't need to feel responsible for abandoning me to live her own life.

I told Finkelman at our next session that I was considering making a permanent move to Connecticut.

"I see," he said. "Now, that's something to chew on."

"A decision I think will work," I said.

Finkelman was now resigned to the fact that I had decided to marry, despite his admonitions that he still felt I needed to "do some work" before tying the knot.

"You're a strong-willed woman, Coco," he said, "a quality that will hold you in good stead, but don't confuse will with reason."

I was amused by Finkelman's bon mots. I had even begun writing them down as possible material for future articles. Finkelman was a cliché in shrink's clothing. I was actually becoming fond of the guy who, despite his intellect, was more transparent than he realized.

In Boca, on the southern tip of the eastern seaboard, Yvonne was getting hot and heavy into my wedding plans even though Parker and I insisted she not get involved.

"Mother," I said, "this isn't the first time around. Please, get a grip."

"Have you given more thought to your dress, Coco?"

"Yes, I've combed the shops," I said. "All I've been seeing are dresses in putrid shades that are so overdone with flounces and fluff. Others came in colors that work well for Crayola, but would look ridiculous on a grown woman. And what about you, Mom? Have you been thinking about your dress?"

"I'm the MOB," she said. "I need to blend into the woodwork."

"MOB?"

"Mother of the Bride, darling. I need to be invisible."

Even when my mother wasn't physically present, she could never be invisible.

"So, I'm doing a complete turnaround: I'm wearing white."

"But I'm the bride."

"That's why you should wear black, darling. You'll set a new trend."

I had to agree: My mother was one of a kind.

As for Bridgette, she was starting to come around and accept the fact that I made her brother happy even if I was Jewish. As for her dress, she confided to Parker that she was feeling slightly frivolous and might want to try something in the salmon mousse or the raspberry truffle family. She had already purchased a strawberry blond wig because she was tired of being a brunette.

"Maybe we should elope," I suggested to Parker.

"Over my dead body," Yvonne offered her two cents when I mentioned the possibility. "Your father and I have already planned a big surprise."

"No surprises, Mother," I said. "And no Rose Harris. Parker's house is already perfect."

"Rose Harris is dead," she said. "She croaked in the D and D building, picking out swatches. And anyway, that's not what your father and I had in mind."

"Give it to me straight, Mother," I said, "so I can start adjusting to it now."

"An all-black wedding cake, sweetheart, with white roses draped along each tier. I want you to have the whole enchilada."

8

"The most dangerous food is wedding cake."
—James Thurber

A Piece of Cake

And it was all that: the whole enchilada . . . and more. On a snowy evening in December, Parker and I got married under a chuppah, or canopy as Bridgette liked to call it. A hundred and fifty of our nearest and dearest attended the wedding and reception at the Seaport Country Club. For weeks before the wedding, Annie splashed paint colors on her canvas until we found exactly the right shade: a deep purple with a touch of red and hint of gray, and voilà! I was a vision in violet, which Annie said was the new black. My dressmaker, Raffaella, agreed to design the dress. I bought the material. It was simple and elegant, tea length with soft varying shades and layers of chiffon billowing at the sides with a scoop neck and long sleeves with tiny buttons up to the elbow. I looked romantically ethereal. Around my neck was a single diamond pendant that Parker had given me the night before. My mother decided to comply with my wishes and stay away from bridal white, opting for her old black Givenchy, which she decided she wanted to wear and would have if my father hadn't threatened to shoot her on the spot. Instead, she found a peach organza gown at Bergdorf's with an accompanying ivory-colored boa that made her look ever-so-slightly like a Creamsicle.

Eliza, looking like a vision in burgundy velvet, walked down the aisle with Hudson's two little girls, Chloe and Isabelle, following behind, tossing rose petals from tiny wicker baskets. Bridgette, in keeping with her original plan, wore her strawberry blond wig and a raspberry silk suit and carried a Judith Lieber bag in the shape of a raspberry. She looked oddly like a transvestite. A justice of the peace spoke eloquently and sentimentally, leaving the women reaching for their tissues before an avalanche of mascara ran amok. Even the men became slightly teary-eyed when Parker and I recited our respective vows on life and love forever after.

The champagne flowed, the room dripped flowers, and outside, a December snow fell gently upon a candlelit evening. The only glitch was my mother's black wedding cake with a slight variation on the theme: Instead of a butter cream black atrocity, she had convinced us to allow her to have a caviar and cream cheese cake that sat on a table in a corner near the hors d'oeuvres. Despite my dismay, it was a huge hit.

"Let's face it, Coco," Annie said. "They don't make mothers like Yvonne anymore."

"Thank God," I said.

~

After our honeymoon in Paris, I moved to Seaport full-time and became officially suburbanized. I had sold my Manhattan apartment right after Thanksgiving and split the money with Mitch, which was part of our divorce agreement. Mitch was now engaged to Maxine, proving once again that glitz over substance sometimes pays off.

"And don't think the big boobs didn't hurt any," Annie reminded me.

I kept my favorite pieces of furniture that fortunately fit perfectly with Parker's décor. Eliza came home from school on occasional weekends, finding Seaport to be less of a drag than she thought it would be. When we all craved the fast pulse of New

York, there was the three-bedroom apartment to provide us with a temporary rush of adrenaline. I was busy working on an assignment for *Parents* magazine, which brought me into the city for occasional meetings with my editor. The rest of the time, I did freelance writing, including occasional children's stories for some of the top kids' magazines.

One morning, over breakfast, Parker said he had played golf with the publisher of the *Seaport Gazette* and had mentioned me.

"John Brooks is a member of the club," Parker announced. "He said he'd be interested in seeing some of your stuff. How does that sound?"

"Interesting," I said.

That same day Parker dropped off a packet of my articles at John Brooks's office and arranged for the three of us to do lunch at the club on Wednesday.

John Brooks was a large man with a hard handshake and a grin that exuded warmth on the spot. We took to each other immediately and the wine that Parker ordered only increased our mutual admiration.

"I like your work, Coco. Have you ever considered a different kind of writing?" he asked over his third glass of pinot noir.

"Such as?"

"We've been looking for someone to write a humor column," John said. "Have you ever thought of trying to tickle the funny bones of your readers?"

Parker kicked me under the table, indicating I should say "yes" no matter what.

"Funny, but I've always wanted to write humorous pieces," I lied.

"What we're after are satirical essays that can reflect the lighter side of life."

For the rest of the lunch, I convinced myself, Parker, and John Brooks that my funny bone was indeed my most important body part.

"Let's give it a shot, then," Brooks suggested. "Write something up and bring it over to our editor, Gillian Monk. The sooner the better."

That afternoon and well into the night, all I thought about was "funny." I went to the library and scanned the works of several humorists. Then, it hit me: the one person who was funnier than them all. The woman who was constantly dishing out her lines and unknowingly providing me with material when she least expected it was my mother, Yvonne. And there on my bed in Seaport, Connecticut, I had a sudden epiphany. I remembered after my divorce, my mother's constant fear that I would die an old maid. I recalled her exact words:

"I just haven't met Mr. Right," I had reminded her.

"How about Mr. Maybe?" she had asked.

And there it was: my idea for that first humorous article. I ran to my computer and at 2:55 A.M., I churned out my first piece, "Meeting Mr. Maybe."

The Seaport Gazette

MEETING MR. MAYBE

It's hard to make a lunch date with my friend Jane these days—hard to find a moment where the two of us can shoot the breeze. That's because Jane has fallen prey to cyber-mating. She has a new boyfriend. The nice part is, she never had to leave home to meet him. All that's required is owning a computer and having lots of time on her hands.

Jane converses daily with her cyber-mate, Hank, whose online call sign is "Big Boy." Jane refers to herself as "Hot Lips."

"Tell me about Big Boy," I asked her the other night when she took a moment out to talk with me on the phone.

"He's wonderful," she said, "intelligent and funny, sensitive and very sexy. I think he just might be my next Mr. Maybe."

"What does Big Boy look like?" I asked.

And then she got serious. "I haven't a clue," she said. "I never laid eyes on him. So far our relationship extends exclusively to the computer."

I tried appearing nonchalant. After all, what did I know? My history of dating involved looking into the faces of real men, which by millennium standards has become a bit passé.

"How did you know that Big Boy was the one?" I asked.

"He and I belong to the same chat group," Jane, I mean Hot Lips, said. "I conversed with many men until one day when Big Boy came aboard and responded to me. The chemistry was incredible."

Computer chemistry. I was intrigued.

"The best part is we're totally compatible. We enjoy all the same things. I ski. Big Boy skis. I like jazz. So does he. I jog and he runs five miles a day."

"Except you never do it together," I said, somewhat puzzled.

"A small price to pay for a meaningful relationship," she said.

"Last week I heard from Big Boy only once," she added. "I nearly panicked. I thought he had tired of me—found another cyber-mate, until he got back online and told me he had the flu and was out of commission. I was so relieved that I sent him chicken soup."

"Wasn't that difficult?"

"I faxed him my mother's recipe. Big Boy said he cooked up a batch. He's feeling better already."

"How often do you and Big Boy talk?" I asked.

"We started out 'dating' twice a week. Now, we're up to three days plus weekends. I imagine we'll be living together before long," she said.

"How is that possible?" I asked.

"Easy," Hot Lips said. "We'll both move our computers into our respective bedrooms and communicate from there."

"Sounds very intimate."

"We couldn't be closer. It's the most fun I've ever had without actually touching."

"Definitely a new approach to dating," I agreed.

"It's our answer to safe sex," Hot Lips confessed. I had to admit: She had a point.

"Big Boy and I send each other love letters every day. It's very romantic. The fact that we can tune out at any time keeps the sparks flying. We never take each other for granted."

"Aren't you anxious to meet each other in person?" I couldn't help but inquire.

"What! And ruin a perfectly good relationship? Never! We prefer things to stay exactly the way they are. We both have our space and it never gets boring."

"Don't you miss the normal dating routine?" I asked.

"I hate the dating scene," Hot Lips said. "It's so ordinary—so bourgeois. It's much more relaxed this way. I never have to worry about what to wear. If I'm having a bad hair day, he'll never know. It's the only way to go."

It sounded intriguing. I envisioned getting up each morning and plugging in to my cyber-mate, never having to brush my teeth or get out of my bathrobe. If I had a pimple on my nose, who would care? Our relationship would be based on the real stuff: the inner person, not outward appearances. I began to think Hot Lips was on to something. I had to deal with disagreements, working things through, and making up. Hot Lips bypassed all that by turning off her computer when the going got rough.

The next day, Hot Lips phoned me, in tears. "It's over!" she cried.

"What happened?" I asked.

"Big Boy sent me his picture."

"What does he look like?"

"He's certainly not a Big Boy," she said. "Not at all what I imagined. He even has a beard. I detest beards."

Hot Lip's bubble had burst. She was now faced with the same problems every other person had to face: imperfect mates.

"What am I going to do now?" she asked.

"I know a man you might like to meet," I suggested. "You and he have a lot in common."

"What does he do?" Hot Lips asked.

"He's a retired pharmacist," I said. "He stays home and plays computer games all day."

"What's his name?"

"His real name is Sheldon Ehrenkrantz. His online call sign is Stud Muffin."

Hot Lips and Stud Muffin have been dating for a few months, now. It's a match made in cyber-mate heaven.

~

The next morning, bright and early, I went over to the *Seaport Gazette* to drop off a hard copy of "Meeting Mr. Maybe," along with some other samples of my work. I enclosed a note to the editor, Gillian Monk, explaining that John Brooks had suggested I try my hand at a humorous piece. I faxed him one, as well. I said I'd enjoy meeting her when she had some time. I heard nothing for a week. Then, on a late Tuesday afternoon, the phone rang. It was Gillian Monk herself.

"I laughed out loud," she said. "Haven't done that for a while. And John Brooks called me, too. Seems to be a fan of yours. Why not stop by tomorrow so we can meet in person."

I called Parker on his cell and told him that our little lunch had paid off.

"I'm seeing the editor of the *Seaport Gazette*," I said. "She wants to talk."

"It wasn't the lunch, Coco," Parker said, always my staunch supporter. "She obviously likes your writing."

"But I'm not a humorist," I said.

"You are now," he said.

The following day around noon, I met Gillian, who decided that instead of talking in her office, we should go out for a quick bite. We drove over to the deli together in Gillian's VW Rabbit. I was immediately impressed by her spontaneity. She was casually dressed and had an easy air about her that made me feel instantly comfortable. In her mid-thirties, she told me she was one of the youngest editors the *Gazette* had ever hired.

"How did you get into the newspaper business?" I asked.

"I started out as a reporter for a small paper in Massachusetts. It was my first job out of college. I did tons of freelance work, too. Then one day I saw an ad for a job as assistant editor here in Seaport. I applied and came down for an interview. They hired me on the spot."

"You must have had great credentials," I said.

"It's funny, Coco, I was editor of my high school yearbook and wrote extensively for my college paper, but other than a few articles here and there, I was pretty green. They decided to take a chance with me. I got lucky."

I sat there eating my turkey on rye, sucking on a sour pickle, and listening intently as Gillian filled me in.

"Then, a few years ago, our editor relocated because of her husband's job offer in Chicago. I was moved into the spot of editor. It all evolved on its own."

"So you got lucky again," I said.

"The reason I wanted to meet you," Gillian said, "is that we're looking for a full-time humor columnist. Frankly, the writer we have now has lost her spark and is not exactly with the times. We want a fresher, more contemporary approach. I'd like to see more of what you do and if you can deliver the goods under pressure. Can you have something on my desk by tomorrow?"

I swallowed hard. "Is this a weekly column?"

"Yes. Every Wednesday you'll have a spot on Op-Ed where you can wax eloquent on any subject that you consider humorous. I'm not hung up on what you write as long as it has generic appeal and gives our Seaport residents a laugh. These days, more than ever, we need a touch of humor in our lives."

I tried to conceal my anxiety. "Any subject?" I reiterated.

"I'll be honest, Coco. I am considering two other writers, but I think you're a natural and you're definitely in the running. Your body of work is impressive, but humor writing is a very specific genre. Not everyone can handle it. So let's see how you do," she said, smiling warmly.

"Write what you know, Coco, and just distort it enough to make it funny."

"I'll have something on your desk by morning," I said.

Gillian treated me to lunch and we drove back to the paper. We said our good-byes in the parking lot. Then, without stopping for anything, I went straight home and plunked myself down in front of my computer.

Suddenly, without warning, I was entering a new phase of my career: humor writing. Whether I had the talent or not remained to be seen. But Gillian was giving me my big chance and I was going to try my hardest not to blow it.

I wrote throughout the afternoon and took a break at dinnertime to phone Annie.

"What's up, kid?" she asked.

"I'm writing a piece for the *Seaport Gazette*," I said. "I'm in the running for the position of humor columnist."

"Go for it, doll," Annie cheered me on. "The paper can sure use a good writer. The one we have now stinks."

"But, I'm not sure I can handle humor," I said. "And especially not on a weekly basis."

"Are you kidding, babe?" Annie said. "Just write your life. It's a piece of cake."

9

"Leap . . . the net will follow."
—Unknown

La Crème de la Crème

I have never cracked under pressure, but tonight my anxiety level had reached its all-time high.

"How the hell can I make this happen?" I asked Parker when he walked through the door that evening.

"Come on, Coco, you're a writer. You've been knocking out articles for years. Just bite the bullet. Stop agonizing, sit down and do it. The editor liked what she saw. Just strut your stuff."

When it comes to humor, trying to be deliberately funny is the kiss of death. Just watch the good comedians and you'll understand that. Timing is everything and the same rule applies with writing. "Write what you know," Gillian had said. The rest, I assumed, would flow naturally.

I stayed up late trying to "flow." By 10:00, I was still trying to write from experience. I pecked away at the keys expecting a miracle to happen, but nothing but banal words filled the page. "Meeting Mr. Maybe" might have been beginner's luck; maybe I couldn't be funny on a regular basis. It just wasn't my style.

Around midnight I needed to veg out, as I knew I might be pulling an all-nighter. I took a break and joined Parker in the bedroom. He was engrossed in some inane late-night film. When I reached for the clicker, he jumped.

"What are you doing?" He seemed startled, repossessing the remote control.

"Nothing," I said. "I was only going to lower the volume so we could talk."

"I can do it. I know exactly the right level the volume should be for conversation."

"What are you watching?"

"Some old film with a group of has-been actors."

During a commercial break, I reached over for the clicker, again. Parker stood firm, protecting his territory.

"What's wrong with you?" I started to get irritated. "I just wanted to change the channel for a second."

"Allow me," he said, defensively.

"Be my guest, I didn't know it meant so much for you to be in control."

"Who's in control? It's just that I was watching this particular movie, so if you need to channel surf, it's better that I do it. It's a well-known fact that men can click faster than women."

Shades of Mitch, who used to covet the clicker as though it were a family jewel.

And with that, I bolted from the room, hotfooted it back to my laptop, and in one fell swoop wrote a humor piece that Gillian just might find funny. And I owed it all to Parker and the rest of the members of his sex.

The Seaport Gazette

KING OF THE CLICKER

There's a question that has been plaguing me for many years, the same one that women all over the place are wondering about: Why can't men surrender the TV remote control, otherwise known as "The Clicker"? I've been observing men for a while now, and I can tell you this: Once a guy gets his hands on one of these little gizmos, he's never going to give it up. Why, he covets this sucker like it's one of the family jewels. Women get boob jobs. Men, if given the chance, would have their remote controls surgically implanted in their hands.

I once asked a man to hand over the clicker and he looked at me as though I had told him to toss me a hand grenade. Then I was put through the third degree.

"What do you want the clicker for?"

"I want to change the channel."

"Why?"

"Because I'm not interested in watching some idiot on some stupid game show feed a piece of pickled herring to a woman in a teddy with a fur boa around her neck."

"But," he said, "if she swallows the herring before the clock runs out, this guy will win an all-expenses paid vacation to the Poconos, along with a bottle of pink champagne."

"Give me that clicker."

"No."

"I hate game shows."

"Let me watch this one couple, then I promise I'll switch channels."

"Why can't I switch channels when the show is over?"

Then he said something that I swear I'm not making up.

"It's easier if I switch channels. It's a known fact that men click faster than women."

If you think I was going to lower myself by having a dialogue about who clicks faster, you're absolutely right. I sat there in my living room telling him that it's a well-known fact that my clicking acumen is as good as his. We argued this point for about fifteen minutes, longer than it took for the woman in the teddy to swallow the herring and for another woman to cover her significant other in whipped cream before the clock ran out. By this time I was so disgusted by the program selection that I got up from the couch and started to walk out of the room in a huff, at which point my friend shouted:

"Since you're up, would you mind bringing me back a

bowl of that chocolate fudge ripple ice cream with some M and Ms on the top?"

To make matters worse, he wasn't even my husband, so by all rights, I didn't have to put up with this nonsense. But by now I was so brainwashed by men with clicker complexes that I knew better than to think I could win a discussion with a remote control freak. There's something about being king of the clicker that makes a guy feel, well . . . like a guy, the same way we gals need to be in charge of the telephone.

Once a man takes hold of the clicker, it's his for life. He's not going to share it with anyone, no matter how hard they plead. He's at the center of a vast universe consisting of over a hundred channels to play around with. Why, he's practically heady from the power. He literally runs the show. He decides what to watch and when to watch it, and God help us if we try to intervene.

If you've ever observed an ordinary couple arriving home after a long day, you'll notice the following scene: He runs for the TV. She runs for the telephone. While he's involved in some serious channel surfing, she's on the phone complaining to her friends that she can't get him away from the tube.

He views TV as his escape from what he fears most in a relationship: intimacy. She views the telephone as her hotline to sanity, a chance to vent to her friends that she's married to a guy who doesn't give her the attention she needs.

A couples therapist once told me that she saw two people whose marriage ended because when confronted with the question, what do you cherish most, the husband admitted it was the TV clicker.

"It's the only way I ever get to feel I'm in charge," he said.

They divorced. She got the house. He got the TV set and the remote control.

Around my house, it's a different story. We have two TVs and two clickers. If my husband, Parker, wants to watch television, I don't get all hot and bothered. I simply retire to my room and watch whatever program I want. He does the same. Our marriage works beautifully. We never get in each other's way. We never argue. We never get into power struggles. That's because we haven't seen each other for days. I'm upstairs watching The Shopping Channel. He's downstairs watching some guy in a pair of high heels and a dress having peanut butter sandwiches shoved down his throat by a woman in a mink bikini holding a whip.

"The idea," he tells me when I pass through the room on my way to the kitchen, "is to see how many sandwiches he can eat before the clock runs out."

"You're sick," I say.

To which he replies:

"Would you mind whipping me up an egg salad sandwich on pumpernickel with a side order of Mallomars and a Sprite?"

I went to bed at 2 A.M. with a satisfied feeling. The next morning, my eyes blurry from lack of sleep, I drove over to the *Seaport Gazette* and hand-delivered "King of the Clicker." Then I went home and napped until noon, when I met Parker at the eighteenth hole for lunch on the patio in the main clubhouse.

"The dirty deed is done," I said. "I dropped off my piece."

"I knew you had it in you, darling," he said.

"Thanks to you," I said, smiling.

And Parker beamed, never for a minute suspecting how after he read my piece he might not be so thrilled. Gillian had said, "Write what you know," and therein lay the secret to my success.

There was a message on my machine the next day from Gillian. I immediately called back.

The managing editor picked up. "Sorry, she's in a meeting," he said.

"Please tell her that Coco Harding called."

"Oh, Coco, our new humor columnist. Hi. I'm Kirk Lawson. Welcome aboard."

A moment of silence followed where I paused to collect myself.

"Really? Are you sure?"

Kirk laughed. "I am definitely sure I'm Kirk," he said. "As for you, I'm afraid it's true. You're one of us now, Coco. Welcome to life on Seaport's fast track."

I laughed. "This is great news."

"Whenever was a weekly deadline great news?" Kirk asked.

"Oh yeah, I forgot about that," I bantered back.

"One question though: Did your husband ever give you back the remote control?"

"He's still clicking away," I said.

"I'll have Gillian call you later. She'll want to go over a few things, but in the meantime, congratulations again and I look forward to meeting you."

I could hardly contain myself. I screamed out to Parker who was working on his stock portfolio in the den.

"You are not going to believe it," I said. "I got the job."

"Go take a cold shower and start writing, sweetheart," he said.

I called Eliza and told her the news. She was elated. "Just don't write about me, Mom," she warned.

"I'll try, honey, but I'm not sure I can promise. You're just too tempting."

Then Annie, who was her usual nonchalant self.

"I don't know why you're so shocked," she said. "You're la crème de la crème. I knew it all the time."

"You did not, you liar."

"I intuitively felt it," she said. "Good news. Now we have a reason to celebrate. Let's do lunch tomorrow. My treat."

For Annie, every occasion in life was cause for celebration.

10

"A terrible thing happened again last night: nothing."
—Phyllis Diller

Sex à la Carte

Every Thursday I schlepped into the city to do lunch, do Finkelman, and do dinner. My "do" list was regurgitating activities. Life was going well in Seaport. I was launched as the *Gazette*'s humor columnist and readers responded by sending complimentary letters to the editor. Gillian was pleased with her decision to hire me and each week I churned out breezy, satirical essays that seemed to evoke the light touch the paper wanted. With that going for me, and more freelance work on the side, I was busy. Several times a week, I met Parker at the club after his golf game and we lunched. Eliza was doing well at school and her emergency phone calls, more prevalent in her earlier years at Wellesley, had trickled down to a few jingles two or three times a week. She was enjoying her final year and thinking ahead to a master's program at some elite graduate school for which the tried-and-true Mitch would shell out the dough. One might say I had it all. Yet, I was restless.

I burst into my session on Thursday. "I've had it," I said. "One more Whammo and I'll die."

"Whammo?"

"Yes, Parker's favorite expletive is 'whammo.' He came home

from his golf game the other day and told me that he hit the ball and whammo it was downhill for the rest of the day."

"Can you be more explicit?" Finkelman asked.

"He uses it to drive home a point. 'I bought the stock at fifteen and wouldn't you know it: Whammo! I lost my shirt.'

"Or when I'm driving: 'Damn it, Coco, if you keep turning corners like that, whammo! This car's history.'

"But, the worst," I said, "is during lovemaking when he's about to climax.

"'Oh yes! That's it, whammo!' and I know it will be another eight hours before Parker will be able to get it up again."

Finkelman never tired of hearing about the inertia in our bedroom. The more I complained, the more he twitched and questioned.

"We all have different sexual styles." Finkelman came to Parker's rescue. "Some people sigh or moan. Others are more vocal in their responses. Parker's is a whammo."

How would Finkelman know? Picturing him under the covers with the missus wasn't a pretty sight. I imagined that after lovemaking he would lie back, pick up his Mont Blanc, and question his wife on every detail of the act.

"Was it good for you, darling?" Finkelman might ask.

"The earth moved," she'd say.

"Can you elaborate more, dear?"

"I'd rather have a cigarette."

"You know that's very self-destructive. Perhaps we need to examine why you need to smoke after sex. Weren't you satisfied?"

"Maybe if you'd shut up and stop analyzing, I could get off," she would reply.

Such mental meanderings kept me occupied while Finkelman tried his best to elicit a response on why Parker and I couldn't generate heat between us.

I began using analogies to move our sessions along.

"Picture a menu," I said. "There's à la carte and then there's prix fixe. Our lovemaking is more of the latter. Parker chooses predictability over unrestricted. There are only certain parts of me he wants to sample and he omits the rest."

"What parts?" Finkelman was nearly salivating.

"The usual: breasts and vagina. A little stroking and then he's inside me. And whammo! It's all over but the masturbating."

"Masturbating?"

"Yes, after we're through, I go into the bathroom for one final go-around. It's actually the best sex I have."

"And the à la carte?"

"Ahhh, that's the best. The whole nine yards. A sexual extravaganza where the two parties feast off each other, devouring every part of their bodies, culminating in exquisite orgasm. With Parker, these parts are off-limits."

"I see. I see," Finkelman said. "Keep going."

"Parker is a prix fixe lover," I said. "He has the appetizer, proceeds to the entrée, and when he thinks I'm aroused, goes for the hot and heavy dessert. He nibbles. He doesn't dine."

"Do you notice how your sexual analogies pertain to food?" Finkelman interjected.

"Yes, food and sex: primal needs," I reminded him. "The two are intertwined."

"You can't live without food," Finkelman said, "but you won't die from lack of sex."

And the sad fact was, Finkelman really believed that to be true.

PART TWO

First Course

(The Seduction)

11

"Careful, the beverage you're about to enjoy is extremely hot."
—Starbucks coffee cup

A Full Plate

And there I was, back to the future. I was four years into my marriage and still working at the paper when Gillian called me in to discuss the article she wanted me to write for the Chaîne des Rôtisseurs's vegetarian banquet. That night at the Chaîne dinner, I had collected most of the material I needed to make the article shine, but Harry had offered to supply me with more information if I needed it. I had tucked his card away in my jewelry box, underneath strands of pearls and funky necklaces. I went through the weekend promising myself I wouldn't call him. But Monday morning, over my first cup of coffee, I weakened. I picked up the phone.

"Dr. Troutman's office," his receptionist, Sabrina, answered.

"This is Coco Harding, I'd like to speak with Dr. Troutman if he's available."

"I'm sorry," came the obligatory response, "Dr. Troutman is with a patient. What is the nature of this call?"

Stumbling slightly, I said, "I'd like to make an appointment."

"Is this your first office visit?"

"This is not exactly an office visit."

"Is it for a consultation?"

"No."

"A digital enhancement?"

And then, because I wanted to cut short the questionnaire, I said, "Yes, I'd like to be digitally enhanced."

"Dr. Troutman can see you a week from Thursday at ten A.M."

"Nothing sooner?"

"Dr. Troutman is booked solid. If this were an emergency, we would squeeze you in, but since you're only being enhanced, you will have to wait, unless, of course, we have a cancellation. Would you like to be on our 'patient waiting' list?"

"That would be fine."

I gave the receptionist all my vital statistics, including my insurance plan.

"Your digital enhancement is not covered by insurance."

"How much is the digital enhancement?"

"Five hundred dollars," she said. "We'll see you on March 19 at ten o'clock."

I was now reduced to a Patient-in-Waiting and it would cost me five hundred dollars to boot.

"Please have the doctor call me," I said, hastily trying to rectify the situation.

"With reference to what?" she asked.

"I met Dr. Troutman last week at a Chaîne dinner and he asked me to call the office to discuss the details. I'm doing an article."

"This isn't *New York Magazine,* is it?" she asked, "because Dr. Troutman is not speaking with *New York Magazine* this week. He's inundated."

"I'm not with a magazine. I'm with a newspaper."

"Not the *New York Post*? Dr. Troutman absolutely refuses to talk to Page Six."

"Just tell him I need some scoop on the Chaîne."

"But you will keep your digital enhancement?" she asked.

"Actually, I just realized, I'm busy a week from Thursday. Maybe I can be enhanced some other time."

"I'll give Dr. Troutman the message to call you," she said.

That same afternoon, the phone rang just as I stepped out of the shower.

"So, a writer's work is never done," a familiar voice said.

I stood there in my bedroom, a towel draped around me as Harry and I began the verbal gymnastics.

"I thought I could use some more Chaîne information from the expert," I said.

"Expert-on-call," Harry said. "The question is, when?"

"What is your availability?" I tried to stay professional.

"I'm unavailable every day, but for you, Ms. Columnist, I'll make an exception."

"I could come in and be digitally enhanced," I said. "That way there's something in it for both of us."

"Do you want to be enhanced?" he flirted back. "Because that can be arranged. I do fantastic digital work."

"Your receptionist had me slotted in for ten A.M. next Thursday, but I canceled."

"I don't like to be canceled," he said. "In fact, I take cancellations very badly. How about drinks after work? When will you be in the city again?"

What I wanted to say was: I can be in by early evening, but instead told him I would make myself available according to his busy schedule.

"Tomorrow, Bemelmans Bar in the Carlyle Hotel. Can you make it at five o'clock? My last appointment is four on Thursdays."

"See you at five," I said.

"And I'm never late," Harry said. "My office is around the corner from the hotel. How will I recognize you?"

"You'll know me immediately," I said. "I'm the one who desperately needs to be enhanced."

That evening, I told Parker I was going into the city the next day to discuss a freelance job and might not be home for dinner.

"Ah, the writer's life," he said. "If it gets too late, you might as well stay over at the apartment."

The best thing about Parker was he applauded my work and never asked questions. I felt a twinge of guilt run through me as I contemplated what tomorrow would bring. When in doubt, I turned to my two reliable sources: Finkelman and Annie. In this case I decided to bypass Finkelman.

"Kiss your wedding vows good-bye," Annie said when I told her I was seeing Harry. "The man has a major reputation with women."

"For God's sake. Don't overreact. It's just drinks. I need more info for the article."

"Yeah, and I'm Madonna," she said.

"Okay, so I'm a little attracted. Is that so terrible? I'll get what I need and I'm outta there."

"I'll bet you'll get what you need," she said. "That's what worries me."

Annie, as free-spirited as she was, also had a practical side.

"Look Coco, this isn't a lecture. All I'm saying is, be careful."

It couldn't be more perfect: Thursday was my New York day so it seemed only natural that I would schedule appointments, including Finkelman, which I wasn't looking forward to. I would hop over to the Carlyle fresh from my session.

"You seem preoccupied today, Coco," Finkelman nailed me within the first ten minutes.

"I'm planning to murder my husband so I can have an affair," I said jokingly.

Finkelman sat back, arms stretched, his palms resting on the back of his neck. He flicked a piece of lint off his brown tweed trousers and sighed.

"Your fantasies seem a bit elaborate today," he said.

"My fantasies are always elaborate."

I wanted Finkelman to work for his money. If I was going to hand out information, I wasn't going to make it easy. And I wouldn't accept any "I sees."

Finkelman was on to me. "If you're going to take your sessions seriously," he said, "don't give me selective reporting."

I held back until the end. "I have a confession to make," I told him five minutes before my session concluded. "I'm meeting Dr. Harry Troutman for drinks after I leave here."

Finkelman, familiar with the cast of characters that inhabited my life, sat up straight in his chair and adjusted his bow tie, one I hadn't seen before.

"So you've saved the best for last, I see."

"Slipped my mind."

"Coco," Finkelman strained to hold back his disapproval. He dabbed some saliva on his finger and reached down to remove a speck of dust on his shoe. "You do know you're not utilizing your sessions properly. It is part of the doctor/patient contract to adhere to proper patient protocol. You seem to be regressing. Am I to assume I'm correct when I tell you that I'm picking up some resistance? Now, what's this about Dr. Troutman?"

"Sorry," I said coyly, "we have to stop."

"Not to mention, extreme defiance," Finkelman said, twitching ever so slightly and giving his bow tie a little tweak.

12

"The best of life is but intoxication."
—Anonymous

Brief Encounter

Harry was tucked away at a small table at Bemelmans Bar when I arrived. In front of him was a single, long-stemmed pink rose, prepared lovingly for me in a small glass flacon and tied with a white, grosgrain ribbon. He was sipping a whiskey sour and stood up when I entered the room. He looked even better than I remembered, dressed in a camel hair sports jacket, dark brown pants, and a rust-colored turtleneck sweater. He took my hand and escorted me to a chair in a corner of the room. The subdued cocktail lighting provided the perfect ambience.

"It's a well-known fact by those in the know that Bemelmans Bar serves the best whiskey sour in town," Harry said, looking into my eyes with a gaze that could melt. "Shall I order you one?"

"I wouldn't miss the experience," I said, trying to sound as relaxed as possible while my stomach did tiny flip-flops.

He picked up the rose and handed it to me.

"Are you always this charming?" I asked, taking a sniff of a pink petal.

"You can't imagine," he said, a smile breaking out on his face.

It was that very smile that had hooked me the night we met and, unbeknownst to me now, would hold me captive from this day forward.

"I suppose we should get down to business," I said, feeling slightly nervous. "That's why I'm here, after all."

"You really want to forgo the flirting?" he asked, running his hand along my cheek. "Because you're so absolutely damn flirtable."

I could actually feel my face redden. I pulled back, dropping my notebook and scrambling to retrieve it. Harry beat me to it. Our mutual heads met below the table and without warning, Harry kissed me softly on my lips. I pulled away and sat upright. And then, because I was caught off guard and could think of nothing pertinent to say, I decided to ignore what had just transpired. Instead, I threw a few peanuts in my mouth just as my much-needed whiskey sour appeared right on cue.

"To adventures, literary and otherwise." Harry picked up his glass and toasted.

We talked our way through another drink and into the dinner hour. When Harry peered over at his watch, it was past seven.

"Do writers ever get hungry?" he asked, "because I'm starved. The last meal I had was a tuna on rye at noon, and not a very good one at that."

"Traditionally, writers are accustomed to starving," I said. "It's an occupational hazard."

"Would you care to make tonight an exception?" he asked. "Because if you would, I know a place that makes a mean pasta putanesca. They custom design it just for me."

The truth was, my stomach was rumbling and some good pasta sounded divine. But I was curious.

"Isn't your wife expecting you for dinner?" I dared to be so bold.

"Éclaire is away for a few days," he said. "She's at Canyon Ranch, 'freshening up.' It's not easy leading such a hectic lifestyle, after all. Our social engagements have run her a little ragged."

I burst out laughing. I would come to learn over the course of the evening that Éclaire frequented spas as often as I had my hair trimmed . . . every six to eight weeks.

"Parker thinks I'm in the city working with a colleague."

"You are," Harry said.

Harry paid the bill and scurried us into a cab and downtown to Lupa. We were greeted by the owner, Mario Batali, who obviously knew Harry and bent over backward to please. The place was bustling and while they didn't take reservations, we were seated immediately when Mario saw Harry.

"*Buona sera,*" the waiter said, pulling my chair back until I was comfortably seated. Harry wasted no time in asking for the wine list and chose a nice dolcetto to accompany our pasta.

"Did you know," he asked me, after his ritualistic sniff of the cork and the first sip, "that dolcetto originates in the cool slopes of the mountains of the Piedmont area in northwestern Italy?"

"Can't say I did," I said, my eyes fixed on his. "Tell me more."

"Love to," Harry said, bumping knees under the table. "The grape is affectionately known as 'the little sweet one' and thrives where others struggle to ripen."

I could feel myself melting on his words.

"Am I to assume there's a metaphor lingering here?" I asked.

"What I'm saying, Coco," Harry continued, "is that I think of you as 'the little sweet one,' too."

"I've never been compared to a grape before," I said, "but I can assure you that unlike the dolcetto, I never ripen without a struggle."

"That remains to be seen," Harry said, pulling his leg away long enough to order a cold antipasto. He then broke off a slice of bread and dipped it into the greenest olive oil I had ever seen.

"There's olive oil and then there's olive oil," he said. "Here, try this." He reached across the table and placed a small piece of oil-drenched bread between my lips. If climaxes could be obtained through the ingestion of food, I was experiencing an orgasmic moment.

I cannot remember anything about our meal except that all the culinary flavors seemed to blend into one glorious gastronomic adventure. The conversation flowed easily as Harry and I savored each morsel that was presented. We lingered long into the evening over espressos and biscotti, discussing our mutual lives: marriage, children, and our respective careers. Harry and Éclaire had one daughter, sixteen-year-old Melissa, aka Muffin, who was struggling with weight issues and unclear as to where her future would lead her.

Harry sat back. "You've seen my work?"

"My dear, some of the best noses in the city are Troutman noses. I know four women with schnozzles the size of sausages, which are now carved to perfection and look very retroussé."

Harry beamed. "I'm just an exterior designer," he said.

It was eleven o'clock when we looked up and realized we were among a handful of people left in the room. Not once was the Chaîne des Rôtisseurs ever mentioned.

"I'm afraid I failed you as a mentor," Harry said. "You were supposed to pick my brain about the Chaîne. I don't think I've been any help, have I?"

"Do I detect a modicum of guilt?" I asked.

"When is the article due?"

"I have a month to get it into working order."

"Then we'll have to work fast," Harry said. "I have an idea. Meet me on Saturday for lunch and I promise that we'll concentrate only on Chaîne-related topics."

"I can't get away on Saturday," I said. "It's my day with Parker. Unless you'd like to join us at the club for lunch; I'm sure he'd find you fascinating."

"Not as fascinating as I find his wife," Harry said.

"Really, come to Seaport," I said. "You and Parker would enjoy each other and we can talk Chaîne together while Parker does his nine holes. It will get you out of the city for a few hours. Maybe even a dip in the pool."

"You're a very convincing woman," Harry said. "How do you know that Parker won't mind the intrusion? He might want you all to himself."

"Are you kidding? Parker thrives on meeting all the new and interesting people in my life."

"Shall I take that as a compliment?"

"More to the point, I've been noticing lately that Parker's eyelids are hanging a tad low. There might even be a job opportunity here."

"Coco," Harry said, "are you always so direct?"

"Only when provoked," I said.

We were standing on Thompson Street in front of the restaurant.

"You know, I could devour you on the spot." Harry inched closer. "What say we have a nightcap and take total leave of our senses?"

"What say we simply take leave?" I said, hailing the first taxi I saw. "But keep Saturday in mind. Call me and let me know. I'll be at the apartment until tomorrow afternoon." I slipped my phone number into his jacket pocket.

Then, feeling just a bit tipsy from "the little sweet grape," I kissed Harry firmly on his lips, closed the door of the cab, and watched him become a stick figure in the distance.

13

"A little nonsense now and then
is relished by the wisest men."
—Roald Dahl (*Willy Wonka and the Chocolate Factory*)

I Want to Be a Bad Girl

Early on, I was told by most of the adult authority figures in my life, my mother and teachers mostly, that I had an uncanny knack for getting myself into heaps of trouble. While I was less than totally innocent, it always looked worse than it was. One Saturday afternoon when I was eleven, my girlfriend Patty and I made a phone call to the local pizza parlor, ordered a pie with all the trimmings, and had it sent to the lady next door, Mrs. Braverman, who hated kids and, with the exception of her three cats, lived alone. Mrs. Braverman was the perfect target at whom our budding adolescent mischief-making pranks were directed.

We watched from my bedroom window as the pizza truck drove up. Mrs. B. came to the door and insisted she had not placed an order. While we couldn't hear the exact exchange, it was apparent that she was less than happy. The pie was taken away, the driver left, and Mrs. B. bolted from her porch over to my house. The doorbell rang as Patty and I cowered in the closet, giggling so loudly I thought I would split a gut. Then the sound of my mother's high heels on the stairs as she made her way into my room, shouting, "Coco, Coco, get downstairs right this minute."

Sheepishly, Patty and I joined my mother and Mrs. Braverman in our living room.

"Mrs. Braverman claims that a pizza pie was sent to her house."

"One that I never ordered," Mrs. Braverman looked sternly at us over her wire-rimmed glasses, "and especially not with anchovies."

"Do you have an explanation, Coco?" my mother asked.

Patty and I looked at each other and, in unison, began to laugh so uncontrollably that we couldn't speak.

"Well, I guess that settles that," Mrs. Braverman said, making her grand exit. "If I ever receive a pizza pie again, the authorities will be notified."

But it didn't stop us. Over the next few years, Patty and I wreaked havoc on Mrs. B., who always tried to catch us in the act, but to no avail.

"Keep that up," she stopped me one day as I was waiting for the school bus, "and you won't amount to a hill of beans."

"I don't know what you're talking about," I said.

"Mark my words: If I ever find the person who nailed my mailbox shut, there will be hell to pay."

That time I was a true innocent and not the culprit. The Friedbauer boys, who lived up the street, were the wanted ones. Mrs. Braverman was open season for us all. But once a prankster always a prankster, and until I moved away from home and left for college, Mrs. Braverman had me pegged.

"You're a very naughty girl, Coco Plotnick," she said, "and you will pay dearly for your peccadilloes. You are nothing more than a scamp."

I went home and looked up "peccadillo" in our *Webster's* first edition. It could be worse.

I left for college on a crisp September morning, ready to begin a new chapter in my life. As I was getting into my father's Cadillac Eldorado, I saw Mrs. Braverman pull her parlor curtains aside and sneak a peek through her front window, watching as I, Coco the neighborhood scamp, vanished into oblivion, leaving a trail of peccadilloes behind me.

Mrs. Braverman paved the way. I carried my peccadilloes well into adulthood. She had dubbed me naughty and so, having been labeled such, I considered it a handicap that I would bear forever, like a large nose or a slight limp. Now, especially where Harry was concerned, the naughty girl image came back to haunt me. So much so, I wrote a column the next day, inspired by my meeting with Harry the night before.

The Seaport Gazette

I WANT TO BE A BAD GIRL

I want to be a bad girl—the type you meet once and never forget. The kind of girl who knows who she is and isn't afraid to show it. The one women love to hate, men kill to love.

Back before Hollywood got caught up in special effects and raw sex, there was a certain kind of woman you don't see around much anymore. Women like Garbo and Lombard, Bergman and Tierney—women who knew how to look at a man and make him feel like a million bucks.

I want to be a bad girl with eyes that smolder like Bette Davis's and lips that are wet like Dorothy Lamour's. I want to walk into a room and have men's blood pressure rise simply because I smiled. Bad girls knew how to walk no matter what they wore. Their clothes moved with their bodies. They clung to their figures, accentuating every crevice and curve. If a bad girl wasn't careful, she would cause cardiac arrest to any man standing nearby. I want to walk with a slouch and toss my hips around like Jane Russell. When I try to walk like a bad girl, I stumble or turn my ankle. When my dresses hug my body, it's usually due to static cling.

I want to be a Siren who makes grand entrances and memorable exits. When Myrna Loy looked into William Powell's eyes, she exuded self-assurance. Myrna didn't need Women's Lib to get what she wanted. She simply cocked her head and William jumped. When she played Nora to Powell's Nick Charles and didn't like what he said, she brushed him off with merely a glance that implied, "Don't be ridiculous, you silly little man." Then, she turned on her heels and sauntered off. Her exit lines gave us all pause.

I want to be a vamp like Jean Harlow. Vamps like Harlow slinked instead of walked. They glided through life as if they were floating on air. Vamps knew how to posture and pose. They stopped men dead in their tracks. The last time I stood with one hand on my hip, the other in the air, my husband draped a pair of trousers over my arm. He said to make sure I got them to the cleaners on time.

I want to have a voice like Bankhead's and Dietrich's: deep, throaty, and sexy. I tried using that voice last week when buying a chicken at the market. The butcher offered me a cough drop and told me to gargle with Listerine.

I want to kiss men with first names of Clark, Cary, and Marlon. I want to be half of that incredibly handsome couple who vows undying love. I want my vowing to take place in the arms of leading men, on chaise longues, on rose-covered verandas. All my life I kissed men named Marty, Lenny, and Herb. You don't get the same results from men with those names.

It is not in my cards to be Rita Hayworth, Joan Bennett, or Hedy Lamar. I am not destined for Casablanca, Wuthering Heights, or Tara. My leading men will never be Leslie Howard, Ronald Coleman, or Humphrey Bogart. It's very hard being a bad girl unless you have a bad boy to make it all possible.

I'm tired of equal partnerships. I want to be called "Babe," "Doll," and "Hey, gorgeous." I long for men who still open doors, hold my coat, and run to the passenger side of their cars so they can assist me in the difficult task of climbing out of the vehicle. When a man sees me stranded on the side of the road like Claudette Colbert, I want him to stop and offer to change my flat tire. The last time I had a flat, AAA told me to hang loose; they'd get to me in about two hours.

Back in the days of rumble seats and roadsters, bad girls rode with the tops down, their hair flying in the breeze. My hair flies, too. That's because it's unkempt. I want to have hair like Veronica Lake's. Veronica's wave was so long it undulated down her cheek. She brushed it away with a puff of her breath. When my hair falls down my cheek, people tell me it's time for a haircut.

I want to live in a melodrama like Joan Crawford and Gloria Swanson. I want to dance like Ginger Rogers and Ann Miller. I want to sing like Jane Powell. The only singing I do is in the shower and even then, I'm told to pipe down.

I want to be a bad girl like Mae West, who used all her equipment to drive men wild. I want to use my equipment, too, but it's never around when I want it. These days, the closest we've come to a new kind of bad girl is Madonna. Madonna likes us to think she is bad, but when you strip away the packaging, she's the girl next door. June Allison and Judy Garland once were the girls next door, except there was always a bad boy around to corrupt them. My next door neighbor, Ed, is a real gentleman. I winked at him once and he asked me if I had gotten something in my eye. Back then, when a bad girl flirted men got the message. I want men to get my messages, too. I want to be provocative and irresistible. I want to have an intoxicating personality in the style of the late Katharine Hepburn. I want strong, silent types to pay me wicked compliments. The last compliment I received was from my dentist. He told me I did a nice job of flossing.

I want to be a bad girl who smoked cigarettes before we knew that cigarettes can kill. Cigarettes made a girl look absolutely divine. I want to sit in dimly lit cafés with a cigarette holder in my hand, drinking pink champagne while my frosted red, pointy fingernails glow in the dark. I want to carry a gold compact and powder my nose in expensive restaurants with my ermine coat draped around my shoulders.

Real bad girls didn't try to be bad . . . they simply were. They exuded naughtiness by the way they lowered their eyes, moved their mouths, or shrugged a shoulder. Real bad girls were subtle, mysterious, and possessed an air of je ne sais quoi. I want some je ne sais quoi, too. I want to be seductively foxy and always on the verge of a mad seduction. Most of all I want to be a bad girl . . . real bad!

~

Harry phoned from his office the next morning.

"Éclaire won't be back until Monday. Can I take you up on that dip in the pool?"

"I'll see you at the Seaport Country Club on Saturday morning," I said. I gave Harry directions to the club and invited him to stay the afternoon.

"Parker will be on the course, but he'll join us for lunch around one o'clock. In the meantime, I'll show you around and maybe join you in a swim."

"Pretty women in swimsuits are my weakness," he said.

But all I could think of was how my thighs would look in my black bikini and would Harry think I was a candidate for a smidge of liposuction.

~

It was late afternoon when I returned to Seaport. Parker greeted me with a martini in one hand and a golf club in the other, as he had just returned from the club. Parker lived and breathed golf, always working on his strokes, always striving for that hole in one.

"So, how's my little writer?" he asked. "Was yesterday's meeting everything you hoped it would be?"

"Better than expected," I said. "And guess what . . ." I wanted to break him in gently. "That Chaîne article I'm doing? Well, that doctor who hosted the dinner is available for an interview. He's an authority on La Chaîne des Rôtisseurs. I invited him up to the club on Saturday. And he agreed to come. I thought he might join us for lunch after your game."

"What's this medical gourmet's name?" he asked.

"Harry Troutman."

"Dr. Harry Troutman, surgeon extraordinaire? Is that who you've been talking about all this time? I had no idea."

"Why, yes, he is a plastic surgeon. How did you know?"

"He did Joan's eyes several years ago," Parker said. "A terrific job."

"Then you and Harry met?"

"Only for a few minutes when Joan was in recovery. Seemed like a nice guy."

"He is," I said, "and now you'll have the chance to find out for yourself."

14

"The glutton digs his grave with his teeth."
—English Proverb

A Match Made in Culinary Heaven

Parker had an eight o'clock tee time. The plan was, I would meet Harry at eleven, show him around, and have a swim. The three of us would then meet back at the clubhouse for lunch at one. This would give Parker time to do eighteen holes, shower, and change.

With great precision I chose my outfit, consisting of a little Diane von Furstenberg sundress whose hem fell just above my knees, showing off my suntanned legs that were helped along with Clinique's bronzing cream. My days of baking in the summer sun were over, but the look of health and vitality was still possible with a good line of cosmetics that feigned a tan while being dermatologically PC.

I was waiting on the porch of the clubhouse, slightly nervous and excited, when in the distance, I saw Harry's Mercedes approaching. My mass of shoulder-length silver hair had been cut to perfection only the day before by my "mane man," Robert of Seaport. A gentle breeze played around my head and lifted a few strands of hair up and around my face. My makeup was applied carefully and I looked slightly demure, while inside, I was practically quivering. Harry pulled up to the entrance, spied me immediately, and waved hello as the valet took his keys and drove the car away, leaving us together on this beautiful June day.

Harry had brought a swimsuit along in anticipation of our morning swim. But first, I asked if he'd like some coffee after the ride from Manhattan to Seaport. He eagerly accepted and we went inside to the dining room where a silver urn of freshly brewed coffee and plates filled with mini Danish sat glowing in the sun. A handful of people moved about, but for the most part, the dining room was empty, leaving us alone to talk.

"I haven't stopped thinking about you since Thursday," Harry said. "You do leave a lingering scent."

"It must have been all that garlic we consumed at Lupa's," I said, laughing.

"Coco, I'm serious, you've touched something inside me and I find, much to my surprise, that you're floating in and out of my head a lot during the day. Why do you think it is?"

I sipped my coffee and toyed with my yellow linen napkin.

"Perhaps you have a crush on me," I said.

"Perhaps I do. Otherwise why would I drive to Seaport on a Saturday morning just to do lunch with you and your husband who I'm sure is a hell of a nice guy, but hey . . . you catch my drift."

Brazenly, I reached across the table and dipped my finger into Harry's cup, pulled it out and raised my coffee-stained finger to his lips.

Harry gently kissed it, then placed my finger between his lips, sucking slowly.

"And now it's time for our swim," I said, removing my finger from his mouth.

Our eyes locked. The pieces were all in place.

Harry and I met poolside after he emerged from the locker room wearing black tightly-fitting trunks that hugged his body in all the right places. I could hardly contain myself as he greeted me at the deep end of the pool. I, too, wore a black swimsuit that showed off my curves and accentuated my bustline to look slightly more ample than it actually was. Harry's eyes danced around me as he took a full-frontal view and pirouetted me around.

"Is this a consultation?" I asked. "Are you checking out my derrière to see if I need some work?"

"I know what you need," he said.

"What?"

"You need to get wet."

And there, standing by the pool at Seaport Country Club, Dr. Harry Troutman placed his hand on my slightly rounded but toned stomach, and with one hefty push tossed me backward into the water. Then he jumped in after me, dove beneath, and gave my leg an underwater tweak.

"Wet enough?" I asked him, resurfacing.

"That remains to be seen," he said.

~

Showered and dressed, Parker met us promptly at one o'clock in the main dining room where, only an hour before, Harry and I had sat and flirted. The room was now bustling with golfers, hungry for lunch after their games. Women, looking spent from their nine holes, bemoaned their golf strokes, while groups of men assembled, slapping each other on the back and tossing out golf terms and plays that had caused their balls to run amok.

Parker spied us seated at a table near the window, overlooking the golf course. With hand already extended halfway across the room, he greeted us, his eyes glued on Harry.

"So, this is the guy who beautifies our world," Parker said, shaking Harry's hand.

Parker was his usual ebullient self as he pulled up a chair next to me and gave me a quick peck on the lips.

"So, welcome to Seaport. Coco says you were most helpful with the article she's been writing."

"Yes," I blurted out before Harry could get a word in, "the

night we met at the Chaîne dinner, Harry couldn't have been more informative. That's why I thought it would be nice to invite him up to the club and give him a chance to meet you."

"Great idea," Parker said, "though I would have liked getting you out on the course."

"I'm a bit rusty in that area," Harry said. "Tennis is more my game."

"Well then, maybe after lunch, you can grab a racket and we'll have a go at it."

Parker was the hail fellow well met. The bon vivant whose mission in life was to make sure everyone's needs were taken care of.

"I didn't realize until just the other day that you were the doc who did my late wife's eyes," Parker said. "But when Coco mentioned your name, I remembered what a great job you had done on Joan."

"Coco mentioned that your wife had been a patient. I'm sorry for your loss."

Well, at least she died without bags under her eyes, I was tempted to say.

"Yes, Joan was one of the best, but, I've been blessed twice." He reached over and took my hand. "When Coco came into my life, the sadness dissipated. I'd say I'm a lucky man."

I blushed slightly. While Parker's adoration was all consuming and sweet, I felt mildly uncomfortable having him extol my virtues in Harry's presence. I caught a peripheral glimpse of Harry, who was engrossed in Parker's accolades, while I sipped my diet Coke. I should have been grateful to have a husband who cherished me so, but being seated between Parker, who adored me, and the man to whom I was wildly attracted, made me feel disloyal even though nothing much had transpired between us except for a few kisses and lots of innuendo.

Harry shifted in his chair. "This is some lovely club you have here," he said. "I understand you own another out on the Island."

"It's been great," Parker said. "I inherited them both from my grandfather and they continue to be quite successful. Helps to pay the bills and keep Coco in the style to which she deserves to be accustomed."

Everyone laughed good-naturedly while Parker, in minute detail, described his Connecticut and Long Island clubs.

"Some country clubs took a hit after 9/11," Parker said, "but we're going strong. In fact, our membership is actually up, what with the increase in the upwardly mobile population of Seaport; the young couples wanted a place to hang out with their kids. Take a look around and you'll see what I mean."

The dining room was filled with attractive women in their thirties and forties who were dressed in their tennis togs and sat at tables flanked by their toddlers and uniformed nannies, munching on chicken fingers and grilled cheese sandwiches, while the moms picked at their grilled chicken salads and the yuppie dads downed cheeseburgers and beer. Here was a microcosm of the rich and lovely. Parker sat back and basked in the glow of his success, all the while making sure that Harry was enjoying a lunch fit for the gods.

The waiter appeared on cue. "Giorgio, tell Chef Henri Pierre that we have a special guest with us today," Parker said. "Have him whip up something original."

"I can easily order from the menu," Harry interrupted. "That turkey club looks inviting."

"I won't hear of it," Parker said. "Henri Pierre can weave magic in the kitchen. Giorgio, have Henri Pierre step out here, if you don't mind."

Giorgio disappeared to fetch the chef. Parker was now in his glory. "You may be a Chaîne member, Harry," he said, "but my man, Henri Pierre, has been known to prepare dishes that draw our members to tears. I discovered him when Coco and I were in Paris a couple years ago and I made him an offer I knew he couldn't refuse. I paid through my teeth to bring him over from France and set him and his family up in a condo near the best schools. I spare nothing where my club is concerned. I only want the best."

My eyes rolled as Parker tried impressing Harry both with his foresight and with Seaport Country Club's bill of fare. Henri Pierre, beads of perspiration on his forehead, came out of the kitchen dressed in full chef regalia and was asked to join us at the table. For the next half hour, Henri Pierre, Parker, and Harry discussed vittles and wine. Harry, now fully engrossed in culinary talk, spouted forth on La Chaîne des Rôtisseurs. Henri Pierre became rapturous as he recalled a Chaîne banquet he had presided over in Provence a few years back.

"It was an evening to remember," Henri Pierre reminisced. "The wine flowed, zee women were gorgeous, and zis gala event won for me an award for my French cuisine. Ah, how bee-u-tee-ful was zis night." He kissed his fingers as he spoke of the many courses he had served. By this time, the three men were so caught up in the conversation, I felt like an intruder. When Henri Pierre was finally called back to the kitchen, Harry asked us to be his guests at the next Chaîne dinner. There was no doubt that Harry and Parker had bonded, and it was food, that common denominator, that had brought them together. Even I couldn't compete with Henri Pierre's apricot soufflé, which he insisted on whipping up for dessert.

Well into the afternoon, Parker, Harry, and I sat in the Seaport Country Club's dining room, drinking imported champagne and savoring Henri Pierre's cuisine. Harry had been wooed into submission by my husband and all the gastronomic delicacies that were placed before him, so that for a while, he almost forgot I was even there. Perhaps it was true: The way to a man's heart *was* through his gut. I had become merely a backdrop—a feminine presence that added a nice touch the same way a decorative piece of art lights up a room. In the end, despite all of Harry's early fawning over me, it was Parker who catered to Harry's appetite, so much so that our little lunch had turned into an all-day dining extravaganza. Harry insisted that when Éclaire got back to town, the four of us should definitely get together for a meal. At 4:30, after Harry and Parker had chatted away the day, and Harry had been given the grand tour of the club, Parker and I escorted Harry to his car and watched him drive away, Parker waving his hand Italian style and shouting "Ciao."

"Now, that's one terrific guy," Parker said. "Wouldn't you say we got along magnificently?"

"I'd say he was your new best friend."

"I owe it all to you, Coco. If it weren't for your Chaîne article, Harry and I would never have met. And aren't you pleased that he suggests we pick up where we left off? If his wife is anything like him, it should be a fun evening."

"I'm counting the minutes," I said, all the while thinking: Men really are such stupid pricks.

15

"Appetite, a universal wolf."
—William Shakespeare

Love at First Bite

I phoned Annie on Sunday morning and filled her in on the latest installment of Harry.

"Parker loved him," I said.

"And what about Harry?"

"It was a match made in culinary heaven."

"Parker is always the consummate gentleman," Annie said. "Why should yesterday be any different?"

"They couldn't get enough of each other."

"Great," Annie said. "I take that as a good sign."

"Parker had Henri Pierre cook him a meal that he'll never forget."

"Why can't he do that for me?" Annie asked.

"I'm jealous," I said.

"Of Parker and Harry?"

"Harry was lusting over me until our waiter, Giorgio, shoved a goose liver pâté under his nose. Then Harry was a goner. I'm telling you, Annie, I've been replaced by apricot soufflés and French champagne."

"My love," Annie said, "you are one lucky broad. You have now unlocked the secret to man's greatest desire: food."

"The man was crazy about me. He told me he couldn't get me

out of his mind . . . until Parker entered the scene and took over. Now Harry wants us to get together again when the missus returns from the spa, so we can all do dinner."

"Coco," Annie said, "invite them both to Seaport and cook them a meal. I promise, it will push Harry over the edge. If you think he's nuts about you now, one bite of your prickly pesto pasta and he'll be your slave forever."

"What are you saying?"

"I'm saying, doll, that Harry's stomach is his most erogenous zone. One way to get him to eat out of your hands is not to play the femme fatale; to really make his fricassee fry, try donning an apron and make his weenie sizzle."

"My God, you're right."

"Sweetheart, that wife of his probably hasn't made a home-cooked meal since the Reagan administration. In a word: Gourmandize him! He'll lap it up and soon he'll be lapping you up as well."

"I thought you wanted me to 'be careful'?"

"I do," Annie said, "just not dead."

Annie had switched positions: She had gone from being the Grim Reaper who told me no good could come from this, to living vicariously. And no wonder; her husband, Saul, was practically comatose, a real coach potato, the typical American male who spent his weekends watching sports while Annie painted in her large studio overlooking the Sound. My life continued to add a dimension of excitement for Annie. She was starting to get caught up in my as yet unconsummated affair.

My conversation with Annie was interrupted by "call waiting" with Harry on the other end.

"Good morning, my dear," a very alert and chipper Harry greeted me. "I'm still on a high from yesterday."

"So glad you enjoyed yourself," I said with a slight edge of aloofness.

"That husband of yours is a real charmer. Not that I'm surprised that you would be married to such a great guy. Lunch was as good a culinary experience as I've had in years. I didn't even need to bother with dinner. The only hunger pangs I had were toward you. I could have eaten you up."

"Parker will be happy to hear this," I said.

"Coco, I mean it: You're driving me a little crazy. What can I do to quell my appetite?"

"Quell not," I said. "Instead, I'd like to invite you and Éclaire to dinner so I can show you that Henri Pierre is not the only one who can titillate your salivary glands."

"Not just another beautiful face, but the woman cooks, too." I could practically hear Harry slurping on the other end. "When Éclaire gets home tomorrow, we'll run through her date book and plan an evening. In the meantime, when do I get to see you again?"

"As soon as you and Éclaire give me the go-ahead," I said, playing it as cool as I could.

I now had Harry sufficiently aroused, which was exactly where I wanted him. Annie was right: Appeal to his palate and the man would be putty in my hands.

"Then we'll have to schedule dinner soon, because I can't be away from you too long."

We ended our phone call with the promise that Éclaire would call in the next few days.

I phoned Annie back.

"What's the verdict?" she asked.

"Guilty as charged," I said. "The man can't get enough of me."

"Wait until he samples your menu," she said. "We'll need to call in the paramedics."

Parker was thrilled that Harry had been so overwhelmed by lunch at the club. He also jumped at the idea of our cooking dinner for him and Éclaire.

"I'll crack open my 1999 Alexander Valley Clos du Bois Marlstone Cabernet," Parker said. "If Harry is the wine connoisseur I believe he is, he'll go wild."

I began planning the menu in my head. It would be a meal cooked to perfection, with which even the great Henri Pierre could not compete. I began poring through my cookbooks in anticipation.

The following Tuesday, Éclaire, refreshed from her week at the spa, and sounding a bit remote but cordial, followed her husband's instructions to call with available dates.

"I understand that Harry was very taken by his day at your club. And he hasn't stopped raving about Parker."

"The feeling is mutual," I said. "And we'd like you to come to Seaport, too. Parker and I want you to enjoy our home and have dinner with us."

"Is cooking a hobby of yours?" Éclaire asked.

"I dabble."

"I used to cook all the time," Éclaire offered, "but it's gotten so that with Harry's crazy schedule, it's easier to eat out. Sometimes he doesn't get through with patients until eight o'clock. Some nights we settle for takeout. I'm all for simplifying life."

"Keeping it simple makes sense," I said, envisioning how complicated my life was becoming by the minute.

After fifteen minutes of weekend dates that wouldn't work, we finally settled on a Saturday night in the middle of July.

"One thing, though, as far as food restrictions are concerned, Harry is allergic to shellfish."

"I'll make it a point not to seat him next to a shrimp," I joked.

"That will be perfect," Éclaire said. "I'll just have returned from my mud bath weekend at The Golden Door and I'll be feeling emaciated and cleansed."

"You'll be ready for a good meal, I'm sure," I said. "There's nothing like a good mud bath to clean out the pores."

"You do mud baths?" Éclaire inquired.

"Can't say I do. But occasionally I exfoliate."

"I can't impress enough how crucial it is to exfoliate," Éclaire said, suddenly perking up. "Harry has a fabulous exfoliating cream that he prescribes to all his patients. Not to mention his seaweed scrub for an absolutely divine full-body treatment."

I could feel myself drifting into that place where all parts of me started to go numb. Éclaire could probably go on like this for hours if I didn't interrupt just as she was getting into the benefits of Restylane and Dysport as alternatives to Botox.

By the time we got off the phone, I was practically an expert on emollients, not to mention the latest scoop on all types of aesthetic procedures. Éclaire, bless her little heart, was a plastic surgeon's dream wife.

That night I sat down at my computer and knocked out a column that would appear in the *Seaport Gazette* the following week: "Put on a Happy Face."

The Seaport Gazette

PUT ON A HAPPY FACE

There's something about facelifts that shakes me up. That's because I have never seen a person who, after his/her face has been lifted—no matter how good a job—looks entirely real. Case in point, my friend, Vera, the authority on all types of procedures. Vera, a woman of substantial beauty, decided to have a little lift. Her face was tightened so securely that her mouth, which used to be charmingly crooked, has been raised a tad too much in a northerly direction. Vera now looks perpetually happy even when she's not. That's the problem: Facelifts not only eradicate wrinkles; they remove all signs of genuine emotion.

The gal across the road had just a bit of rearranging. She was nipped and tucked by the biggest and the best. She emerged from her bed looking ten years younger. She's slim, she's toned, she's liposuctioned. Her breasts are augmented and her derrière is as tight as her face. My fear is that one false move and she might actually break.

People are more up front about cosmetic surgery than they used to be. Bandaged noses sprout up everywhere. But, it wasn't always this way: Men and women, who were once vain, submerged for a while only to resurface a few weeks later, looking surprisingly "new."

"Charlene," I said when I saw my friend at the supermarket, "you look very . . . uh . . . well rested."

"Yes," she said, "I've been on vacation for a while. On a scale of one to ten, with ten being my ultimate best, how rested would you say I looked?"

"Completely restored," I said, "not to mention, quite taut."

Charlene's face was so tight that when she spoke, all that moved were her lips. The rest of her face remained completely intact, much like a puppet. All she needed were the strings and she could be manipulated beautifully. She was so perfect a specimen of female pulchritude that it seemed as though she had been molded into place by Crazy Glue. And the sad fact was, Charlene used to appear interesting and offbeat. She had her own look that could not be replicated. Now, the new Charlene followed in the footsteps of many other bevies of beauties who had "gone cosmetic." They all looked artificially perfect.

Today, we are all rushing to join the Beautiful People's Club. Wrinkles that used to be a natural process of aging are being Botoxed into oblivion. When I first heard about this phenomenon that is now sweeping the country, I was shocked.

"Buttocks?" I asked naively. "Who wants buttocks on their face?"

"Botox, honey, not buttocks," the ladies told me over lunch.

"It's the latest thing. A quick shot into your forehead and those 'surprise lines' you have will disappear."

I checked out my face in my compact mirror. Yes, it was true: a fine narrow line appeared across the length of my forehead. But, frankly, it never bothered me before. Now I was being scrutinized differently, as somewhat of an outcast. I went home and researched Botox. Here's what I learned.

Botox injections cost between $500 and $2,000, depending on the areas that need to be injected and the depth of the lines. Botox, which really is a botulism toxin, is injected into the muscles of the face, causing temporary paralysis. And I was worried about old canned food going bad? Now, I realized a little botulism could add years to my life.

Aha, I thought, this is just what I'm looking for: a nice case of facial paralysis. But, the good news was, it would prevent my skin from wrinkling. Moreover, it would reduce the appearance of my frown lines, forehead furrows, and my all-time favorite: nostril flaring. My goodness, not to ever flare again. Why, it was too good to imagine. And if that weren't exciting enough, Botox could also be used underneath arms or on palms to prevent sweating. I could toss my deodorants out the window. I was intrigued enough to take it a step further. I made an appointment with a plastic surgeon.

"My dear," he said, after going over my body with a giant pair of magnifying goggles, "the good news is, like a fine vintage car, you're holding up quite well."

I held on to the side of the table, poised for his next remark.

"But, that's not to say a little aesthetic adornment couldn't help things along. Take your face, for example: In addition to Botox, some laser skin resurfacing can go a long way."

"Do tell."

"Yes, my cutting-edge laser will burn off the outer layer of your skin, causing new cells to regenerate. The results are amazing."

"Any side effects," I asked.

"Your skin will be permanently sun-sensitive and there is a risk of uneven pigmentation patterns."

In lay terms, this meant I could never go to the beach again and I might end up with a polka-dotted face. I hotfooted it out of his office and into that of another cosmetic guru whose name I had been given by Vera-the-Magnificent.

Dr. Lookgood, who was not only a plastic surgeon but a gynecologist with a new calling, greeted me with a wide smile revealing a set of pearly-white laminates. His hair had been transplanted, he told me, from an actual mink; his chin had been implanted and looked ever-so-slightly askew. His lips had been filled with collagen and his eyelids lifted, giving him a lecherous stare.

"I'm into the natural look," he told me.

"I can tell," I said.

This gyno-gone-wild was an expert on wrinkle-plumping.

"We can take fat from your butt," he said, "and inject it into your face to puff up any wrinkles you have."

Buttocks, again!

"I don't want butt fat on my face," I said. "It's unseemly."

I envisioned men giving me the once-over and admiring my tight rear without even looking down. It was more than I could handle.

On the way home, I recalled a conversation that I had once overheard when my friend's mother, Estelle, saw a woman on a Fifth Avenue bus. After staring at her for ten minutes and not being able to contain herself, she walked over and sat down next to her.

"Tell me," Estelle whispered, "by any chance, have you had your eyes done?"

The woman, taken aback, leaned over and said, "Well, frankly, I have."

"You'd never know," Estelle said.

I went home and stood naked in front of my full-length mirror. True, if I looked closely, I was less than total perfection, but I wasn't that bad, either. The next day, I called my friends who had recommended the Botox King and the Butt Plumper.

"Thanks," I said, "but I've decided to stay naturally imperfect."

"Not even a dash of silicone?" Vera asked. "Not a teeny chemical peel?"

So as not to let the ladies down completely, the next time we lunched, I was as tight as a triple martini lunch.

"You've been done!" they shouted in unison.

"Well, yes," I said, "in a way I have."

I was now one of the girls.

The truth is, I hadn't the heart to tell them that for $3.50, I had purchased a roll of duct tape, lifted the skin adjacent to my chin, given a little pull, and strategically placed a piece of tape behind each ear to hold my face in place.

"You look incredible," they said. "Who did it?"

"Ace Hardware," I told them.

16

> "I just love Chinese food. My favorite dish is number 27."
> —Clement Atlee

No Turning Back

For the next several weeks Harry phoned regularly wanting to see me.

"Please," he said, "I can't wait until July. Come in to the city and we'll do dinner."

It was hard for me to stay away, for each time I heard his voice, I melted. Finally, I succumbed.

"I'll be free on Thursday after my therapy appointment," I said.

It was the first time I had told Harry about Finkelman.

"But you're so together, Coco. People like Éclaire need shrinks, but a gal like you has all the answers."

"Yeah," I said, "that's why you and I are having dinner and my husband has no clue."

"So, Coco Harding is on the couch," he teased.

"Not really. I do my shrinking in a very uncomfortable leather chair."

"Same time, same place?" he asked.

Bemelmans Bar had now been dubbed "our place." Promptly at five, I found Harry sipping his whiskey sour and by 5:15 we were holding hands in a far-off corner of the room.

"This can be dangerous. We could run into people," I said, disengaging my hand.

"I'm not allowed to have a drink with a friend?"

"Sure, who's your friend? I don't see any friends."

Harry leaned over, looking at me longingly.

"I want to kiss you, Coco," he said. "I want to kiss every inch of you. I dream of us making love."

I pulled away in the nick of time, just as a chipper voice interrupted.

"Is that you Coco, darling?"

"Oh my God, Erica."

"Steve and I are in town for a long weekend. We're visiting my folks who are in from Atlanta and staying here at the Carlyle. I just got back from shopping and thought Steve might in here having his own Happy Hour."

"Wonderful to see you. This is my friend, Dr. Harry Troutman, who's helping me with some research on an article."

"Dr. Troutman, of course. My friend Wendy can't stop raving about you. She's sporting the nicest breasts in Scarsdale."

Harry turned bright red. "I'm glad your friend is pleased. I enjoy making women happy."

"Happy? She's ecstatic. You changed her life," Erica gushed. "So, Coco, how *are* you and Parker and how is life in the burbs? Frankly, I never thought you'd make the move. You're soooo Big Apple."

"We're all doing fine, Erica," I said.

"And that gorgeous daughter of yours?"

"Finishing up her Ph.D. work."

"Well, the next time you get in to town, give me a call and we'll do lunch. Nice meeting you, Dr. Troutman. Gotta dash. Steve and I are doing an early din-din and then we're off to theater. Here's my card, Coco. Give me a jingle."

Erica vanished as quickly as she had appeared, leaving me momentarily stunned.

"As I was saying: We could run into friends."

"She's a friend?"

"More of an acquaintance."

"Then there's nothing to worry about."

Dr. Harry Troutman might possibly be the most unscrupulous man I had ever known.

"Do you think Erica saw us?"

"Doing what? Reading my mind?"

"This makes me nervous, Harry," I said. "We've got to be careful."

"I'm always careful. That's why I carry condoms."

"Oh that's cute, really cute."

"Relax darling," Harry said. "All we're doing is having drinks."

"You have a reputation to uphold. We could get caught, you know."

"Are you always this nervous, Coco?"

"I don't know. I've never done this before . . . have you?"

"I've been faithful to my wife for twenty-two years."

"How long have you been married?"

"Oh Coco, darling," he said, laughing, "you just might drive me crazy."

Then, looking around the room and checking for sudden imposers, Harry took my face in his hands and kissed me long and passionately on my lips.

"You taste like a peanut," he said, "very salty."

And because I was so caught up in the moment, I wanted to believe every word that Harry said.

~

From the Carlyle, we taxied down to Chinatown for dim sum at the Golden Unicorn. We climbed the stairs to the third floor, getting immediately caught up in the cacophonous roar of the crowd. I quickly scanned the room, checking to make sure no one I knew was there. That was the price one pays for illicit dining: looking over one's shoulder for sightings of familiar faces. Secure in the knowledge that the coast was clear, I sat back and enjoyed dinner, sipping Chinese beer and caught up in the gaiety of the evening. Despite all the potential danger, once I allowed myself to relax, Harry and I had a glorious time. Harry enjoyed educating me on foods of all nations and tonight's focus on Chinese was no exception.

"The Golden Unicorn is known for its dim sum," he said. "It's actually Cantonese for 'heart's delight.'" He put a steamed vegetable dumpling between his chopsticks and placed it between my lips. The aroma exploded upon first bite.

"Hmm, delicious," I said. "I want more."

"I'm here to serve you, my love. My mission is to fill you up yet keep you begging for more."

Each bite was a delicious metaphor of sexual connotations, all washed down with the beer that flowed nonstop.

"This is the best dim sum I've ever had," I said. "I never know what to expect with you."

"My job is to keep you constantly surprised," Harry said, punctuating his words with a slight burp.

"Éclaire must be constantly experiencing new taste treats. Is she as adventurous a diner as you?"

"Éclaire's idea of an exciting meal is some lettuce leaves and a granola bar."

And then it all started to make sense: Harry and Éclaire were gastronomically incompatible. She was à la carte. He was prix fixe. She grazed. He gorged. Exactly what I had tried to convey to Finkelman about Parker's and my sex life, except with Parker, it was I whose hunger pangs were never quite satisfied.

"Perhaps that's how she keeps her lovely figure." I jumped into Éclaire's arena. "Some women simply prefer nibbling."

"Éclaire considers food a necessary inconvenience. She likes going to trendy restaurants, but more for the ambience, less for indulging her culinary fancies. And then there are those expensive outfits she likes showing off. No, sadly, Éclaire and I are not on the same page where dining is concerned."

I registered this piece of information in the back of my brain as I would come to do each time Harry handed me another marital tidbit. Harry had married a woman who was his quintessential arm candy, but when it came to real substance, she was missing a few necessary components. I, on the other hand, seemed to pique his intellectual interest. Our conversation flowed, and during dinner we talked on a wide range of topics: art, travel, the latest theater worth seeing, the last book we enjoyed and, of course, our mutual attraction to one another.

"Coco, it must be obvious by now that I can't get enough of you."

Ignoring Harry, I cracked open a fortune cookie and peeled the strip of white paper from between its crisp wafer-thin lips. I sat back in amazement.

"You know," Harry said, "the protocol with fortune cookies is to add the phrase 'in bed' to the end of the message."

"Really? Well, hold on to your seat."

"Don't tell me: 'A day without laughter is a day without sunshine,'" he said.

"In bed," I added.

"What *does* it say?"

"A new adventure with a charming stranger will soon take place."

"In bed," Harry said, smiling.

That night, still reeling from dinner, I decided to play it safe and not invite my "charming stranger" back for a nightcap. In fact, I promised myself I would never invite Harry to my apartment since my doormen, Walter and Jasper, were even bigger gossips than my mother's canasta group in Boca. One time, after the delivery boy from Gristede's dropped off a bag of groceries, Walter said:

"Seems the kid stayed longer than usual."

"I was looking for tip money, Walter," I said.

If Harry even so much as entered my building, their eyes would roll and they wouldn't be able to keep their mouths shut.

Instead, Harry and I parted company and I drove back to Seaport full of dim sum and on an emotional high. Dr. Harry Troutman had completely won me over, heart and soul, and there was no turning back now.

17

"Anybody who believes that the way to a man's
heart is through his stomach flunked geography."
—Robert Byrne

A Piece of Puffed Pastry

For the next few weeks, Harry and I met three times on each consecutive Thursday, following my sessions with Finkelman who, after I had confessed all, said my marriage was on the road to destruction if I weren't careful.

"Coco, this attraction for Harry is fraught with danger, not to mention that you are veering out of control. We need to examine why you choose to live so dangerously."

During my last session, Finkelman, looking quite dapper in his new polka-dot bow tie, spewed forth a diatribe of analytic analects geared to make me think twice about my impulsive behavior.

"Coco, we are all endowed with free will, but as with all qualities, that freedom is not unlimited. There is a dynamic involved in any relationship . . . an energy that powers it, and in an interdependent world, which for better or for worse, is the one we live in, we need to be mindful of the immutable reality of Newton's second law: 'For every action, there is an equal and opposite reaction.'"

Finkelman was certainly up on his facts. Although I could hardly stifle my yawns, he sounded somewhat erudite. He continued.

"I liken this interdependency to the tectonic plates deep

under the oceans. When one shifts even a bit, it rubs against another one, ultimately resulting in earthquakes or tsunamis, which do no one any good. You have a spouse who truly cares for you, and while at times there may be temptations to stray, when all is said and done, in order for a healthy marital relationship to survive, the main emotional focus must be directed in such a way so as not to detract or devalue that mature and committed relationship."

Finkelman, having completed what he considered quite an impressive tap on the knuckles, poured himself a glass of H_20 and sat back in his chair, awaiting my response. His performance had been so sterling, so eloquent, I wanted to applaud, but instead, looked out on a sun-kissed Central Park with an expressionless look on my face. At $200 an hour, at least I got "a spew with a view."

"Furthermore, Coco . . ."

Oh no, I thought, not a "furthermore."

"Once a decision has been made to engage in a marital union, the best effort should be made to uphold and nurture it. You have a lot to be grateful for: a lovely daughter, a career that is flourishing, friends, family, extended and otherwise . . . what more does a woman need?"

"A good fuck," I wanted to blurt out, but I held my tongue as I thought it might push Finkelman over the edge and only encourage more intellectual regurgitation, or even worse, another "I see."

The fact was, during all my time with Harry, I had not once succumbed to my sexual desires. I had remained strikingly and dutifully the faithful wife that Finkelman was imploring me to be. But, giving up Harry was out of the question. We shared a synchrony too compelling to relinquish, a spontaneity I had not found with any other man. And in the end, it was exactly that lively, self-actuating relationship that held me captive, not to mention our long, romantic evenings when we sipped and supped at some of New York's finest eateries.

~

As we inched toward July and the upcoming dinner party with Harry and Éclaire, I was both edgy and excited. I spent time poring through cookbooks, imagining every forkful of food that Harry would be ingesting. I wanted each bite to be memorable. There was something about feeding a man who appreciated food that increased the excitement, not to mention that my need to spoil him had reached mammoth proportions. My hope was that once he tasted my cooking, I would become irresistible in an entirely new way. Harry was my constant challenge. Now, a new culinary adventure would add a new dimension to our already overheated relationship. Perhaps the writers of fortune cookies really knew their stuff.

Parker and I took off to the Berkshires on weekends, where the lilting strain of classical composers wafted over the lawn of Tanglewood and onto our deck as we sipped one of Parker's latest wine acquisitions. On one particular Saturday night, a week before "the" dinner party, Parker opened a bottle of Puligny-Montrachet he had been saving for "a special occasion"—a wine that he described as elegant and harmonious. While we sat under the stars on a balmy summer night, thoughts of Harry filled my head, and even though Parker did all he could to make life as "harmonious" as the wine we drank, our marriage lacked that "vibrant and lingering aftertaste" that stayed with me long after Harry and I parted.

"What is the special occasion?" I asked Parker.

"Summer, the night, being here with you. What can be more special than that?"

I smiled, while pangs of guilt momentarily pushed all thoughts of Harry out of my head. I was in constant conflict: On the one hand, Parker was the ever constant, all-adoring husband. And then there was Harry, bigger than life itself, who I carried along with me day and night, an omnipresence too compelling to resist. And of course, Finkelman, whose bottom line message was: You can't have your cake and expect to eat it without some repercussions.

Parker was thrilled that I showed so much interest in our upcoming evening with Harry and Éclaire.

"It's wonderful to see you so involved in the menu," he said.

"Each course will be a little meal unto itself," I promised.

"I'm looking forward to meeting Éclaire. I have a mental image of her in my mind."

"Like what?"

"Like a piece of puffed pastry, as her name connotes."

"You're in for a surprise," I said.

All week I busied myself with work, nudged by the constant reminder that in only a few days, Harry and Éclaire would be dining at our home. I had decided to go Tuscan and would prepare an Italian feast reminiscent of the country's flavor. One taste of my risotto and Harry would be mentally transported from Seaport, Connecticut, to the dark cypress trees amidst scented olive groves, and winding, dusty roads leading from flowered hillsides to checkered clothed tables in small trattorias. Each course was designed to create a mood that would stay with Harry long after the evening was over. And I, of course, would dress the part: my simple form-fitting red cotton Donna Karan jersey dress with a shawl tossed around my shoulders, exploding in an array of colors reminiscent of the Tuscan countryside—a splash of yellows, greens, aubergine, and salmon. Smart but elegant. Colorful yet soft. A woman ready to wow the pants off Dr. Harry Troutman.

18

"Cooking is like love. It should be
entered into with abandon or not at all."
—Harriet Van Horne

Prelude to the Seduction

Bright and much-too-early on Saturday morning, before Parker left for his 8:30 golf game, the phone rang. It was Bridgette calling from Cape Cod, where she had been visiting a friend for a week. Parker picked up. I sat up in bed, poised for any unforeseen calamity designed to put a blemish on the day I had been planning for weeks. All I wanted was to be left alone to cook, set the table, and pamper myself for a few hours before Harry and Éclaire arrived.

"Bridgette!" Parker sounded elated. "Well, of course, dear, you should stop by on your way from the Cape to New York. What time can we expect you?"

I grimaced and shot him a dagger indicating that under no circumstances did I want to be interrupted by his sister.

"Well, yes, I am just running off to the club, but yes, Coco will be around. She'll be busy with dinner preparations but she'd love to see you." Pause. "No, I don't believe she needs any help, but thanks." Pause. "Yes, well, uh . . . I can't see why not. Drinks sound nice." Pause. "No, I don't think you would be intruding if you stayed through the cocktail hour. The more the merrier. See you around five o'clock, then."

I threw a pillow at Parker along with a few unsavory expletives.

"Damn it, Parker, why tonight?"

"For God's sake, Coco, what was I to say? That my own sister isn't welcome in our home?"

"But, hell, of all nights. Why?"

"I didn't realize this was an exclusive 'members only' evening."

"I just wasn't planning on a whole entourage."

"Come on, dear. Bridgette can be quite charming. She'll enjoy meeting the Troutmans and they'll probably find her to be delightful."

Of all the words to describe Bridgette, "delightful" did not immediately come to mind. I hadn't even brushed my teeth and already Parker and I were arguing. He picked up his clubs and headed toward the door. I threw in a few last-minute parting shots.

"Bridgette's visit won't lend itself to an intimate type of evening. You know how she gets, name-dropping and all. Frankly, she can be an embarrassment, and well, I was hoping for a quiet evening, just the four of us."

"Can't you be more flexible? It is only drinks, after all. Not dinner. What's the harm?"

"Trust me," I said. "Drinks will turn into dinner. We can't ask her to leave."

"So she'll stay for dinner, big deal. What's gotten into you, anyway? With that menu you've created, there's certainly enough for an extra person."

The big deal was that I wanted no uninvited guests. I wanted one couple. In truth, I wanted half of one couple. I wanted Harry, and being petulant seemed to be my new modus operandi.

I stopped pouting long enough for Parker to give me a quick kiss good-bye before he left the house.

"I'll see you later, honey. Eighteen holes, a quick lunch with the boys, and then I'm all yours."

I lay in bed for a while, the day stretching out before me. The mellow glow under which I had glided through the week suddenly began to dissipate. Bridgette had unknowingly thrown a curveball, and while under normal circumstances sharing the cocktail hour with my sister-in-law was certainly not inappropriate, I was so intent on carrying off the evening my way that even the slightest variation on my well-planned theme put me in a bad mood.

But there were errands to run, flowers to buy, a table to set with our special china and crystal, and while Hedy, our German housekeeper, the angel that she was, would assist, I wanted to be in charge of it all. Each hour leading up to Harry's arrival was a kind of foreplay to be blissfully savored. The last thing I needed was Bridgette making her grand entrance, upstaging my well-planned performance.

I threw on jeans and a shirt, tied up my hair in a ponytail, and with grocery list in hand, I headed to the market for last-minute items that could not be bought until today. My first stop was my favorite Seaport market: "How Green Is My Salad." Exotic foods of all nations lined each shelf. Freshly cut flowers dripped from wicker baskets. A room devoted only to cheeses sent their ripe perfume drifting over into the pâté department. Here was a feast for the eyes as well as the stomach.

It was only 9:15 and already the parking lot was filled. Young moms with children rustled about their SUVs while their golden retrievers and other Lab derivatives, relegated to the backseats, barked their hellos through slivers of open windows and into the morning air. The temperature was already in the eighties and a scorcher had been predicted for the day. I had told Éclaire to make sure she and Harry brought along bathing suits for a dip in the pool before drinks. They were to arrive in the late afternoon and could be on a collision course with Bridgette. The image of the three of them arriving en masse created a momentary angst, but I dismissed the idea quickly. There was no room in my head for anything but happy thoughts. With that in mind and basket in tow, I waltzed through the aisles en route to my feast Italiano:

fresh loaves of crusty breads, vine-ripened tomatoes, lettuce as green as the Tuscan hillsides. I sorted through the olive department, carefully choosing khaki-colored olives with bright sprigs of pimento peeking through the tops. The pastry counter was already bustling with action: a squealing toddler begged for a freshly-baked croissant; fresh samples of the day's pastry selection lay in bite-sized chunks on a plate to be grabbed up by hungry shoppers who had not yet had breakfast. I took a piece for myself and then bought my bread and some petit fruit tarts fresh from the oven. I chose the freshest of fruits that would accompany the chocolate tortes and zabaglione that I would later whip up for dessert.

My menu was planned with precision. We would begin with a cold antipasto, served poolside and prepared with great simplicity to include some dry finocchiona sausage, a coarse liver pâté. Imported prosciutto with a firm flesh surrounded by a fragrant layer of ivory-colored fat would be entwined with small segments of ripe honeydew melon. Next to the prosciutto would be the plate of fresh figs whose stems had been trimmed then carefully peeled back to form the illusion of petals. Olives, anchovies, baby artichoke hearts, Italian salami, and red peppers the color of poppies would rest among a variety of Italian cheeses: fresh mozzarella, a tangy Caciotta, and provolone. A basket of fresh bread and crackers would be readily available as we sat on striped green-and-tan lounge chairs, sipping cocktails and soaking up the late afternoon sun with intermittent dips in the pool to wash away the July heat that was forecast well into the evening.

I sniffed and fondled the melons, selecting only the roundest and the ripest. The prosciutto was thinly sliced for me by Antonio, who assured me it had been cured on the bone, hard to find in America. I chose the cheeses with care, each one bursting forth with its own pungent aroma.

I was having a field day moving through the market, gathering up my goodies. I then wended my way to the glass-enclosed flower atrium, awash with color. Black-eyed Susans and white-

and-yellow daisies filled mammoth vases. Sunflowers that looked as though they had first been lying in Tuscan fields served as a backdrop to buckets of daffodils, blue delphiniums, peonies, irises, bowls of gardenias, tulips, lilacs, and marigolds. Walking among this floral display elevated my spirits as I plucked a few long-stemmed roses and some ferns, picked up several bouquets of wildflowers, a few sprigs of lily of the valley and Virginia bluebells. Then some violets, primroses, and anemones that would later be arranged in my Waterford and Baccarat vases to enhance their beauty even further.

I was caught up in my shopping spree, purchasing items with wild abandon, guaranteed to create the right ambience: assortments of greens would make their way into the salad; focaccia dough oozing olive oil was ready to find repose in my bread basket; mushrooms as white as moonstones headed for my orecchiette pasta; and the largest and freshest eggs were chosen for my zabaglione. By the time I left the market forty-five minutes later, I had enough edible ammunition to drive Harry into gastronomic ecstasy.

The rest of the afternoon was reserved for last-minute arrangements: setting my table, a hair appointment followed by a massage, and then home for a long and leisurely bubble bath and nap. Parker returned after lunch as promised and spent an hour in the wine cellar selecting tonight's choice bottles, including a sublime sweet dessert wine to accompany the zabaglione and platter of fresh fruits and tarts. The rest, he said, would be a surprise. Parker took his wines as seriously as did Harry and in doing so would immediately win him over.

My mother interrupted my nap with a phone call at 3:15.

"Darling! Why are you answering the phone in the middle of the day?"

"I was sleeping?"

"Why? Are you ill?"

"I'm relaxing before our dinner party."

"How lovely. Who's coming?"

"Dr. Harry Troutman and his wife."

"You mean *the* Dr. Harry Troutman? That's who I wanted to send Aunt Pauline to."

"Aunt Pauline had work?"

"Yes, she had her buttocks lifted. They were hanging so low, she could have dusted her floors without a vacuum cleaner. She saw some butcher in Miami, instead, who did some liposuction and then lifted them so high, she can hardly sit down. I told her to see Dr. Troutman but she went to her best friend's son-in-law's cousin who doesn't know from tushies. How do you know Dr. Troutman?"

I explained that I had met Harry at a Chaîne dinner I was covering and that we had become fast friends. My mother was instantly impressed.

"Well, it certainly can't hurt to know someone like that," Yvonne said. "You do know he's the Tiffany of plastic surgeons?"

"Yes, I know, Mother. He helped me with some terminology on a food-related article I just finished writing."

"On plastic surgery?"

"No, on food. Harry's avocation is feasting."

"Maybe one day he can take a look-see at me. My wattle is drooping again. I can't believe you and Dr. Troutman are doing an article together."

"He's only consulting with me, Mother."

"While you're at it, maybe he can give you a once-over. Why not take advantage of a golden opportunity?"

"Thank you, Mother, but for now, it's strictly a working relationship."

I had done a good job with the Chaîne article and convinced Gillian to let me do a two-part series on the "real food" of yesterday compared to the trendy, fat-free, tasteless foods of today. It would have a humorous bent with a serious subliminal message and serve as a lead-in to the Chaîne article that would follow in the next issue. Gillian went for the idea. I would have it in her hands the following week. I had some time to read it over before getting dressed.

The Seaport Gazette

MY YEARS OF EATING DANGEROUSLY

I grew up on Betty Crocker's buttermilk biscuits dripping with preserves. I devoured Aunt Jemima's pancakes with a vengeance. So where did I go wrong? When did I stray from the path of incredible edibles to the calorie-conscious fat gram freak I am today? The sad fact is, I haven't tasted real food since the 1980s.

I'm that same person who, as a young girl, tripped from restaurant to restaurant accompanied by my parents—two people who worshiped at the culinary altar. If it were Tuesday, my dad-the-dentist's New York day, it was steak at Danny's Hideaway when we spent an evening on the town. "On the town" meant we would eat two baskets of garlic bread, followed by salads oozing Roquefort cheese dressing, rare steaks, and a dessert that nearly drove us into calorie arrest.

Dinner with my folks meant dining at the best spots: Romeo Salta, L'Aiglon, La Petite Marmite, The Sea Fare, or, if we wanted to eat lightly, we'd grab a salad at Longchamps. Dining out was an occasion. We dressed to eat. Theater nights included dinner before the show and a snack afterward when we topped off the evening with ice cream sundaes at Rumplemeyer's or with slices of cheesecake too large to accommodate our mouths at Reuben's, where beautiful women in low-cut dresses sat next to their sugar daddies, toying with sandwiches named after famous celebrities.

The days of my youth were laden with epicurean delights. I collected matchbooks from every restaurant I visited and sometimes sneaked home a menu and I sat for hours reading over the bill of fare, deciding what my next selection would be. When I look back, I can't remember ever eating as well as I did during those years with my parents. They believed that introducing me to different taste experiences was part of my education, and I, the willing student, if graded, would have received an A in Restaurants 101.

But that was before the world went a little crazy and people started being careful. It all began with Metrecal, that magic liquid guaranteed to shed pounds on those who considered themselves a bit too well-endowed in the wrong places. The mothers of the '50s all drank that stuff. They raised daughters who, after years of being exposed to the finest foods, suddenly were admonished for eating too well.

"You don't need the French fries, darling," my mother began whispering in my ear when we ordered cheeseburgers.

"I like French fries," I said.

"Well, you can't have it both ways," she replied, and suddenly my nice, secure, happy eating days were over and I was relegated to a store to buy, in my mother's words, "an adorable little panty girdle" to hold in what she referred to as baby fat.

Yes, it's true. I went to my Sweet Sixteen party at the Chanticleer in New Jersey in a to-die-for putrid-pink strapless gown wearing a padded bra to accentuate what I lacked on top and a panty girdle to hold in what I had an abundance of on the bottom. Then, with my body properly secured in all the right places, I gave a toss of my perfectly coiffed, cardboard-stiff hair sprayed flip, danced a few rounds with my date, and spent the rest of the night eating everything in sight.

Back in the '50s, eating was my thing. Raiding the refrigerator wasn't an avocation, but a full-time job. Ah, those evenings I sat with my friends in my kitchen, bolting down bags of Oreos, Drake's coffee cakes, and cans of colas loaded with so much sugar they weighed more than hand grenades and were probably even more lethal.

When I recall those bittersweet days, what I remember most is the food: macaroni and cheese, peanut butter and Wonderbread sandwiches, my mother's meat loaf served with mashed potatoes and gravy, and my father's rendition of tuna surprise made with half a jar of Hellmann's mayo, which he spread liberally on a hard roll with a cream cheese door. (I licked through the "door" to get to the tuna.) And oh, the lamb chops with their greasy, delicate little bones streaked with fat that I gnawed on five nights a week. There was something about them that our mothers couldn't resist. They were the staples of our youth along with Ritz crackers and logs of Velveeta cheese.

Those were the days when moms stayed home and never left their kitchens—when aromas wafted through the air and lingered long after mealtime was over. Each house had its particular odor. Mine reeked of sautéed onions, it was burned toast at Jane's, and Angela's house smelled wonderfully Italian with a pot of sauce bubbling away on the stove.

"My mom always has sauce going," Angela said. "My father likes it. He pours it over everything. She changes it every day by adding either sausages, onions, or peppers."

Angela was the luckiest girl I knew. She got to eat spaghetti seven days a week. With me, it was always those darn lamb chops! I consumed so many that I secretly believe the sheep police had a warrant out for my arrest.

Life is different now. Eating is no longer as much fun as it used to be since we've become fanatically diet-conscious and dull. The smells of yesterday are no longer. Our meals are now prepared in microwaves where baking a potato takes less than ten minutes. We live in aroma-challenged homes where the only fragrances are citrus-laced detergents in place of real food. Where once we lingered in the kitchen until the meal was ready, we now satisfy our hunger pangs in seconds flat with a mere press of a button. Is it any wonder social discourse is diminishing? Instant gratification has replaced that wonderful feeling of waiting for dinner and arriving at the table deliciously famished. Now, we often eat on the run and cram meals in between busy schedules. Long, leisurely dining has become an intermittent indulgence.

Today, a popular pastime is poring over labels: lite, fat-free, and artificially sweetened, ingredients that add nothing to our hips and even less to our taste buds. Mealtime has become a series of games, my favorite being "On the Side," where food arrives unadulterated and we are in total control of every morsel we put in our mouths.

I miss the days when we didn't use words like "macrobiotic" or "trendy" to describe a salad. When cleansing our palates wasn't known as "intermezzo" but a good burp. Oh, how I miss my mother's chocolate cake made with real eggs and not egg substitutes, and fried chicken, where leaving the skin on the bird wasn't considered a major culinary sin.

Last night I had a dream: I was being chased by a giant cheeseburger, dripping with grease, onions, tomatoes, and a pickle, which forced its way into my mouth until I consumed the entire thing. I awakened feeling slightly peculiar. Whatever happened to real food? I'm starving.

19

"There is no sight on earth that is more appealing
than the sight of a woman making dinner for someone she loves."
—Thomas Wolfe

Dinner at Eight

I began getting dressed at 4:00, tossing a sarong over my swimsuit. Parker was to greet our guests at the door and direct them to our patio where hors d'oeuvres and drinks would be waiting. Promptly at five, the Troutmans' Mercedes pulled into our circular driveway and following behind them, as ominously predicted, was Bridgette. It couldn't have been worse timing. I had wanted at least a few minutes to get Harry and Éclaire settled before Bridgette descended upon us.

"Darling!" Bridgette got out of her Beamer convertible and ran over to Parker. "I made it in less time than expected. And let me say, I've had enough of the Cape. All that saltwater was starting to ruin my complexion. You know how I get when I'm out in the fresh air too long. And those goddamn seagulls. They poop everywhere. I need a drink."

Parker, gently moving his sister aside, was more concerned with being the consummate host where Éclaire and Harry were concerned.

"At long last." Parker extended his hand to assist Éclaire from her car. "Your name is practically a household word around here. Harry couldn't stop talking about you, not to mention my wife who has been looking forward to this evening for weeks. I'm so pleased to finally meet you. And you, old fella," he turned to Harry, "welcome back to Seaport and, most especially, to our home."

Bridgette undulated herself between them, making her presence instantly known.

"And this is my sister, Bridgette, who just breezed in from the Cape and will be joining us for drinks."

Bridgette eyed Éclaire up and down, taking in her face, hair, dress, shoes, and handbag.

"Good God, dear, how the hell do you stand up in those high heels? You obviously have good feet."

Éclaire, unaccustomed to the likes of Bridgette, offered no retort, but instead put on her faux smile to match the faux pas. One sting from the WASP, Bridgette, and the JAP, Éclaire, didn't stand a chance.

"Well then, come along all of you," Parker said, escorting the three to the back patio where I sat in a chair, looking as though I hadn't moved a muscle all afternoon. As they approached, I rose, my sarong swaying behind me in rhythm to the late day summer breeze. I had spritzed a touch of Marc Jacobs perfume, the same fragrance that Harry had said drove him wild the last time we were together, and the one that made Parker sneeze violently.

After kiss-kisses and the obligatory oohs and aahs over our home, we settled in for drinks around the pool. Feeling particularly festive, Parker cracked open a bottle of champagne that brought squeals of delight from Éclaire, who looked absolutely adorable, if not just a tad "busy" in her Emilio Pucci.

"Why is it that champagne always tastes better in summer than any other time of year?" Éclaire chirped.

Éclaire was famous for interjecting conversational stoppers that gave one momentary pause.

"It doesn't," Bridgette said, taking a swig that emptied her glass in one fell swoop. "I've been known to drink it for breakfast, any day of the year. Champagne is mother's milk to me."

"Well then, here's to a bubbly summer," Parker chimed in, clinking glasses with Éclaire.

Harry, handsome and sporting a healthy bronze tan, glanced over to me, giving me one of his furtive smiles that made me melt. I smiled back as he raised his glass to me in a silent but understood toast. Seeing Harry after a brief absence only reinforced my desire and made me want him all the more. On this particular afternoon, having downed a glass of champagne too quickly, I felt a sudden high. I could have devoured him on the spot, but remained poised and calm—and, above all, controlled.

Cocktails went off without a hitch. Bridgette went to her car, dug a swimsuit out from her suitcase, and hit the pool before any of us, splashing around seemingly without a care in the world. And why not? She had inherited a ton of family money and another big wad from her ex-husband Boris H. Whitney, who, besides being one of "the" Whitneys who had collected rare art and polo ponies, gave Bridgette new meaning to the words "gay divorcée." Now in her late fifties, Bridgette could live out the rest of her days enveloped in a hedonistic glow, as evidenced by her frivolous need to spend money, stay at the finest resorts, and shop 'til her closet doors bulged from excess. Today, fresh from The Chatham Bars Inn, where she had mixed and mingled all weekend, and now a little drunk from three glasses of champagne, Bridgette had to be watched like a hawk, lest, in an unforeseen moment, she aim a verbal arrow at any of us with one of her acerbic remarks.

All was going well, despite Bridgette's effort to charm the pants off Harry, when Éclaire picked up a petal-shaped fig and yelped, "Oh my God, it looks just like a little vagina."

Stopping dead in our analysis of the Middle East, all of us turned our attention toward the figs, emitting slight smirks of recognition. Harry took a knife, and smeared some goat cheese in the center of one, and ever-so-carefully, placed his tongue along the red slit, licking and savoring it before relegating it to his mouth and swallowing it whole, all the while watching me watch him.

Oh yes, I thought: We were in for a memorable evening.

Around 7:00 and two bottles of Dom Perignon later, Harry and Éclaire excused themselves to shower and change in the cabana a few feet from the pool, surrounded by a cluster of hydrangeas and wildflowers, landscaped by our gardener, Emilio. Fresh towels, mini-bottles of body lotions and Frédéric Fekkai shampoo lay in small baskets for our guests to enjoy. Bridgette, champagne glass in hand, sauntered off to the house to use the indoor guest room facilities, while Parker and I went upstairs to prepare for the evening ahead. My dress lay on the bed and my scarlet red Manolo Blahniks on the floor ready, in Cinderella-style, to caress my feet. A quick shower, a towel wipe of my curly silver mane, a dash more of perfume, and I was ready to tend to our guests. Again, as predicted, Bridgette had wormed her way into a dinner invitation. When halfway through cocktails, Parker said, "Bridgey, you can't possibly leave us now," she lowered her eyes and said, "Well, if you really don't mind, I'd love to stay for din-din." And stay she did.

Dressed and hungry, we assembled in the dining room, lighted candles around the well-appointed table with petit glass vases holding a single bud above each plate. Harry flanked me on the right and Parker sat at the head, with Éclaire on his left. Hedy scurried to set a place for Bridgette, who was well turned out in one of her weekend ensembles: a little Isaac Mizrahi that still had Cape Cod dune sand caked inside a pocket from a Friday night walk along the beach with a handsome stranger whose name eluded her. She rewound the tape, sparing us no details.

"I was so full of margaritas last night that I have no idea who he even was," Bridgette laughed. "All I know is he said he'd be phoning me next week for dinner. Other than that, I assume I'm still a virgin."

Éclaire shifted uneasily in her chair. "I adore the Cape," she said. "Harry and I haven't been there for ages; what with our East Hampton house and all, who has time to gallivant?"

"So, you're 'Hamptonized,'" Bridgette said. "Personally, I find the Hamptons a bit too flashy for my taste. I prefer roughing it."

"Bridgette's idea of 'roughing it' is staying at a five-star hotel and not ordering room service," Parker jumped right in.

This solicited laughs, even from Bridgette, who accepted it good-naturedly. Bridgette might be the Queen of the smart-ass remark, but, to her credit, she could take it as well as dish it out.

Hedy placed a basket of warm bread on the table, steam still rising from its pores.

"Don't tell me you stayed in and baked bread on a hot July day?" Bridgette asked me.

"I'd like to take the credit," I said, "but no, I'm afraid I left that up to the bread elves."

"Coco isn't the 'kneady' type," Parker said. "But let me say this: My wife is one hell of a cook, as soon you'll see. She whipped up this entire Tuscan menu and her polenta with wild mushroom sauce will send you into rapturous bliss. But first, before we get you too excited, take a piece of this bread and dip it into our Tuscan olive oil and tell me you're not transported back to Italy on a late November day when the olive harvest is in full bloom, the finest time to be in Tuscany, I might add."

Each of us reached for a slice of bread, Harry beating me to it. He placed a crusty piece on my plate and dribbled it with the olive oil. I placed it to my mouth, some oil lingering on my lips. While the others followed suit, Harry leaned over. "I should be licking this off your mouth," he whispered.

"You see my point?" Parker continued, oblivious to Harry's little aside. "Tuscans produce some of the finest extra virgin olive oil in all the Mediterranean."

He then went on with a dissertation on Tuscan olives, stating that the best oil comes from under-ripe olives, still green and just starting to turn reddish black, and they must be harvested by hand, then rushed to the press within forty-eight hours of being picked. Only then will the true aroma and flavors come through. Parker made it a practice to enlighten his guests on pertinent trivia, providing what he considered an additional flavor to the meal. His plethora of culinary tidbits added to the merriment, and as we hung on his every word, Harry managed to entwine his left leg around mine. A flowery cotton tablecloth, dripping along the floor, concealed what would certainly qualify by old Mrs. Braverman as a "peccadillo" of the highest order. I responded by locking my leg around his, so that we made a perfect pretzel. All during the first course of a papardella al sugo d'anatra (ribbon pasta with duck sauce) until Hedy cleared the dishes, Harry and I stayed connected, Harry occasionally moving his leg slightly, rubbing up and down mine, as Bridgette recapped her Cape Cod weekend and moved on to her itinerary of the Greek Isles she would be visiting in August.

"Harry and I adored cruising the islands," Éclaire said, "despite the fact that I got food poisoning eating a fish of unknown origin. I have a very delicate stomach."

"Darling, why do you think they invented Lomotil?" Bridgette asked, somewhat bemused. "I intend to travel the world before I croak, and that includes places a nice girl like you would dare not trespass."

"Harry and I went to India once," Éclaire defensively snapped back.

"And I'm sure you adored the Taj Mahal," Bridgette said.

"That white marble would go great in our bathroom," Éclaire said.

~

Dinner went beautifully. Parker served wines that were perfect companions to each course, with Bridgette getting drunker with every sip. My sea bass was grilled to perfection and served with the polenta, accompanied by fresh asparagus with a nutmeg hollandaise sauce with Parmesan shavings. My bocconcini salad with balls of mozzarella made from water buffalo's milk, arugula, and Belgian endive was tossed with a light olive oil and balsamic vinegar and a splash of lemon juice. The oven-roasted potatoes with rosemary and garlic arrived at the table on a ceramic platter surrounded by warm caponata topped with pine nuts and raisins. The aromas blended together into a heavenly scented mixture of garlic, onions, mushrooms, and tomatoes that filled the room. Outside the French doors off the dining room, little lights twinkled around the pool and patio. Nina and Tim Zagat would have given us a 30 on atmosphere alone. By the time dessert arrived, Bridgette was pronounced legally drunk and Éclaire and Parker were engrossed in conversation on Italian art. As for Harry, he was in ecstasy over my zabaglione, served with a raspberry sauce that Hedy placed before him, while I ladled fresh fruit into small glass bowls to cut the sweetness of the bittersweet chocolate and the white chocolate curls used as a garnish. Bridgette remarked that the fruit tarts were similar to those she had sampled before and I simply couldn't have baked them. Parker introduced a sweet ice wine to add the finishing touch to the meal and, ever the faithful husband, admonished his sister for thinking the tarts were store-bought.

"My wife is a marvel with cakes," he said. "I watched her bake these tarts with my own eyes."

"Get a life, Parker," Bridgette said, lighting up a cigarette and walking outside to the "smoking section."

Only once during dinner did Bridgette get slightly out of hand, when she turned to Harry and asked him to examine her profile.

"So, what do you think, Doc?" Bridgette raised her chin northward.

"What is it you're hoping for?" Harry asked.

"Have you got a couple of hours?"

"For God's sake," Parker interrupted, "the man is enjoying dinner. Office hours are over."

"Oh, shut up, Parker. It's conversation, not consultation."

With that Bridgette practically thrust her boobs in Harry's face.

"And these mamas," she said, "definitely need a little lift. They've been hanging around my waist too long."

"A mastopexy is standard procedure," Harry said. "We do a lot of them."

"I believe my sister has had a tad too much of the bubbly," Parker said. "Bridgette my dear, let's get off your imperfections and onto another subject."

"Oh pu-leeze," Bridgette said. "It's not like we're not grown-ups."

"Harry gets inundated with questions all the time," Éclaire said. "He's just too irresistible to resist, plastic surgery-wise, I mean."

"Never mind, never mind," Bridgette said. "I've lived with my esthetically challenged bod this long. I can put a lid on it tonight."

"You'll have to excuse my sister," Parker said. "She's intoxicated with the exuberance of her own verbosity."

Harry swallowed another spoonful of zabaglione and bit into a kiwi and custard tart.

"Have I died and gone to heaven?" He turned to me. "Or does it get better than this?"

"That depends on your definition of heaven," I said.

20

"Life itself is the proper binge."
—Julia Childs

You Are Now Entering Dangerous Territory

It was my shining hour. Aside from the provocative Bridgette, it had been a perfect evening. The stage had been set. All of us talked well into the night before Bridgette announced around 1:30 A.M. that she needed her beauty sleep and wanted to go home. Parker insisted she was in no condition to drive and escorted her to the guest room where, in a hazy stupor, Bridgette prostrated herself on the bed fully clothed and fell into a deep sleep on top of the chintz bedspread.

Éclaire, stifling another yawn, gave Harry her oh-my-God-it's-so-late look, and to us, exclaimed, "Oh, my goodness, where did the evening go?"

Good-byes were exchanged with promises to get together soon. At the door, Éclaire said that she must get the recipe for those sweet little tarts, which she actually believed I had baked. Somehow, the thought of Éclaire standing in front of a hot oven and ruining a perfectly good manicure was more than I could imagine. Éclaire was the kind of gal who was so perfectly put together that any activity that caused breaking a sweat was out of the question. No, baking tarts was not part of Éclaire Troutman's repertoire.

At around 3 A.M., after Parker and I had discussed the evening in minute detail ranging from Éclaire's chiseled looks to Bridgette's big mouth, we fell asleep, only to be awakened five hours later with a knock on our bedroom door from an angry Hedy who threatened to quit on the spot.

"Miz Harding," she wailed as I threw on a robe and met her in the hall, "I just don't have to put up with the likes of *that* woman."

That woman, of course, was Bridgette who, upon rising, had demanded that Hedy run her a bath.

"Who does she think I am anyway? In all my years I've never been ordered around by *anyone* and most especially *not* someone who treats me with such disrespect."

I calmed Hedy down, assuring her that no baths needed to be run and all requests by Bridgette should be ignored.

"Mr. Harding's sister stayed the night," I explained. "And she'll be leaving soon. In the meantime, I'll tend to her needs so don't you worry."

"Thank you, my dear," Hedy said. "Frankly speaking, Mr. Harding is a wonderful man, but that sister of his needs a few lessons in manners."

"Hedy, don't give it another thought. You just go downstairs and relax a while. Mr. Harding and I will prepare breakfast."

"Oh no, Miz Harding, I've already taken care of breakfast. There's fresh coffee waiting and I heated up those sticky buns you like. I can make some eggs, too, and serve them whenever you're ready. Then I'll be off to church."

"Thank you, Hedy," I said, "but we can manage. Go to church and then why not have lunch and take in a movie? Mr. Harding and I are just going to sit around the pool and relax."

"You're an angel, Miz Harding, but that sister-in-law of yours, well, if she was my employer, I'd quit the same day. Would you believe that she even asked me to steam her clothes? I mean, that sister-in-law of yours doesn't know her place."

I apologized profusely while visions of a column ran through my brain. As soon as Hedy's feathers were unruffled, I sat down at my computer and began composing a piece for the following week.

The Seaport Gazette

COMING CLEAN

Another cleaning lady has come and gone. But it's not my fault. I blame it on personality differences: My house and her attitude were incompatible. So I went on the prowl for a new person, someone who doesn't think she is a domestic goddess and isn't afraid to get her hands dirty. A week ago, a nice lady answered my ad. She came over to be interviewed and it was love at first bite. By bite, I mean, she tasted one of my sticky buns and said she'd work for me straightaway if I kept the buns coming.

Up until now, the cleaning ladies I had didn't know how to clean. They just pushed the dust around for a while, stopped for a coffee break, waxed whatever was in their way, and then called it a day.

"There's a reason you've never had much luck with cleaning ladies," my husband, Parker, reminds me. "And that's because you don't rule the roost with an iron hand. You need to be decisive. You need to establish authority."

He said this when our last cleaning lady, Lucille, sat down to watch a soap in the middle of the afternoon.

"You don't understand," I said. "Lucille doesn't think of herself as a cleaning lady. She thinks she's royalty."

There was no doubt that Lucille had her own style. She appeared at my door every week, dressed to kill. She made me hand over the sixty bucks straightaway, which she stuck in her cleavage. Then she made herself a cup of coffee, after which she pulled the vacuum cleaner out of the closet and went about her business, humming show tunes from all her favorite Broadway shows.

A vacuum cleaner was the only machinery Lucille ever operated. She explained that too much heavy lifting could tip her uterus and make her infertile. If she needed any heavy cleaning done, she always asked me.

"After all," she once said, "your childbearing years are over. Your uterus won't mind a sudden jolt. But I'm still in my prime."

Rather than get embroiled in a gynecological discussion, I figured it was easier to succumb to Lucille's wishes.

One day in the middle of her humming "What I Did for Love" from A Chorus Line, *Lucille let out a loud yelp.*

"I've done it again," she shouted. "I broke a nail cleaning out your tub. These abrasives are killing my hands."

I rushed into the bathroom with my expensive jar of hand cream. While Lucille sat on the toilet seat anointing her hands with Estée Lauder, I scoured the bathtub, sprayed the tiles, and spritzed the mirrors.

Lucille had her own way of tidying up the house. If she couldn't get a spot out, she rearranged the furniture so the spot wouldn't show.

"Why is the loveseat sitting in the middle of the living room?" I asked her.

"I accidentally spilled some of your nail polish on the rug when I was doing my nails," she said, "so I changed the décor and now you can't see the smudge."

It was remarks like that that made me think that perhaps I needed to rethink Lucille.

Although I liked her style, I loathed her attitude. Once Lucille had a bad case of the flu. She came to work anyway.

"You could have stayed home," I said.

"Domestic Goddesses never shirk their responsibilities," she said. "All I need are two Tylenol, some chamomile tea with

your imported honey, a sticky bun, and a short nap, and I'll be fine."

While Lucille relaxed in the guest room for a few hours, I cleaned out the refrigerator and ended up catching the flu.

Lucille made me sign a contract before she started working for us. It included two weeks' paid vacation. That's when Parker went a little crazy.

"What do you mean, paid vacation?" he asked. In a fit of rage, he threatened to fire her.

"Not so fast," I calmed him down. "Finding good help isn't as easy as you think. And she's so honest."

"So was Abe Lincoln," Parker said, "and he couldn't clean, either."

That's when I hired Hedy, who is sweet, smart, and doesn't hum show tunes. She's not afraid of a little hard labor and she makes a mean bed. But she is hooked on my sticky buns and refuses to start her day until she has downed a few. Other than that, she's perfect.

A few weeks ago, a minor accident occurred. Hedy told me she had twisted her wrist lifting the microwave oven. I helped her wrap her wrist in an ACE bandage and told her to sit down, have a sticky bun, and relax.

Then I attacked the microwave oven myself. It was so heavy I could feel my uterus tip.

Parker is a happy guy since Hedy entered the scene. He extols her virtues whenever she leaves.

"This house never looked so good," he says. "I love staying home."

And that's what life is like, lately: We sit around admiring Hedy's cleaning and getting high on "Lilac Rain" room deodorizer that is so strong I've had a sinus infection for two months.

After awakening, Bridgette took a quick dip in the pool and said she must be heading back to New York. Neither Parker nor I tried to dissuade her.

"You're welcome to stay for breakfast," I said.

"Darling, people with hangovers never eat breakfast, but a spicy Bloody Mary might help."

"I think not," Parker interrupted.

"I hardly remember a thing from last night," she said, "except that Harry Troutman is drop-dead delicious and has more than a slight crush on Coco."

"Don't be ridiculous," I jumped right in.

"Then why did he pat your fanny on your way to the loo?" she asked me.

"You're delusional," Parker said.

"I second that," I said.

"Hey, it makes no never mind to me, but I'm just telling you, the man has the hots for your wife, Parker. And what about that wife of his? Tell me: How many facelifts has this creature of loveliness had?"

"I don't know. She looks pretty natural. Hard to tell," I said.

"I can tell you this," Bridgette said, "she definitely had a boob job."

"How do you know?" Parker asked.

"Are you serious? What woman over twenty-five has breasts like that?"

"Like what?" he asked.

"So high, they practically reach her chin implant."

The fact was, as soon as Éclaire had arrived, Parker couldn't take his eyes off her.

"I think someone went a little heavy on the collagen injections, too," she said. "No one has lips like that except for Angelina Jolie."

"Only her plastic surgeon knows for sure," Parker said, smiling. "But I must agree, she's a very handsome woman."

"*Very* handsome," I acknowledged, "and just think: If you gave her a mustache, she'd be even handsomer."

"My, aren't you two the wicked little witches," Parker said.

I glossed over this with a quick change of subject and reminded Parker that the pool could use a cleaning and to call our guy. Once Bridgette was on the road heading back to Manhattan, I returned to my bedroom and hung up my dress from the preceding night, which I had haphazardly tossed over the back of a chair. It was then I discovered a piece of paper crumpled inside the pocket. On it was an e-mail address with a little note: "Try this on for size." This was such a typical Harry maneuver and I chuckled at the image of him surreptitiously sneaking in his address when I wasn't paying attention. After I showered and slipped into a pair of shorts and T-shirt, I sat down at my computer and wrote to SkinDeep@northbell.com:

> *Dear SkinDeep: Please note that I never accept e-mail addresses from strangers. In this case, I will make an exception. Please identify yourself if you wish to continue this correspondence.*
> *CocoPuff@atlanticline.net*

Parker walked in just as I was closing my laptop.

"You don't really think that Harry is coming on to you, dear?" he asked.

"Please sweetheart, your sister is just being the usual troublemaker. Harry seems the perfect gentleman," I lied through my teeth.

"With a beautiful wife who seems to adore him," Parker added.

"Exactly," I said. "Éclaire is lovely."

"Her husband wouldn't have it any other way, I'm sure. I think I'll do a few laps. Care to join me by the pool?"

"Maybe after I finish my column," I said.

I waited for Parker to change into his swim trunks and leave the room. Then I opened my laptop and lo and behold, there he was: the newest member of my buddy list. Establishing that we were electronically connected, he continued:

Dear CocoPuff,

Well, well, so you want to know who I am. Try picturing a guy, 6'2", dark hair, slight tan, and eyes that smolder every time you're near. I don't think I can stay away, so I'm resorting to instant gratification. Let's stay connected. SkinDeep

I was back on in a flash.

CocoPuff: This tells me nothing. I know several men who fit your description.
SkinDeep: But, CocoPuff, darling, are these men madly in love with you?
CocoPuff: Define madly.
SkinDeep: Do they melt on the spot?
CocoPuff: They leave pools of water at my feet.
SkinDeep: I can't eat or sleep since I've seen you. Help! I'm wasting away.
CocoPuff: What can I do?
SkinDeep: Feed me.
CocoPuff: I believe I did last night.
SkinDeep: I'm hungry for more. Please say we can meet.
CocoPuff: What do you have in mind?
SkinDeep: Breakfast. Lunch and dinner.
CocoPuff: What are you most in the mood for?
SkinDeep: Eating you.
CocoPuff: You're disgusting. Maybe dinner. When?
SkinDeep: How about tonight?
CocoPuff: Don't be daft. Neither of us is free.
SkinDeep: When can you break away?
CocoPuff: Can't say. I'm a busy gal.
SkinDeep: Don't make me beg.

CocoPuff: Salivating will do.
SkinDeep: Give me a date.
CocoPuff: Next Thursday and it had better be worth it.
SkinDeep: Cocktails, Mark Hotel. 5:00. Dinner to follow.
CocoPuff: Stay frozen until then. No melting allowed.

We were off and running, now involved in the most dangerous game of all: e-mailing. More lives have been wrecked due to irresponsible technological communications than rolls in the hay. Safe Sex, sure, but Computer Condoms: That's what this generation needs.

The rest of the afternoon I spent writing by the pool, later switching over to some light reading, while visions of Harry intruded upon me at every turn. All I could think about was our next meeting and how Thursday just couldn't come soon enough.

21

"A Pap smear is kinda like a throat culture, only you don't gag. Unless maybe if you're really short."
—Sarah Silverstein

Invitation to a Pap Smear

For the next several days I put the finishing touches on my Chaîne article for Gillian. It was coming along nicely, even without Harry's help. The lead-in article in last month's *Seaport Gazette*, "My Years of Eating Dangerously," was received well and I had gotten letters from eager fans who couldn't wait to see the second installment that was due next month.

On Thursday, I drove into Manhattan early for my annual doctor's appointment. A visit to my gynecologist was preceded by a reminder mailed to me a month earlier:

"Our records show you are due for a gynecological examination. Please schedule an appointment at your earliest convenience."

The card arrived on cream-colored classic linen stock with black lettering that looked like an invitation to a special event. It all sounded so cozy, so inviting, that I often wondered if I should buy a new outfit befitting the occasion. But considering that the doctor never saw me fully clothed and hardly remembered my face, I decided to pass on the duds. Instead, I spritzed on a dollop of cologne so when he walked into the examining room and found me wrapped in a paper gown, my scent would jar his memory.

"Oh yes," he would sniff, "my L'Air du Temps."

While I waited amongst a group of other middle-aged, pre-menopausal women, I scribbled away at a column about a visit to the gynecologist that was guaranteed to bring a smile to the female residents of Seaport. By the time I was called in, I was already halfway through the article, and would have shared it with Dr. "Feelgood," except if he took offense, I might flunk my Pap test.

The Seaport Gazette

"HI YO, SILVER"

For years I have been a member of the Silver Stirrups Club that allows women to ask themselves this question as they embark on their annual gynecological visit: Is this experience absolutely necessary? The first time I saw a pair of these metal gizmos, I was reminded of the first time I mounted a horse, except with the horse, I had reins to hold on to. In the case of the gyn exam, all I can do is white-knuckle the sides of the examination table and shout, "Hi Yo, Silver!" To make matters worse, it isn't politically correct to offer the doctor sugar cubes or oats to get him to halt. What makes this event so unique, so memorable if you will, is that all parties involved pretend that something else is going on than what actually is. It's a little like a Disney World adventure where everything seems a bit surreal, yet not altogether a fantasy either.

A few months ago I received a note in the mail resembling an invitation. It was neatly engraved with block lettering on a cream-colored card, and read: Our records show that it has been a year since your last gynecological examination. Please call the office at your earliest convenience to schedule an appointment.

I quickly ran to the phone and booked a slot for early July.

It all seems so elegant, so festive, that I always wonder if it's necessary to bring along flowers.

I arrived at the office on a hot, muggy afternoon, dressed to kill. Women always dress for their gynecologists even though as soon as we arrive, we're out of our duds so fast we don't know what hit us. Some gals even have their hair done for the occasion or buy new shoes. There are no lengths to how far a woman will go to look good. What follows next is the routine procedure involving travel accommodations between various rooms.

The Waiting Room. *This is where all sisters unite, pretending not to have a care in the world about what is to happen next. A feeling of camaraderie is in the air. Some keep to themselves, reading magazines. Others exchange conversation, ranging from weather reports, child rearing, vacation spots, and fine dining experiences. Everyone is in a state of denial and never discusses the reason they are actually here.*

The Dressing Room. *This is where we remove our clothes in exchange for a paper robe or a white sheet, and I'm not talking the designer couture collection. This is wrapped around the completely naked body, sarong style, and worn en route to the next room,* The Loo, *where a specimen is left and magically whisked away by invisible elves.*

The Examining Room. *This is where it all happens, center stage with three main characters: the patient, the nurse, and the doctor who plays the leading role.*

Nurse: "Hello (eyes the chart) . . . Ms.----------. You're looking well."

Me: "Thanks. White sheets become me."

Nurse: "Why don't we hop up on the scale?" Followed by "Why don't we hop up on the table?"

After a series of hops, I am positioned properly and the nurse hums chirpily while I ask for a cup of water so I can pop a few Valium brought along for the occasion. She tells me to take a deep, cleansing breath. It is at this precise moment the doc enters, smiling widely while simultaneously slapping on a rubber glove.

"Hello (he eyes the chart) . . . ----------." He greets me with the same enthusiasm as Regis Philbin on Who Wants to Be a Millionaire? *Under normal circumstances, he might even be a nice guy, but on this auspicious occasion, it's business as usual. And here is where it gets particularly funky. Neither I, the nurse, nor the doctor addresses the matter at hand: the exam. Instead, we lapse into intensive rounds of small talk designed to make everyone present feel more relaxed, when you can actually cut the tension with a knife.*

Doctor (sitting on a little stool and shining a 900-watt spotlight under the sheet): "So, how's the family: the kids, the grandchildren, the dog, the cat?"

Me: "Really well, especially the cat."

Nurse: "I have two cats. Their names are Fluffy and Smokey."

Doctor (fidgeting around with a lot of paraphernalia): "I'm a dog man, myself."

Nurse: "I have a goldfish. Very orange, with a white stripe down its back."

Me (counting the holes in the ceiling tiles): "Did you know there are two hundred and fifty-eight holes in one ceiling tile?"

Nurse: "Gee, I never knew that. Did you, Doctor?"

Doctor (probing and prodding): "Can't say I did, but that's an interesting piece of information. You must be a real trivia buff."

Me: "Yes, I've always enjoyed counting holes in ceilings. It's become a hobby."

Nurse (handing the doctor a Q-Tip the size of a shish kebab skewer): "Do you think it will rain?"

Me: "Eventually it will, but not today. Today it's sunny with a smattering of clouds and no possibility of precipitation."

Doctor rises from under the sheet and steps back, tosses his gloves with perfect aim into the trash can. He then spends the remainder of the time surveying the other half: my upper landscape. He nods approvingly. "You can get dressed and I'll meet you in my office" or what I refer to as the "Now-we-can-act-like-real-people" room.

The Real People Room. *I wait ten minutes until the doctor saunters in, holding my chart and announcing in medical terms, "You're doing very nicely. I'm pleased with my findings." I have now regressed to age five. I feel like a model patient who is about to be awarded a prize for good behavior. At the very least, I expect a lollipop. I now proceed to the final stop on my trip: the Pay-on-Your-Way-Out Room.*

Pay-on-Your-Way-Out Room. *It is here I must hand over my money, when, for what just transpired, I think they should be paying me. I am told to have a good day and to call the office in a week for the results of my tests. Something else to look forward to. I go home and down a glass of wine. I have survived yet another visit to the Silver Stirrups Club. I hope to be invited back next year. I have passed with flying colors. "Hi Yo, Silver!"*

From there I stopped off for a grilled cheese and tomato sandwich at Jackson Hole and headed toward the Metropolitan Museum, a favorite spot to decompress for a while. My appointment with Finkelman was at 3:00 and I was already dreading my session where, in Hercule Poirot fashion, he would ask me to reveal all.

When I burst into Finkelman's office, a blast of cold air hit me, a relief from the burning sun and heat that enveloped all of Manhattan on this last Thursday in July. I flipped through the latest copy of *Elle* left by the previous patient. Finkelman's magazine collection had no fashion magazines in its repertoire and consisted of more tony selections: *National Republic*, *Smithsonian*, and endless copies of *JAMA*. The occasional *Reader's Digest*, so out of character, was a welcome find.

Finkelman, dressed in a striped blue-and-white seersucker suit from Brooks Brothers and navy bow tie, was wiping his head with the proverbial handkerchief. A woman from the previous session bolted from the room, sobbing and mumbling a few obscenities under her breath. Finkelman had his work cut out for him. Unlike my gyno, who had only to stare at female genitalia all day and could forgo the mental abuse, poor Finkelman was ever the target of his patients' transferences. No wonder he always looked so washed-out, so frazzled.

I sat back in the chair and commented on the weather, something I couldn't care less about and never discussed.

"It's a real scorcher out there today," I said.

"I see," Finkelman said.

"Hot as hell," I reiterated.

"Hmm."

"But I am keeping my cool."

"How is that?"

"Well," I said, "things have heated up a bit."

And with that, I sailed off into the sea of analytical metaphors and presented Finkelman with a blow-by-blow of the previous Saturday night dinner party and my most recent acquisition: Harry's e-mail address.

"I see," yet again.

"And . . . we've begun e-mailing."

"Is that all?"

"He wants to see me."

"Uh-huh."

"And I've agreed to a casual dinner."

Silence.

"So we agreed to meet and agreed to eat."

"That's a lot of agreeing."

"Yes, but . . . uh, he's a big help, with my article and all."

Finkelman blew into the same hankie that only minutes before swabbed his brow and all I could think of was: Will he brow-wipe again or will he switch to another handkerchief?

"Is your mind wandering, Coco?"

"It is actually, but getting back on track, Harry has become a regular fantasy figure."

"It seems that your fantasy is fast becoming a reality," Finkelman aptly noted.

"Do I get demerits for speaking the truth?"

"Your sessions are paths to enlightenment," he said. "The work you do in here lays the groundwork to life outside this room. Unlock the key to your unconscious motivations and you'll be free to move ahead in a direction that serves you best. Free associate, please."

"My dinner party was a huge success."

"Elaborate."

"The meal was cooked to perfection. My sister-in-law showed up. Éclaire looked exactly like a plastic surgeon's wife should. Parker thought she was a real looker. Bridgette thought she was a ditz, but Bridgette can be cruel and unrelenting. She got drunk and stayed over. She also caught Harry giving my butt a friendly pat. Is that the free-associating you were after?"

"How did that happen?"

"What?"

"The butt pat?"

"Harry is very spontaneous. He sees a good piece of ass and he feels compelled to pat it."

"Coco." Finkelman shifted legs and lifted his chin from his shirt collar, gave a cough, wiped his brow (same snot handkerchief), and cleared his throat again. "You need to stop seeing him."

"Oh?"

"There's no room in your marriage for two men. And since your husband is the primary love object, you must stop seeing

Harry immediately. Also, and we haven't touched on this: It's difficult for me to treat you professionally when you're running around half-cocked."

My mouth nearly flew open. "Half-cocked?" Freud must have been turning over in his grave as he said it.

"Nice psych terminology," I said.

"Coco, once you sever the relationship between you and Harry, we can examine the ramifications of your behavior, which is a throwback to your adolescence and needs careful, not to mention honest, appraisal and analysis. In short, Coco, you need to stop acting out."

"Parker is not my primary love object," I said. "That's the problem."

"I'd like us to replay an earlier tape, Coco. Please, if you will, take a trip with me and examine again the relationship you shared with your parents."

"Sam and Yvonne? Please, I won't be able to stay awake."

"Indulge me for a moment. You should recall that you were always vying for your father's attention."

"No, I was trying to save him from Yvonne's clutches. The man couldn't make a move without her. Still can't."

"Yes, and your job was to save him from this horrific fate."

"No, my job was to have some quality time without the intrusion of my mother."

"Quality time?"

"Sam and I shared peak moments without Yvonne," I said.

"Enumerate."

"Movies. Dinners. Baseball games. Father/daughter moments."

I sat back and allowed my reverie to take hold. It was true: I had invested large amounts of time "playing up" to my father. As an only child, I wanted to attract his attention, be the apple of his eye, and I learned early how to win him over. While Yvonne encouraged our relationship, she was often threatened by the special bond that had developed over the years. I had sharpened my baby teeth on my dad so that by the time I was a budding adolescent, I had perfected the art of seduction through my intellect, humor, and ability to read men. Finkelman might have a point: I *was* vying for my father's attention, and was my life a constant struggle to be noticed and adored?

Now, years later, I am that same "child," now dressed in designer clothes and shoes living in a dream house, with a dream daughter and a doting husband, and had found a daddy-substitute on whom to focus her attention. Was Harry my father replacement and was Parker the good mommy who encouraged me to move forward and grab every opportunity that came my way? Forty-five minutes later, Finkelman, rising from his chair, congratulated me on a job well done.

"Now, Coco, this is what I call a session put to good use. Keep this up and we'll soon have you as good as new . . . psychoanalytically speaking."

As I rode down the fifteen floors, I mentally reviewed my session. Yes, I would need to give up one man in place of another. I decided that if I wanted Harry in my life, the man who had to go was Finkelman. The following session I would tell him I wanted to terminate my therapy.

Having decided to give Finkelman the heave-ho, I was a free agent. My actions were now completely my own and no longer were up for scrutiny by a judgmental shrink. But Finkelman was right: I was acting out and I felt amazingly like the child that he was harping on me to address, the one who, as an adolescent, had taken great joy in circumventing my mother's warnings about almost everything I did, especially where men were concerned.

To this day, her words came back to haunt me. "Coco, remember, if you give away the milk, why would he need to buy the cow?"

Similarly, when I had married Mitch, she had thanked God that her daughter had ended up with such a prince.

"Darling," she reminded me on my wedding day, "if you keep

the home fires burning, your husband won't seek warmth on other hearths."

It was just too good to resist. Taxiing over to The Mark, I made a few notes for a column: "Letter to a Newly Married Daughter," a tribute to my mother, the perfect maternal cliché. I would put the finishing touches on it this week and have it appear in next week's issue of the *Gazette*.

The Seaport Gazette

LETTER TO A NEWLY MARRIED DAUGHTER

Coco darling,

Now that you are a newly married lady, I want to say a few words as you embark on the threshold of a new adventure with the man of your dreams. As you and Mitchell begin married life together, remember those three little words that will always hold you in good stead: Joint Checking Accounts. Your money is always your money and Mitch's money is your money, too. That's the democratic way of doing things.

When you fall on difficult times and you and Mitch have words, and your first inclination is to pack up your Louis Vuitton luggage with your monogram on the front, and come home to Daddy and me, my advice is: Bite your tongue, count to fifty, and most important, percolate! There's nothing like a good cup of coffee to make a man come to his senses, unless it's instant. I find that Savarin, "the coffee they serve at the Waldorf Astoria," is my favorite and works best with your father and me.

Don't expect every day to be sunny. There will be occasional downpours, if you know what I mean. That's when you must remember that a smile is your umbrella and, as "Annie" says, "the sun will come out tomorrow" if you play your cards right. Things are never as bad as they seem and every marriage can be saved, except maybe Aunt Lillian and Uncle Mike's who have been bickering for years, which Uncle Mike blames on the fact that his dentures are killing him.

Another point to keep in mind is that men aren't as smart as women. They are grumpy by nature. They were born that way. Never let on. Women should always pretend their husbands know more than they do. That way, there will be harmony in the house, which is good for the children and the pets, not to mention your plants. You can tell a lot about couples by their plants. A droopy Wandering Jew says all.

Some words of wisdom: Never let Mitchell see you without makeup. It won't do a thing for your marriage. Only natural blondes from the Midwest can get away with that, not dark-haired girls from New Jersey. Even if it means getting up at the crack of dawn to put on your face, do it. A pale wife is not a pretty wife. As I've told you a hundred times, Estée Lauder makes a very nice night cream that was tested on live crows to dissolve their crow's feet and tighten their necks. Never squeeze your pimples. You can get a brain tumor.

Honesty is not the best policy. Never tell your husband everything. What Mitchell doesn't know won't hurt him. This business of communication is overrated and was drummed up by some old spinster psychoanalyst who hated men. From day one, I never told your father anything and just look at us.

Always keep a little mad money under the towels. You never know when you'll need it, but believe me, you will. Also, keep some sachets inside Mitchell's socks. The way to a man's heart is through his nose, not through his stomach as otherwise suggested. Saran Wrap is a girl's best friend whether it be for storing a pot roast or wrapping around Mitchell's head when he snores.

It is expected that you should occasionally cook a meal. That's why microwaves were invented. Once a week, make a meat loaf. It will last for days. The rest of the time, make reservations. Eating out promotes mental health. No woman needs to stick her head inside an oven or put her hands in a dishwasher. It will ruin your manicures. Too much time spent in the kitchen will give you hot flashes. For years, I thought I was menopausal until I figured out I was standing in front of a 500-degree oven.

Coco sweetheart, I realize you never worked a day in your life, but until you get pregnant, maybe you should think about getting a little part-time job at the makeup counter at Bloomies, from ten to one, just so you won't get bored and can feel productive. Mitchell will respect you for having a career.

As for housecleaning, my suggestion is: Hire a cleaning lady. Housework can be extremely dangerous. Daddy and I didn't send you to a Junior College to breathe pollutants. There are more important things to worry about than what's lurking behind your toilets. Let someone else deal with wax buildup. This reminds me, always wax. Never shave. Never use Mitchell's razor or you'll grow a beard on your legs. Now that Mitchell has a thriving dental practice, one gold crown should take care of your maid expenses for six months.

If you heed my advice, Coco, you are guaranteed to have a marriage like Daddy's and mine. Stay off the diving boards and out of public pools or you'll catch polio. Drink only bottled water. Why you and Mitchell had to go to Nicaragua in the first place is beyond me.

Daddy and I wish you both a very happy life. Remember, if things get really bad and Mitchell proves to be the jerk your father thinks he is, your bedroom will be waiting for you. I haven't touched a thing. Not even your poster of Albert Schweitzer. Now, that's what I call a real man.

Much love and hugs to you, the best daughter in the world who has brought Daddy and me much joy and the occasional migraine headache. And don't forget: Make sure you practice safe sex. By that I mean, use a bed with a good mattress or else you and Mitchell will throw your backs out.

One last thing: A sense of humor goes a long way in marriage. Your father has been telling me the same stupid jokes for over forty years. I pretend they're wonderful. We all know that Mitchell is not naturally funny. You must laugh at his jokes anyway. This will make him feel loved, and a loved man will do anything for his wife . . . except put the toilet seat down, but who's perfect?

We will be waiting at the airport when you return. I pray to God you don't get hijacked. Wear nice underwear in case you're body searched. And don't forget to bring along a surgical mask. I heard that Nicaragua is very dusty. If you need to reach us any hour, day or night, I'll be sitting by the phone, but don't feel you have to call. Of course, it would be a nice gesture to let us know you're still alive, but I'm sure you have better things to do than think about your parents. Oh, and if you have a free minute, get started on your thank-you notes, especially to Grandma who has never gotten over the fact you never even acknowledged her gift of that possum coat she gave you when you went off to college.

Coco precious, Daddy and I will be thinking of you every minute of every day until you return home. Love from the person who knows you best in the world,

Mummsie

P.S. Always carry rubbers . . . you never know when it might rain!

22

"Before we got engaged he never farted.
Now it's a second language."
—Caroline Rhea

The Big Bang

"SkinDeep" was waiting when I arrived. I sat down and ordered a Cosmopolitan.

"CocoPuff, I presume," Harry teased.

"Pleased to meet you," I replied. "And am I to assume you are SkinDeep?"

"In the flesh," Harry said with a broad smile on his face. "So happy to know you."

We followed each other's lead and played off each other beautifully. Carrying the thought further, I could only imagine the simpatico we would experience in the bedroom.

"You look exquisite," he said, "glowing as usual."

"It's called summertime. I'm as hot as hell."

"Exactly the way I want you."

And in front of a packed room, Harry leaned over and kissed me passionately.

Two Cosmopolitans and two gin and tonics apiece, and I was feeling no pain.

"SkinDeep," I said, "I want to see the place where you transform beasts into beauties."

"Office hours are over, darling."

"Please," I said, "I need to know all about you."

"And if I were to agree?"

"You'll be rewarded handsomely."

And with that, the check was ordered up and paid, and Harry and I were on our way up to 75th and Fifth and his penthouse office.

Manhattan doormen, with the exception of my Walter and Jasper, are the most discreet people in the world: They pretend to know nothing, but understand everything. Harry's doorman, George, was no exception. As we stepped from the taxi, George gave us his obligatory nonchalant nod and led us over to the elevator alcove. One button push away and we were whisked up to the twenty-second floor and into a waiting area that looked like a small hotel lobby. Sleek brushed aluminum chairs surrounded a gigantic oval glass table where perfectly arranged magazines lay in neat piles, far different from the literary selections that Finkelman subscribed to. Off in the corner were shelves containing photo albums of before and after shots of Harry's success stories. Original pieces of art hung on the walls, revealing Harry's eclectic side: a small Chagall in the hallway, a Picasso over the reception desk, off to the corner a Daumier, a Miró, a Jasper Johns, and a Warhol. Down a long hallway with examining rooms on each side, was a large Rauschenberg leading to Harry's consultation room—the room where life-altering decisions were made daily. The man had an eye for art as well as fine food and wine. Everywhere I looked, I was treated to a visual banquet of paintings. My favorite was Harry's latest acquisition, a middle-aged woman staring out at what, I couldn't be sure.

"It's a John Currin," he said. "A newcomer on the scene, but a master at capturing the essence of the postmenopausal woman. Like Currin, I, too, am fascinated by the beauty of the older woman. This one serves as a model for all those who come through these doors."

Harry continued.

"I consider a woman's imperfections to be the best part about her, it's what makes her real, adds character. But most of my women patients won't agree. They want to be 'corrected'—changed. My job is to ever so slightly tweak her so-called flaws, keeping her image intact, so that after surgery, she still looks perfectly natural while having been enhanced, but not made different. For me to be successful I must give the woman what she wants, but not compromise my philosophy on beauty. I refuse to turn out cookie-cutter, plastic molded facsimiles of the so-called 'perfect woman.' My job is allowing a woman to remain herself with slight alterations. When the bandages come off, what is new must also be familiar. Plastic surgery, unless we're talking about extreme physical handicaps, should never be a jolting experience. I let my patients go gently back to their lives bearing some semblance of their prior selves."

How could you not love such a guy?

"Please," I said, "show me around the rooms where these miracles take place."

"Contrary to what you may have heard, Coco, I'm not a miracle-worker. Just a doctor trying to make my patients happy."

"How about those who aren't your patients?"

"Especially those," Harry said. "Come here, you."

And right there, next to a Mary Cassatt of two women, Harry and I kissed. Still kissing, Harry backed me into an examining room, the only illumination coming from the outside hall light. There in the dark, surrounded by glass shelves on all sides, Harry moved me gently over to the examination table, covered with a thin layer of disposable white paper, reminiscent of Dr. Feelgood's office earlier today. Slowly, deftly, Harry positioned me down on the table, his hands deliberate, but gentle. My body stiffened slightly.

"Shhh, darling," he whispered, "don't stop me."

Harry stood at my side. He was in no hurry. His only intent was in pleasing me.

"I want to know how you feel, Coco. I want to explore every crevice—every inch of you."

And there in the same room where hundreds of other women

had lain before me, Dr. Harry Troutman gave me the examination of my life, his hands inching beneath my sweater, moving up my torso to my breasts. I inhaled deeply, tightening my abs so my stomach would appear flat. Even at moments like these, vanity reared its egotistical head.

"We can't have any intrusions," he said, reaching behind me and lifting me ever-so-slightly, enabling him to remove my bra.

"Harry . . ." I sat up.

"Oh, Coco, my love," he said, molding his hands to my breasts. "You're perfect."

"Am I? I don't know that."

"I know."

"Harry?"

"Yes, darling?"

"I want to touch you, too."

The next sound I heard was the quick "zip" of Harry's trousers, a swish of belt being pulled from its loops, shoes being kicked across the room. "Come with me, sweetheart," he said, taking my hand. "I'm taking you up to my recovery suite."

"But I haven't even had the anesthesia."

"I want you fully awake," Harry said. "I promise, you'll feel no pain. Only ecstasy."

"I don't know. We haven't even had dinner."

"Better to eat you on an empty stomach, my dear."

~

And as I was being maneuvered up to the recovery suite, only one image entered my mind: my mother, Yvonne, sitting on her deck chair in Boca, imploring me to make the most of this moment. "At least, while your clothes are off, darling, so it shouldn't be a total loss, let the doctor take a look and make a few recommendations."

I quickly dismissed the thought as we entered a small elevator. Harry pushed a button and in seconds the door opened into a magnificent recovery suite. Subdued lighting appeared with the flick of a switch and soft music with another. Celadon-colored floor-to-ceiling duvets lined the room with lime green and pimento red carpeting at our feet. The room was dressed for serenity and had a soothing spa-like effect for post-op patients whose immediate goals were to find relief amidst any discomfort they might sustain from their surgeries.

And then, the mind-demons appeared, those unwelcome guests, those nasty intrusive destroyers of the perfect moment who interrupted my passion with a barrage of questions:

1. Was my breath fresh?
2. Was I simply glowing or was I downright sweaty?
3. Was the KY jelly from this morning's gyno invasion still intact or could I use a quick dab? ("There's nothing like a dry pussy to kill the sex," Annie liked to occasionally remind me.)
4. Would my boobs appear too flat in the missionary position?
5. Would my boobs droop too much if I were on top?
6. I should have had a snack at The Mark as my stomach was growling uncontrollably.
7. Would my hair feel soft to the touch? Did I use enough conditioner?
8. I should not have cancelled my leg-waxing at Georgette Klinger.
9. Would my moaning appear too guttural or my screams too vocal?
10. Would my blow job be adequate or would I be too rough?
11. Would my vagina seem velvety smooth?
12. Would I be a lousy lay?

Harry kissed me hard on my mouth as the next minutes became a blur of exquisite mutual arousal. Just as he finished caressing every part of my being, kissing, rubbing, nibbling, tasting—just after I had followed along, licking and sucking and sliding my mouth up and down his perfectly erect cock, he was now jumping on my bones, slipping on a condom as he readied himself for the "Moment of Impact." It was then the worst moment of my life came into play. Suddenly, as his gorgeous penis slid into me, a sound, not unfamiliar, but certainly surprising, caught me off guard and filled the air. Was it coming from me or from him? It was hard to tell, but just as we were about to experience mutual orgasm, the culprit became known: I had let go with the biggest, loudest, most explosive fart of my life. And the rest, as they say . . . is history.

23

"The better to eat you with, my dear."
—The Big Bad Wolf

Setting the Stage

There are those moments in life that are better off left alone. Moments so horrible that they could tear a relationship to shreds if one dared to trespass upon them. Harry and I never spoke about that night except to say it was, for lack of a better word, a "blast."

The following morning, after having spent the night in Harry's recovery suite, I called Annie on my cell to recap the fart fiasco.

"How soon will you be back in Seaport?" she asked.

"I'm on the FDR Drive. With no traffic, around ten o'clock."

"Meet me at A Scone's Throw," she said.

An hour later, I appeared at our favorite coffee shop, slightly disheveled and at loose ends. I was wearing last night's clothes and was on the verge of tears.

Annie was downing a grande, quad dry cappuccino when I arrived. I insinuated myself on a maroon velveteen chair and threw my hands in the air. "It's all too gruesome to even report," I said.

There were a few minutes of silence when Annie broke in: "When you say 'fart,' do you actually mean that you passed wind?"

"Wind is too nice a way of putting it," I said. "Picture an eruption so loud . . ."

"Perhaps he was so caught up in the moment that he never even heard it."

"Stop trying to placate me, for Christ's sake. It was ear-splitting. I'm telling you, it was the loudest goddamn gastric emission you can imagine. The man must think I'm a fucking one-woman volcano."

"So you had a little gas? Big deal. I mean, he's a doctor and all. I'm sure he's heard a fart or two in his life."

"He's not a gastroenterologist, Annie. His patients might have a few wrinkles, drooping eyelids, sagging breasts, and fat butts, but I can tell you this, not one of those butts couldn't control itself. And, I'd bet money that the lovely Éclaire never farted a day in her perfect little life."

"Maybe he thought you burped," Annie consoled. "A fart and a burp can be interchangeable."

"A fart doth not a burp make. He'll never call me again," I wailed, as I downed my woes in a triple quad venti vanilla soymilk latte.

By the time I got home, there was an e-mail from "SkinDeep" who thanked me for the most fascinating evening of his life.

"What did I tell you?" Annie said, when I phoned. "He never even noticed."

"He'd have to be deaf," I said.

The matter was then dropped, never to be referred to again, except at those rare moments when Annie and I wanted a good laugh and pulled the scene from our "Life's Worst Moments" list and howled.

~

That night, Harry and I had set the sexual stage for some of the best lovemaking to follow. He was thrilled by my uninhibited behavior. I was grateful for his discretion, meaning he had the good sense to ignore yet another one of my "peccadilloes." And so, we moved on to our weekly illicit meetings, preceded always with cocktails and dinner at some well-chosen spot not likely to be frequented by friends or acquaintances who, like pop-up book characters, might spring up unexpectedly. Occasionally, we threw caution to the wind and took chances, figuring if we did run into people, we would tell them that Harry was assisting me on a book project I was doing on plastic surgery.

Parker often asked when we could see Éclaire and Harry again. I brushed this aside with a curt: "soon." Then, one morning in early August, out of the blue, the telephone rang. A breathless Éclaire was on the other end. I panicked. Had we been caught? When? Where? How? I tried to remain cool.

"Hello Coco, this is Éclaire Troutman. Harry and I would like to invite you and Parker to join us at our home in East Hampton."

My heart nearly jumped out of my chest.

"Oh, Éclaire . . . hi . . . how lovely . . . well, yes, uh, of course . . . yes, we'd be thrilled." I stammered on each effusive word.

I gushed. I cooed. My ebullience was revolting. "Let me get my date book."

"I'll hold on," she said, puffing ever so slightly. "I just gave my toenails a touchup. I'll blow while you get your book."

I ran over to my desk where an e-mail from SkinDeep had suddenly materialized. Back to the phone.

"How does Labor Day weekend look for you?" Éclaire inquired. "You can come out on Thursday afternoon and stay through Monday. We'll be inviting others, as well."

"Others-as-well" sounded perfect. "Others-as-well" would allow for the necessary amount of anonymity to get me through the four days. "Others-as-well" would defuse the issue and allow Harry and me to blend nicely into the woodwork.

"Actually, we're very free," I said with emphasis on the *very*, "and what could be nicer than a weekend with you and Harry. Parker will be *ecstatic*." With Éclaire it was easy to lapse into superlatives.

"Well, good then . . . and Coco . . ."

Oh God, just like Finkelman, there was an "and"? I held my breath.

"Perhaps, we could meet for lunch before then."

"Before then would be nice."

"This Thursday after my hair appointment with Serge would work for me."

"I'm often in on Thursdays," I said. "How much fun would that be?" I was becoming more banal by the moment.

"So let's say we meet at one o'clock at Geisha. You do *do* sushi, don't you? I make it a practice to eat lightly at lunch. I like saving my calories for din-din."

"Sounds great," I said. "See you at one on Thursday."

"And Coco?"

"Yes?" I quivered.

"Maybe some shopping après sushi?"

"By all means. I do some of my best buying après sushi. Nothing like some raw tuna to get the retail shopping genes in gear."

I hung up and ran to my computer. I couldn't wait to respond to Harry's morning love note.

"CocoPuff, it's Monday morning. Wipe the sleep from the corners of your eyes and tell the good doctor how you are."

I e-mailed straightaway: "Three guesses who wants to do lunch on Thursday. CocoPuff."

Next a call to Annie, the daily recipient of the ongoing saga of my life.

"Hold on to your panties," I said. "Number one: We're doing the Hamptons over Labor Day weekend . . . at the Troutmans'."

"The plot thickens," Annie said, "and you're in over your ass."

"Number two: Éclaire and I are doing lunch on Thursday."

"My God, if it weren't for you, I'd have no life at all. How the hell did *that* happen?"

"She called me not more than ten minutes ago."

"Does Harry know?"

"I just e-mailed him."

"He'll croak."

"Harry likes living on the edge. He probably has an erection just thinking about it."

"Go girl go!" Annie said.

On Thursday, fresh from Serge and with every hair clipped to perfection, the lovely Éclaire in her Thierry Mugler suit was ready to down some sushi.

"This is the only place in the city where I do raw fish," she said.

"A regular risk-taker," I thought, smiling, not wanting to appear too sarcastic for fear that Éclaire, whose sense of humor was not her strong suit, might take umbrage.

She ordered a tea of scented jasmine leaves wrapped around a rosebud.

"Presentation is everything," Éclaire said, practically squealing from delight. "I actually prefer green tea, but the aroma of jasmine is hard to resist. Green tea, you know, gets rid of the body's impurities. Harry touts its virtues. He recommends a green tea scrub to all his facelifts. Some of the best day spas in Manhattan will soon be carrying his line. I myself am religious about using it and my skin never looked better. Look at my pores."

I had to admit: Éclaire's face, which Harry had once confessed when he was tipsy, had been nipped twice, looked as uptight as she was, but it had knocked enough years off her life to give her that baby-doll look, putting her somewhere between late thirties and mid-forties, depending on the day. Today, well-coiffed and made up, she could pass for under forty, although as of her last birthday, Harry had also mentioned, she had hit forty-five.

We ate and small-talked our way through lunch, never once discussing Harry on a personal level. Conversation included the latest hot films and books. We then moved on to our respective children and our upcoming weekend in East Hampton.

"Are you a pool or an ocean person?" she asked. "Our house sits on a bluff overlooking both. The sunsets are amazing."

"Parker detests sand," I said. "As for me, I've always been a saltwater gal."

"Salt water is a natural exfoliant," she said. "If Harry could bottle it and sell it, he'd make a bloody fortune. Ask him, he'll tell you that salt water, like aspirin, cures everything."

"I'll make a point of it," I said, imagining swallowing a tablespoon of salt water every time I had a headache.

"Après sushi" we hit the shops with a vengeance. The raw fish had given Éclaire the jolt she needed to dish out the loot for "a nice little nightie" at Bergdorf's that made her feel "quite whimsical." She also found Barney's to be her oasis in which to drop a bundle on two pairs of leather sandals and a Prada tote. So I shouldn't feel left out of the loop, I treated myself to a Chanel Gossamer lipstick for that high-beam gleam the salesgirl told me I couldn't live without. We parted company at 4:00, giving me two hours to catch my breath before meeting Harry at Nick's. When we had talked earlier, he said he was "feeling like a pizza."

Between Éclaire and Harry I had reached my allotted calorie count of the day, but knew I'd be burning them off in bed later. Pizza, in fact, was the perfect antidote for killing off the lingering flavors of the eight pieces of sashimi I had consumed earlier, accompanied by a pungent seaweed salad. By the time 6:00 rolled around, Éclaire would be back in Bronxville, nibbling on a lettuce leaf and soaking in her nightly bubble bath while Harry and I were feasting off each other.

24

"The ornament of a house is the friends who frequent it."
—R.W. Emerson

A Weekend in the Hamptons

As pizza goes, Nick's is as good as it gets. Harry pulled off strings of mozzarella with his fingers while I burned my mouth on the fiery-hot and subtly sweet sauce, biting into the puffy, blistered crust, even daring to swallow an anchovy, which normally I never did. The pepperoni was slightly charred and the mushrooms, wild and steamy. This was a pizza fit for the gods and its tangy *formaggio* aroma made the experience worth my walk from Fifth over to Second. We doused our throats with a classico chianti and shared a salad brimming over with roasted peppers and black olives.

"So, how did you and the lovely Éclaire enjoy lunch?" the ever curious Harry asked.

"She's a very nice girl," I echoed my mother's summation of friends who seemed pleasant enough, but offered little else in the personality department.

"So you've made a new best friend, then?" Harry asked.

"Bound by common interests," I said. "And to her credit, she even eats raw fish . . . with chopsticks, no less."

"That's about as exciting as it gets," Harry said, peeling away a pizza crumb from the corner of my mouth.

"She's looking forward to our Hampton weekend," I said.

"Bring the black bikini. If I can't touch you, at least you can help embellish my fantasy."

"You love all this, don't you?"

"I love you," he said, and right there at a table at Nicks's, in between pepperoni-filled bites of pizza, Harry dared to declare his feelings openly.

"Is that the chianti talking?" I asked.

"Shut up and eat your pizza," he said.

Walking out into the August air, we were hit with a blast of humidity, adding a sultry touch of ambience to our already heated passion. Harry and I had become the best of lovers, learning all the innuendoes and private places that longed to be touched and aroused. When we weren't together, I would rewind the erotic mind tape of our sexual encounters so that by the time Thursdays rolled around, I could hardly wait to throw myself on Harry's supple bones. There were even those nights when Harry and I couldn't hold off and found another option for instant gratification: the ladies' room where, inside a cubicle, magnificent—though awkward—quickies took place. We even had our favorites and rated each, according to its size and amount of wiggle-room necessary for our brief and wild sexual encounters.

One particular evening, before Le Cirque closed its doors at the Palace Hotel, Harry and I met in the lobby for an 8:00 P.M. dinner. Our game plan was in motion, me starting off with a trip to the loo, his cue that I was ready for action.

"Excuse me for a minute," I said. I sauntered over to the ladies' room. It was well-appointed with ample cubicles, serving as a perfect invitation to a momentary tryst. I nestled myself into one and waited. Moments later: footsteps, knock on the door. I, poised and ready, greeted my lover who, in less time than a flush of a toilet, embraced and entered me while I, hand ready to detonate the flusher, let out squeals of delight in time to the sound of water churning wildly in the bowl, a perfect musical accompaniment to mutual orgasmic satisfaction.

Then the sound of high heels entering the room: an imposer arriving on the scene. Harry and I remained motionless and spent, he, seated atop the toilet seat, I, on his lap, my feet wrapped around him like a pretzel, while the woman in the next cubicle peed, flushed, gave her hands the obligatory wash and wipe, and exited. Giggles abounded, moving into hysteria as I untangled myself from Harry's torso, slithered to the floor, and lay there until I could regain my composure. Then Harry was out the door. I retouched my lipstick and blush and appeared at the entrance of Le Cirque fresh as a daisy and feeling none the worse for wear as we were greeted by the maître d' and slipped into chilled martinis to cool us off. Such were the moments that added to the merriment of our affair and convinced me, without question, that I was falling deeply, and quite madly, in love with Dr. Harry Troutman.

The Hampton weekend arrived, and as the Weather Channel promised, the temperature was a glorious 86 degrees and sunny. My new "best friend" Éclaire was outfitted in a caftan over her Lagerfeld swimsuit as she welcomed us into their "little-house-by-the-sea" as she had so described it over lunch. "The little house," as it turned out, was six thousand square feet of rambling splendor, including a rounded turret that housed the dining room on the first floor and the master bedroom on the second, taking advantage of the pool and ocean view. Maximizing water views was, in fact, the key element in the design of this Hampton extravaganza and a romantic feeling was achieved with curved lines, dormers, and a guest cottage in the back constructed of brick with a slate roof. As Parker and I pulled into the circular paved driveway, we had entered a bit of paradise, paid for by Harry's able hands, which not only redefined beauty for his patients with a flick of his scalpel, but enabled him to hire the top architects and landscape artists to create a Hampton home that had won accolades in *Architectural Digest.*

"Welcome, welcome," Harry joined Éclaire and greeted us, martinis in hand. "Please, don't worry about touching a thing. Our houseman, Gregor, will see to your grips and set them up in the guest cottage. All you need to do is follow us to the pool and leave reality behind."

With that, we were whisked off to a back patio with an ocean view that extended for miles. Mango martinis were waiting in a silver shaker. A basket of cheese and bread fresh from Citarella's lured us into culinary submission while Éclaire, calm, cool, and eager to please, didn't know what to do first. She pirouetted around like a ballet dancer about to assume an arabesque pose.

"The others will be arriving shortly," she said. "There's a darling couple from Manhattan, my best friends, Alice and Charlie, and our dear, dear chums, Leslie and Tom, from Scarsdale. The six of you will be staying in the cottage out back."

The cottage was a mini-mansion of architectural opulence. It had a great room downstairs and four bedrooms above, each one designed and decorated with flair and guaranteed to put all guests, no matter how high their stress levels, into a tranquil frame of mind.

"It's all just too-too fabulous." The voice belonged to Alice, who came breezing through with Charlie, her very significant other, on her arm. "My God, Éclaire. Love the renovations. It's all so Paradise Lost . . . and Found."

Introductions were made as Alice, looking very chic and bubbling over with enthusiasm, checked out the new patio addition.

Alice was a jewelry designer whose line of "Jeweled Vegetables" was the current rage with the major department stores and boutiques. Her line sold for more than any produce item ever should. She was wearing a smashing orange carrot with a green stem that practically reached her cleavage.

When questioned about her one-of-a-kind pieces, she explained.

"Jeweled Vegetables are the new bling," she said. "They're flying out of the stores."

She turned to Éclaire.

"I see you've gone completely wild. I absolutely adore the zebra fabric on the patio furniture and *oh my God,* you've added a gazebo."

Charlie, a successful Manhattan attorney, stood there nodding in approval. He was so tanned and toned, he looked like a bronzed statue who had just walked off the pages of *GQ* and landed in the Hamptons. He was so perfect a specimen of male pulchritude that I wondered if he was actually real.

Following close behind, not five minutes later, were Leslie, a cabaret singer, and her hunky-hubby and investment banker, Tom. The two couples, brought together by Éclaire and Harry, had known each other for years. Leslie had also brought along her favorite fashion accessory, "Marshmallow," her white toy poodle who periodically nipped at our ankles and had a whiny yelp that drove all of us to distraction.

"I don't care what it is, as long as it's cold," Tom announced to Harry who handed over a shaken-not-stirred martini.

"Oooh! I adore the view," Leslie said, belting out a few lines of "Isn't It Romantic?"

Leslie, as it turned out, sang her way through life.

"This view was special ordered just for you," Harry-the-charmer said. "FedEx delivered it this morning."

"And you, Éclaire darling," Leslie hugged Éclaire who turned her head away to avoid a lipstick kiss, "you're wearing my absolute favorite perfume . . . don't tell me, let me guess . . ." She sniffed Éclaire's neck. "It's so familiar. I know . . . wait . . . it's coming to me . . ."

"Chanel Number Five," Éclaire said.

"Of course," Leslie said, "it's so you."

"Actually, it's so Coco," Éclaire said.

"Oh, Coco," Leslie returned to me, "you and Éclaire wear the same fragrance. That's soooo girlfriendy."

"Coco Chanel," Éclaire corrected.

"Whatever." Leslie quickly turned to me. "And *you* must be *the writer* we've all been hearing so much about."

"Award-winning writer," Parker jumped in. "You should read her column."

And then the barrage of questions came pouring out: "Where does it appear? How often? Do you write about real people? It must be such a pressure to be on constant deadline . . ."

Harry intervened. "Let *the writer* get at least a little drunk," he said, "before you start the interrogation process."

"But I simply adore writers," Leslie said. "They're so absolutely *Sex and the City.* You must be a Carrie."

I winced and shot Parker a look that had "get-me-outta-here" written all over it.

"And that would make you . . ." Alice said, pointing to Parker, "Mr. Big!"

"Ladies," Éclaire said, "you must try the fresh clam dip."

"Don't tell me, you and Harry went clam digging this morning?" Charlie tried interjecting a humorous note.

"'Fraid not, old boy," Harry said, "but these clams did come straight from the market not three hours ago and I guarantee they were swimming in that ocean before we grabbed them up. Not for me though. One clam and I'd puff up like a blowfish."

And then, without missing a beat, Harry turned to me. "While you people settle in with your drinks, I'm going to take this woman away from her admiring fans and give her the old house tour. Parker, please join us, if you'd like."

"No thanks, I think I'll stay out here and soak up the view, if you don't mind."

With that, Harry offered an arm and escorted me off the patio and into the house while Éclaire disappeared into the kitchen to see if her cheese pastries had puffed.

"Oh God, is this all right?" I asked. "Should we be doing this?"

"It's a house tour, baby," Harry said, pushing me toward the stairs. "Don't you want to see the bedrooms?"

We walked upstairs and down a long hall filled with family photographs on the wall. Some were of Harry and Éclaire when they first were married. Another of Éclaire in her bridal gown followed by photos of Muffin, grandparents, and travel scenery, most of which had Éclaire feigning smiles as she stood in front of an iceberg in Alaska, a mountain in Switzerland, on the bow of a sailboat in Maine, and one where she looked particularly bored as she held a fishing rod with a slimy bass on the other end.

"And this," Harry said, directing me into the master bedroom, "is my favorite. Every element of this room is designed to take advantage of nature's gifts. Look up. The skylight offers a dramatic view of sunrises and sunsets. Look out the picture windows and you'll see the landscape below including the ocean. The pastel color scheme softens the wood and glass surfaces and brings peace and quiet into the environment. At the end of my busy week, it's my retreat. It combines contemporary with Old World."

"It's beautiful," I said.

"The bed is an original Louis the Sixteenth," he said. "The chandelier is Italian and the needlepoint rug is from Spain. Come here, darling," he whispered.

"Harry . . . not here . . . not now."

"Yes, here. No one is around. The guests are all sucking up to Éclaire and Éclaire is busy playing hostess with the mostest."

"But she'll notice we're absent. She might come looking for us."

"She's got three men downstairs to flirt with," he said. "She wouldn't miss out on that."

"I'm feeling a little uneasy."

"Touch this," Harry said, taking my hand and placing it on his crotch. "See what you do to me? I want this inside you right now."

"In your bedroom?"

"Yes."

"What would Louis say?"

"He'd be thrilled, I promise," he said, going over to lock the door. "Stand right there, sweetheart."

And there in Harry and Éclaire's to-die-for bedroom, on top of the voluminous antique white comforter with a patchwork quilt at the foot of the bed, Harry flung me down, lowered himself on top and reached inside my panties.

"My God, I love it when you're so wet."

"Make me come . . . now," I said.

"I want to taste you."

Harry pulled down my panties and retreated toward my legs, moving them slightly apart. He inched down further, his head now between my thighs. "Yes . . . yes . . . darling," I said, "that's it . . . move your tongue around . . . harder . . ." I grasped his hair. "Yes, right there, exactly the right spot . . . suck on me . . . harder . . . oh yes . . . that's it. Faster, faster."

"Harry!" Éclaire's voice shouted from the first floor landing, "for God's sake, are you coming or what?"

"Yes," Harry screamed back. "Yes, we're coming."

"Good," Éclaire hollered up, "because my spanakopita are getting dry."

And then, Harry moved up my body and gently inserted himself deep inside me, climaxing in a most exquisite orgasm.

"Harry, I mean it . . . come right now," Éclaire said. "I need you to carry in the tray."

"I'm coming now," he said. Then he kissed me hard and fast while I stifled a gasp, jumped up, zipped his pants, and was out the door of his bedroom, as I ran into the bathroom and splashed a handful of cold water on my flushed cheeks. Five minutes later I was back on the patio, asking Parker to please refill my martini, which he said had definitely put a glow in my cheeks.

By the time Labor Day arrived, Harry and I had managed two more fabulous fucks, one in the guest cottage after my swim while the others were off playing tennis. There I was, fresh from the pool when Harry snuck into my room, pulled off my bikini bottom and bent me forward over a chair and humped me doggy-style.

Then, on Monday morning before breakfast, Éclaire insisted we take a tour of East Hampton and stop by the pond to feed the ducks.

"I'll take a pass," Harry said. "Say, Coco and Parker, let's whip up a special egg dish. When you guys return, breakfast will be waiting."

"I could really use a few more winks," Parker said. "All that wine we drank last night has got me pretty hungover."

"Pile into my SUV," Éclaire told the others. "I'll be your tour guide."

Alice and Charlie and Leslie and Tom, like perfectly matched bookends, did as they were told.

"We'll be back in less than an hour," Éclaire said.

"Take your time," Harry waved them off. "We'll be cooking away."

Parker retreated to the cottage for a nap leaving Harry and me to cook up a storm.

"Surprise me," Parker said. "Do something exotic."

Complying with his wishes, Harry and I moved into the library of the main house and screwed our heads off while the old literary masters (first editions, no less) eavesdropped upon us.

A weekend with this gang had given me another idea for a column. All this talk of food had made me hungry. When the others were asleep, I retreated to the den and wrote my next piece, "Life Among the Radical Chic."

The Seaport Gazette

LIFE AMONG THE RADICAL CHIC

You really want the veal parmigiana, but decide on the tournedos Rossini. For openers you choose the pamplemousse because it sounds oh-so-chic. When a grapefruit arrives at the table, your husband is sure it's a mistake. You kick him under the table, a signal to keep quiet and pretend he understands French.

The endive salad rémoulade tastes bitter. You secretly prefer iceberg lettuce with Russian dressing made from Hellmann's and ketchup, but if anyone ever knew, you'd be banished from the in-group, pronto. You have finally arrived, and among your new circle of friends, you are considered gastronomically savvy. You have given up the things you love most for image, nouvelle cuisine, and so-called good taste.

The cooking lessons you took cost more than three months of grocery bills, but you can now make a mean soufflé that doesn't droop and a chocolate mousse that outdoes even the chef at Daniel. You know the difference between croque madame and croque monsieur. When the wine list arrives, you can tell at a glance that a Chambertin is a sensible choice and a perfect accompaniment to your husband's filet de boeuf en croute.

You have learned to dress properly, trading last year's Calvins for this year's Guess jeans. "Guess what?" your husband asks. "I don't get it." But get it or not, unless you have George Marciano's "?" on your tush, you are not in vogue, proving that it's not always what's up front that counts.

You read the latest fashion magazines so you know what style is all about. Overkill can ruin a look, while subtlety and a strand of cultured pearls are always in. When in doubt, the little black dress worn with a fabulous brooch can make you look like the radical chic woman you are striving to become.

Your raison d'être is to fill your home with accoutrements of class. You are trying desperately to replace clutter with minimalism, but will never make it until you shed the pack rat image. Your magazine rack is correctly filled with issues of *Smithsonian*, *Forbes*, *Architectural Digest*, and *Gourmet*. The covers of *Travel & Leisure* that adorn your coffee table lure you to paradises that you someday hope to visit. You can talk travel with the best of them. Last night, over Cosmopoli-

tans, you casually mentioned that the chef at St. Bart's newest restaurant is your best friend's second cousin, once removed.

You are well read and are able to discuss politics and the new best-sellers with ease and aplomb. You are appropriately under-tanned, as no wise person over thirty ever sits in the sun without a caftan. You use a zinc-laced #38 sunblock and a dollop of Retin-A to keep your skin healthy and wrinkle-free. Your pedicures match your French manicures. Your haircuts are by Charles of the Chic. You exude élan and are determined to make the grade at any cost. And cost you, it will.

You have taken to arguing in dulcet tones and have given up hollering for leaving the house until the mood passes. You are amazed at how tranquil you have become, and find that Prozac does a real good job of keeping you well balanced. After all, it is déclassé to shriek like a banshee or scream at your kids. Stylish super-moms don't threaten. They simply guide and gently prod. Being a 'noodge' is definitely not a class act. Your children, ages two years and three months, are already on the waiting lists for the biggest and the best private schools.

You are certain a new car could give you the right image, but you are rather fond of your old Honda, even though your neighbor's Mercedes, panther black no less, has appreciated the value of your neighborhood considerably. Still, the real radical chic knows the key to being cool is understatement. While desperately seeking style, you know the real truth: You are a closet bourgeois. Although you are hoping to shed that image, your plebeian behavior often erupts without warning. For instance:

Last Sunday, you were seen at a cocktail party pilfering exotic hors d'oeuvres and other savory selections, which you surreptitiously slipped into your purse to enjoy during Sex and the City. *Last month, while attending a wedding, you were so carried away you began wrapping up some of the large buffet items. A waiter, catching you in the act, asked if he might be of some assistance. Totally embarrassed, you explain you are scavenging food for your Great Dane at home. "I think I can help you," he says accommodatingly. He walks back into the kitchen and returns with two large paper bags. They contain bones from the prime ribs served at the wedding dinner.*

But real style is inbred, not acquired. It is increasingly apparent that your attempt at savoir faire needs some major overhauling. That is why when a friend goes into your newly designed kitchen one afternoon for a glass of Evian and finds a box of Velveeta next to the brie, Mallomars next to the Petit Beurres, and Ritz crackers instead of Carr's water biscuits, you are so humiliated you nearly faint dead away.

"I would never have thought it of you," she declares, her nose pointed northward.

You retire to your room, a wet compress on your brow, and pick up your latest issue of the New Yorker. *It is obvious that you still need practice. With a little more effort you will have your radical-chic role down to perfection. In the meantime, when no one is looking, you kick off your Ralph Lauren sneakers, remove your Rolex, and lie down on top of your monogrammed comforter. You unwrap a Snickers bar you keep locked inside your night table drawer and pick up a steamy paperback novel. The road to radical chic may be paved with good intentions, but at your very core, you are still the same old girl your mother taught you never to become.*

25

"The nature of the work is to prepare
for a good accident."
—Sidney Lumet

Running into an Accident

There are few obsessions like two people in the throes of overheated sexual intoxication. I couldn't get enough of Harry or him of me. My normal life became a series of daily inconveniences to be squeezed in between our meetings: trips to the cleaners, grocery shopping, hair appointments, doctors visits, golf with Parker, even writing my column were mere diversions leading up to Thursdays with Harry. And through it all, never did Parker or Éclaire suspect anything. Parker understood that Thursday was my day in the city and always suggested I stay over, as he hated the thought of my driving home late at night.

Similarly, Thursday hospital meetings, which often ran late into the night, offered Harry the chance to grab a bite and stay over at one of Manhattan's smaller and choice hotels. Only once did Éclaire balk, and when she whined too much, Harry, the dutiful husband, obeyed and our plans were squelched.

With enough initiative and creative thinking, Harry and I made quite the team indulging in our guilty pleasures. During daylight hours we were productive members of society. Harry listened intently to the trials and tribulations of some of the richest women (and men), appealing to him for only one thing: eternal youth. My column and freelance work made the hours fly. Éclaire kept me on her roster and called regularly to see if I could come out and play.

"What can you do? She likes you," Harry teased. "The friendlier you two are, the less obvious we'll seem."

Partners in crime, Harry and I played out our respective roles to the hilt. Parker insisted that Harry occasionally join him for a game of golf and invited him up to the club on his days off to do nine holes. While golf left Harry cold, he managed to work his way into a handicap of eighteen. Whatever Harry tried, he succeeded at. We both agreed to be appropriately social to throw off the scent. Lunches with Éclaire became regular, monthly obligations and when the four of us dined together in the city, we looked like the happiest of couples, dining and drinking and laughing all the way through the evenings. It was all so revoltingly perfect.

One afternoon in September, the fall foliage dripping its red and orange grandeur over the golf course, I joined Parker and accidentally slipped on a rock, sustaining a large gash just under my left eye. Within seconds, Parker was on the phone to Harry's office.

"Dr. Troutman's office. This is Sabrina. How may I help you?"

"It's an emergency," Parker said. "My wife and I are personal friends of the doctor."

"Dr. Troutman is in surgery. May I have your name and the nature of the call."

"Parker Harding. My wife, Coco Harding, met with some adversity on the golf course."

Parker articulated the event down to its last detail, while I sat under a tree, blood-stained tissues pressed against my cheek.

"For God's sake, just give her the condensed version," I said.

"I'll page Dr. Troutman," the well-programmed Sabrina said.

Five minutes later, Harry phoned and told Parker he was just finishing up in the OR and would meet us in his office in an hour.

"Don't do anything until I see her," he said.

"What about ice?" Parker asked.

"Preferably over gin with some tonic water and lime," he quipped.

At 3:30, we were in Harry's examining room, the very one where we had had our initial encounter. Harry slipped on rubber gloves and had me lie on the table with Parker, the ever-faithful husband, by my side, dousing me with comforting words.

"Nasty cut," Harry agreed, "but with a few stitches, no one will even know you attacked a rock."

I was anointed with an anesthetic with Nurse Krystle, a bosomy work of art, assisting the doctor and smiling widely throughout my procedure. Harry's bevy of nursing beauties, obviously chosen for their looks, were there to calm the patients while he snipped and sewed. All I could think of as Nurse Krystle hovered over me was: Were her jugs her own God-given attributes or the work of Master Harry? Twenty minutes later, the final stitch was put in place as Harry stood back and admired his handicraft and Parker lapsed into gushing accolades, thanking Harry profusely.

"Take the patient home and cater to all her needs," he told Parker. "I'll see Coco back here on Friday morning."

Nurse Krystle assisted me off the table, her cleavage spilling over onto my lap.

"Will there be a scar?" I asked the typical question.

"Your secret is safe with us," Harry said.

Once again, Harry the Miracle Maker had come through.

On Friday, I arrived alone and early at his office. Harry personally escorted me into his examining room, where he closed the door and drew me to him, kissing me gently on the lips so as not to disturb the bandage.

"I can't leave you alone for a minute, can I?" he asked. "What were you doing on the golf course anyway? You hate the game as much as I do."

"Trying to be the typical Seaport wife," I said. "I like pleasing my husband."

"Stop trying to make me jealous." Harry sat me down on the table. "All right, let's take a look."

Slowly, carefully, Harry removed the patch that had adorned my face for the past few days. "Beautiful!" he said. "It will be a bit red for a week or two, but after that you'll never even notice." He handed me some ointment, which I was told to apply several times a day. "The idea is to keep it clean and stay out of the sun for a few weeks. That means no pool, no golf, no sunbathing. Stay indoors and write."

"What about food and water for good behavior?"

"I'll supply that when I see you on Thursday," he said.

"Yes, Doctor."

Then Harry kissed me, his hand kneading my breasts while he pressed himself against me. I moved into his body and had the phone not intruded, we might not have been able to stop. Harry picked up. "Yes? I'll talk with Mrs. Grossman. Put her through." I sat and listened.

"Good morning, Mrs. Grossman. Yes, dear, it's perfectly normal to itch."

Silence.

"No, Mrs. Grossman, do not scratch. Just leave your face alone and follow the post-op instructions."

Silence.

"Sexual intercourse? Only if Mr. Grossman doesn't touch your face."

I giggled in the background, Harry shushing me and smiling.

"Absolutely not, Mrs. Grossman. You shouldn't even be thinking such carnal thoughts."

Silence.

"I know Mr. Grossman can't resist you. You have me to thank for that. I'll see you on Monday. Enjoy your weekend and remember, hands off the face . . . and all other body parts as well."

Silence.

"Enjoy your eightieth birthday party, dear, and send my best to Mr. Grossman. Good-bye."

Harry and I broke out in loud guffaws.

"Beauty knows no limits," Harry said. "Mrs. Grossman, a lovely woman, has the figure of a sixty-year-old and soon a face to match."

I had to hand it to Harry: He absolutely has a way with the ladies.

~

The following week I stayed home and followed Dr. Troutman's orders to the letter. Plastic surgery on my mind, I churned out a column on extreme makeovers, based on the popular reality show and my recent mishap on the golf course.

The Seaport Gazette

EXTREME MAKEOVER: TV'S CUTTING EDGE

It has taken me months to build up the courage to admit that I am a closet TV viewer. I'm not talking respectable TV like the local news channels that dish out blood and guts on a daily basis. No, I mean the real disgusting stuff, like The Bachelorette *and my all-time favorite,* Extreme Makeover, *which can be a death-defying experience.*

For those of you who have never tuned in to this hour-long regurgitation-inducing show, here's how it goes: Take reasonably semi-normal-looking people who are dissatisfied with most every part of their anatomy and rearrange them so they emerge looking nothing like themselves. Then send them back to their families, who are waiting in some grand ballroom of a local hotel, and watch their reactions. Why, it's all so excruciatingly nauseating that you can't pull yourself away from the tube. And if that's not bad enough, around the middle of the show, just after the first commercial for a popular antacid, giving you enough time to go get a snack, the person of the week has consultations with a plastic surgeon, and a reconstructive dentist who appear simultaneously, wearing dark glasses so 1) they won't be recognized and sued and 2) they won't throw up when witnessing their patient in his or her original state.

From then on it's riveting, hold-on-to-your-seat drama, leading up to the climactic moment when the patient, having been put through hell, emerges and makes contact with his or her loved ones who demand fingerprints, proving that this person really belongs to them.

I recently tuned in to this show, the treat of the week being a woman who was unhappy with her looks, but appeared to me like a normal middle-aged gal who, like the rest of us, seemed a bit beaten up by life and whose husband had pretty much stopped noticing her. The presurgical interview went as follows:

Interviewer: *"Tell us, what makes you a candidate for* Extreme Makeover*?"*

Woman (*teary-eyed*): *"I'm just not the woman I once was. I've raised three kids who never leave me alone, my husband no longer thinks I'm sexy, and I've gained thirty pounds from consuming too many Twinkies because I'm bored stiff with my life. My skin is losing its elasticity and my butt is too big. In short, I gross myself out every time I look in the mirror."*

Interviewer: *"That's why we have decided you qualify for an* Extreme Makeover.*"*

At which point every other middle-aged woman in America has only one thought in mind: "Duh, what makes this broad so interesting when all of us look even worse and have lives that make hers seem like a walk in the park?"

The woman, who is now in a state of utter euphoria, is then whisked off in a limo to a five-star hotel where she will be sequestered for six to eight weeks, after receiving consultations by the biggest and the best physician, dentist, nutritionist, personal trainer, couturier, and hairdresser in America. She will then be put through physical and mental torture, necessary to achieve the extreme and awesome appearance of being permanently altered.

For one hour, while I munched away on high-caloric snacks, hanging on the edge of my chair, I observed every in-depth, minute surgical procedure no person who isn't a physician has any business being subjected to. And yet, enveloped in these horror-gripping medical moments, too compelling to resist, my own, yet-untampered-with eyes stayed glued to the TV screen. No matter how hard I tried, I could not turn away from the slice of the scalpel as the doctor peeled away layers of skin, liposuctioned every fat cell, lifted every drooping, sagging, wrinkled layer, readjusted the nose, pinned back the ears, and lifted the scalp. If that weren't enough, the woman's boobs which, before the show, resembled two oranges, were now siliconed into two ripe melon-sized doozies. I mean, it was enough to send me over to the Yellow Pages to look up the local Body Shops.

After the operation, which was done in one fell swoop since the program had a limited time allotment of only one hour, the woman lay in her hospital bed, tubes hanging from every orifice, mumbling obscenities similar to those I shouted during childbirth. The next day, which followed after the next commercial for a popular tranquilizer, she was sitting up, managing a few swigs of ginger ale and a cup of warm sorbet. Soon thereafter, she actually moved a few limbs, looked like she had fallen off the Empire State building, and was starting to utter real words like: "Oh S—t!" A week later, after a final commercial for a popular anti-acne moisturizing face cream, the still-camouflaged doctor appeared, removed the woman's bandages, and held up a mirror to show her how magnificent she now looked.

The moment of truth was upon her and the rest of the TV viewing public, the big question being: Would she be made ecstatic by her new persona or would she throw the mirror at the surgeon's Botoxed forehead, causing his immediate demise for which she would be sent away for life where nobody would give a damn how she looked anyway?

"Oh my God!!" she shouted, as the surgeon and nurse backed off, just in case. "I can't believe my eyes."

"Do you love the new you?" the doctor asked nervously.

"I . . . I . . . I don't know what to say," she chirped, "I'm absolutely . . . dumbstruck!"

"I assume," the doctor said again, "that means you're pleased."

"Not pleased . . . I'm overwhelmed. I'm floored. I'm a new woman."

"I take it, then, that you're happy with the results."

"Yes, yes," she squealed, reaching over to kiss the doctor with her collagen-laced lips. "I'm stunning! Now my husband will notice me again."

Three weeks later, after being given a new wardrobe, a new hairstyle, a new body-by-Lance, the personal trainer, her gallery of family and friends gathered in the grand ballroom for the moment of impact.

As the husband and kiddies hovered together, the glass doors parted. The music swelled as Ms. Gorgeous appeared down the velvet-carpeted runway. "Ooohs" and "Aaahs" reverberated through the room as this perfectly coiffed and well-dressed vision of loveliness slithered forward.

The crowd cheered, the children wept, as the husband, overcome with awe, uttered the words: "Darling, is it really you, my wife and mother of our three little monsters?"

"Yes, my love, it is I: the Extremely Made-over woman of your dreams."

For the next month, life was sheer bliss. The husband couldn't get enough of his new bride. He catered to her every wish. He made love to her every night. Then, as reality would have it, they settled in to life as it always was: The kids began to misbehave, the husband resumed his usual couch potato position and began ignoring his wife. She became depressed and lost sleep. She stopped working out and felt sluggish. She lost her vibrant glow and her demeanor was dull. She gained back all her weight and started to droop. In short, her extreme makeover fell by the wayside. The moral of this story is: "Beauty is only skin deep, but eating Twinkies is a joy forever."

26

"If it doesn't work on my face,
I can put it on my toast."
—Coco Harding

I Am a Fruit Cocktail

As Harry assured me, I healed perfectly, a faint, barely visible fine line the only evidence of my accident. A dab of makeup took care of that. By the end of September, unless I studied myself up close under bright lights, I couldn't even tell I had been injured.

Parker and I were scheduled up to our eyeballs with a new season of social engagements; theater, art openings, the usual Seaport fundraisers would keep us hopping well into autumn. Harry and I were also well "into each other." Éclaire was off to another spa, this time, Canyon Ranch in Tucson. Over lunch at Asiate in the Mandarin-Oriental Hotel just before she left, we picked over our crab salads and betal leaves while Éclaire extolled the virtues of frequent spa vacations.

"Coco, you should really join me sometime. Do you ever spa?"

I never even knew that spa was a verb.

"Truthfully," I told her, "basking in the muck of mud baths and seaweed scrubs leaves me cold."

"You haven't lived until you've been massaged with tangerine extract followed by a warm bath filled with flower petals."

"I can't sit still that long," I said.

"Coco, your problem is you don't allow for enough downtime. You're entitled to a little diversion now and then."

She should only know that her husband was the most full-blown diversion of my life.

"One day I'm taking you with me. I won't take no for an answer."

Then she studied my face. "Oh God, I never noticed before, but did you know that your T-zone is in severe trouble?"

"What T-zone?"

"The major zone areas of your face seem to be filled with oily patches."

"You know that for a fact?" I was slightly alarmed.

"Just looking at you I can tell that your epidermal lipids and your sebaceous oils are incorrectly balanced. To put it simply, Coco, in some places, your skin acts oily. In others, it acts dry. It's obvious what the problem is: Your face has a split personality."

"I have schizophrenic skin?" Perhaps it was time for another session with Finkelman.

"You need to put your skin on a training program until the root causes of its confusion are addressed."

Éclaire was a walking encyclopedia of dermatological information.

"I had the same issues before Harry sent me to a skin guru. Now, I'm putty in the doctor's hands. She told me that as skin matures, cell reproduction seems to lag. Much like an old car that's lost its oomph."

I pictured myself as a beat-up old Chevy that needed some work.

"Let's face it, Coco, the way we live takes a toll. The sun, wind, and free radicals pave the way for lines and wrinkles. Your skin's support system needs a boost."

Forget Finkelman. Maybe group therapy was the answer.

I gnawed on a cherry tomato and hung on her every word.

"I'm not kidding, Coco, if you could see what I see sitting here, you would throw a paper bag over your face."

I pulled a pocket mirror from my bag.

"Oh my God," I said. She was right: There was a pore over my left nostril that was as big as my mother's mouth, not to mention a blackhead that looked like a tick.

"After lunch, we'll run over to my favorite day spa, Dream Girls, and you'll have a consultation with my personal esthetician, Swan. She can perform wonders."

Éclaire had a gallery of "personals" to get her through any situation: a personal shopper, personal trainer, personal masseuse, and now Swan, whom she promptly phoned to see if I could be squeezed in.

"Of course, Mrs. Troutman," the receptionist said, "Swan will always see you and yours."

Éclaire had one thing going for her: clout. She was received graciously by all the maître d's in the city, given the best tables in restaurants, could get theater tickets from her "personal" scalper, and now Swan, who she promised would make magic with my face.

Swan, the clone of Ivana Trump, greeted Éclaire as though she were her best friend.

"Dahling, you look absolutely divine. But I can tell your face is ready for some of our Precipitation."

I looked around for a meteorologist, but none were in sight. I soon learned that Precipitation was nothing but a moisturizing lotion that would keep a face dewy, damp, and soft.

"I'm here with a friend, today," Éclaire introduced me. "She needs, uh . . . a little help. Maybe she could use some Precipitation, too."

"Sit right here, precious," Swan said to me. "I need to take a look with my magnifying glass." I took a seat. "Hmm. Oh yes . . . oh indeed, yes, you do need some help."

"Will it hurt?" I asked.

"Angel, what I have here is a mixture of clove buds, apple emollient, avocado balm, seaweed flakes, banana extract, peach kernel, and papaya nut palmitate . . . all blended together into one economy-size jar of a magical whipped potion."

All someone had to do was put me in the produce department

of a supermarket, stick a maraschino cherry in my mouth, and I'd make a handsome fruit cocktail.

I envisioned sharing this adventure with Harry later and smiled to myself at how amused he would be. For now, I went with the flow, chalking it up as good material for a column.

After Swan was finished screwing around with my face for fifteen minutes, she handed me a mirror so I could witness the transformation. She insisted that already I looked cleaner, fresher, and exuded a youthful glow. The truth was, I looked red and blotchy. The only reason I looked somewhat younger was that I now resembled a teenager with a bad case of acne.

"Admit it," the admiring Éclaire said, "you look well sloughed."

Some compliment. The last slough I had seen was hanging by its toes at the Bronx Zoo. But, I had to hand it to Swan: This gal knew her epidermis like I knew my Ben & Jerry's ice cream flavors.

Then, the pièce de résistance: Swan unscrewed a jar of pink gel and rubbed it between her French-manicured fingers.

"I've saved the best for last," she said. "For our final touch and to give your face the simonizing it needs, I'm about to offer you our very own beauty secret, an exclusive with Dream Girls day spa only. It was handed down by an Egyptian queen."

Éclaire was all atwitter. She hung on Swan's every word. We both took a whiff and let out a loud "Yuck." A small group of women, fresh from their massages, had now gathered around us to witness my shining moment. This glop smelled exactly like a cross between rotten eggs and Lysol toilet bowl cleaner. Swan spread a handful on my face. I held my breath. Suddenly, my skin felt very tight. I was afraid to open my mouth for fear it was permanently sealed.

"Well ladies," Swan addressed the crowd. "You'll never believe it: It's Nefertiti's placenta."

"The actual one?" a woman asked.

"How did you preserve it for so long?" another chimed in.

"It's placenta extract, dears," Swan said. "It was kept in a frozen vat in Egypt for hundreds of years. History has it that

Akhenaton, Nefertiti's husband, fell in love with her skin and kept the formula with him until he died. He took it with him to his grave. Years later, a dermatologist in Perth Amboy, New Jersey, got his hands on it and sold it to our cosmetic company for millions of dollars."

"My second cousin, Naomi, lives in Perth Amboy," a woman with an extra-tight facelift said. "She could use some of this."

"I can sell you a jar right now," Swan said.

I was awed by Swan, who worked the crowd so well it was worth spending money just to see how far she would go. Éclaire was, of course, lapping it up. "See what I mean?" she whispered to me. "Aren't you impressed? You look better already."

Swan swabbed me with a citrus emulsion plus a few other necessary tonics and ointments, and threw in a sample of Nefertiti's umbilical gel as well. The entire package put me out $350.00.

"If it doesn't work on my face, I can put it on my toast," I told Éclaire.

"Shhh," she said, "Swan might hear you."

"Now dear," Swan told me, "every night before bedtime I want you to rub these assorted emollients on your face. Follow this with our chaser of grapefruit enhancer and some orange essence and lemon grass toner. In no time, you'll look younger and more refreshed."

I honestly thought I saw a squirt of citrus emanating from my pores.

"And sweetheart, don't forget the avocado balm and papaya flakes. They'll work wonders."

Yes, I thought, they will be a nice addition to my salads. Parker will love it. I thanked Swan, who was now busy selling beauty products to all the passersby and ignored us completely.

"This is the biggest bullshit I've ever seen." I grabbed Éclaire's arm. "Let's blow this place."

"Coco," Éclaire said with a parental tone, "you've really got to have a more serious skin attitude. None of us are getting any younger, you know."

I relayed the entire scenario to Parker that evening who told me that Éclaire meant well and was only trying to help.

"A spa's not a bad idea," he said. "You could benefit from a little pampering. You ought to think about going with her sometime."

"An entire week with Éclaire is more than I could handle. Just getting through lunch takes fortitude."

Parker, a definite Éclaire fan, took umbrage. "Darling, try not to be so hard on your friends. After all, Éclaire has some wonderful qualities."

"Name two."

"She's a very gracious hostess and she always smells nice."

It was at moments like that I knew exactly why I needed Harry in my life.

The Berkshires in autumn is a visual treat. In early October, we invited Éclaire and Harry up to our house in Lenox to see the leaves in full regalia.

Éclaire, back from Canyon Ranch, high-glossed and well-oiled, jumped at the chance for a weekend away from the city's clamor. Parker insisted he be in charge of the cooking and Harry said he'd bring along the wine.

"There's a Beaujolais I want us to try. It's amiable and casually refreshing. It's meant to be drunk young. Éclaire and I picked some up just last week."

"It's very fruity in a plummy sort of way," Éclaire added, smacking her lips together and trying to sound very in-the-wine-know. "It's relatively light, straightforward, and uncomplicated, not to mention quite yummy."

Parker seemed impressed. Harry and I cringed on the "yummy."

Long walks through leaf-lined trails, lunch al fresco at a quaint restaurant overlooking a pond, followed by late afternoon cocktails at the Red Lion Inn in Stockbridge, provided just the interlude we needed before returning home for dinner. That morning, Éclaire had insisted we visit the "I-Just-Love-Norman-Rockwell-Museum," so, yet again, Parker and I took the tour along with our guests.

Back at the house, Parker, donning a chef's apron, set to work in the kitchen. Éclaire stood by, tearing lettuce leaves in preparation for her famous salad that she said we should be prepared "to-die-from."

"Éclaire does do a mean salad," Harry agreed. "In fact, it's what she does best, culinarily speaking."

I, not part of the cooking team, slipped from the kitchen and outside to catch a view of the sun going down behind the green and purple hills. Harry was out there in a flash, waving to Parker and Éclaire through the window, but they were both too busy with the menu to even register our presence. Slowly, Harry and I meandered down the path and into a glen off to the side of the road, hidden by patches of myrtle and wildflowers among the coverlet of autumn leaves.

"If I don't kiss you immediately, I might die," I said.

"No deaths to ruin our weekend," Harry said, scooping me up in his arms and pressing me against a tree trunk.

We kissed like two lovers who hadn't seen each other in weeks, though it had only been a few days since we had slept together. Two insatiable animals in heat, we sent off a series of love-sounds: moans, heavy breathing, muffled expressions of our affection in time to the rustle of the early evening breeze. Harry placed his arms beneath my sweater, fondling my breasts, then bent down to kiss them. I, in turn, slid my arms around his waist. We fell to the ground, a blanket of leaves beneath us, as we rolled around, entwined in an embrace that led to the sound of respective zippers being pulled down, exchanging cloth for skin, as I reached inside his khakis, feeling him growing in my hands. We switched positions so that Harry was now on his back and completely in my control as I pulled down his underwear and moved my tongue down the length of his muscular legs, my head coming to rest between them, my mouth fitting perfectly around his hard cock, and then stopped.

"Don't leave me like this," Harry moaned. "I can't take it. I want to feel your mouth on me."

He had relinquished all power to me. I became increasingly aroused as I watched him writhe beneath me. Then, when he could stand it no longer, I moved my tongue up and down and around the tip of him in slow, steady, circular motions. Harry called out my name as my mouth became a vessel into which would pour the elixir of his love.

"Coco, darling . . . please, I want us to come together."

But this time, I was calling the shots and loving every moment. I wanted to be the voyeur, watching as he climaxed into my mouth.

I took full command, playing him all the way to the point where he could not hold back any longer. With a deep, manly groan rising from his throat, he raised his buttocks slightly as I milked him gently and deeply feeling the full length of him grow even harder and then exploding into the most intense, exquisite orgasm as he emitted one final, guttural gasp. My mouth overflowed with semen as I tasted him and then swallowed.

"I love the way you taste," I said. "I love experiencing you this way."

I moved my mouth to his, some cum still remaining on my lips so that he could taste himself on me, too. The connection between us was stronger than ever, more intense than I could ever recall. We lay together for a few minutes, oblivious of anything around us except the sun fading behind the hill, the temperature dropping suddenly, signaling us to move indoors.

"I wanted you to come, too, Coco," he said.

"I did. If you could feel me, you'd see that. As soon as I tasted you, I came."

And even if I hadn't climaxed completely, I felt a spiritual coming together in such a profound way that I felt satisfied and complete.

"We'd better get back to the house," Harry said.

We unruffled ourselves, brushing leaves from our clothes to obliterate any telltale signs of our indiscretion.

"I love you, Dr. Harry Troutman," I said.

"And I you, darling," he whispered back.

We strolled back to the house, two lovers sharing one shadow, watching as the last streak of daylight fell into evening.

"We're just about ready for dinner," Éclaire announced when we walked through the back door. "I don't know about you, but I'm famished."

"I already ate," I wanted to tell her.

~

A Williams-Sonoma cloth graced the table. I dug my fork into Éclaire's salade deluxe, tossed a few avocados and accolades around, and nearly chipped a tooth on an olive whose pit she had forgotten to remove. Éclaire might be considered the salad maven of Bronxville, but maneuvering one's way through her greens could end up being a dangerous if not costly dental experience.

The main course, a gibelotte of rabbit, one of Parker's specialties, included curried Thai basil and eggplant stew, sprinkled with a smidgen of saffron that Parker was not ashamed to say cost him ten dollars for only a small vial. He served this in our deep, country-style soup bowls that we had schlepped back from Italy a few years ago.

"The secret ingredient is the saffron," Parker said. "Without it, the rabbit can fall flat on its face."

We tasted and cheered. I wasn't sure if a Standing O was called for, but Harry did get up from his chair and bow.

The Beaujolais, as Éclaire had described, was indeed "yummy" and was a perfect match for the slightly spicy sauce into which we dipped large chunks of crusty bread. The meal ended with a light raspberry nut cake surrounded by a bowl of fresh raspberries I had brought with me from Seaport, and a platter of cheese and crackers. The temperature had dropped drastically for an early October night and Parker felt a fire was in order. For the next hour, the four of us lounged on the couch or in oversized stuffed chairs. Parker pulled out his favorite brandy and offered it to us. After only two sips, he promptly fell asleep, as did Éclaire, whose little brush with cooking had left her exhausted. I looked over at Harry. "What's wrong with this picture?" I whispered. Then I got up, walked into my bedroom to draw a bath, leaving my unconscious spouse in the living room with the slumbering Éclaire. In five minutes, Harry, en route to the guest room, made a pit stop at my room, grabbed me, and was undoing my bra and working his way down to my panties when I stopped him cold.

"This is cutting it just a little too close, darling," I said. "In other words, scram."

I went into the bathroom and turned on the tub faucet.

"How about a *bain à deux*?" he asked, following me in.

"How about a quick exit," I suggested, giving Harry a peck and literally pushing him out the door. A few minutes later, both Parker and Éclaire, who had risen zombielike from their after din-din naps, were on their way to bed.

"Now that's what I call a fabulous meal, if I do say so myself," Parker said. "I could tell they loved it. Harry even had thirds."

"Harry never can get enough of anything," I said. Then I stepped into the tub and soaked a good twenty minutes before Parker's snores put closure on any chance of his wanting sex. I felt relieved. There was only so much a gal could handle in one evening.

27

"I come from a family where gravy
is considered a beverage."
—Erma Bombeck

Talking Turkey

October came and went with breakneck speed and we were now pushing toward Thanksgiving. Hudson, Susan, Chloe, and Isabelle would be arriving from California for the long weekend along with Clark. Eliza and her new boyfriend, Josh, who was from Philadelphia and a medical student at Mt. Sinai, would be there. Of course, Bridgette rounded out the ensemble.

"Don't say no," Éclaire called me three weeks before, "but Harry and I just found out we'll be sans children for Thanksgiving and we'd love to spend the holiday with you, if you're available, that is. Muffin is going skiing in Tao."

"We'll be with family," I said, "but of course you'll join us."

"We won't be imposing?"

"You and Harry will be a most welcome addition," I said. "We'll be doing Thanksgiving at our home."

"I'll bring the salad," Éclaire offered.

"Without the olives," I said.

"My, but aren't we getting just a tad incestuous?" Annie asked when I told her the latest. "You've been upgraded from social to holiday friends. It's all getting cozier by the minute."

"You and Saul should come, too. Why not witness madness in the making?"

"We just might take you up on this."

"We wouldn't have it any other way," I said.

~

The guest list reached fourteen and made Thanksgiving dinner a formidable challenge. Everyone wanted to bring something, but the majority of the meal fell into my hands. Hedy worked with me on the menu, insisting that she prepare and cook the turkey and make her special stuffing. I didn't say no. Parker spent the previous weekend combing the wine cellar in search of the perfect turkey accompaniment, choosing a pinot noir from Burgundy, and for those who preferred a white wine, an iconoclastic, dry Semillon. He carried bottles of these upstairs along with champagne and robust and sweet port and Madeira for dessert. The liquid refreshments were all in place. The rest was up to me.

There is nothing more congenial than congregating around a table with "Big Bird" as the centerpiece. It evokes nostalgia. It encourages warmth. It's a scene right out of a Norman Rockwell painting. Except ours was the antithesis of a Norman Rockwell Thanksgiving. In fact, had poor Norman been present, he would have gone into immediate cardiac arrest. Even Disney couldn't have done it better. Our guest list might as well have included Mickey and Minnie Mouse, Donald Duck, nephew Huey, Bugs Bunny, Elmer Fudd, and all of the Seven Dwarfs. The only difference was that our cartoon characters had other names.

Extra table leaves had been added to accommodate all. The table was set to perfection with an autumnal theme of reds, yellows, and oranges. Flowers graced the table, but did not obstruct views or hinder conversation. Bridgette managed to down two vodka and tonics before dinner, the effects of which had loosened her tongue. She was in rare form, ready to engage in verbal combat whenever a moment presented itself. Her first and favorite victim was Éclaire, who was just too irresistible to ignore, and who was wearing her cinnamon-colored lenses in honor of the holiday.

"Darling, your eyes go perfectly with the stuffing. You must have lenses for all occasions. Tell me, what happens if you want to emulate the squash?"

"I'd look exactly like a tiger, with sharp claws ready to attack." Éclaire slung her sharp, well-manicured claw in Bridgette's direction.

Parker told his sister to keep her venom on ice, and chill.

It was not a Thanksgiving for the weak of heart. The banter continued through each course and there was no controlling Bridgette.

"Tell me, dear," she now addressed Eliza's friend, Josh. "What will your specialty be and don't tell me radiology."

"I've been tossing that around. How did you know?" Josh asked, nonplussed.

"I know the type," she said. "Thin and bony. Well, there's still time to change your mind."

"Why would I?"

"I'm only suggesting, dear, if you don't mind looking at pictures all day, it's a real hoot. As for me, I'd rather go to the cinema."

With that, Bridgette took a hearty gulp of wine. That was only a sampling of how far she could take an insult and run with it.

Annie lapped it all up while Saul sat back in disbelief, removing himself from the table at regular intervals to check the score of the Army-Navy game.

Hedy, accustomed to Bridgette's antics, could barely look at her.

"I know I'm out of place, Miz Harding," she told me when we had a moment alone in the kitchen, "and God forgive me, but if it were up to me, I'd lace your sister-in-law's sweet potatoes with strychnine."

"Bite your tongue, Hedy," I said, the two of us grinning knowingly.

The rest of the evening played out like a French farce with Bridgette being the lead character. Eliza was in tears because Bridgette had insulted Josh. Josh spent the evening reassuring

Eliza that he couldn't care less. Éclaire was royally pissed off by Bridgette, who harassed her well into dessert, and Harry was doing a slow burn because I locked the bathroom door when I went to pee, so he couldn't sneak in for a quick feel. Parker spent the evening trying to rein in his sister, who was so drunk on wine that she wet her pants. Annie contended with Saul, who fell asleep during the soup course, dropping his head in the pumpkin bisque and nearly ingesting a pearl onion. Hudson and Susan retired to their respective guest rooms early. Chloe had vomited after eating a chestnut and Isabelle was coming down with a cold. Clark had laryngitis and never said a word all evening, but sat around sketching architectural renderings of his latest project. Eliza and Josh decided to stay at Mitch's apartment in the city, since he and Maxine were doing Thanksgiving with her folks in Buffalo.

"Mom," Eliza explained, "we just can't spend the night in this nuthouse. It's better this way."

"I'm sorry," I said.

"It's not your fault, Mrs. Harding," Josh said. "Eliza and I think it will be a lot easier to be in the city. We have plans to see some friends tomorrow and we're doing a matinee on Saturday."

"I apologize for Bridgette," I said.

"Mom, the woman is completely mental."

Éclaire and Harry chatted with Eliza and Josh after dinner, with Harry offering to assist Josh any way he could with his medical plans.

"I'd be happy to write a recommendation, when the time comes," he said. "I was a medical student once myself and it always helps to know someone in the field. And don't rule out plastic surgery, either. It's been a great ride. Every day offers new challenges."

Éclaire took me aside after they left. "Eliza is absolutely darling and that boyfriend of hers is drop-dead delicious. It looks very serious."

She said "serious" in such a way it seemed almost fatal.

"Yes, they are a cute couple," I agreed. "My guess is, they'll be engaged before long."

"I wish I could say the same about our Muffin. She can never sustain a relationship. Perhaps Eliza and Josh might know some eligible men."

"I'll put the idea out there," I said.

"Muffin is a very nice girl," Éclaire said. "She's been working on her weight issues, and we've been after her to get her nose done, although she wants no part of it. She's a real rebel. Can you imagine, her father being a plastic surgeon and all? We put her on the diet patch, but she said it made her itch. Would you believe we have a daughter with body image issues and we, with our designer genes."

I blinked.

"She takes after Harry's side of the family. His mother was a large woman with a real beak. She was as stubborn as Muffin, refusing to alter her appearance. 'What I came into this world with, I'm leaving with,' she told Harry."

The truth was, according to Éclaire, who confessed all to me, that Muffin Troutman was a nice girl, but not a thin girl. She wasn't what one could call pleasingly plump or still carrying around an excess of baby fat. No, Muffin Troutman was downright, unequivocally fat, and much to Éclaire and Harry's chagrin, she didn't give a flying fuck, her exact words. The name "Muffin" didn't help any, either. It only served to accentuate her flaws and was an open invitation to be mocked by her peers. She was given the name when, at age four she became hooked on blueberry muffins and couldn't get enough. Éclaire thought it would be ever-so-cute to call their then-skinny child by a name resembling a tasty treat.

"My two sweets," Harry would say when referring to his wife and daughter.

At the time everyone thought it was darling. But as time passed and Muffin grew into an economy-size pastry, Éclaire suggested she use her birth name, Melissa.

"Muffin, angel," Éclaire said, "perhaps, you've outgrown that nickname. Melissa is so much more sophisticated."

"I like Muffin," Muffin said.

"Darling," Éclaire continued, "it's unbecoming and, while I hate to say it, being a bit overweight doesn't add charm to that name. In fact, it brings attention to the fact you're fat. There, I've said it."

To which Muffin stood up from her lounge chair at the club pool, and with chair imprints running down her chubby, sweaty thighs, looked at Éclaire and said, "Frankly, Mother, I don't give a flying fuck," loud enough for all in the immediate vicinity to hear.

"After that," Éclaire said, "I never made reference to my daughter's name, again. The subject was closed forever. Oh, and Coco, all of this chitchat is our little secret, of course."

"I never heard a thing," I assured her.

PART THREE

Intermezzo

(Foreplay)

28

"Let us eat and drink,
for tomorrow we shall die."
—Isaiah XVII, 13

In a Stew . . . The Plot Thickens

Little did I know that Thanksgiving dinner was to be our version of the Last Supper, a turning point in all our lives. On Wednesday afternoon, after arriving home from his golf game, Parker sifted through the pile of mail on the marble table in the foyer. Two plain white envelopes sent to each of us, and bearing no return address, caught his eye. He took the letter opener and sliced away at his envelope with the precision of a surgeon. He was jolted by what he read:

To Whom It May Concern:

This is to inform you that I have been retained as counsel to bring to a discreet closure certain events of which you may or may not be totally aware. My client, who wishes complete anonymity, has hired me to see if there is any truth regarding a matter concerning an indiscretion between two parties close to you. I have been instructed to inform you that in the event that this matter cannot be resolved, the names shall be disclosed, and a lawsuit will be pending.

You may contact me via e-mail with any questions. If you choose to do so, utmost discretion will be exercised and names will not be disclosed. The purpose of this letter is to avoid un-

necessary damage, both monetary and emotional, regarding the parties involved.

jacquescuze@opton.net

Parker crumpled the letter and stuck it in his pocket. Then he went straight to the bar and made himself a Jack Daniels on the rocks. A half hour later, I appeared from the cleaners, Parker's starched shirts standing at attention like cardboard soldiers on wire hangers.

"Hello, darling," he said.

My eyes, in typical fashion, went directly to the mail. "Anything interesting?" I asked.

"Yes, actually there is," Parker said. "You have one, too."

"Have one what?"

He handed me the white envelope, retrieving his shirts from my hands. "Here, read this."

I went into the den and sat down. Parker joined me on the couch, first refreshing his drink. I studied each word, trying to act cool, appropriately baffled, and seemingly unaffected.

"What is this about?"

"Obviously someone is doing something with another someone," Parker said, "and it looks like someone else ain't happy about it."

"It's probably one of those sickos out there," I said, "the same type who makes crank phone calls."

"You really think so?"

"I don't know." I read the letter again, trying to keep my composure.

"You know what I think?" he asked.

I braced myself.

"I think someone we know is having an affair right under our noses."

"What someone?"

"You tell me?"

"How should I know?"

"Close friends, perhaps."

I threw out a barrage of innocuous names, indicting our neighbors across the road and other random fantasy suspects.

"I mean very close friends, Coco, people we know intimately. People in our lives. Those with whom we have tight connections."

"Oh Parker, really," I said, trying to sound dismissive, "aren't you making more out of this than is warranted? It's probably a joke . . . a bit sick, but a joke nonetheless. I mean, really, this can't be taken seriously."

"Oh, it's serious, all right."

"Then who's the culprit?"

"The culprit who hired the lawyer or the culprits who are having the affair?" Parker asked.

"All of the above, I guess, but honestly Parker, this is the stuff movies are made of."

"How do you think they devise the plots for movies? It's called real life."

"Well, I'm going to take a shower. I'm exhausted," I said. "I just want to unwind a little before dinner."

"You seem so casual about the whole thing."

"Don't you get it? The person who sent these is obviously trying to ruffle our feathers, start something. The best thing to do is just ignore it."

I went into the bedroom and turned on my computer. SkinDeep's message was waiting.

CocoPuff: Did you find a little something in the mail today? I did. It arrived in a white envelope. It took my breath away . . . and it's not anthrax, though just as lethal. SkinDeep.

Oh my God, I thought, this is starting to be not-so-funny.

I wrote back immediately.

SkinDeep: My mail runneth over. What do we do now?

Parker followed close behind. I slammed down the computer cover. "I will get to the bottom of this, you know," he said.

"How?"

"I'm not sure, but this is too intriguing to ignore, don't you agree? I would think this is right up your alley, being the curious writer that you are."

"I don't have time," I said. "I prefer to chalk it up as one of life's little mysteries that have no answer."

"Oh, I see: the Ostrich Maneuver . . . hide your head in the sand and you'll never need to know."

"Frankly, I don't care."

"Coco, when did you *not* care about anything?" Parker asked.

I slipped into a warm shower, figuring I'd wash away the day and toss my worries down the drain. But I was frightened. Harry and I had been caught, and someone knew everything, but just how much everything, I wasn't sure. I awaited his reply.

As I was toweling myself off, Parker sat down on the small bathroom stool with yet another refill on his bourbon.

"You're not getting drunk, are you?"

"No reason for me to get drunk," he said. "I'm not the guilty party. But someone out there ought to be as drunk as a skunk because someone out there is guilty as hell."

"Maybe you should contact the e-mail source."

"Maybe I will," he said, taking a long swallow of bourbon.

If I acted suspiciously, Parker would know the jig was up. My modus operandi was to assume a naïve affect. In other words, behave like Éclaire who, when life took a turn for the worse, went shopping or to a spa.

After I finished applying my makeup and Parker had jumped into the shower, I called Annie and filled her in on the mysterious letter.

"I'm just going to pretend nothing is wrong," I said.

"Nothing is wrong."

"What the hell are you talking about?"

"Everyone is guilty until proven innocent, Coco, and that includes all of us. How are you?"

"Peachy-keen," I said. "My life is about to go up in smoke. Harry e-mailed me. He got one, too, and my guess is, so did Éclaire. I answered him, but I haven't heard back."

"Listen to me, whatever you do, don't act weird."

"Weird? I sound like I'm practically catatonic. Parker is the one making an issue, not me."

"Meet me nine o'clock tomorrow at our place."

"If I haven't been tarred and feathered by then," I said. "I think Parker knows."

"You see, you *do* sound guilty. For Christ's sake, lose the attitude or he *will* suspect you."

"You're forgetting something," I said.

"What?"

"I am guilty," I said.

After dressing for dinner, we decided to go to Positano, one of our favorite Seaport spots overlooking the water, where familiarity would have a soothing effect on Parker's frazzled nerves. Deciding to forgo the usual bottle of wine, we settled instead on glasses of a light and understated pinot grigio.

I studied the menu, chatted briefly with Giuseppe, the owner, and gave our favorite waiter, Carlos, my order of Pollo Terra Mare, as anything heavier would wreak havoc on my already upset stomach. Parker ordered the Chilean sea bass and said very little during dinner. Over coffee, he announced, "I wonder who else received copies of the letter."

"I'm sure we'll find out," I said. "Until then, let's just get on with our lives."

"Seems as though our lives are getting on with us," Parker said. "You know, it honestly wouldn't surprise me if Harry Troutman was fooling around behind his wife's back."

"Our Harry? The man is a workaholic. He spends practically every waking hour in the OR."

"He's around women all day. That's temptation enough, don't you agree?"

"A veterinarian is around animals all day," I said. "That doesn't mean he's screwing the cats."

The next morning Annie and I sat at A Scone's Throw trying to piece together the jigsaw puzzle. Not only had Parker and I received letters, but Harry and Éclaire as well. Even Dr. Finkelman had gotten into the act and left a message on my cell phone to call him back as soon as possible. The plot had thickened into a stew of suspects.

I phoned Finkelman on the spot, intending to leave a message. Instead, he picked up.

"Dr. Finkelman?" A question mark at the end.

"This is Coco Harding."

"Coco, an unusual letter has come into my possession," the ever-precise Finkelman said. "I have a four o'clock Thursday available."

Bless his little shrinky heart. My Thursday slot was still open.

"I suggest we meet for a session. This is a matter of grave concern."

"Oh that," I said, trying to sound nonchalant. "Our nearest and dearest have all received copies."

"Then I'll be seeing you on Thursday next?" Finkelman inquired.

"I'll pencil it in," I said.

"Shall I take that to mean a yes?"

"Yes, I'll be there."

"I see," Finkelman said.

"I love it," Annie said. "Even the shrink has gotten into the act. It doesn't get much better than that. A little Hitchcock with a touch of Neil Simon thrown in. I always adored a comic thriller."

~

There is a small hotel, the Franklin, on 87th between Lexington and Third, described by Allen Sperry in his *New York's 100 Best Little Hotels* as an updated version of where Philip Marlowe might have stayed in a Raymond Chandler story. Its darkly elegant marble lobby makes for a clubby atmosphere—the perfect spot for Harry and me to meet to sort out the repercussions of our misdemeanors. Harry had left his office early for "a lunch that might last well into the afternoon," he told Sabrina. In truth, we met at the Franklin to try and sort it all out.

And sort it out we did, in between two hours of steady lovemaking, three orgasms apiece, and a nap.

"We're history, Harry," I said, opening my eyes an hour later.

"Baby, we're just warming up. But that's what I love about you. You get all worked up over everything."

"So, you're cool with this?"

"Cool? I'm practically frozen," he said.

"What about Éclaire?"

"What about her?"

"What was her reaction to the letter?"

"She never even saw it. I intercepted it before she ever got to it."

"So she doesn't know."

"Éclaire doesn't have a pulse, darling. If she did happen to hear rumors, she'd ignore them. Don't you understand? I've made all the national magazines including *The Enquirer*. It's been suggested by New York's biggest gossips that I've been having affairs for years."

"Have you?"

"Shut up and have another orgasm," he said, tossing me back beneath the covers and nibbling on my ear.

And so, with a twinkle in his eye and some slight trepidation on my part, I complied with the good doctor's wishes.

Harry and I never did solve the problem of what our next move should be. Lost in each other's arms, we lusted our way into the afternoon, interrupted by a call on my cell at 3:00 from Parker, inquiring as to my whereabouts. I figured I had better pick up.

"I'm in the city on my way to see Finkelman," I said. "What's up?"

"You can add Bridgette to the list. She called me a few minutes ago. Her letter was sitting in a pile of mail for two days, but she was away and didn't see it until now. She finds it all so intriguing. Hasn't had such excitement in years. She fancies herself to be a modern-day Nancy Drew and says she'll figure it all out. The guilty parties always leave clues. So darling," Parker changed the subject, "after Finkelman, will you be staying over in the city?"

"I haven't gotten that far," I said. "But I've got to jump. We'll catch up later."

"The lady vanishes," Harry said. "You're going to be the mother of all sessions with that shrink."

"And you?"

"I have a four-thirty consult with a Teaneck matron with bags under her eyes, followed by a digital enhancement for rhinoplasty at five-fifteen. And drinks at six with the object of my affection."

"And whom might that be?" I asked.

"You'll find her at Bemelmans Bar. Then we'll move on to dinner."

No matter how many restaurants we frequented, the one we always returned to was Dumonet at the Carlyle Hotel, an easy walk from his office. He and Chef Jean-Louis Dumonet enjoyed bantering about the latest wines and on occasion, the chef had prepared exquisite dishes for Harry and his dinner companions, be it Éclaire, friends, colleagues, or me. The newly renovated dining room and updated menu would be the perfect backdrop to "get a footing" on the cause célèbre of the moment.

I had to admire Harry for his seeming nonreaction to the letter. I, who had to work at being cool, marveled at his insouciance.

"The idea, Ms. Worrywart," he had told me back at the Franklin, "is, when you have something to hide, the best thing to do is be obvious. No one will ever suspect." With that in mind, we had tooled around town for months, dining discreetly, but ever the constant target for idle gossip from passersby who knew Harry. Often when people stopped at our table, I was introduced as the writer with whom he was working. They always begged to know more. For a while, Harry explained that I was a columnist in Connecticut who was doing an article on cosmetic surgery. Soon, bitten by the writing bug, he got into the act himself. "I'm tossing a few ideas around," he began saying. "Ms. Harding and I are brainstorming."

"And that's all I can say," he once brushed off a stunning redhead who stopped by our table at the Four Seasons with husband in tow—a woman with whom it appeared Harry might have had more than a nodding relationship.

"Oh, Dr. Troutman, I knew it: You're writing a book. Please tell me, am I in it?"

"It's too soon to reveal anything," Harry said, shaking hubby's hand and dismissing them as quickly as possible.

"Don't tell me. I know," I said when they were out of sight. "I'll just bet you 'did' her."

"I'll never tell," he teased. "But I will say, a little rearranging might have taken place."

The fact was, Harry had taken this reasonably attractive suburban housewife and turned her into a raving beauty. Hubby was so pleased that the first question he asked when his wife was roused after anesthesia was, "When can she have sex?"

"You might want to wait a few weeks," Harry had told him,

smiling. "Your wife is still swollen. And when you do, make sure she's the passive partner."

When husband and the beauty returned for her final office visit and saw the results, she threw her arms around Harry's neck and kissed him.

"I meant that the sex should be with your husband," Harry said.

Such moments were few and far between, but Harry was high profile and no matter how alone we thought we were, I always sensed that invisible spies were breathing down our necks.

29

"Great food is like great sex.
The more you have the more you want."
—Gael Greene

The Usual Suspects

Promptly at 4:00, I was back in Finkelman's office. Sitting in my old chair, looking out at the same view, staring at Finkelman's bow tie, I was overcome with déjà vu. I had not seen him for several months and upon first sight, he looked tired and worried.

"Coco, I would like us to turn our attention to this most disturbing letter that fell into my hands."

I envisioned the envelope landing through the open window during a session and knocking Finkelman for a loop, while some unsuspecting patient rambled on about his or her life's petty annoyances.

Finkelman whipped open the envelope and read the letter word by word, stopping to pause and give his forehead a wipe from the same snot-filled handkerchief I remembered so well.

"One must admit, this is most distressing," he said.

"Most," I said.

"Now tell me, have others been privy to its contents?"

"Yes."

Finkelman paused. "I see," he said, "and who might the others be?"

"Well, Parker, of course, and Harry and Éclaire."

A flood of "I sees" came tumbling forth. I counted. Five consecutive ones and a few more to follow. And with each, a wipe of the brow, blow of the nose, scratch of the head, finger inside the ear, and a sip of his water; Finkelman became more fidgety than I had ever seen him. He was downright coming apart at the seams.

"The repercussions can be grave," he said, "with dire consequences. For me as well as the others. Tell me, Coco, can you shed light on this unfortunate turn of events? Who do you think is responsible for such a heinous act?"

I girded my loins. I stood firm. "The usual suspects," I said. "Someone who is out to get us."

"This is scandalous, reprehensible, and slightly depraved. I am not going to mince words, Coco, when I say that such errant behavior is the work of a jealous and scheming individual whose wrath knows no boundaries. Tell me, are you frightened? We should discuss your concerns before we delve further into this contumelious and nefarious state of affairs."

He went on like this for another five minutes, dropping three- and four-syllable words to emphasize his point.

"The situation must be resolved, Coco. Lives are at stake here. And because I am personally involved, I might add, my reputation could be in jeopardy. If my patients ever got wind of this . . . well, you can only surmise."

Finkelman pulled the ends of his bow tie so tightly, I thought he might strangle himself. He gave a little cough and sat upright in his chair, removed his glasses, and wiped each lens with a spittle-laced Kleenex.

"What I'm saying, Coco, is this affair must cease, and it must cease now. I have obviously been chosen to act as mediator to convince you to see the error of your ways. There is no other reason for me to have received this letter."

He cleared his throat. "I believe the perpetrator will be the first to contact Mr. Jacques Cuze. He or she will set up an anonymous e-mail address just as Cuze did."

"Then we may never know whodunit," I said.

"Exactly, but that's not the point. Someone wants this affair to stop. Once Cuze is satisfied that it will, he will contact the source and the entire incident will be dropped. It is imperative that you take this threat seriously. And Coco, my advice is that you must be the one to contact Cuze, under a pseudonym, of course. Then, you can get back to your life and put your affair behind you."

"And if I don't?"

Finkelman pulled his chair up close to where I sat. He looked around the room, as though some uninvited presence was hovering nearby. He pointed his fleshy, hairy-knuckled finger at me.

"If you don't, Coco Harding . . . there will be hell to pay."

Bottom line: Our affair didn't cease. Bottom line: Someone was on to us and I needed to find out who. Bottom line: I was more curious than frightened. I went over to Kinkos, obtained an anonymous e-mail address, hooked in to their Internet café, and composed a letter to Jacques Cuze.

Dear Jacques Cuze,

As a recipient of your letter, I am asking that more information be provided as evidence that an actual affair is taking place. You may reach me at the attached e-mail address: curious@atlanticbell.net.

Anonymously yours,
Innocent but Curious

I e-mailed it off to Cuze that same afternoon. That evening, I checked in at the Internet café and found a response:

Dear Curious,

Didn't you know that curiosity killed the cat?

Be forewarned,
Jacques Cuze

Two could play this game. I responded again, this time more determined.

Dear Jacques Cuze,

Please provide the cold, hard facts. Otherwise, I shall assume this letter is a sham.

Innocent but Curious

I heard nothing for several days. When I told Harry I had been in contact with Jacques Cuze, he told me I had missed my calling as a sleuth and to give it up.

"Someone is toying with our heads. I refuse to play the victim."

"That may be true," I said, "but someone knows that an indiscretion is going on. Aren't you worried?"

"If I gave credence to every sicko out there, Coco, I wouldn't be able to leave my house. Forget about it, darling, and just get on with your life."

But my life as I had known it wasn't the same. Parker was watching me like a hawk, checking for telltale signs of guilt. Finkelman phoned, breathing heavily into my cell phone, asking if the shenanigans had stopped. I could practically feel his perspiration pouring through the receiver.

30

"I adore seafood, especially saltwater taffy."
—Milton Berle

Nantucket: The Pause that Refreshes

Through it all, Éclaire waltzed through her days as though in a golden haze, never even bringing up the subject of the letter. Only once, during one of our monthly lunch dates, did she suggest that "something funny" was going on and asked if I had received any strange mail.

"Oh that," I said, nearly choking on a piece of radicchio. "Those letters are becoming such a bore."

"Harry tried concealing the first letter from me. He's so damn protective, never wanting me to worry my head about things, but I found it and read it." She inspected her freshly manicured nails. "Who has time for such pish-posh anyway?" she said. "But Coco, do you really think any of this is true?"

"It's one of those stupid chain-type letters that are sent around to stir up trouble. I've heard this happens a lot. A friend of mine from Chicago said they were circulating for months, accusing people of all sorts of things. Believe me, it will pass if we just ignore it."

"Well, I have more important things to worry about," Éclaire said.

Like which spa had the best seaweed wrap, I thought.

What I found most astonishing yet reassuring was Éclaire's

total lack of interest. This was her best character trait—one I came to heavily rely on. As long as she wasn't rattled, why should I be? As for Parker, his suspicions grew daily as he speculated on Jacques Cuze's next move and who the guilty party might be.

And so, Harry and I bounced back and forth between food and fornication as if every fuck was to be our last. On a February Thursday when Éclaire was off to another spa, this time with Muffin in the hopes she could inspire her daughter to shed some weight, and with Parker en route to California for a long weekend to see his kids, Harry and I drove up to Woods Hole, hopped a ferry to Nantucket and a small and uninhabited B&B, his "Nip-It" license plate blazing like a beacon along the highway.

"I don't like leaving at a time like this," Parker had said, as though he were abandoning an exciting TV show whose next installment might provide the clues he needed to solve the mystery. But leave he did as family commitments won out.

It was over dinner that first night at Nantucket's Brant Point Grill that the chef, happy to see some newcomers enter the restaurant in the middle of a dead season, emerged from the kitchen with a plate of his special North Carolina shrimp in a light curry coconut broth adorned with avocado, sweet potato, and tomato. He offered Harry a forkful. Harry pulled back.

"Get that crustacean away from me. If I so much as inhale a shrimp, I'm history."

The chef withdrew the fork with sincere apologies.

"Please," Harry said, with an apologetic note in his voice, "you caught me off guard. Join us for a drink."

Obligingly, the chef pulled up a chair and asked the waiter to bring him a scotch as Harry regaled us both with a story of his first encounter with shellfish.

"I was seventeen and away with my folks at the Jersey shore. I was happily clawing my way through a broiled lobster when, within minutes, my face blew up to the size of a small Volkswagen. Had I not been immediately delivered to the emergency room, my throat would have closed up. No thank you, but these sea creatures and I are never destined to become friends."

By now, all traces of shellfish had been removed by the waiter for fear that Harry might go into anaphylactic shock right there at the table. The chef finished his drink and disappeared, promising to prepare a lovely dish for us sans seafood. I was reminded how I had never seen Harry ingest shellfish except for one instance.

"What about that stone crab salad that Éclaire served us in the Hamptons last summer?" I asked. "I could have sworn I saw you eat it."

"Those crabs were as fake as her acrylic nails," Harry said. "No, Éclaire knows better than to poison me with shellfish."

He turned his attention to a wine list that resembled a novella. Harry considered menus and wine selections as exciting as a best seller. After uttering a few hmms and ahas, he asked if I was in a red or white mood.

"I can swing both ways tonight," I said.

While I perused the menu of culinary delights, Harry went off on the pinot noirs.

"Pinot noir is a very fussy grape and needs careful handling. New World pinot noirs tend to be slightly fuller in body and flavor than, let's say, red burgundies. They're soft and smooth, yet intense and long-lasting . . . just like the perfect woman." He winked at me.

Noticing Harry's intense wine scrutiny, the waiter appeared.

"One of my personal favorite pinot noirs," he offered, "is this beauty, with a flavor reminiscent of black cherries and a deep floral aroma that adds to their charm. It will go perfectly with the duck that the chef is preparing for you this evening."

Harry was immediately impressed. "By all means, bring us a bottle."

"This wine is worthy of exaltation," the waiter said, sizing up Harry on the spot.

I expected a host of angels to ascend from on high, with gold trumpets and hallelujahs resounding.

There is no greater aphrodisiac than spending time in a popular resort off-season when the population takes a nosedive from bustling to barren. Harry and I found Nantucket to be more charming than ever. The February weather was bleak, the winds blustery, adding even more ambience to the picture. We walked the beach in our down parkas, arms locked, separating only to gather shells that had been washed ashore. The next day, we lunched at a quaint café, kept open all year round catering to the Nantucket townies who made up a small percentage of the residents. The rest were retired doctors, lawyers, business tycoons, artists, and writers whose goals had gone from top-of-the-heap to permanent "down-time" dwellers.

After lunch, we sauntered back to our B&B and made love on a goose-down comforter beneath a white canopy that required a step stool to accommodate my ascent from floor to bed. Outside, the sky had moved from an azure blue into slate gray, darkened by late afternoon clouds that guaranteed that a pending storm would keep us in our room for the rest of the day. As the clouds rolled by and whipped up the ocean waves, Harry and I snuggled beneath the covers. Spent by another round of lovemaking, talk turned to the infamous letters of Jacques Cuze. While Harry didn't even flinch, I always suspected the worst.

"What the hell are they all about anyway?" I asked, as I lay on the bed while Harry stroked my freshly waxed leg, flung haphazardly over his thigh.

"What they're all about, my dear Ms. Worrywart, is that a very frustrated somebody, aka Jacques Cuze, is resorting to scare tactics."

"So this is one big, ugly joke then," I said.

"Darling," Harry said, nibbling on my nipple, "what can possibly happen?"

"I don't know," I said, "but murder immediately comes to mind."

"You *do* have a very active imagination, Coco." Harry stopped playing with my breast to pop open a bottle of champagne that had been chilling on ice all afternoon. We toasted to "unexpected adventures at every turn" while I pretended not to give a damn, secretly thinking that in only a matter of days, one of us could be obliterated by some unknown pistolero hired to off us in the most gruesome of ways.

Parker called my cell promptly at 6:00 P.M., California time, to chat. I had alerted him to the fact that I might go up to Lenox for the weekend, and the best way to reach me was on my cell. Harry and I were finishing our dessert when he called.

"I just tried the house in Lenox," Parker said, "but no answer."

"I'm having trouble with the phones," I lied through my teeth. "I think the storm knocked out service."

"There's a storm in Lenox?"

"Five inches of snow," I said with authority, as I had called ahead to the Berkshire Chamber of Commerce and found out they had been hit hard with a mammoth snowstorm. If I was going to live dangerously, I had learned to cover my tracks.

"The best way to reach me is on my cell," I reiterated.

"Thank God for modern technology," Parker said, letting it go at that. "We're all having a ball on this end. Wish you were here, dear. The kids want to say hello."

One by one, child by child, we exchanged pleasantries, while Harry dipped his spoon into his chocolate decadence mousse and fed me a bite.

"I'm starting to have some interference," I said. "You're becoming fuzzy."

"All right then, darling," Parker said, "I'll try and reach you in the morning. Good night from San Francisco all the way to Lenox, Massachusetts. Stay warm and cozy. And why don't you build a fire?"

"Great idea," I said.

After dinner, Harry and I retired to our room and followed Parker's advice: We tossed a log into the fireplace and drank brandy from plastic cups until the warmth of the Courvoisier eradicated all sense of guilt.

"We can't go on like this forever, can we?" I asked Harry. We were back on the bed once again, two nude bodies aglow in the light of the candles I had brought along to enhance the mood. As if we needed any enhancement. I could have been in a coldwater flat and the sexual energy Harry and I generated would have been enough to light up the world.

"Why *can't* we go on like this forever?" Harry parroted my remark.

"I don't know. Won't we get caught? I mean, somebody is already on to us."

"You're not back on Jacques Cuze again, are you?"

"I'm sorry, but I just can't be as cool as you are."

"That's because you're blister-burning hot, baby," Harry cajoled.

He leaned over me, one hand running through my hair, the other barely brushing my neck as he moved slowly down toward my breasts.

"Oh Harry, don't stop," I pleaded.

Lips met lips and parted, tongue merged with tongue and danced playfully around our mouths. Harry's kisses were strong and passionate as his tongue moved away from mine and began making a tour of my body, pausing first at my breasts where his hands had just been, and circling the aureole of each one. He then grabbed the small pillow with "I Love Nantucket" stitched across the front and placed it under me. Even in the heat of passion, Harry was a man of details. In simultaneous rhythm, one hand found the soft crevice between my legs and gently began circling his palm against my vulva, stimulating me from the mound above until my legs parted widely. With the other hand, he placed a finger inside me. Slowly, deftly, moving that finger in and out of my well-lubricated vagina in perfect time to my undulating hips which rose into the air, my feet still positioned on the bed. Suddenly, Harry was all hands, probing, manipulating, stroking me into submission as I cried out into the night, "Make me come, now."

"We're just getting started, sweetheart," he said. "We're just warming up." And with those words, his finger went deeper inside me as my legs lifted into the air, moving as far apart as they could. My body was no longer mine. I had relinquished control to Harry, whose only job was to savor me completely.

And savor me he did. Suddenly, with one finger still inside me, the other hand moved to my buttocks as he reached between my cheeks, searching for my love knot that accepted eagerly another finger of his other hand. Now, in perfect motion, Harry worked me from both ends until I could hardly breathe. My voice came in gasps. I could hear myself moaning like a wild animal begging for mercy, but Harry would not free me from my own desires. And then, when I could bear it no longer, his tongue found my clit and circled it slowly, pausing occasionally to place the tip of his tongue inside my vagina, then returning to my clit, which was now the size of a cherry. He then changed position, fell back on the bed, and pulled me on top of him. I reached for his cock, which I longed to caress with my mouth, but Harry held me back. Instead, he positioned my wet pussy on to his throbbing shaft as he entered me from below, I thrusting up and down from above, as we moved in time to our own pleasure, but not yet climaxing.

Keeping the pace, we shifted from the bed to the "Tranquility" hot tub with its built-in surround sound system and magnetic jets, sending a variety of sensations to all parts of our bodies. The high-tech audio system directed sound waves through the tub, creating a wavelike effect, heightening our lovemaking even more. As we moved in time to Frank Sinatra belting out "In the Wee, Small

Hours of the Morning," rotary nozzles sent a jet stream to our private parts, giving new meaning to Bed, Bath, and Beyond.

With a sudden burst of almost intolerable ecstasy, we exploded together in simultaneous orgasms until the hot tub practically overflowed. In the end, it was those very orgasms that allowed me to risk everything, including my marriage.

31

"There is evil in every berry of grape."
—The Koran

Coming to My Senses

Parker phoned me several times that weekend, asking if the Lenox phone lines were still down. His final call came on Sunday morning.

"It's been a rough few days," I said, "but at least I had electricity." Harry smiled. "I'll be home tonight just in time to greet you at the door when the limo arrives in Seaport. But I did get a lot of work done. I finished next week's column and am working on an article for *Gourmet* magazine. Lenox is the perfect writer's retreat."

Parker lapped up every word as he pictured his wife, burning the midnight oil, the perfect example of fortitude meets creativity.

"I should send you to Lenox more often," he said. "You never sounded more productive."

"And sated," I said. "Let's not forget completely sated."

"That's what happens when you let yourself go," Parker said. Who could argue with that?

Early Monday morning after Parker's return from San Francisco and my return from Lenox/Nantucket, the phone rang. It was

Finkelman urging me to come in that afternoon. I rubbed the sleep from my eyes and held the phone tightly against my ear so as not to awaken Parker, who, jet-lagged and snoring softly, hadn't gotten to bed until after 2:00 A.M. Carefully, I slipped slowly from beneath the covers and into the bathroom.

"Coco, this is urgent, nay critical. I must see you here in my office at five P.M. sharp. A matter has come up that requires immediate resolution. Can you be here?"

Still groggy, I acquiesced. "Five it is," I said. I dragged myself back to bed.

"Who was that?" Parker, half-awake, turned over and asked.

"Nobody, just Finkelman. Go back to sleep, dear."

I tried falling back to sleep myself, but to no avail. I was still on a high from the weekend and the exquisite time Harry and I had shared in Nantucket. I was constantly operating on two levels: one, my adoration of and sexual obsession with Harry, and two, my affection and respect for Parker, who was a man of integrity and source of strength, who loved me unconditionally. But sadly, he could never satisfy that emotional and sexual itch that constantly needed to be scratched. The guilt I felt had become a permanent part of my psyche, the price I paid for my indiscretions. Would I ever be truly happy, I asked myself over and over again, and why wasn't Parker enough? I hated myself for succumbing to desire when what Parker offered was to be cherished and revered. How low I had stooped in the name of passion. I was disgusted with myself for being so conniving and indiscreet—for taking my marriage for granted, all in the name of libidinous cravings. I was a weak woman who didn't deserve a man like Parker. And so, while I waited for my next liaison with Harry, fantasizing every minute detail of our last encounter, a part of me loathed him as well for being the object of my sexual dependency.

That feeling was short-lived. I had only to see Harry and I was immediately transported from naughty little girl to even-naughtier grown woman, the latter of which always won out. But first there was Finkelman to contend with. I spent the morning writing a column and then met Annie at our favorite Seaport restaurant, "V," where we were treated like royalty and could linger for hours without impatient stares from the help. The manager of "V," Mark Goad, ever the attentive host, sat me at a corner table where many of my columns had been composed. There was nothing like the coupling of fine food sprinkled with creative juices to make this place enjoyable. I considered "V" (named for vino, vineyard, and all things wine-related) my little lunchtime oasis where I could linger, undisturbed.

Today was different though. Annie appeared promptly at 1:00, a bit disheveled from the windy February day, prostrated herself in a chair, and waved for a waiter.

He appeared on cue and Annie ordered a glass of chardonnay, not her usual modus operandi. She guzzled it down as though it were water.

"Okay, let's talk this through," she said.

Annie and I had "talked our way through" our entire friendship, dissecting any and all issues without censorship. We let all our emotions hang out and, in doing so, became as close as any two sisters. And we always found solutions to all problems. But today, we were both stymied as to what to do next. To top it off, more letters had arrived, each one growing more and more threatening. If these letters held any merit, were our lives in danger? The last one was a real whopper:

To Whom It May Concern:

Beware the lethal kiss of death.

Jacques Cuze

"Finkelman called," I said, momentarily changing the subject. "He asked to see me this afternoon."

Annie raised her glass. "Let's eat, drink, and make merry . . . before one of us is a goner."

We observed the situation from all its various angles until we started to get slightly tipsy and turned our attention to lunch.

We poked at our chop chop salads preceded by a plate of crispy fried calamari and coconut shrimp.

At least if one of us was going to be ousted, we might as well go to the dogs and eat ourselves into oblivion. With that in mind, we ended our lunch with a slice of three-layer blackout cake and two forks, so we could share the calories equally.

"Will there be anything else?" the waiter asked.

"A gun," Annie said.

I had to hand it to her: Annie kept her sense of humor intact through any situation.

~

Finkelman opened the door to his office, perspiration emanating from every pore on his face. In all my years at the gym, I had never broken such a sweat. He escorted me in, wiping his brow as I took my position in the chair from which I had unloaded my entire life story. Finkelman began fanning himself with Jacques Cuze's letter.

"You've seen this, I trust?"

"Yes. My guess is everyone has a copy."

"Death threats have been made, Coco. We can no longer sit idly back and ignore the severity of these letters. I was afraid to turn on my car ignition this morning for fear I would blow up."

I was impressed. Finkelman did have fantasies, after all, negative though they were.

"Why did you ask to see me?"

Finkelman scratched the tip of his nose, gave his left earlobe a tweak, and batted his eyes five times in succession. "I am asking . . . no, pleading that you come to your senses. You must cut off your little peccadillo with Dr. Troutman or I shall be forced to intervene. You are in grave danger."

There it was: another peccadillo.

"Intervene how?"

"I shall report him to the AMA."

"And tell them what?"

"That he has debased the Hippocratic oath. That he is cavorting with a patient and that his medical license should be revoked."

"I am *not* his patient," I said. "But I am *yours.* And, I might add, if you make any more threats, I will report *you* to the AMA. Don't dare to interfere in my life or *you* won't have a practice to worry about."

Finkelman stared out the window at his Central Park view and said nothing. A few more bats of his eyes and a nervous little cough as we sat there in silence for a few minutes while he digested my words.

"I see," he finally said.

"Look," I said, playing shrink to my shrink, "I still don't understand why you are so worked up over all of this."

"I'm in a precarious position," Finkelman offered. "I know too much. With that comes a responsibility to protect my patients. If, for a moment, you can allow yourself to take Jacques Cuze's threats as real, you might acknowledge that this is no laughing matter."

"Who's laughing?" I asked.

I sat back in the chair ruminating over the usual suspects. "Certainly, Harry and I *are* the culprits here. I suppose that either Parker or Éclaire, if they got wind of this, might not be too happy."

"Aha," Finkelman interjected.

"Then again, sister-in-law Bridgette is not exactly my biggest fan. She'd probably love to see me out of the picture."

"Hmm," Finkelman uttered another erudite response.

"So, I suppose, if anyone is in danger, it could be either Harry or me. But let's not forget Hedy the housekeeper who sees all, but keeps to herself, except for that one time when she was about to quit over Bridgette's improprieties."

"I see," Finkelman said, "and what 'improprieties' would you mean?"

"Nothing serious. Last July at our dinner party, Bridgette drank too much and began ordering Hedy around, demanding that Hedy be her personal attendant. Hardly grounds for murder, I'd say."

I felt as though I was a prime suspect in the board game Clue. The Parker Brothers, bless their homicidal little souls, could have a field day with this one.

"I suggest you think long and hard, Coco," Finkelman said, "and start to pay credence to Jacques Cuze's letters. I must confess that I have begun losing sleep over this and have even thought it might be a matter for the police."

"The police?" I perked up. "What good would that do? There's not evidence here, only lame threats and speculation. No one can trace Jacques Cuze's letters. The police will dismiss it on the spot and spend their coffee breaks having a good laugh. I think you're making too much out of this."

"I'd like to continue seeing you, Coco, until this matter is put to rest." Finkelman looked over his date planner. "You are in serious denial and we need to discuss why you prefer to hide from reality. We can take this up on Thursday at eight P.M. I'd be willing to see you after dinner hours."

"Sorry," I said, "that would interfere with dinner with Harry."

"Have you always been this infrangible, Coco?"

I knew that Finkelman was scared. His fancy words dripped from his tongue like a verbal avalanche.

"Thursday at eight," I said.

"Good, and try to come to your senses between now and then."

Finkelman was starting to sound annoyingly like my mother.

A hint of spring was in the air when I left Finkelman's Central Park West apartment building. The days were getting longer, and as I drove onto the West Side Highway the sun was setting and cast its glow on the buildings that flanked the highway. Thoughts of warmer days ahead should have added a sense of relief, but instead, a feeling of dread welled up inside me. Within days, our lives could all change.

When I walked inside the house at 7:30, Bridgette, who was passing through Seaport on her way back from a New Haven art tour, came to the door, a drink in her hand.

"Welcome to death row," she said.

From the start, Parker and Bridgette banded together in sharing the news of Jacques Cuze's letters. As soon as Bridgette received one, she phoned Parker and vice versa. Their sibling alliance was growing stronger by the letter as they vowed that together they would get to the bottom of this charade.

Parker appeared with a Jack on the rocks. "I made an eight o'clock dinner reservation at the club."

"I see you two have already gotten started," I said. "You can pour me a glass of sherry."

Bridgette's hostile leer was piercing. I was convinced she knew something, but instead of being direct, she plied me with innuendo in the hopes of breaking me down and whipping me into admission. I would not budge, not even under the accusatory stares of her piercing eyes, as intense as the bright lights of an interrogation room under which criminals confessed all.

"Bridgette thinks she may be on to something," Parker said.

"Or someone," Bridgette said, pinning her eyes on mine.

I could see we were off to a bumpy night.

At dinner, Bridgette announced after two vodkas and a glass of wine that she had scheduled an appointment with the renowned Dr. Troutman. She waited for an obligatory reaction from me, but I remained cool and poised and didn't respond.

"Yes," she pressed on, "I'm thinking of having a boob reduction. These bazookas have been getting in my way for years."

The thought of Bridgette baring her breasts in front of Harry was at once disturbing and amusing. One look at Bridgette's knockers and Harry might opt for early retirement.

"That's my Bridgey," Parker broke in, "never willing to settle for anything less than perfect."

"I'm tired of having jugs that jiggle," Bridgette said. "I need a smidge of tightening, and since you've all been touting Harry's needlework, I felt I should give him the opportunity to work wonders with me. I'm interviewing him tomorrow at nine A.M. sharp."

I hated to tell her, but if there was to be any interviewing to be done, it was the other way around. I could hardly wait to hear the outcome of her consultation.

"A little fine-tuning and my cups shall runneth over," she said, "only not as much as before."

On those words hung, not only Bridgette's breasts, but my next week's column. That night after everyone was asleep, I sat down and wrote: "My Cups Runneth Over."

The Seaport Gazette

MY CUPS RUNNETH OVER

Yes, ladies, it's true: Bosoms are back. We may now put our derrières behind us and concentrate on what's up front. For those well-endowed women this comes as no great revelation, as they are accustomed to flaunting their merchandise. For others, such as I, you can only imagine the fear associated with this piece of news. Does this mean I must suddenly hit Victoria's Secret and buy myself a push-up bra, or do I face the fact that I am simply not going to make it as this year's answer to Dolly Parton?

For years, I've accepted my limited accoutrements and was quite happy living out my life with the minimum daily requirement of chest. Why complain? What was lacking on top I made up for on the bottom. But now it is being brought to everyone's attention that you ain't really got it, if you don't have it where it counts the most: up front.

"Relax," my husband Parker tells me, "what's the big deal? I'm a leg man myself."

Men who got shortchanged make remarks like that. Men who tell their wives such whoppers are really closet breast men. I know because we once went to a party where Parker's eyeballs left their sockets for a brief moment, and it wasn't over anyone's legs. Clearly, it was a matter of mammary glands.

Some women I know headed down the "Silicone Valley" route years ago to get what nature failed to provide them. They returned from their visits looking perkier and sporting knockers the size of watermelons. So naturally my ears perked up (my only perky organs) as I also learned that couturiers will be designing their clothes with the full-torsoed woman in mind. This means if a dress is enhanced by melon-sized boobs, kumquats will simply not do. Let's face it, I am not going to turn heads wearing a skintight T-shirt that houses a couple of Ping-Pong balls when soccer balls are the rage.

It was not always this way. Back when I was a blooming adolescent, parts of my anatomy stuck out. I was coming into my own and breezed through puberty with a certain amount of cleavage and clout. To accentuate my attributes even more, I squeezed myself into tight-fitting Merry Widows, an elongated bra that came equipped with bones that temporarily cut off my air supply. The main attraction of a Merry Widow was to give us all nineteen-inch waists and bust lines that ended just beneath our chins. Merry Widows took the ordinary and turned them into extraordinary. To this day, I owe everything to what that contraption did for me, more than my entire college education.

But boobs are funny things: As we change, so do they. What reached great heights one day can shift positions the next. Where I once offered the world a double feature, I now present a couple of short subjects and no coming attractions. So when the news came out that chests are once again receiving "top" billing, my only recourse was to take up this matter with the woman in charge of bringing the maximum out of the minimum: the salesperson at Victoria's Secret.

"I need to know Victoria's secret," I said.

"Rubber foam," the salesgirl said. "It performs miracles."

Easy for her to say. She had a chest that would never know from padding, a chest that was clearly a 36D and climbing.

"There's nothing to be ashamed of," she continued. "You are what you are."

"That's the point," I said. "I need to change my persona."

She dragged out a couple of bras that she guaranteed would make me firm and fully packed. I tried on the first. I looked like I was wielding two ballistic missiles beneath my sweater. If people accidentally bumped into me, they could be maimed for life.

The next bra was filled with a synthetic material that smelled funny.

"That's petrified rubber," she said. "It goes through a high-velocity treatment. Then it's injected with high doses of silicone and welded into shape by our own Victoria's Secret seamstresses. Only they know the real secret. But we promise, you will have years of success."

"Success with whom?" I asked.

"Men!" she said. "Isn't that what this is all about?"

"Forget it," I said. "My husband is happy with me just the way I am."

"He probably told you he's a leg man," she said.

"Howdyaknow?"

"Honey," she said, shaking her maracas, "I was once married to a leg man, except he really wasn't. He pretended to like legs only to console me. So one day, I surprised him: I went to see my cousin Sheldon, a plastic surgeon in New Jersey, who turned me into a vision of loveliness. Now my cups runneth over. And everybody's happy."

"Do you have Cousin Sheldon's phone number?" I asked.

"Sadly, Cousin Sheldon passed on. He was in the middle of a breast augmentation when he got hit with a flying piece of silicone. It blinded him in his left eye."

"Death by silicone?" I was horrified.

"Actually," she said, "he got hit by a bus on the way to his car."

This gave me pause. If silicone was responsible for Cousin Sheldon's demise, who needed it?

On the way home, I had trouble seeing over the dashboard because my chest, which had now risen to new heights, blocked out my view of the road. I went through a couple of red lights. An officer stopped me a few blocks from my house.

"Let's see your license, lady," he said.

It took me five minutes to even be able to reach over my bag to retrieve it. He reprimanded me for not wearing my seat belt. I tried explaining they don't make seat belts to fit around a push-up bra and that a woman in my condition needs extra compensation. He wanted no part of it. I received a ticket for driving under the influence.

"The influence of what?" I asked.

"Dangerous underwear," he said.

The next morning, promptly at nine, Bridgette was in Harry's examining room, wrapped in white paper like a giant loaf of French bread, waiting for her breast evaluation.

"Well, good morning, Bridgette," Harry said, joined by Nurse Krystle at his side. "So nice to see you. The last time we spoke was in the middle of July at Parker's and Coco's house."

"Yes, well, since last summer, my breasts have dropped another inch. At this rate, they'll be down by my waist by summer." She let out a coy little giggle.

"All right, then," Harry said, "let's take a look and see what can be done to improve the situation."

Harry parted Bridgette's paper gown, exposing two full breasts with large brown aureoles and nipples as big as pencil erasers. She thrust her chest forward for Harry to admire as Nurse Krystle hovered at the far end of the room, pretending to be invisible.

"Yes, well, I do see what you mean." Harry gave a reassuring, but professional smile. "Some reduction could improve the situation and give you the lift you're after. I will need to do a breast examination before we continue."

He invited Bridgette to lie down on the table while he probed for any unusual lumps. Satisfied that Bridgette's breasts were healthy, if just a bit bulbous, he sat her up and told her to get dressed so they could discuss the procedure in the privacy of his office.

"What do you think, Doctor? Are they too ample for your liking? Or do you prefer smaller breasts, like my sister-in-law's, for example?"

Harry reddened, ignoring her remark. "It's all a matter of proportion," he said. "For a woman of your stature and build, I think you can accommodate larger breasts. Smaller women might prefer less accentuated ones. Personally, I think a reduction is in order here."

Bridgette got dressed and met Harry in his office. An 8 x 10 family portrait sat in a silver frame on his desk.

"What are you doing about your daughter's weight? She seems just a tad obese."

Harry was taken aback by Bridgette's bluntness. "Melissa has been grappling with weight issues all her life," he said, "but Éclaire and I are addressing the problem."

"You should." Bridgette added, "Such a pretty face, but much too puffy."

Harry would rue the day that Bridgette walked into his office.

After poring through books of photos of other patients with similar issues, Bridgette was confident that Harry was "her man."

"We can schedule surgery within the month," Harry said. "My agenda is full, but my secretary can work you in as soon as an opening presents itself. Are you in a hurry?"

"I've lived with these ripe old melons for a long time," she said, "a few more weeks won't make a difference."

Then, she leaned over the desk, her voice softening. "Coco tells me that you're the best in town. That you have golden hands and know just how to use them."

"Well thank you, Bridgette," Harry said, "I will try not to disappoint you."

"I'm sure you won't." She rose from the chair, giving Harry a little peck on the cheek and exiting his office.

~

Éclaire, fresh from a week at Canyon Ranch in Lenox, had decided to take up art, her new avocation, and signed up for classes with a Monsieur Mars, alias Marvin Hershkowitz, an aging reject from the Paris art scene, who took pointillism to new heights. Mars, age sixty-five, had recently arrived in New York. In order to pay his rent, he offered classes at his little home-based Tribeca studio, consisting mostly of postmenopausal women with time on their hands and a desire to let their creative juices spill over their canvases. Éclaire had heard about Mars from her friends, Alice and Leslie, who knew someone who was married to Mars's ex-wife and said he was the best art teacher in New York. Mars also taught a class at the Art Students League and was known for fast-talking budding young artists of either sex into bed.

Éclaire was enchanted and inspired by Monsieur Mars, who complimented her brushstrokes as he leaned over her, trying to sneak a peek of cleavage. She always made a point of wearing low-cut sweaters so as not to disappoint the great master. After class, Éclaire, Alice, and Leslie had lunch together and discussed art ad nauseum. Then, they went shopping.

Éclaire came home after the first class, lit up like a Christmas tree.

"It's like doing needlepoint on canvas," Éclaire beamed as she held up a small painting of a fruit bowl laden with grapes, apples, pears, and one large banana, composed of tiny dots.

"Lovely, darling," Harry said. "Keep up the good work."

"Maybe you can hang this in your office."

"Why not?" Harry cringed at the thought.

"Your patients will think it's a Seurat," Éclaire said.

~

While Éclaire was busy dropping oil paints on canvas, Harry and I sampled our own private artistic delicacies at Café des Artistes, where we dined on asparagus crisped in beer batter and accompanied by a crème fraiche dip. The restaurant was celebrating its annual asparagus festival so that each stalk was particularly tasty at this time of year. The lovely dinner took the edge off Jacques Cuze's latest missive.

To Whom It May Concern:

Every murderer is probably somebody's old friend.

Jacques Cuze

"For tonight, darling," Harry said, "we will put Jacques Cuze out of our mind."

"I'll go along with that," I said.

In the middle of Harry's pot au feu and my tea-smoked duckling with buttery confit and braised, cinnamon-stoked cabbage, owner George Lang appeared at our table to greet us. As usual, I was introduced as "the writer."

"George knows us," I smiled. "Parker and I have been regulars here for years."

"And how *is* your husband?" George asked politely. "Are the country clubs doing well? Please, send my regards and tell him we should plan some tennis this summer and of course, dinner, the four of us."

"I'll pass that along," I said.

"And I'll have Chef Neimenin whip up his famous Chocolatissimo for two."

George, the consummate gentleman, knew exactly how to pamper his customers. He and his lovely wife, Jenifer, had been friends of Parker's for years and had dined with us on several occasions. After some pleasantries, he left us to our meal. As we nibbled our endive-Stilton salads and sipped our spicy Trimbach Gewürztraminer wine, Harry seemed a bit nervous.

"I just can't take you anywhere, now, can I? So you know the Langs?"

"How will we explain this one?" I asked Harry.

"Easy, darling," he said. "I'll simply tell Éclaire and you'll tell Parker that we had dinner here."

"Ah, the honest approach for once," I said, smiling. "How original."

~

The murals of wood nymphs in the buff on the restaurant walls lent themselves to romance. Café des Artistes was in itself an aphrodisiac, a temple of seduction guaranteed to inspire grand lovemaking that followed in one of Harry's recovery suites immediately après dinner. I felt rejuvenated if not just a tad full after not only the Chocolatissimo, but macadamia tarts, which George threw in as an added dessert bonus. All I wanted was to fall asleep in Harry's arms. I inhaled his Devin cologne, whose scent perfumed my body, and begged him to "do me" again. Obligingly, he inched down and finding my most receptive love spot, rolled his tongue up and down in rhythmic motion until I came.

"You taste very ripe tonight, darling," Harry noted, "with a slight hint of pepper."

"It must have been the Stilton," I said.

Harry not only rated restaurants, but vaginas as well. Zagat could have a field day with this.

It was Annie who had once told me that when women ate certain foods, their vaginal fluids reflected the particular taste.

"Shrimps are the best," she said. "Eat a couple of shrimp and you'll be a regular chicken of the sea."

Shrimp? Harry would break out in hives as soon as he tasted me.

Harry's suggestion of telling our respective spouses that we had dined together made perfect sense. The story went: I was working on an article on "Olive Oil: The Other Botox" and solicited Harry's expertise. Certainly, Parker would have suggested I ask Harry and Éclaire, who was now so engrossed in her art that she couldn't see past her canvas.

"Olive oil?" Parker erupted. "You can replace Botox with olive oil. Since when?"

"Harry said they've been doing a study on this for years. A team of plastic surgeons in Romania, headed by Dr. Florentina Fleischmann, are presenting a paper in one of the journals. This is a hot topic."

"And you're doing an article as well?"

"With Harry's help, of course," I said.

"You're certainly on the cutting edge of the latest cosmetic trends," Parker added.

"One has got to grab the hot ones as they surface. Harry was kind enough to share this with me and I thought I'd give it a try. One of the food magazines could be interested."

There was no end to how far Harry and I could stretch a creative lie.

32

"When women are depressed they
either eat or go shopping. Men invade another country."
—Elaine Boosler

Up to His Ears in Breasts

"Spring—when a young man's fancy lightly turns to thoughts of love." Shakespeare: Now there was a guy who knew the score. Harry was up to his ears in breasts. Brides all over Manhattan were having their boobs augmented or reduced before their wedding day.

"Pre-wedding plastic surgery has become the rage," Harry said. "I'm booked all through July. Facelifts, tummy tucks, name it: These women want to walk down the aisle completely renovated."

"Thanks for another column idea," I said.

The Seaport Gazette

HERE COME THE BOOBS!

Brides and grooms everywhere are doing it: not just tying the knot, but having pre-wedding plastic surgery. The New York Times *Styles section bared all. The article began with the November wedding of a couple, both of whom had nose jobs, while the bride also threw in a bit of liposuction for her cheeks and the groom, an implant in his chin to make it look square. After all, who wants a rounded-chin groom? Topping it off, he had his teeth whitened so his smile would be as dazzling white as his bride's gown.*

"It is something we both wanted to do," the bride announced, saying that she loved her fiancé with his crooked nose, but adding, "Now I love him even more. Now he is hot."

Let's face it, why look "typically bridal" when "hot" is an option?

Groom Greg (my friend's son) confessed he was shocked when his bride greeted him at the altar looking like a completely different person.

"I wasn't sure I was getting the same girl," he confessed to me later, when I, a wedding guest, commented on how different "Jane" looked.

"She wanted to surprise me," Greg said. And that she did. She had a pre-wedding makeover including a breast augmentation that resulted in having to have a last-minute gown reconstruction to accommodate her new boobs.

This new trend got me thinking: If a little rearranging here, a shot of Botox there, can insure love-ever-after, why not go for it? At least that's what bride Wendy's mom, Annie, had to say when not only Wendy went under the knife a few months before her wedding, but Annie did, as well.

"I looked in the mirror one morning," Annie said, "and what I saw shocked me. I no longer looked young."

"That's because you're not," I said. "Why can't you accept the aging process gracefully? You happen to look terrific."

That may be true, but "terrific" wasn't good enough. Several months before Wendy's wedding, Annie had a complete facelift and tummy tuck, and tossed in a Brazilian butt lift to complete the package.

"When I walked down the aisle, all eyes were upon me," Annie said. "I was nipped and tucked from front to rear. I looked and felt as beautiful as my daughter."

Gone are the days when the mothers of brides and grooms all wore beige and gray. Today, these women are competing to look as stunning as their offspring. And if that isn't bad enough, one mother I know wore white to her own daughter's wedding and renewed her vows at the same ceremony.

"It was a real deal," Joan said. "A two-for-one lump sum wedding, and it was quite sweet. When the groom slipped the ring on Amanda's finger, my Harry followed suit and placed a wedding band on my finger, too. I was a bride all over again."

"Didn't your daughter mind your infringing on her day?" I asked.

"We considered it a bonding experience," Joan said. "I will admit, the mother of the groom didn't see it that way, but she's easily rattled by everything."

The pre-wedding makeover has now become the rage. When reserving the hotel for the reception, the bride now books a consultation with her plastic surgeon, as well. Operating rooms are as busy as bridal salons. It used to be that a bride would awaken on her wedding day and all she needed to worry about was her hair and makeup. That has now taken a backseat to major overhauls.

My friend Judy and I were discussing this over lunch. "As far as I'm concerned," Judy said, "plastic surgery should be part of a divorce agreement, not a pre-wedding requisite. Isn't it better to end the marriage on an 'up' note and go out into the world as a stunning divorcée?"

She has a point: Coming into a marriage, the bride has already snagged a husband, but leaving the marriage, she is once again a single woman where drop-dead gorgeous really counts the most.

Apparently, lots of women agree. One gal made her soon-to-be-divorced husband include a complete makeover as part of the agreement. She left the marriage looking tired and downtrodden. She emerged a month later, refreshed, renewed, and rejuvenated, having been "rearranged" by one of New York's finest.

"What happened to good, old-fashioned values?" my friend Susan wants to know.

"They reinvented themselves inside the doctor's office," I said.

"Having good values is one thing, being valued is another." So said thirty-year-old bride Samantha, who looked gorgeous even before she went under the knife. "When I tried on wedding gowns, I just didn't feel right," she said. "My rear end was sticking out too far, my tummy had an ugly little bulge, and my breasts weren't perky. I just wasn't bridal material."

And so Samantha, along with her rear end, tummy, and her "un-perky" breasts, hotfooted it over to a plastic surgeon who took inches off her tush, got rid of the tummy bulge, and allowed Samantha to shimmy down the aisle like a model on a runway, looking pert if not just a tad plastic.

Men are getting into the act, too. Like the groom with the chin implant, another guy thought it was time to get rid of his beer belly. "I've been a couch potato all my life," he said. "Now that I'm getting married, my fiancée wants me to turn the other cheek."

That's exactly what he did. Brian turned off the sports channel, rose from the couch, and had his cheeks liposuctioned and lifted, both on his face and his rear. He threw in a hair implant, too, plus a little repair on his deviated septum, resulting in a nose that could adorn the cover of GQ. The Brian I knew fell to the wayside while the new Brian looked svelte and sexy. His bride was ecstatic. She had a bit of cosmetic enhancement, too, so much so that when she smiled I was afraid her face might break. But they did make a stunning couple, even if they didn't look entirely real.

The bridal gown industry agrees that it's made all the difference. One bridal consultant said that pre-wedding plastic *surgery has increased her sales. "Brides who have 'had some work' have a new lease on life. They look great. As a result, they don't mind spending more on a gown. They've already dropped a bundle for the surgery. A few more bucks won't even make a dent."*

"Boobs," my husband says, "they're all a bunch of boobs."

"In more ways than one," I say.

~

Harry and I had our own variation on spring, as well. For us, thoughts of love turned to thoughts of exquisite food and sex.

Finkelman dubbed Harry a "polyphagiac."

"The man's id exceeds his superego, Coco. He has no restraint. He's a slave to his libidinal and gluttonous cravings. His gratification knows no boundaries. And he's bibacious, to boot."

With Finkelman, one needed to bring a dictionary along to the sessions.

But I, who basked in Harry's excessiveness, was loving every grand, gourmandish, and sensuous moment.

As April approached, Éclaire had swimsuits on her mind and, having devoured one too many lettuce leaves, was feeling bloated. She asked Harry if a smidge of liposuction was in order.

"It's only gas," he assured her, "not fat. Maybe if you ate some real food for a change, your abdomen wouldn't bulge. If I even attempted to suction you, I'd be vacuuming air."

But Muffin Troutman was another story. She had grown a whole dress size over the winter and Éclaire was beside herself.

"Darling," Éclaire cornered Muffin one morning, "Daddy and I were thinking: How would you like to lose your tummy this summer?"

"I'd rather lose my virginity," Muffin said, stuffing a blueberry scone into her mouth and retreating to her room for the rest of the afternoon.

And then, to add more insult to the already harsh reality, another letter arrived:

To Whom It May Concern:

Spring is short-lived . . . and so are you. Take heed.

Jacques Cuze

I phoned Harry and told him that Cuze was back in business.

"Toss it," Harry said. "Trust me: None of us is going to an early grave."

Finkelman had a different take. "One of us will not get to see September," he said.

A sudden reprieve of warm weather and with it the arrival of tulips, robins, and Bridgette's new breasts. One day we had ten inches of snow, the next thing we knew, all of us were still alive and well, while being warned on a weekly basis to cease and desist from hanky-panky. The first weekend in May, Bridgette came up to Seaport to do nine holes and show off "Harry's breasts," as she now referred to them. She cornered me in the restroom, undoing her blouse.

"Take a look at these babies." She practically tossed her boobs in my face. "Aren't they flirty?" I had to agree, Bridgette's breasts did look perky. Harry had downsized her from a 36D to a well-proportioned 34C. Bridgette had new ammunition with which to work her wiles. There would be no stopping her now.

On a lighter note, Éclaire and "les girls," Alice and Leslie, were turning into artistes extraordinaire . . . or so Monsieur Mars told them. Every week, he salivated over their paintings and pecked their cheeks on either side as they left his studio, their little "Seurats" in hand. Éclaire invited me to join them for lunch after their last art class of the season. I agreed to tag along.

"And, Coco, my dear, dear friend Lynn from California is in town, so she'll be coming, too," Éclaire said, beaming. "You'll just love her."

I hadn't seen Alice and Leslie since last summer in East Hampton and could use a little idle chatter in lieu of all the pending doom that Jacques Cuze was tossing our way.

I met them at DB Bistro Moderne, the more informal "little sister" of Boulud's uptown Daniel.

Alice looked even more fetching than I had remembered her. Her new wash-and-wear closely cropped "do" was reminiscent of a flapper-goes-millennium. She wore a stunning zucchini around her neck that she and her daughter, partners in Dana Designs, had created. Even my mother, Yvonne, had begun collecting some of Alice's pieces and attended all of her Boca trunk shows.

"I'm wearing an Alice today," Yvonne called regularly to tell me. "Today it's the pinto beans surrounded by little rhinestones. I'm a regular one of the girls."

Leslie, still doing her stints as a cabaret singer, was also sporting a necklace by Alice and greeted me effusively, as though she had seen me only yesterday. I had to admit: Éclaire's pals were, to borrow my mother's phrase, "the Tiffany of friends." While we waited for Lynn to arrive, we ordered Cosmopolitans to celebrate their artistic achievements with Monsieur Mars.

Many giggles and two Cosmos later, the maître d' appeared at our table with Malibu Barbie on his arm, looking as though she was airbrushed to perfection. If this woman were a drink, she would be Dom Perignon champagne.

"Oh my Gawd!" Éclaire let out a little yelp. "Look at *you*! It is *really* you hiding in there, or is it a Fig Newton of my imagination?"

"Do you love it or do you love it?" Lynn said, pirouetting slightly.

"I *love* it," Éclaire squeaked. "And, don't tell me . . . let me guess . . . you did the boobs, too."

"The whole nine yards," Lynn squealed. "Am I a hottie or what?"

"You reek glam," Alice said.

"Ditto on that," Leslie chimed in, with a few bars of "Isn't She Lovely?"

"And . . ." Éclaire interrupted her superlatives to introduce me. "This is the Coco from Seaport I've been telling you about."

I had never been dubbed a "the" before.

"Oh yes," Lynn gushed, "Éclaire has told me soooo much about you."

Lynn was all woman in the sexiest sense of the word—the kind who turned men's heads when she entered a room. She was wearing a pair of "Fuck Me" shoes and her entire persona oozed lust. Her blond mane draped behind a perfectly proportioned body—a body that had been sculpted magnificently by a top Beverly Hills plastic surgeon. By all rights, she should not be walking the streets, but be posed on a pedestal as an exquisite specimen of womanhood. Even Harry would be hard-pressed to find any flaws.

Yes, Lynn was sizzle and glitz personified, yet was blessed with just enough brains to destroy any notion of being a hard-core bimbo. By the time I made it through my cheese-tomato tarte Tatin, I was actually becoming fond of the woman.

Lynn was between husbands and working on her fourth. A man named Mickey G. from Las Vegas who was in "the business" had tried slipping a diamond on her finger, but Lynn had declined his offer.

"When I asked Mickey G. what his business was, his answer was, 'Don't ask.' That's all I need—a goomba in my life . . . if you catch my drift."

Perhaps Mickey G. was exactly the man we needed to set Jacques Cuze straight.

Clinking our glasses, we toasted to friendship. Éclaire invited us all out to her Hampton house for the Memorial Day weekend. Shades of last summer drifted through my mind. Here we were, nearly a year later, and Harry and I were still going strong, under the eerie watch of one Jacques Cuze, of course.

Éclaire broke in. "Did you know, ladies, that Coco is writing an article on olive oil as a wrinkle replacement? Harry is helping her sort it all out."

"I think I heard about that," Lynn said, her own Botoxed face dewy and smooth. Her smile reflected da vinci porcelain veneers that even Mitch couldn't rival. Ruminating on this latest statistic, Alice and Leslie dabbed a few drops of olive oil on their own cheeks.

Talk then moved from Botox to Barney's.

"I need some new thongs," Alice said. "Charlie keeps ripping them off me."

More giggles and a tiramisu "for the table" later, and we were hitting the stores for underwear. At Barney's, as I watched the ladies go at it, I took notes in my scribble book for my next column.

"Aren't *you* going to 'do' a thong, too, Coco?" Lynn asked.

"I already ate mine," I said.

The Seaport Gazette

THE BOTTOM LINE

Underwear is serious business. I never knew quite how much until I recently paid a visit to a local and rather posh lingerie shop to purchase what, under normal circumstances, I wouldn't be caught dead buying: a thong. A thong, as all women know, is a minuscule piece of material the size of a large Band-Aid that is supposed to give one a clean, sleek look and remove all signs of a V.P.L. (Visible Panty Line).

While I have never given much thought to my V.P.L., I was instructed by a saleswoman at Ann Taylor, after purchasing a pair of white linen pants, that I needed a politically correct undergarment to go along with them.

"Honey," she said, with an ever-so-slight Southern drawl, "unless you wear proper drawers, everyone will know you're wearing panties."

"I am wearing panties," I said.

"That's supposed to be your little secret. Don't you know that the no-panty look is what you should be aiming for here?"

I was enlightened.

"Sweetie," she continued, "go get yourself a thong and you'll never leave home without it."

I zipped over to the lingerie shop, where a bevy of beauties who know underwear the way my husband knows sports couldn't wait to get their hands on my bottom and ply me with an assortment of thongs that guaranteed that no more V.P.L.s would invade my life again.

"Have you ever worn a thong before?" the salesgirl, Cindy, inquired.

"Frankly, I'm not the thong type," I admitted.

"You will be after you leave here," she said. She planted me in a dressing room while she went to select a few choice thongs. She returned moments later, carrying with her a handful of what I thought were handkerchiefs.

"Here," she said, "slip these on over a panty liner from the box and you'll see the difference between these and ordinary panties. A favorite among the ladies is our thong called the Hanky Panky." She held up a white piece of lace and handed it over.

I closed the door, fearing that at any moment she might return and catch me in the throes of this despicable act. Following her instructions exactly, I positioned a hygienically sealed liner in place as I held my knees together, securing it so it wouldn't go askew. Juggling the liner in conjunction with the thong was an act so intricate and gymnastic, I was sure I could be hired as a performer in the Big Apple Circus. The only problem was, I wasn't sure which was the front and which was the back. I called after Cindy, who was lurking outside the room.

"Sorry," I said, "but does this little thingy actually have an instruction manual?"

"It's easy," she said, barging in and holding up the thong. "Simply place the sliver of material in the back."

"The back of what?"

"Your buttocks," she said.

"But it won't cover my buttocks."

"That's the idea. That way no one will ever know you have anything on. You'll exude nakedness."

"Is that a good thing?"

"It is," she said, "if you're wearing see-through clothes. A fatal fashion flaw is a V.P.L."

I was becoming savvier by the moment.

"I can stay in here and observe if you'd like," she said.

"No thanks," I said, banishing her from the room. "I prefer doing underwear alone."

I stood there for ten minutes before I started to get the hang of it. I needed something like a Global Positioning System, designed for intimate apparel. Once the thong was in place, I felt an odd sensation, as though my body had swallowed a foreign object. Was there a Heimlich maneuver for this sort of dilemma, I wondered, as I envisioned the EMS crew bolting into my dressing room.

"Hey Joe, it's another one of those thong jobs."

"Yeah Mike, seems this one is in real deep."

My nightmare vanished when Cindy returned.

"Having any luck?" she asked, as I gave one hearty pull. I heard something pop and prayed I hadn't removed a major part of my anatomy along with the thong.

"I was hoping for less traumatic underwear," I said.

"You'll get the hang of it," Cindy assured me. "Buy this pair and go home and practice. By the end of the week, you won't be wearing anything else. And," she continued, "I'm ordering you a few more in nude to wear under your extra-extra-sheer garments. They've presently flown out of the store and we need to restock. I'll call you when they come in."

Not wanting to argue, I paid the fourteen bucks, went home, and tossed the thong in back of my dresser drawers.

A week later, my husband said that while I was out, he had received a strange phone call from a woman telling me that my Nude Hanky Pankies had arrived.

"What did that woman mean?" he asked. "Is she promoting porn? And, what's a Hanky Panky?"

"A thong," I said.

"A rubber flip-flop beach shoe?"

"Underwear," I said. "To erase my V.P.L."

"What's a V.P.L.?" he asked, somewhat startled.

"A girl thing," I told him.

After an hour of trying on thongs of various colors and fabrics, we moved on to makeup, where we spent another half hour discussing the merits of one cream foundation over another. La Prairie won out over Chanel. After Barney's, we crossed over to Bergdorf's for some more R&R. These women didn't just shop. They had consultations. Each pair of Manolo Blahniks, Christian Louboutins, and Jimmy Choos was scrutinized with care. For them, a pair of shoes was a bonding experience. When we got to the swimsuit department, however, it got a bit hairy.

We hit the dressing rooms with our little "Band-Aids" masquerading as bikinis. We began trying them on, alternating with a series of sighs and groans emanating from each cubicle. Occasionally, one of us would prance out and ask for an opinion. Lynn was the first to appear in one that covered only her bare essentials.

"So, whatdayathink?" She turned full circle to give us a complete view of her perfectly toned body.

Whatdawethink? Was she kidding? At forty-eight, not an ounce of fat, not a drop of cellulite, not a loose muscle adorned her frame. Her breasts were high, her tummy flat, her hips, though undulating, were in perfect proportion to the rest of her. Her Brazilian butt lift dazzled the eye with just a hint of cheek sneaking out from under the bikini bottom. Her waist was no more than twenty inches and her legs went on forever, her pair of $1,000 Alessandro Dell'Acqua heels enhancing them even more.

Éclaire was no slouch either, having been chiseled to perfection by Harry's master hands. Her body molded perfectly to a Laura Urbinati bikini. The array of swimsuits was designed with these women in mind. Alice took to a floral bikini and Leslie found a leopard skin in actual velvet that made her resemble a jungle beast. She paraded in front of the three-way mirror, letting out a little roar.

As for me, I managed to bring life to a one-piece black swimsuit that had conservative written all over it.

"For God's sake, Coco," Éclaire admonished. "You have a great body. One-piece suits are so our mothers."

I slipped my feet into the Delman wedgies I had purchased only moments before and had to admit, I looked hot. The shoes created the total look, and I decided if I kept them on at all times, the entire package could work beautifully.

Our retail therapy completed, except for a pit stop at Fendi for a little pouch that Éclaire couldn't resist, we parted company, planning to meet again at the Troutmans' house in the Hamptons in only a few weeks.

After a day of shopping with Éclaire and the girls, momentary pangs of guilt invaded my thoughts. On the one hand, I was breezing through the day acting as "one of the girls," while every chance I could, I was bedding down with Harry. The price, I told myself, was that I would ultimately get caught. Finkelman had been trying for days to get me to see this. By 5:00, our shopping spree complete, I walked away, not only with shoes and swimsuit, but a large dose of Jewish guilt that my mother had spent a lifetime trying to cultivate.

33

"A gourmet is just a glutton with brains."
—Philip W. Haberman, Jr.

Golf Is a Four-Letter Word

May 30. Memorial Day, and there we all were, once again, stretched out on chaise longues on Éclaire's and Harry's palatial patio, overlooking the ocean: Alice and Charlie, Leslie and Tom, and Parker and me. Lynn, back in California, unfortunately could not join us. We couldn't have asked for better weather. Decked out in our new swimsuit attire, we slapped sunblock over our arms and legs, sipping pineapple margaritas freshly prepared by Harry.

"Here you go, ladies," he said, adding a touch of frivolity to the drinks with slices of pineapple and kiwi. "One of these and all your troubles will melt away."

If only, I thought.

Éclaire, bouncing about in a green and white striped caftan and looking somewhat like a flapping awning, carried lunch out to the poolside table. "I'll have one of those drinky-poos, too, darling," she cooed.

"Of course you will," Harry said. "Éclaire has been slaving away in the kitchen all morning creating one of her luncheon masterpieces."

Alice shot me a look that had "Yeah, right!" written all over it.

It couldn't have been a more idyllic setting: the eight of us chatting away under the afternoon sun, sharing stories, and laughing among ourselves.

"It's a tough life, but somebody's got to do it," Parker said.

"You'd better relax now, guys," Harry said, "because tomorrow I'm going to whip the pants off all of you."

Knowing that Parker, Tom, and Charlie were all avid golfers, Harry had arranged for a 7 A.M. tee time at the Maidstone Golf Club, where he was a member.

"I've been touting the Maidstone for years," Parker said. "My own country clubs can't even hold a candle to this golf course."

"In that case," Harry said, "it will be early to bed tonight for me, so I can be up and at 'em at the crack of dawn."

"Yes," Éclaire agreed. "We're all rather pooped. Harry and I made dinner reservations at Della Femina for seven thirty. Then, beddie-bye for me, as well."

Harry shot me a look. Beddie-bye for Éclaire meant playtime for Harry.

After a lunch of Éclaire's Caesar salad and spinach quiches and fresh fruit from Citarella's, we basked like lazy animals by the pool, catching up on our favorite books. A weekend in the Hamptons was the perfect antidote for frazzled nerves and the internal combustion that Jacques Cuze's letters had wrought.

Around 5:30, I excused myself to retire to our guest room for a short nap and shower before dinner. Éclaire had escorted Parker over to the stone wall at the far end of the property where they sat, wineglasses in hand, watching the ocean whip up frothy waves as a late afternoon breeze came up. The rest of the gang had strolled down the winding path toward the rose gardens, leaving Harry to tend to drinks and hors d'oeuvres. Once everyone was safely out of the house, Harry abandoned his chores. He climbed the stairs to my room and knocked gently on the door. Hearing no response, he turned the knob and walked inside.

"Am I disturbing you?" he asked.

"All that rest and relaxation wore me out," I said. "I was just trying to catch a few winks, but I haven't been too successful."

I was stretched out on the chintz comforter in only my silk bathrobe. Harry walked over and sat down on the bed. As he leaned over to kiss me, his hand undid the sash.

He began nibbling my ear, working his way down, his hands and mouth probing inside my robe.

"What a tasty morsel," he hummed.

I had now morphed into an hors d'oeuvre, more edible to Harry than even the spanakopita that were nestled in the oven, becoming as overheated as we were. If not for the sound of Éclaire and Parker returning to the house, Harry would have "eaten me alive," his last words to me before Éclaire shouted from downstairs, "Yoo-hoo, anybody home?"

As quickly as Harry had appeared, he suddenly vanished, always on call for Éclaire's sudden appearance.

The rest of the weekend sped by with golf games, tennis, lunches, and dinners interspersed by brief encounters with Harry whenever an opportunity presented itself: a grope in the garden, legs nudging legs beneath tables, and on one star-infested evening while the others surrounded the piano, shouting out their show tune requests to Leslie whose voice lilted out to the patio, Harry and I grabbed a moment in the moonlight. Anyone observing us would see four happy couples enjoying life, impervious to the layer of doom that lay beneath the exterior of frivolity. And then, before we knew it, the weekend was over and Parker and I were in the car and back on the road heading back to Seaport.

~

The first Saturday in June, Parker joined his cronies on the golf course. The early morning sun cast a hazy glow on the green. It was one of those perfect days when all seemed right with the world. Parker was decked out in his Maidstone Golf Club golf shirt, a gift from Harry, and with a seven handicap, he was counting on his expertise, mixed with an ounce of luck, to shoot even par. He pulled out his driver and smacked the ball into submission, landing it within an easy wedge of the first hole. His game was going perfectly until the fifth, a long par three over the duck pond. Parker took an iron out of his bag and just as he swung, another blast of wind circled the course and Parker's ball fell short, landing in the water.

"Wouldn't you know it?" Parker slapped his leg while the guys snickered. "You can't mess with Mother Nature. She's gonna do what she's gonna do and she's obviously playing dirty today."

He grabbed his ball retriever from his bag and lifting it out, he stopped dead in his tracks. Attached to the metal claw of the retriever was a bright red thong.

Parker held the thong between his fingers as though he had hooked a moray eel. "What the hell is this?" he asked aloud.

"Way to go, Harding." Dan Atwood slapped him a high five.

"Is there something you want to tell us, old man?" Pete Gillespie guffawed.

"We never knew you had it in you," Steve Campbell, the worst golfer in the group, applauded. "That wife of yours certainly has a sense of humor."

"Yeah," Parker played along, "Coco will stop at nothing to get me off the golf course."

But, in his heart, Parker knew that I had nothing to do with this mischievous little prank.

They resumed, with Parker's game taking a nosedive for the rest of the morning. By noon, having reached the eighteenth hole, he shot an embarrassing ninety-three.

"Guess your heart's just not in it, today," Pete continued to bait Parker.

"Not when he has more important business at hand," Steve winked. "Let's see that thing, again."

"It's not a thing, it's a thong," Dan said. "All the gals are doing them."

"Doing what?" Pete asked. "What the hell do you do with one of these except maybe blow your nose?"

It was the perfect exit line. Parker said his good-byes and

drove off the green in his golf cart and over to the clubhouse to drown his misery in a couple of Bloody Marys. Completely ignoring the thong incident was impossible. Somebody was obviously going for the jugular.

Just as I turned into the driveway of Seaport Country Club to join Parker for lunch, my cell phone rang. I picked up and a deep, muffled voice came on.

"*Don't risk it,*" the caller said and then hung up.

I immediately redialed the number. It rang continuously.

I walked inside the club and over to the dining room.

"Darling." Parker rose in acknowledgment of my arrival.

"Shit!" came my response.

"I'm glad to see you, too."

"I just received an ominous phone call. And how is your day?"

"I played like your mother."

"That bad, huh?"

"So, what was the call about?" Parker inquired.

"*Don't risk it,*" I said.

"Don't risk what?"

"I don't know. That's all he said. I tried calling back, but the number was obviously coming from a pay phone. This guy is no dummy."

"How do you know it was a guy?"

"The voice was deep and throaty."

"So was Marlene Dietrich's."

"I don't think it was Marlene."

"What I'm saying is, you can't be too sure these days."

~

A Scone's Throw was bustling on Sunday morning when I met Annie for breakfast.

"That's all he said, don't risk it?"

"Those three little words, and don't ask me why I think it's a guy."

"Maybe it's Bridgette in drag," Annie said.

"Bridgette, now there's a thought."

"I wouldn't put it past her. I don't trust that woman."

"Neither do I, but do you really think she's making threatening phone calls?"

"Are you kidding? The woman would stop at nothing to break up your relationship with Harry."

"So she really does know about us?"

"Hello?"

"Maybe I can get Mickey G. to whack him."

"Who's Mickey G.?"

"Éclaire's friend, Lynn, has a Mafioso boyfriend."

"Sounds promising," Annie said.

"Don't get all excited," I said. "It's just a fantasy."

34

"A raisin is a worried-looking grape."
—Anonymous

Up Close and Personal

Parker later told me that he decided to keep the thong incident "under wraps" and let it be his dirty little secret, adhering to the philosophy: When life gets tough, the tough go into denial. Everything was fine for a couple of weeks; no phone calls, no threatening letters from Jacques Cuze, and then it all came to an abrupt halt.

On Tuesday afternoon, Hedy was preparing our clothes for delivery to the dry cleaners. Sweaters, trousers, suits, and skirts lay in a pile on a bedroom chair. She reached in to check each pocket, retrieving randomly deposited items: theater ticket stubs, throat lozenges, scraps of paper with phone numbers, two Viagra in Parker's slacks, and a shirt button in mine. Suddenly, she stopped short. There in Parker's windbreaker pocket was the red thong. Hedy had never made eye contact with a thong before and was more surprised than shocked. She waved it in the air, inspecting it, wondering how it was anatomically possible for any woman to squeeze her rump into one of these. She walked over to the mirror, lifted her uniform and placed the thong against her own abundant, thickly veined thighs. Just for a moment, she allowed her imagination to run amok, picturing herself in one of these. Then, embarrassed by the thought, she collected herself and crumpled it into a tiny red ball, shoving it into her own pocket. She went about her chores, checking the thong periodically. Two questions flooded her mind:

1. Whose thong was it?
2. How did it get into Parker's pocket?

Hedy tried recalling if she had ever seen a red thong in my underwear collection. A mental inventory of my intimate apparel turned up nothing. She rummaged through my drawers, but no, my panties and bras were all in earth tones or muted shades of pastels, with the exception of a purple lace panty that I had bought when I was feeling particularly frisky. But red was not my personal fashion statement, as far as Hedy knew.

That same evening, Parker found himself ruminating over the thong. His windbreaker now lay in a bin at the dry cleaners. In a fitful, sleepy stupor, he awakened at 4 A.M., panicky that Delores at the cleaners would find it and call the house. He would phone Delores the first thing in the morning and ask her if any miscellaneous items had turned up.

"No, Mr. Harding," Delores assured him, the next day, "we go through each and every pocket before cleaning the clothes. What exactly are you looking for?"

"My red tie. I may have left it in my windbreaker."

Delores told Parker to hold while she checked the bundle of clothes that had arrived yesterday.

"No red ties today, Mr. Harding, but I'll keep an eye out and call you if it turns up."

"Thanks, Delores. I probably just misplaced it."

Try as he might, Parker could not put the missing thong caper to rest. He believed with the firm conviction of a skeptical man that it had not simply vanished, but was removed by a suspicious party. He decided to play dumb, asking no questions. But periodically, when I was unusually quiet or introspective, he asked me if anything was wrong.

"Why do you ask?" I questioned.

"You seem subdued."

"I'm fine. I've been working late."

The subject was dropped and buried . . . at least for now.

~

The mystery of the missing thong kept Parker searching for answers. Meanwhile, Hedy had hidden it inside the overnight bag that she kept on the top shelf in her room. What she would do with it, she didn't know, but her interest was piqued. She was waiting for someone, anyone, to drop a hint. If Parker so much as inquired as to the thong's whereabouts, she would hand it over and await an explanation. But Parker remained mute, knowing if he even dared to confront Hedy, asking if she had happened to see some missing underwear, all hell could break loose. So it became one of those elephants in the living room that both Hedy and Parker refused to acknowledge.

Occasionally, Parker would tiptoe around the house, rummaging through drawers, peering inside boxes, checking the washer and dryer periodically to see if, as if by magic, the red thong would materialize. It didn't.

~

There comes a time when the obvious can no longer be ignored, when the tension is so thick and distracting, the consequences so potentially grave, that all parties in question are sufficiently, to quote Eliza, "freaked out."

I had been seeing Finkelman weekly, each session becoming a breeding ground not for self-analysis, but for sleuthing.

"I'll admit I've been a bit jittery lately," I said.

"As well you should," Finkelman acknowledged. "But is it enough to make you stop seeing Harry?"

"I'm not that scared," I said. "Anyway, I'm in too deep to stop."

"Someone may very well stop you, Coco," Finkelman added, adjusting his latest bow tie atrocity.

"Why do you have such a vested interest?"

"I'm your psychiatrist. It's my job to be vested. Your mental health is of major concern."

"My mental health is just fine," I said, sitting back and recalling last night's sexual escapade with Harry, who had given me record-breaking orgasms in the space of only two hours. I couldn't quite bring myself to share this piece of news with Finkelman, however, for fear he might become so excited, he would either have to leave the room to masturbate, or blurt out a series of "I sees," neither of which I could handle. Then Finkelman got serious.

"I have reason to believe that Jacques Cuze speaks the truth," he said. "You can no longer assume you are not in danger. He might have tangible evidence of impropriety in the making. What I am saying, Coco, is that the ending to this macabre tale can be grim."

But what was really grim was the thought that Harry and I would permanently cease to fuck.

35

"Giving chocolate to others is an intimate form of communication, a sharing of deep, dark secrets."
—Milton Zelman, publisher of *Chocolate News*

Sex by Chocolate

Breaking the somber mood, on my way home I got a call from Annie on my cell. She sounded euphoric.

"What's up, doll?" I asked.

"My life just took a turn for the better."

"You and Saul finally had sex?"

"Honey, Saul and I haven't had sex for so long, my KY jelly has expired. No, this is even more exciting: Dr. Andrew Weil is my latest hero. I was rummaging through his book, *The Healthy Kitchen,* only to discover that he advocates chocolate."

"Sometimes the gods do look down on us," I said.

"Chocolate is a portable, highly concentrated source of nutrition. So I went out and bought an entire box of Godiva. It's all dark chocolate, which has lower amounts of sugar, and most of the saturated fat comes in the form of stearic acid, which is converted in the body to oleic acid—the main fatty acid in heart-healthy olive oil."

"Maybe we can start rubbing chocolate on our faces, too," I said.

"Plus," Annie said, biting into a chocolate liqueur, "it's loaded with antioxidants. If old Andy Weil can eat an ounce or two every couple of days, why can't I?"

"You're a regular walking encyclopedia of information," I said.

"I haven't been this excited in days. Health by Chocolate is my new mantra."

"Go for it, and save a piece for me."

"You've got Harry," Annie said.

Annie had said a mouthful. Talk about chocolate. The following Thursday, Harry and I gave new meaning to the word bittersweet. We were lunching at La Vineria, a shoe-box-size restaurant that Zagat had described as "so small you can sit at more than one table simultaneously." I told him about Annie's new affair with chocolate.

"And, to add to that," I whispered as we knocked knees under the table, "I have a tote bag filled with the elixir of the gods: chocolate mousse straight from the chocolate capital of New York City."

I had made the tour of several bakeries featuring their own special brand of mousse: white mousse, chocolate mousse, chocolate addiction mousse, chocolate decadence mousse, raspberry mousse, death by mousse, and, if that weren't enough, a black-and-white decaffeinated mousse in case we needed to come down from our chocolate high.

For three chocolate-filled hours, we doused our bodies in chocolate mousse mania. We smeared, we licked, we anointed, we savored. I had even included, as part of our sexual foreplay, chocolate-covered strawberries so no orifice would be denied. By 3:00, Harry and I were drowning in chocolate debauchery that would have left Lady Godiva herself exquisitely exhausted.

While Harry and I were becoming human bonbons, another kind of excitement was brewing back in Seaport. In the midst of changing the bed linens, Hedy suddenly doubled over in pain and grabbed her right side. She let out a refined but audible scream, but to no avail. She was alone in the house. Releasing her hand, she felt another jolt of agonizing pain and began to perspire and become slightly nauseated. Frantic, but with her wits intact, she picked up the phone on the night table and rang up the Seaport Taxi Service.

"I need a taxi immediately," she burst forth, with a modicum of composure, ever the perfect lady.

"It'll be about twenty minutes," the dispatcher said. "Where ya headed?"

"It's an emergency," Hedy said. "I'm in severe pain and need to get to the hospital." She continued pressing her fingers deeply into her right side, between her groin and abdomen.

"Lady, you don't want a taxi. You want an ambulance. Call nine-one-one."

"No, ambulances are much too intimidating, I insist that a taxi be sent over. I'll wait by the front door until one arrives."

"Lady, I'm tellin' you. Call nine-one-one."

"I refuse," she said. She presented the dispatcher with her name and address and, bent over in pain, she made it to the foyer, where she sat on the wicker bench until a taxi arrived.

Ten minutes later, a cab pulled up in our driveway. A disgruntled cabbie got out and rang the bell. Hedy emerged looking a bit piqued and still holding her side.

"What took you so long?" she grumbled.

"Lady, three years ago, I practically had to deliver a baby. I hope nothing funny is going on here."

"Young man," Hedy said, "I am not pregnant. I am merely suffering from acute appendicitis. Now, take me to Seaport Hospital and don't stop for red lights."

When she arrived at the emergency room, by mere coincidence, Bob Satin, chief of surgery, was checking the charts. Hedy walked up to the main desk, gave the receptionist her vital statistics, and when asked for her address, said that she was employed by the Hardings. Dr. Satin looked up.

"Parker and Coco Harding?" he asked.

Hedy nodded.

"Parker and I go back to when we were both pups," he smiled. "I knocked him dead on the golf course a few weeks ago."

He then personally escorted Hedy into an examining room and had her in the OR within the hour, prepped and ready. By the time I was back in Seaport, Hedy was out of surgery and there was a message on my cell asking me to deliver some of her personal belongings to the hospital. Parker was away for the day at the LI club and wouldn't be back until dinnertime.

"I'll be unreachable all afternoon," he had told me. "I'm meeting with the big boys to discuss wiring the club for Internet access. My phone will be turned off." For entirely different reasons, my cell had been off all afternoon, too.

"Mrs. Harding," Hedy's message said, "I have been trying to reach you. I'm at Seaport Hospital. Please deliver a few articles of clothing, my nightgown, and my bathrobe. And you can add my Polident and my bottle of cologne. Thank you."

I went into Hedy's room and pulled her suitcase from the shelf. Opening it, I began placing her undergarments into the bag when suddenly, crumpled in the corner, there was the red thong. I paused and stared. Hedy? A red thong? The combination didn't seem plausible. Collecting her sundries and a few more items, and leaving the thong in its place, I snapped the suitcase shut and headed over to Seaport Hospital. On the way over, I called Annie.

"Wait till you hear this," I said. "Hedy wears thongs."

"Looks can be deceiving," Annie said. "I always suspected that underneath that German exterior lurked a fräulein oozing passion."

"I can't even imagine our Hedy in sexy lingerie. I've never even seen her with a man, except our gardener, Emilio."

"Aha! Who knows what evil lurks within the flower beds?"

"It's highly unlikely. Hedy has never been married and is probably still a virgin."

"Nothing shocks me," Annie said. "Gotta run. Saul and I are catching dinner and a flick. Auf Wiedersehen."

Hedy was just out of recovery and in her room by 8:00. I had finally gotten hold of Parker and told him to meet me at the hospital on his way home. Hedy, slightly incoherent from the anesthesia, mumbled a few words and smiled when she saw me.

"Dr. Satin took out my appendix," she said. "He's a very nice man."

"Aren't you lucky?" I said. "It takes weeks to even get an appointment with Bob Satin. I brought your bag and a few magazines."

"Did you throw in my bunny slippers?"

"Of course."

"Good, these disposable hospital booties are for the birds."

I had wanted to say that I had included her red thong, too, but kept quiet. Once Hedy was settled with a nurse at her side, Parker and I left, promising to return in the morning.

"Can you keep a secret?" I asked Parker over drinks at the club.

"Is it worth keeping?" he asked.

"You decide. Here it comes: Hedy is a femme fatale. I found a red thong in her suitcase."

Parker stiffened slightly, downing his bourbon and water in one swallow.

"Those German broads are hot babes," Parker said. "Look at Eva Braun: She had Hitler eating out of her hands."

"Eva Braun didn't wear red thongs," I said.

PART FOUR

Entrée

(Climax)

36

"Hungry men have no respect for law,
authority, or human life."
—Marcus Garvey

A Bad Horoscope Day

The cast of characters was all in place and holding their own except for Finkelman, who had grown more paranoid by the week. It had gotten so bad he had taken to popping Zoloft on a daily basis to take the edge off our sessions. Thankfully, no one had received any more letters or calls. We were grateful for small blessings.

Parker, seemingly more nervous than usual, was spending more time between his two clubs, often bringing Bridgette along with him. Her new boobs had snagged a man from Watch Hill, Rhode Island, whom she had met on a sailing weekend with her old college roommate and husband. Seems that the hubby's best friend, Willie Fitz, a retired Brazilian shoe tycoon, came along for a sail, took one look at Bridgette's new knockers, and practically proposed marriage on the spot. With that in mind, Bridgette announced to Parker over brunch that her sex life had suddenly blossomed and that she was now considering a vaginoplasty to go along with the rest of the package.

"I wonder if Dr. Harry would be interested in doing my wa-wa?" she posed.

"For Christ's sake, Bridgey," Parker said, "not in the middle of my eggs Benedict. Can't you keep those thoughts to yourself?"

Bridgette picked up her mimosa. "Bottoms up!" she said.

Back at the ranch in Seaport, the good news was that Parker was having more and more trouble getting it up and was losing his sexual edge. This meant I had a breather in between Parker and my escapades with Harry. God knows, Parker tried and felt guilty when I couldn't raise an orgasm or he, his penis.

"I'm letting you down," Parker said.

"I'm fine."

"A woman like you deserves to have regular orgasms."

"I can always masturbate."

(A sudden pause.)

"Do you?"

"On occasion."

And then Parker hit me with the sexiest question he had ever asked:

"Can I watch?"

"Would that help you to get an erection?"

"I don't know, but it's a good place to start."

And right there in our bedroom as the late afternoon sun came streaming through the windows, I gave myself a state-of-the-art, full-blown, lollapalooza orgasm and Parker and I came separately/together, while he let out with one loud, hard, hand-on-dick Whammo!

The following week, after Harry had left for a medical convention in Arizona, Éclaire phoned to say she was having a bad horoscope day and needed a massage badly.

"Let's do lunch and then we'll head over to Bliss. I need to have the bitch in me tamed."

We met at Fred's in Barney's and then taxied over to Bliss where, for the next two hours, the savage beasts in each of us were reduced to purring cats. Standing there in our underwear, Éclaire in a lemon yellow bra and thong, I brought up Hedy.

"My housekeeper, Hedy, is also into thongs," I said. "I found a pair in her suitcase when I was packing it up for the hospital. I think she's leading a secret life."

"I have these thongs in every color," Éclaire said, "except, come to think of it, I'm missing my red one."

I dismissed the comment as quickly as it came, only to have it resurface as I was lying in bed that night. In the first blush of morning light, it came back to haunt me. Don't be ridiculous, I told myself, what's the big deal? Hedy's red thong and Éclaire's couldn't possibly be one and the same. Still, the idea amused me. I tossed it off as a minor piece of trivia that bore no impact on my life in any way.

Yet that same week at exactly 1:55, I was en route to a dental cleaning with a protégé of Mitch's who could shine teeth whiter than a strand of Mikimoto pearls. The taxi stopped for a light at 82nd and Central Park West directly in front of Finkelman's building. Coming through the front door was none other than Alice. I resisted the urge to roll down the window and shout hello. Instead, I watched as she retrieved her cell phone from her bag and headed toward the Museum of Natural History.

"Now that's what I call a real coincidence," I told Annie later.

"And that's what I call 'something smells fishy,'" she said.

The next day another letter was waiting at home:

To Whom It May Concern:

When the cat's away, crime does not pay.

Jacques Cuze

I e-mailed Harry about it, but no reply. In fact, there had been no contact the entire time he was away. It was only when he was back in town that my Blackberry suddenly kicked in.

Tell me you still love me.
SkinDeep

It stopped me cold. Two could play the same game.

Out of sight, out of mind.
CocoPuff

And so it went.

Absence makes the heart grow fonder. Allow me to show you.
SkinDeep

When?
CocoPuff

Dinner on Thursday. Café Gray.
SkinDeep

Sounds like an offer no sane woman could ever refuse.
CocoPuff

The view from the Time Warner building at night is dazzling and Chef Gary Kunz at Café Gray had prepared a salad mélange of marinated vegetables followed by lamb chops with a carrot-curry emulsion for me and a salted cod laced with lime and port, for which Harry sent accolades back to the kitchen. It was Thursday night. Harry looked particularly sharp in a dark blue pinstripe suit and striped silver-and-gold tie attached to the collar of a baby blue shirt. The color made his eyes pop. Harry had recently attended another Chaîne dinner and as the story went, I was doing an article on spec for *Gourmet* magazine. Éclaire was dining with Muffin and Parker was playing bridge. Excitement was in the air when Harry announced that he was going to be away all next week at a medical convention at the Arizona Biltmore Hotel and Spa. I squealed with delight at the possibility of joining him, but he never asked.

"No rest for the weary this time, darling. It will be one medical seminar after another."

"I can work on my tan line," I said. "And it so happens that Parker will be away all next week. He's been invited to participate in the Weston Hills golf tournament in Florida."

"I'd be too distracted," Harry said. "Even Éclaire wanted to join me, especially after hearing about the Biltmore's famous spa attractions."

My mood dissipated when Harry handed me a small box tied with a shocking pink ribbon. Inside was a diamond-studded star on a silver chain with small rubies adorning each of the six points. The card read: *"My heart, my love, my shining star. Forever, Harry."* He attached the pendant around my neck. It twinkled as brightly as the lights that lined the apartment buildings along Central Park South. My dismay over not being able to join Harry in Arizona slowly fell away as we enjoyed each delicious course, including a chocolate crumble with raspberries and oatmeal and a caramelized pear surrounded by olives, pistachios, and fromage blanc sorbet. Harry introduced a forkful into my mouth which I reluctantly tasted and then swooned over.

"Ply me with gifts and fine cuisine," I said, "and you have me eating out of your hands."

"And all stops in between," he grinned.

Harry had reserved a room at the Ritz Carlton on Central Park South where, after dinner at Café Gray, we screwed our brains out for several hours.

"Does that tell you anything?" Harry asked.

"You should go away more often," I said. "But how did you manage to get a tan when you were in seclusion all week?"

"I grabbed a few rays in between the Otoplasty and the Blepharoplasty seminars."

"Ooh, you know how I love it when you speak a foreign tongue, which reminds me: Your favorite client, Bridgette, is planning to see you for a little tightening."

"What now?"

"Hold on to the sheets . . . she's met the love of her life and she wants a rejuvenated vagina."

"There's only one pussy I care about rejuvenating," Harry said.

With that, he pulled me on top of him. My star pendant flying across my breasts, I mounted him. We writhed together in one glorious, vocal, star-spangled, bombs bursting in air, orgasmic eruption.

~

I didn't stay in the city that night and was home by eleven. Parker had left a note: *Something's come up at the club. Don't wait up. See you before the cock crows. Parker.*

Parker was spending more and more nights out. Since the club was undergoing renovation, all his attention was going toward a new spa he was putting in.

"I'll be the first one to try it out," Éclaire had said when the four of us last dined together.

"I've designed it with you in mind," Parker cajoled. "I'm hiring the best massage therapists and estheticians."

"Make sure you include the mud baths," Harry said. "My wife comes alive when submerged in mud."

"She's a regular farm girl," Parker said and laughter filled the air.

When Parker finally arrived home at 2 A.M., he joined me in bed, smelling faintly spicy: a combination of pipe tobacco and a slightly familiar perfume scent.

"You smell sweet," I said.

"It's my new aftershave. Go back to sleep."

"Smells like Chanel Number Five," I said sleepily.

The following Thursday's session with Finkelman bordered on the absurd. His patent leather oxfords were shinier than ever as he paced around the office, flicking particles of dust from his suit jacket. His lips were pursed and his beady eyes darted around the room. On the table next to his chair was a copy of Agatha Christie's *Ten Little Indians,* which he quickly concealed beneath his handkerchief. He then sat back in his chair, emitting a few nervous coughs.

"Coco, indulge me for a moment. Of course, I'll add a few extra minutes to our session. But, I need to wax eloquent."

"As eloquently waxed as your mustache?" I wanted to ask, which was caked so heavily today that I thought if he sneezed, it might actually break.

"The greatest tool for crime solving is the mind. One needs no other clues. Did you know that, Coco?"

I played along.

"It is a profound belief that if you can induce a person to talk to you for long enough, on any subject whatever, sooner or later they will give themselves away. Do you know whom I am quoting, Coco? None other than the great Hercule Poirot himself. And I might add that Poirot appeared in thirty-three of Agatha Christie's novels and sixty-five of her detective stories."

Finkelman's alter ego, Poirot, was in rare form today.

"Have you read any of these books?"

"I'm not a fan of the mystery genre," I said.

"I see. The reason I tell you this is that while I am not a sleuth, per se, I am intrigued and motivated by those little gray cells, the same as Hercule Poirot. So, tell me, Coco, what do you make of Jacques Cuze's last message?"

"All rubbish," I said.

"Perhaps not. It piqued my interest, Coco. *When the cat's away, crime does not pay.* Think about it. What clue is Jacques Cuze sending us?"

"*I* haven't a clue."

"Allow me to tweak *your* little gray cells. Think for a moment: To which cat is he referring?"

At $200 a pop, I wasn't interested in indulging Finkelman's fantasy.

"Why are we doing this?"

"You refuse to see the error of your ways, Coco, that's why. Perhaps, by addressing Jacques Cuze's double entendres, we can piece together the crime."

"What crime?"

"The inevitable crime that is about to happen. If I've done nothing else this session, I have brought to the surface the bizarre turn of events that are already in motion."

"Do you know something I don't know?"

"I will say only this: None of us can afford to take any more chances. The suspects are in place and everyone has a motive."

"It's official," I told Annie. "Finkelman has gone bonkers. All he needed was the Belgian accent and he'd be Hercule Poirot reincarnated. That's all he talked about all during my session."

"I hope you charged *him* the two hundred bucks," Annie said.

37

"Hunger, like lust in action, is savage,
extreme, rude, cruel."
—Betty Fussell

Sleepless in Seaport

The next morning, a very anxious Éclaire phoned before 9:00 A.M.

"We need to talk," she said. "There's something I want to ask you."

Éclaire could put people on the defensive from her first hello.

"Are you all right?"

"I think so, I'm not sure. I could use a little help here."

"Of course," I said. "I'm working on deadline, but I can break for lunch. Would you consider meeting me in Connecticut?"

A slight pause.

"The shopping's great in Greenwich," I added, luring her in.

"Well, maybe that *could* work," she agreed. "I need to buy a few gifts."

Versailles on Greenwich Avenue is a perfect spot for a quiet and refined lady's lunch, neither of which qualities Éclaire was exhibiting when she walked in.

"You look peeved," I said.

"I need wine."

Drinking at lunch was not part of Éclaire's repertoire, nor was it a good sign, especially when used as mental fortification.

"What's up?" I asked, bypassing the small talk and getting to the heart of the matter.

"Let me ask you a question, Coco. What would you do if you discovered your husband was cheating on you?"

(Yes, a glass of wine was definitely in order.)

"Death immediately comes to mind," I said with an air of frivolity.

"I'm not joking."

"Who's joking?"

"What I am getting at, Coco"—Éclaire looked around and leaned in—"is that I have the most uncanny suspicion that Harry is having an affair."

"What makes you think so?" I felt my stomach jump.

"A hunch."

"Hunches can be dangerous."

"He was away last week at a medical convention."

"Really?" I said, feigning innocence.

"Yes, at the Biltmore Hotel and Spa in Phoenix."

"A nice spot."

"I've never cared much for those conventions," Éclaire said. "But I asked to tag along this time, mainly because the spa is divine."

"And?"

"And, Harry refused me on the spot. I told him I would lay low. I wouldn't get in his way, but he was adamant. No wives are coming, he said, this is strictly business all the way."

"Disappointing," I said, firsthand.

"There's more," she continued. "I phoned Harry's office yesterday to schedule an appointment for a friend of mine who is coming in from Texas in October and needs her eyes done. Sabrina, his bimbo receptionist, was on vacation and her cousin, Candy, Sabrina's even dumber clone equivalent, was filling in. I decided to go straight to Harry's head nurse, Krystle, who knows his schedule better than anyone.

"'Sorry, Mrs. Troutman,' Candy said. 'Did you forget that Krystle is with Dr. Troutman in Arizona?'

"I flinched," Éclaire said, "but tried to sound normal. Yes, of course, it completely slipped my mind, I told her. Then I hung up in a rage, the likes of which I have never known before."

Éclaire may have been enraged, but I was practically vibrating. It was one thing for Harry to be sleeping with his wife, but to be doing Nurse Krystle was intolerable. I could hardly contain my anger, but like Éclaire before me, I tried keeping my cool so as not to appear obvious.

"Now you can see why I am livid."

"I can't argue with that," I said, "but I'd guess it's strictly a business relationship."

"Stop defending Harry. This isn't the first time he and Krystle have been away together."

"How do you know?" My fury was raging out of control.

"Several years ago, before you knew us, Harry was away at his Chaîne event at The Breakers in Palm Beach, and who do you think joined him?"

"I'm all ears," I said.

"Two blond beauties."

"A ménage à trois?"

"I have it on the best authority. While he and the girls were making merry beneath the palm trees, an acquaintance of mine and the biggest gossip in Bronxville, Bernice Stillman, and her husband were vacationing at The Breakers. She spied Harry lunching on the veranda with two girls."

"How did she know for certain it was Harry?"

"Harry did her boobs several years ago. She and her husband were checking out that same day. As soon as she got home, she told me she had seen Harry with a couple of bombshells. I played along.

"'Oh, it must have been Harry's nurses,' I told her. 'They accompany Harry to lots of events.'

"'Not only that,' Bernice said. 'I caught them feeding hors d'oeuvres to Harry. Looked very intimate if you ask me.'

"'Who's asking?' I said."

(By this time, I was practically spitting fire, but said nothing for fear my voice would crack.)

"What should I do, Coco; confront him or play it cool?"

"Cut his balls off," I said with the firm conviction of a jilted woman. "The man is a cad through and through."

"Not to mention," Éclaire continued, "that we've all been getting those vile letters. What if Harry is the one in question?"

It was the first time I had ever even considered that Harry might be cheating with someone else. I had now reached my boiling point.

"Please, not a word about any of this. I need to figure it all out. Any suggestions?"

"Kill the bastard," I said.

The waitress appeared. We both ordered the salade niçoises. When they arrived at the table, I picked up a fork and stabbed a piece of grilled tuna so hard, I practically broke the plate.

"You need a plan," I told Éclaire. "Let me mull this over."

In the meantime, I would need to come up with my own version on how to deal with Harry-the-two-timing-rat-fink-low-life-slimeball-womanizing snake.

When in doubt, all roads lead to Annie. We were at lunch a few days later when I spilled the beans about Éclaire's suspicions.

Annie, the ever-rational woman of the world, had an immediate solution.

"I'd be happy to boil him in hot oil," she said.

"Even death is much too good for Harry," I said. "Slow torture is more what I had in mind."

"So, he's been schtupping the bodacious, blond, buxom, bimbo beauty. I didn't think he would actually stoop that low."

"The man obviously can't resist a good piece of ass when it's standing in front of him. I'll bet he and Krystle have been going at it for years."

"Lorena Bobbitt had the right idea," Annie said.

~

I decided to go cold turkey and have no contact with Harry. Instead, I retreated to the Berkshires to think, telling Parker I was working on a piece and needed to have some solitude.

Harry called hourly, but I wouldn't answer my cell. He left eighteen messages on my e-mail and my Blackberry bulged with mea culpas, asking if he had done something to turn me off. I continued to ignore him for the next five days.

~

In the meantime, back in Harry's office, Bridgette was coming out of anesthesia and was in recovery, having undergone what she had been threatening to do: an LVR (laser vaginal rejuvenation), a one-hour surgical procedure to enhance her sexual gratification.

Bridgette told Harry pre-op that she was multiorgasmic, and Harry retorted by promising her better muscle tone than she had ever had before.

"Overall optimum architectural integrity of the vagina is my first priority," Harry said.

Bridgette practically had an orgasm on the spot as he uttered those words.

"You're a 'cunning-linguist,'" Bridgette said, before drifting off to sleep. "Just remember: Willy Fitz is a connoisseur of life's most sensual pleasures . . . my vagina in particular. I want you to make me as tight as a triple martini lunch."

But a month later when Willy Fitz tried entering Bridgette, she was impenetrable.

The next day, Bridgette stormed into Harry's office.

"For Christ's sake, when I said tight, I didn't mean closed for business. Only after I used an entire tube of Astroglide did Willy Fitz even make a dent. And then, when I changed into a more comfortable sexual position, he accused me of fracturing his penis."

"I promise, your vagina will loosen up," Harry assured her. "It just needs to be broken in."

"It's not a goddamn pair of Manolo Blahniks," Bridgette screamed so loudly, the entire office could hear.

For once, I was on Bridgette's side. I was so furious at Harry that I jumped at any excuse to hate him. When she came for dinner and recounted this encounter to Parker and me, I actually applauded.

"Good for you," I said. "I'm glad you gave the bastard hell. He deserves it."

Bridgette was taken aback, not quite trusting my sudden leap into loyalty.

"Well, well, aren't we a couple of bitchy babes," she said, cunningly. "Frankly, Coco, I didn't think you had it in you to ever utter a bad word against Harry."

I stabbed my fork into a chubby brussels sprout, wishing it were Harry's eyeball instead.

All contact with Harry ceased and I busied myself with my writing, taking on more freelance work than I had in years. Every means of communication was closed off and every feeble attempt of Harry's to see me was unsuccessful. He finally resorted to calling Annie and asking what was wrong.

Annie, the ever-faithful friend, told him he was persona non grata and to go take a flying fuck. Then she slammed the phone down.

Back in Seaport after a month of sleepless nights, I decided that letting Harry off the hook so easily was much too good for him. He needed to suffer as I had and I wanted to make his life as miserable as possible. The truth was underneath it all, I missed him terribly . . . especially the sex. I sent him an e-mail:

We need to talk.
CocoPuff

He must have been checking his messages hourly.

I'm at your beck and call.
SkinDeep

Thursday. 6:00. Bemelmans Bar.
CocoPuff

I love you.
SkinDeep

Don't even go there.
CocoPuff

Harry was already on his second whiskey sour when I arrived at the Carlyle. I sat down, looking as frosty as the crushed ice in his glass, and ordered a white wine.

"I'm not staying and I won't mince words," I said. "I just want you to know that it's over."

I sounded like a character in a bad Grade B movie, but I didn't care. I pulled the star pendant out of my bag and slammed it down on the small cocktail table.

"Here, take it. It no longer means anything to me."

"Coco . . . darling." Harry reached out his hand toward me. I pulled mine away.

"It's one thing to be cheating on your wife," I said, "but fooling around behind *my* back is unforgivable."

"What are you talking about?"

"Oh, stop it. I know the truth."

"I'm confused."

"That's not how your sweet little wife told it."

"What *did* she tell you?"

"That you were at the Biltmore with none other than your bimbette, Krystle."

"Éclaire said that?"

"Yes, and that's not all. She knows from a reliable source that you and a couple of blond beauties seemed quite cozy a few years ago at the Breakers."

"Hold it right there, Coco," Harry said. "I have news for you. For your information, my wife doesn't know what the hell she's talking about."

"Shut up, Harry."

"I beg you to hear me out."

Harry looked so pathetic sitting there with a puppy dog look on his face that I felt my anger momentarily wane. I was also curious as hell.

"Okay, explain."

"This is not going to be easy and I am probably going to regret telling you this, but there is a lot you don't understand."

"Try me."

"Éclaire has been bedding down with someone, too."

"What?"

"Yes, and Coco, I wish I didn't have to tell you this, but the object of her affection is none other than Parker."

"You're crazy."

"I swear it."

I sat back, stunned. I reached for my water glass, not knowing whether to laugh or cry. Parker and Éclaire? How was that even possible? The limp and languid penis I had known was obviously standing at attention where Éclaire was concerned.

"How do you know all of this, and what does that have to do with you and Krystle?"

"Coco, Krystle was asked to come along to the Biltmore to take notes at the seminars. But we weren't alone. I had arranged for Krystle and her husband, Joe Kowalski, to join me. They hadn't had a real vacation in years and I thought a week at the Biltmore could work well for all of us and give Krystle and Joe a chance for a little holiday in between work."

"What about the Breakers, where you were seen doing some culinary cavorting?"

"My God." Harry sat back and laughed aloud. "A man isn't safe anywhere. Sorry to disappoint you, baby, but one of those two gals was the Chaîne director, Priscilla Griscomb, and her lesbian lover, Aurora. They've been an item for years. We were sampling the tasting menu and obviously somebody got the wrong idea. Coco, sweetheart, I swear to you, that I love and adore you, and while my wife thinks I am cheating, and she's right, the only one with whom I am involved in any guilty pleasures, is you."

Harry was throwing so much at me that I could hardly assimilate it. Questions filled my head.

"How do you know about Éclaire and Parker?"

"I've always suspected. Parker was flirting with Éclaire the minute he saw her. Don't you know that?"

"Frankly, I was too ga-ga over her husband to notice," I said.

"But that's not what clinched it. One afternoon, I received a call from a strange party—a man I didn't know. He never left his name, but warned me that my wife was involved with a man from Connecticut. Then, before I could question him further, he hung up. But it was enough to convince me that something was up, that my original suspicions were correct."

"My God," I said. "I can't believe it. This is pathological."

"Coco, please, listen carefully. You and I had already begun seeing each other and I figured, what the hell: It's a perfect situation. Let my wife have her fling and we can have ours."

"Why didn't you tell me?"

"What? And ruin all our fun? No way. This was one secret that was worth keeping to myself. That way, no one would ever get hurt."

"Why should I believe any of this?"

"Because I love you, Coco, and I wouldn't lie."

"No, you just wouldn't tell me the truth. I can't figure out which is worse. And I honestly refuse to accept that my husband has been cheating on me all this time . . . with Éclaire, of all people."

"Parker has never satisfied you the way I do, Coco."

"No, but he loves me as much as you do, if not more."

"And he still does. But let's face it, you and he haven't exactly been whooping it up beneath the sheets."

"Oh, and he and Éclaire have?"

"Éclaire has the libido of a piece of Muenster cheese and Parker, from what you've told me, comes before you're even out of your nightie. It's a match made in hell and they love it."

"Do you think they know about us?"

"Trust me, Coco, if they did, we would have heard about it long ago. That kind of information doesn't stay concealed for long, not with my wife."

"Why would you believe some crank caller, anyway?"

"Because this so-called crank caller obviously knows something we know, and he happens to be right. Please darling, tell me you're not still angry."

But, the truth was, I was furious with them all: Harry, Parker, Éclaire, and even with Harry's mysterious caller whose identity might never be known, but who seemed to have control over all our lives. Who was this person and could he have anything to do with the ominous letters that had been circulating for months? I sat back, sipping my wine and saying nothing.

"Coco, are you all right?" Harry broke my reverie.

"Not quite," I said. Then, I rose from my chair, but halfway out the door, I stepped back. The hell with it, I thought. I walked back to Harry and seeing the star pendant still on the table, I grabbed it.

"You've changed your mind," he sounded elated.

"I might as well get some compensation for a broken heart," I said.

Then, turning on my heels, I walked out of the Carlyle and into the first available taxi. I headed over to my apartment and there I spent the night, refusing to answer the telephone for anyone, especially Harry.

~

When I reported back the dialogue that had transpired between Harry and me, Annie actually registered a foreign emotion: shock, less over Harry's display of innocence, more because of Parker and Éclaire.

"That sly little bugger," she said. "Frankly, I never would have thought that he had it in him, or that Éclaire was even his type."

"And frankly," I said, "I thought that Parker's genitalia were permanently out of commission. But getting back to Harry, I can't believe he never said a word about any of this."

"That makes sense to me," Annie said. "Why would he want to ruin two perfectly sexy relationships? He was having his cake while Parker was eating his, too. I don't know who the biggest weasel is."

"Both of them. Men are jerks . . . except for Saul."

"Saul doesn't count; he was whipped into permanent submission by his mother."

"The funny thing is," I said, "Harry sounded so damn convincing."

"Which part?"

"That he hasn't been screwing Nursey or any of his other stable of beauties. I was even starting to feel empathy for the scoundrel . . . while still wanting to kill him, of course."

"You're missing one important element here," Annie said. "You may wish Harry dead, but at the same time, you really don't want to hate the poor bastard."

"How can you say that?"

"Face it, sweetums, where else can you get a fabulous fuck and a facelift almost simultaneously?"

"The man is never laying his filthy paws on me again," I said.

~

I decided to lay low and clear my head. I was still not certain that any of Harry's stories gelled. I was as shocked as Annie, though, oddly, not humiliated or even as angry at Parker's "peccadillo" as much as I was furious with Harry's need to enlighten me about Parker, and by doing so, ruining everything. That much truth I didn't need. Yet in some absurd way, despite the fact that Parker was a cheating, lying bastard, I admired his ability to pull off an affair without my knowing it. He was more conniving than I had given him credit for and in some inexplicable way, it even turned me on. All those nights he was away at his club meetings—all those evenings Éclaire was enjoying her "I want to be alone" time while Harry was out and about, the two of them were trysting their hearts out. But Harry was another story. He, who had women from Boston to New York trailing after him, insisted he was faithful to me while my white-bread husband was the real culprit. And who was the man who had called Harry? Could it be the same one who had placed that call to me only weeks ago, telling me not to risk it?

My mind was a hodgepodge of loose ends I tried piecing together. First, the thong that ended up in Hedy's suitcase. How did it get there and why? Was this Parker's attempt at hiding the evidence? And why was Alice coming out of Finkelman's building in the middle of the day? Dare I confront Finkelman with that piece of information? But as confused as I was, the truth was out. I was now armed with ammunition I could use any time I wished.

I was in control. I had the goods on Éclaire and Parker and could deal the cards any way I chose. For the moment, I decided to do nothing, but sit back and revel in the glow of owning a sliver of information they had no clue I even had. It was my one, true defense against the indefatigable fury that burned deeply inside me.

Harry, of course, continued to call and leave messages. Éclaire phoned twice, asking to see me. I didn't return her calls . . . not yet. Parker moved through his days, the ever-adoring husband, planting kisses on my cheek and telling me he'd see me later. I smiled back and told him to "have a good time." I was tempted to confiscate "Hedy's thong" and hand it to him, watching him writhe in the delicious agony and the sheer horror that would force the truth out of him.

I was lapping up every second of this grand moment and the sweet smell of revenge, which I played to the hilt—even better than Finkelman's mystery guru, Agatha Christie.

~

The first victim on whom I would cut my teeth was Éclaire. After four messages, I returned her call, cheery as ever, and made lunch plans for the following day. I would play my role to the hilt. Crocodile tears fell into her shrimp salad, as she went off on Harry and how she was thinking that while divorce was an option, she had gotten accustomed to her cushy lifestyle and didn't want to divide her fortunes with a divorce attorney.

"I will never leave him," she said. "I'll just have to think of another way to get back at him."

"Have you tried confronting him?" I played along.

"Forget it. He'd never admit the truth."

I marveled at the way Éclaire could take her life and manipulate it as she saw fit.

And then, she hit me with the coup de grâce.

"What would you do if you knew that Parker was cheating on you?" she asked.

I needed to play this one carefully. I sat back in my chair and pondered the question.

"That's easy," I said. "I'd probably have him killed and the woman, as well."

Éclaire blanched. "You mean, hire a hit man?"

"Of course. How else? You don't think I'd actually get mixed up in deadly weapons, do you? No, I'd make sure to find the best in the business, one who believed in slow torture before death actually took place."

"I do know a hit man," Éclaire countered. "Remember, my friend Lynn's boyfriend, Mickey G.? Well, he's been known to get involved in some dirty dealings. Lynn once told me, *entre nous* of course, that one night when they were dining at a restaurant, some guy looked at Lynn funny. Mickey G. walked over to his table and broke his nose."

"Just for looking?"

"Yes. Mickey G. has an uncontrollable temper. One call to Lynn and for the right price, Mickey G. would spring into action and Harry would be history."

"He wouldn't just do it out of friendship?" I played along.

"Of course not. It's a career move. The man has got to make a living," Éclaire said.

"There you go," I said. "The perfect murder."

"Coco, you're not really serious?"

"This is simply girl talk," I smiled. "Anyway, my Parker is as faithful as a puppy dog. He'd have no reason to cheat on me."

"You're absolutely right," Éclaire said. "You're his one and only."

~

As for Parker, I decided to play the adoring little wife and not let him out of my sight. When he mentioned he was off to his Long Island club, I offered to come along and keep him company.

"Darling, that's sweet, but I'll be tied up in meetings all day."

Ah, the eternal meeting: man's greatest tool for infidelity.

"I insist, darling. I can swim and sunbathe while you're engrossed in work."

"You never sunbathe, sweetheart," Parker said. "That's what keeps your skin looking like porcelain."

"I'll use an umbrella, honey," I said.

For the next two weeks, I was Parker's faithful companion, the woman who wouldn't leave his side, his better half, his trusted hombre. We were the reincarnation of the Lone Ranger and Tonto. And he had no choice but to pretend he was enjoying every moment of my sudden Johnny-on-the-Spot routine.

"Don't you need to work on your article?" he asked me over breakfast three weeks later when I was dressed and ready to spend the day golfing. "And I never thought you actually enjoyed golf."

"It's my new thing," I said.

"I'm very busy today, Coco," Parker said, with a hint of exasperation. "I can arrange for Tim at the club to help you with your strokes."

"It's so much nicer when you teach me," I said. "You know all the right moves." I even tossed in a little batting of the eyes to complete the picture.

Despite his daily barrage of messages and e-mails, I had not seen Harry since I walked out of Bemelmans Bar that Thursday, weeks ago. I was keeping a low profile, making him suffer by my absence, so that at any given moment, he could only surmise, but would never know exactly how I was feeling. It was another one of my well-orchestrated moves. Let them all squirm, I thought, while I went about my business planning my next modus operandi.

But the truth was, I missed Harry, missed our dinners, and most especially, our lovemaking. I had come to rely on those times with Harry as the bright spot of my week. Parker inquired as to why the Troutmans had suddenly vanished into thin air.

"Busy schedules," I said, dismissing it as simply as that.

Now that I had relegated Harry to the back burner, I turned my attention to getting even—my antidote to anger, the only key to my salvation.

I decided to throw Finkelman a bone, which would have him salivating on the spot.

When I told him the following Thursday that my affair with Harry was over, he jumped to attention and seemed relieved.

"You'll be the better for it, Coco," he said. "You can now move on and turn your attention to life, as you once knew it: as a writer and the wife of a man who loves and adores you."

And then, I socked it to him:

"The man who loves and adores me is having an affair," I said.

"I see." Finkelman raised his hairy eyebrow, practically panting at the bit.

"The man who claims he worships the ground I walk on has been sharing himself with another woman."

"I see. I see." Finkelman was getting excited. He popped a Zoloft.

"This man, my faithful and adoring husband, has been getting it up on a regular basis with . . . ta-da, drum roll, please, none other than . . . Mrs. Harry Troutman."

Finkelman sat up in his chair and pulled at his mustache, the wax buildup coating his thumb and forefinger. "That is a harsh accusation, Coco. What is it you're saying?"

"I'm saying that while Harry and I were off and running, little wifey back in Bronxville was screwing her head off with my husband."

Finkelman reached for his water and slugged down half a glass.

"You know this for a fact?"

"I don't, but Harry does. Seems he received a phone call confirming what I'm saying."

"I see. Did he know the caller?"

"Of course not. But it was a man who seemed to know what he was talking about."

"I see. Well, it was merely a phone call. That doesn't prove anything. From what we've discussed, Parker seems to be a most dedicated and responsible husband. Not a man who would jeopardize his marriage for a . . . how shall I say it . . . for imprudence and foolhardiness. But all that aside, I am relieved that your breach of marital etiquette has been put to bed, so to speak."

"And Parker? What do I do with the knowledge of his affaire?"

"It's unfounded hoo-ha, that's all it is," Finkelman said. "Dismiss it and get on with your life. It is your behavior I am concerned with, not that of your spouse. Keep the home fires burning and your husband will have no reason to stray."

My mother's voice echoed through the room.

"If in a month's time," Finkelman added a caveat to his statement, "you suspect that Parker is withdrawing, we can discuss an alternative plan of action."

"Such as?"

"Such as couples counseling."

"I had something better in mind."

"Oh? And what were you thinking?"

"Murder," I said.

"Even as a joke that isn't funny," Finkelman said. Then, he took out his trusty hankie and swabbed down his forehead, which was covered in perspiration.

"Éclaire was probably getting back at Harry by screwing my husband. She's convinced he's sleeping with his nurse. Harry swears he's innocent, but she's not swallowing any of it."

"Do you suppose that Éclaire suspects you and Harry?" Finkelman asked the obvious question.

"I thought about that myself, but Harry assured me that if she did, she would have acted on it when she first suspected."

"I see. I see," Finkelman said, while I knew he didn't "see" at all.

38

"No party is any fun unless seasoned with folly."
—Desiderius Erasmus

A "Fete" Accompli

A week later, out of the blue the phone rang as I was about to leave the house for my tennis clinic. It was Éclaire.

"Coco, is it really you? It's been forever. Listen, I'm having a do. So grab your date book and jot down in pen the evening of September ninth."

"Oh, Éclaire, hi," I said, coolly.

"Harry says he can no longer live without you . . . and Parker, too, of course."

"Of course."

"So say you'll come. It's going to be a bash and everyone who is anyone will be there."

"My date book is in the car." I played hard to get.

"Well, I simply won't take no for an answer. Consider it done."

And right there on a Saturday morning, life resumed a sense of normalcy, once again. All the players were back in action as though no ill will had ever transpired between us. I had not seen Harry in six weeks, which also meant I had not had a real orgasm in six weeks, either. Éclaire and Parker had cooled their jets mainly because I was now spending most of my evenings with my husband. Time, the best equalizer of all, had saved us all from ourselves. I decided to accept the invitation, the real reason being that I was dying to see Harry, who still left daily messages on my machine. When I passed on the news to Parker, he was elated.

"Well, that's more like it," he said. "I've missed the Troutmans."

I'll bet you have, I chuckled to myself.

By now, my anger had dissipated significantly. What I was left with were only positive and erotic thoughts. Harry was dancing around my head day and night. I fantasized about his hands all over me, his kisses, the smell and taste of him, the most intense lovemaking the likes of which I had never known. September 9 could not come quickly enough.

Parker, too, seemed renewed and excited. As far as I knew, he had not seen his lovely Éclaire, either. Like two heartsick lovers who were about to reunite, Parker and I talked incessantly about the Troutmans. Each of us had our own hidden agendas, trying not to show too much emotion though we were noticeably overheated.

When an e-mail from Harry arrived the day before the party, I was thrown off-kilter.

Coco, I am counting the hours.
SkinDeep

I was excited, but decided to keep it friendly and cordial.

Parker and I are looking forward to seeing you and Éclaire.
CocoPuff

Are you still as sexy as ever?
SkinDeep

I ignored his comment completely.

Parker and I will see you at 7:00.
CocoPuff

I'm having an erection.
SkinDeep

I shut off my computer, slipped into bed early, and masturbated myself into one glorious orgasm. It was the next best thing to being in Harry's arms.

~

The Troutmans' guest list included many of their friends from all over the map. Lynn and Mickey G., still an item, were coming in from California. Aside from them, and Alice and Charlie, we would not know anyone.

"It will be an entirely different group," I told Parker. "I'm sure many of Harry's colleagues will be there and tons of the Bronxville Field Club crowd. Then there's that Manhattan set they hang with and the Hamptons contingent. You know, the amazing, artificially sweetened couples you so enjoy."

Parker was practically delirious.

"It's just like the good old days," he said. "Pick out an appropriate little gift to bring along."

Perhaps a thong, I wanted to suggest.

Instead, I kept quiet and sat down and wrote a column on the beautiful couples I imagined we would be meeting on Saturday night.

The Seaport Gazette

THE AMAZING, ARTIFICIALLY SWEETENED COUPLE

That's us: the amazing, artificially sweetened couple. We are decaffeinated, cholesterol-free, and not salty to the taste. Our fat grams have been reduced by daily aerobic workouts. We lift weights to turn our flab into muscle. When my husband kisses me, he remarks how spicy my lips taste.

"It's my all-natural, herbal lip balm, darling," I say, "with a hint of tarragon and oregano."

When I kiss him, he tastes vaguely of spearmint from his sugar-free, nonadditive toothpaste.

We remember the way it used to be when we consumed food with gusto. We awakened to breakfasts of strong black coffee, two eggs over lightly, a rasher of bacon, and a dollop of heavy cream.

Now we maintain a different lifestyle. We are anti-oxidized, calcium-carbonated, and are highly potent due to our intake of multivitamins with a mineral formula that ensures our health will be perfect. We have an abundance of energy with which to get through our politically correct day.

We are the New Age couple. We are vital and aware of everything we put into our Listerine antiseptic mouths. We live in a temperature controlled, radon-free house that lacks character—a small price to pay for a safe environment. A long time ago, our kitchen had aromas that wafted through the rooms. Our home is now fragrance-free. We have even given away our microwave oven and eat only foods that are blended in our state-of-the-art food processor. We prefer products that emanate from homegrown fields rather than magnetic ones. We have exchanged culinary aromas for the smell of Lysol spray.

Our home sparkles from constant care. Our bathrooms contain no mold spores or ring-around-the-tub. We use fresh towels after each shower. We bathe twice a day. This necessitates doing a daily load of laundry with phosphate-free detergent. We spend our evenings folding underwear, while watching public-supported programming, the Discovery Channel, and CNN. We contribute large sums of our life earnings to saving the whales and other endangered species. We don't discuss politics for fear of stress, but then there is always Prozac or Paxil to get us through our difficult days.

Our children are overly scheduled and know how to behave. They must leave their shoes by the front door and enter the house in their socks, which have been sprayed with an antifungal solution. Dirt makes us edgy. We wash our hands after sorting the mail. We buy self-adhesive stamps that don't require saliva. We are terrified of anthrax and use a mask when opening any envelope.

We use our cars only when necessary. We are opposed to high-viscosity levels in gasoline. Thermal breakdown frightens us. We walk everywhere, but on weekends enjoy our mountain bikes when we commune with nature, wearing a #32 sunblock.

Our animals, which we love dearly, have been adopted by caring neighbors who are not allergic to dander and shedding. We miss them, but our new lifestyle does not allow for pets. We pick our friends carefully. Before they come to call, we make certain they are not carrying communicable diseases. We will pay any amount of money for a flu shot. We are philosophically opposed to the common cold. If anyone coughs or sneezes, we ask them to leave. We like all visitors to sign our guest book, listing, in chronological order, the dates of their immunizations. When they leave we scour our doorknobs and wash our hands with antibacterial soap.

When dining out, we are extremely careful. After making our reservation, we send along a questionnaire to be filled out by the proprietor.

#1: Is the food fresh? Provide time and date of produce and meat. Expiration dates are important to us.
#2: Please name the natural spring from where your bottled water emanates.
#3: Do your chef and kitchen staff wash his/her hands after handling food? Do they wear masks?
#4: Is your fowl antibiotic-free? Is your salmon farmed or wild?

#5: Does your establishment employ a staff physician who is on the premises at all times?
#6: Are all members of your staff proficient in the Heimlich maneuver?
#7: Is the garbage picked up daily? Are there roach motels stationed in the kitchen?

When we travel by air, we like to know that our pilot has had eight hours of sleep. We require that the pilot's urine be tested for drugs and he/she has taken a Breathalyzer test to measure any traces of alcohol in his/her system. Several airlines have told us we are being excessive. We know better. We keep our seat belts fastened until the plane has landed and has safely reached the terminal.

When staying at luxury hotels, we bring along our own linens, blankets, and pillows. We never order room service for fear of contamination and airborne germs that might be present in elevators. We don't use Jacuzzis for fear that microorganisms might invade our bodies. Air vents frighten us because of the threat of Legionnaires' disease. Public swimming pools are out. We get tetanus shots regularly.

Once a year, we have physicals with doctors who are the biggest and the best. We are never exposed to radiation. We prefer diagnosis to be made by gut reactions rather than invasive procedures. We always practice safe sex. Celibacy is our favorite means of birth control, except for birthdays, anniversaries, and the Fourth of July, and then, we move very carefully. We use only latex products, including disposable gloves. We are tamper-resistant. We do not make physical contact if our protective seals are broken.

This year, we are planning to renovate our house. Our plan is to add a hermetically sealed bubble off the den where we can throw lavish parties and serve hors d'oeuvres from our organic garden.

Most people think we are crazy. They suggest we go for counseling. We tried it once, but our therapist told us we were being uncooperative when we refused to lie down on his couch without a plastic cover. Who knows who was there before us?

The therapist told us that we are the two most interesting people he has ever met. We told him we are simply products of the twenty-first century and are trying to adjust to the changing times.

He prefers that we pay in cash. We tell him we never touch money, as it's covered with germs. He says we could benefit from two sessions a week and thinks we're in denial. We think he's not dealing with a full deck. He calls us "neurotic." We prefer the term "radical chic."

After all, we are simply the Amazing, Artificially Sweetened Couple who, at any moment, can be blown to bits. With the way things are going, we can't be too careful.

Harry and Éclaire's Bronxville house dated back to the turn of the century—a Tudor masterpiece, set high on a hill looking down over the sleepy village of church steeples, the school, quaint shops, and restaurants. The leaves were beginning to turn, while the sultry breath of summer hung lazily in the air. Driving up to their house, we were greeted by a valet who took our car and wished us a happy evening. It was 7:30 and Parker and I were just on the verge of being fashionably late. There in the foyer, standing as pruned and perfectly coiffed as her well-tended shrubs, was Éclaire, her hair tied up and pinned to the side with a diamond barrette. Her strapless dress barely draped the floor with a trail of crushed material cascading behind her, so when she walked, the dress glided along with her. Thanks to her latest lens collection, her eyes looked like two pieces of blue topaz.

Parker was immediately mesmerized by such a vision and commented on how well she looked. I imagined them in sexual play and felt a momentary tug of jealousy sweep over me. But who was I to talk? Then Harry joined the array of guests, looking better than I could have ever imagined. The six-week hiatus had obviously not erased any of my feelings, for the minute he stepped into the room, I could feel my heart begin to beat wildly.

First, the obligatory hellos to his other waiting guests, then he shifted his way toward us, his eyes fixed on mine. I felt giddy and slightly heady as he moved closer—close enough for me to smell his aftershave, the familiar scent bringing back in one split second those nights when he lay close to me, stroking my hair and falling asleep in my arms.

He extended a hand to Parker and then, kissed me lightly on the cheek, whispering, "I've missed you terribly, darling."

And in that fleeting moment I knew that nothing, save death, would ever keep us apart again.

Trays of hors d'oeuvres from foods of all nations were passed methodically around the rooms. On tables sat little "parmesan baskets" filled with Montrachet goat cheese, and next to them, crispy oysters and Prince Edward Island mussels.

Handsome young boys looking *très* gay in their tuxedos sashayed about, offering champagne, wine, or sparkling water. Parker requested his trusty bourbon while I sipped champagne and observed the faces of the rich and beautiful, kiss-kissing their way among the crowd, the women all fashionably dressed and looking perfectly suctioned and augmented in all the right places.

One young woman, on the rim of forty, was probably on her second facelift while others, their bosoms heaving, their butts hard as rocks, mingled about me. They plucked tidbits from the trays, and ever so carefully holding them between their manicured nails, nibbled at them between perfectly laminated teeth. Did these doll-like creatures of loveliness ever actually consume food, or were they nourished purely on the approval of others? I had never seen so many striking faces in one house as I did that evening.

An attractive Asian woman as delicate as a Ming vase, and

with an avid interest in golf, lured Parker to the opposite side of the room upon hearing that he owned two country clubs.

Lost among a maze of guests, some with foreign accents, I practiced my fractured French on a young Parisian boy and his mother. Suddenly, I felt a hand on my arm.

"There you are. I've been looking for you," the voice commanded. I excused myself while Harry guided me through the room and out to the patio.

Obediently, I took his lead, maneuvering through the crowd and being led through several rooms until I was directed through large French doors and outside, where more guests hovered about.

"I needed to get you away from the traffic jam," Harry said.

He directed me over to the side of the patio, then turning a corner, I found myself stepping down some stone steps and inside a small, cramped storage room filled with dusty and discarded porch furniture, folding chairs, and pool accessories. We were alone in this dark stone chamber with only the din of the guests above us.

"You look so stunning, it's really a shame to mess you up," Harry said. He held me tightly in his arms and kissed my hair, my eyes, his hands running down the length of my new Armani.

I knew if I stayed, I would be back where I started and the last six weeks would be for naught. My instinct was to pull away before he kissed me. As Harry's mouth drew closer to mine, his arms pulling me in toward him, I could not move. Then, his lips gently found mine as his tongue probed the inside of my mouth. We were locked in an embrace that left me woozy.

"It's been hell these past few weeks," he said.

We kissed again, Harry backing me up against an old Ping-Pong table. He lifted me up, positioning me on the edge. Slowly, he lifted my dress past my knees, and up around my thighs. I fell back, my legs parting while Harry slowly removed my panties and bent down to kiss my pulsating vagina. I moaned and writhed under his mouth while he tasted me. Then, unzipping his trousers, in one deft move, he was inside me, thrusting in and out as I began to scream with desire. Harry covered my mouth with his hand.

"Shhh, darling," he said. "Save that for when we're alone."

And, in one intense and heightened moment of ecstasy, I came right there. As far as I could remember, Ping-Pong had never been so exciting.

Locked in each other's arms and temporarily lost in the magic of the moment, I could hear distant laughter and muffled voices coming from the patio above.

"You need to get back to your party," I whispered to Harry. "A polite host needs to make sure his guests' needs are attended to."

"And are they?"

"More than you can even imagine, sweetheart," I said.

I brushed off furniture dust from my dress and straightened my hair. Our quickie reunion had left me askew and feeling slightly disoriented. Harry zipped up, kissed me, and disappeared out the creaking door, up the stone steps and back into his life.

And then, caught up in the moment, I suddenly thought I saw a face peering through the small window near the top of the stairs, but when I blinked, it was gone. I figured my imagination was working overtime, my neurotic impulses even more.

I waited a few minutes, reapplying my lipstick and wiping away any telltale signs of impropriety, and then I carefully opened the door. I ascended the steps, turned the corner to the patio, and standing right there among a group of guests, champagne in hand, was Éclaire.

"Coco, where ever have you been?"

"Just exploring," I giggled. "I think I made a wrong turn."

"I'll say. You're covered with dust bunnies." She plucked a ball of lint from my hair. "You shouldn't wander off into unknown places. You could get hurt."

"I'll keep that in mind," I said. "Excuse me, I think I'll get some more champagne."

I could feel Éclaire's eyes burning into me as I turned and walked away, leaving a faint powdery caking of dust trailing behind me.

For the next hour, Parker and I were introduced to many of the Troutmans' friends. Éclaire flitted about, the ever-engaging hostess, then disappeared like fairy dust to the kitchen to make sure that all was running smoothly. Empty glasses were whisked away by conscientious elves and replaced by refills. There was not a used napkin left awry, not a bare plate abandoned on tables. The hired help were the most trained and proficient. Éclaire would tolerate nothing less than perfection.

Parker and I separated and for a while, he was nowhere to be seen, but as I well knew, in a house of three floors and eighteen rooms, including eight bedrooms, one could disappear without a trace. Fifteen minutes before dinner was served, the lovely Éclaire, as in a scene from an old Bette Davis film, descended the long staircase with Parker following closely behind her. He made his way over to me.

"Éclaire was just giving me a tour," he said.

(Of what, I wondered: her house, her bedroom, her body?) Oddly, I felt nothing—not hurt nor anger. All that seemed to matter was that I was back with Harry Troutman, and Parker's infidelity only served to fuel my passion with Harry and eradicate all sense of guilt.

"The house is magnificent," Parker said. "You should see the art on the other floors. Each one, a gem."

"Éclaire and Harry have exquisite taste," I agreed.

"And the people. I was just talking to a princess."

"You must mean Éclaire," I said.

The dining room glittered with candles standing tall and tapered in their silver candelabras. Each painting was illuminated with small lights, so that while we dined, we sat among the greats of the art world, past and present. I was seated beneath a small Matisse. Éclaire had assigned the seating according to her whim, pecking order determined by a list of her personal Who's Who or legends in her own mind. This meant that she would be near enough to Parker to flirt, but closer to the rich and famous, to drop a few names. He would be seated directly across the table from Éclaire, next to a Bronxville matron who was deaf in one ear, hardly spoke a word, and looked hideous in a gown that did nothing for her. Parker's only recourse would be to stare longingly at Éclaire and play a little footsie under the table while she charmed the pants off the biggest art dealer in Manhattan.

The menu had been chosen with care and each course was a delicacy. Harry had taken a poetic description of each course from Le Confrérie de la Chaîne des Rôtisseurs. He then had it written calligraphically on scrolls of parchment paper, tied in ribbon, and left on top of each plate as a little keepsake of the evening.

The chicken liver pâté was served country style, and girded with cornichons, fresh thyme, butter, heavy cream, and scallions recently picked from the Troutmans' garden. A hint of Napoleon brandy could be detected by those in the know. With that was served a brut rosé.

Next, the fish course, a crusted halibut plated with a delicate mound of steamed spinach and olive oil perfumed with extracted exotic lemon juice. No ordinary lemons were good enough for the Troutmans. These were crated and sent from the orchards of California. A Pouilly Fumé, Clos des Chandoux accompanied the meal.

In between courses, Harry introduced the guests and gave a brief history of his and Éclaire's relationship with each of us.

"And, these are our dear friends, the Hardings from Seaport, Connecticut, and the Berkshires," he lifted a glass. "Parker, the owner of two golf clubs, and his lovely wife, Coco, a writer extraordinaire with whom I share a working relationship. Coco often writes about food, and we all know who the gastronomic guru is in that department . . . or shall I say gourmand?"

"Yes, it's true," Éclaire interjected, "Harry is Coco's mentor on all culinary matters. They often break bread together."

"Yes, darling," Harry acknowledged his wife's comment, "and let me say, that many food fights have ensued in the course of an evening."

Laughter abounded and he moved on to more introductions. We then resumed dinner.

To cleanse the palate after the fish, a vertical intermezzo featuring a mango sorbet was placed before us in tall fluted glasses, sprigs of mint adorning the rim of each one.

The salad course was a meal in itself. Locally nurtured and cultured lettuce combined with a smidgeon of Applewood smoked bacon and poached potato surrounded by, as Harry made sure to mention, a fried quail ovum.

"But, not to worry, dear ladies, these eggs cannot rival those each of you have harvested."

I sipped my Riesling and sat back and enjoyed the performance. Harry was not only plastic surgeon to the rich, but a raconteur whose wit and charm could hold an entire room captive. The women hung on his every word and gushed and giggled; the men lifted glasses in salute, knowing they could never be as dashing as he.

And then, the pièce de résistance of the evening: a roast suckling pig that dazzled and delighted. It was wheeled to the table on a cart, the obligatory red apple in its mouth, as the guests applauded in unison. Harry rose once again and read from the scroll:

"My dear friends, this fine porcine skin, not to be confused with porcupine (more laughter), has been seared, the complete corpus then slow cooked for six hours with a mirepoix. The end product has then undergone a deglazing with red and white wines, thence to be served with scallions from our garden, apples, and touches of rosemary."

"I'm Rosemary," a redheaded cutie at the end of the table, broke in.

"And I am sure if we had used this Rosemary on the sow," Harry said, pointing to her, "our meal would be that much tastier."

I groaned silently. Yes, Harry could charm the pants off his guests . . . and I was one to know.

A lovely cabernet made the pig go down smoothly. Harry had spent weeks researching this meal and the wines that were paired with each course were, according to Parker, outstanding.

We were all stuffed and had literally "pigged-out." While the dining room table was being cleared, we were asked to join our hosts on the large glass-enclosed sun porch where pink and white roses were scattered about in large, glass vases and a harpist sat in the corner of the room, entertaining us.

The guests, sated and happy, listened intently as the music filled the air. Harry kept a distant and watchful eye over me. I glanced over occasionally and caught his stare. On the opposite end of the room, Éclaire lowered her eyes when Parker snuck a quick peek her way. Hearts were high and the whiff of indiscretion was in the air.

A half hour later, the Troutmans' housekeeper entered the room, announcing that dessert was being served in the arboretum off the dining room. Parker and I caught up with Alice and Charlie, whom we hadn't chatted with all evening.

"Oh, Coco, I simply adore your dress. You look so fetching," she said.

Alice herself was dressed to the nines and wore a chunky

cherry quartz choker, embellished with an assortment of diamond-studded veggies.

"Well, that's certainly a necklace to die for." Éclaire appeared from nowhere. "Perhaps you can design one for moi."

"Darling, it's yours." And right there in the middle of the room, Alice undid the clasp, removed the necklace, and handed it to Éclaire.

"Oh my God . . . what can I say?"

"That you'll accept this in the name of enduring friendship, that's what you'll say."

"I can't."

"You must. It's rude to refuse a gift."

"Friends forever, then," Éclaire said, embracing her friend while I stood there between them and practically puked.

Dessert was a mélange of fresh fruits in glass bowls with the largest strawberries I had ever seen. Dipping bowls of white and dark melted chocolate lay next to each one. A cut glass tureen the size of a punch bowl was filled with a clear fruit consommé. Guests could pour themselves a cup and add to it berries and bite-size pieces of melon. Platters of assorted cheeses and breads were spread about the room along with trays of cookies and biscotti. Port and sherry were served and more champagne for those who wanted to sustain their festive high.

Harry greeted me at the dessert table.

"Now, here's a self-expressive dessert," he said, placing a strawberry between my lips. "Bite and savor."

"I prefer mine with hot, melted chocolate," I said.

"Oh yes, I should have remembered." He plucked another from the bowl and, coating the entire berry with chocolate, circled my lips.

I licked it off slowly, my tongue sliding up and down the berry.

"I wish that were me, darling," he said.

He twirled the strawberry teasingly along the rim of my mouth.

I could feel myself getting moist as I nibbled the last remaining piece of berry.

Little did I know this would be the last time that Harry would ever feed me.

39

"What is food to one may be fierce poison to others."
—Lucretius

The Party's Over

The morning after the party was warm and sunny. Parker and I later heard that the final guests had left by 2:00 A.M. and Harry and Éclaire had not gotten to bed until after three. Harry was still sleeping when Éclaire floated trancelike out onto the patio at ten. Breakfast had been laid out earlier by the Troutmans' housekeeper, who, after completing her chores, left for her day off. Two vases of cut flowers from the previous night sat on the tables by the pool. More bouquets adorned the breakfast table, a lovely complement to the linen cloth, patterned with large cabbage roses of various colors. An occasional hummingbird lighted on the edge of the birdbath while the last remaining sounds of summer could be heard in the distance. The sun rose high in the sky and the scent of freshly cut grass still lingered in the air. The weather, holding at 75 degrees, was perfect.

Harry's favorite meal was Sunday brunch and Éclaire had ordered an array of his favorite delicacies from Zabar's. Alice had picked them up yesterday morning when she was in New York and delivered the trays last evening. On a table under a shaded oak tree were platters of smoked fish with slices of beefsteak tomatoes from the garden. Next to them were plates of red and white onions and several varieties of cream cheese, fish spreads, and sliced American cheese. Pickled herrings piled high in cream sauce rested in a large glass bowl next to a basket of fresh H & H bagels. Razor-thin slices of smoked salmon glistened in the sun with hearty wedges of lemons ready for squirting. Fresh berries rested in a cut glass bowl. Pitchers of freshly squeezed orange juice would be a welcome treat to the palate after last night's sumptuous dinner. This could have served a small army, but this morning it was only Éclaire and Harry.

Éclaire stretched herself out on a chaise longue and lay poolside with the latest issue of *Elle.* She was hoping that Harry would soon awaken and whip up a pitcher of his famous Bloody Marys. No one made a Bloody Mary like Harry, with just the right amount of Tabasco sauce and cilantro and one secret ingredient to make it memorable. No matter how hard friends tried to wheedle the recipe out of him, he never weakened.

Éclaire dozed off for a while. A half hour later, Harry appeared in his bathrobe, the *New York Times* in hand, and scanned the breakfast table. Pouring himself a glass of OJ, he joined his wife on a neighboring chaise, and flipped open the paper. Éclaire stirred and opened one eye.

"So, you're finally up."

"Can I freshen your orange juice?" Harry asked.

"No, but if you're making a Bloody Mary, count me in."

Éclaire seldom imbibed this early, but feeling exhausted after all her hard work of party planning, a Bloody Mary seemed the perfect start to a lazy Sunday morning.

"Sounds good to me," he said.

The ingredients were already laid out so all Harry had to do was mix his potion and voilà . . . the drink was ready for tasting.

They sat and sipped their way through the next hour, discussing the guests and the evening that was. Before long, Harry grew hungry and, eyeing the table of brunch edibles, inquired if Éclaire was ready to eat.

"I think I'll go up and shower," she said. "But don't wait for me. Help yourself and I'll be back in a while and join you."

On her way into the house, Éclaire plucked a rose from the vase and secured it to her hair.

"Relax," she told Harry, blowing him a kiss, "I shall return."

Ten minutes later, stomach growling, Harry picked up a plate and helped himself to a bagel, slathering it with some fish spread, a slice of tomato, a piece of onion, and a slice of smoked salmon to clinch the deal. He took a hearty bite, lay back on the chaise longue, and resumed reading the paper.

Upstairs, Éclaire took her time. She emerged from her leisurely shower and towel-dried each part of her body with utmost care, applying a layer of après-shower cream to her arms and legs. Checking her toenails, she decided to give each one a second coating of polish. She would have to remind Charlene at the salon to make sure to add three coats instead of two at her next pedicure. She finger-dried her hair, making sure that each curl fell exactly where it should and added a dollop of mousse for good measure. Recently waxed, her body felt smooth to the touch. She checked her teeth for whiteness, her breath for sweetness, and applied her makeup with painstaking precision so that she looked as close to perfection as possible. She popped in her green lenses to match her Sunday stay-at-home leisure outfit and checking herself in the mirror, was pleased with what she saw. Slipping into a pair of flats, she sprayed some Chanel No. 5 on each of her pulse points.

She then arranged a bowl of flowers and moved them from her nightstand to a table over by the window. She breezed through some women's magazines, deciding if she should stay with light reading or nourish her mind with the latest issue of *Atlantic Monthly.* But it's Sunday, she thought. Why tax her brain so early in the morning? She settled on a book she had been reading for the past month, but never got around to finishing. She turned on her state-of-the-art stereo music system and chose a favorite station. Music instantly poured through the house, and even outside to the patio where Harry lay. Éclaire would join him soon, but not before she checked her date book for the following week's events: lunch at Jo-Jo with Babs and Margo on Monday, tennis at the club on Tuesday morning, and lunch at Balthazar with Alice on Wednesday. Tuesday was her four-week hair appointment with Serge, a manicure and massage with Brie on Thursday afternoon, her day spa appointment with Swan on Friday morning, and the Bronxville Field Club dinner on Friday night. Then it was off to the Hamptons for a dinner party on Saturday, followed by a brunch the next day, and finally Sunday again, when she could collapse before returning home to Bronxville on Monday morning. Éclaire yawned just thinking about it all. Then, grabbing her basket of needlepoint—her therapy—she returned to the patio and to Harry, who lay basking in the sun.

Éclaire gently shook Harry's arm, but when he didn't budge, she decided to leave him be. She began eating without him. She scooped some melon and berries into a small bowl, and dressed her bagel lightly with smoked salmon and a smidgeon of cream cheese, garnishing it with a slice of tomato. A half hour later, observing Harry more closely, she noticed his face looked particularly red and his lips were engorged. Some spittle was coming from the side of his mouth.

"Harry," she tried rousing him, "Harry, wake up."

But Harry seemed dead to the world and didn't move a muscle.

Éclaire let him lie there while she poured herself half a glass of Bloody Mary. She dipped her toes in the pool and skimmed a few pages of her book, not really taking note of the words. Emotionless, she walked over to Harry again, this time, checking his pulse. Even under the scorching sun, his body felt cold and clammy. It took Éclaire another few minutes to contemplate her next move. Then she dialed 911.

"Too bad," she thought, "he never even got to finish his Bloody Mary." She stooped to pick up a half-eaten bagel under Harry's chair and awaited the arrival of the EMS.

~

Sunday evening, Éclaire, too upset to talk to anyone, had asked Alice to make the obligatory calls to the Troutmans' nearest and dearest, including Parker and myself.

"Coco," came the somber voice of Alice. "I'm afraid there has been a terrible tragedy."

Was there any other kind?

"Coco, there is no other way to say this than to be direct. This morning . . . oh my God, Coco . . ."

"Just say it, for Christ's sake."

"Coco."

"Yes?"

"Coco, darling . . . it's our beloved Harry."

"What about Harry?" I could feel my stomach tighten.

"Harry . . . he . . . he . . . retired."

"Retired? From work?"

"From life, angel. Harry retired from life. He is no longer with us."

"What are you talking about?"

"Coco . . . Harry croaked."

And the rest, as they say, is history.

~

As soon as I heard the news, I dropped the phone and shrieked. Parker came running.

"It's Harry," I said, sitting down on the bed.

"Harry? On the phone?"

"No," I said, through an avalanche of tears, "Harry is dead."

"What?" Parker grabbed the phone and resumed the conversation with Alice.

"Yes, it's all terribly true. It happened this morning when he and Éclaire were home alone enjoying brunch."

"It just can't be."

"Arrangements have been made. The funeral is on Tuesday at Frank E. Campbell's," Alice said.

"Oh, poor, poor Éclaire. Who's with her?" Parker asked.

"Charlie and I will be staying with her, and of course, her daughter, Muffin, will be here all week."

"She can't be alone," Parker said. "Maybe I should come down."

Over *your* dead body, I thought through my tears.

"What happened?" started the flood of questions.

"According to Éclaire," Alice said, "she found him lying on the chaise longue, a bagel at his feet, a piece of which he ingested and aspirated."

"Harry died eating a bagel?"

"I'm afraid so."

And even though the moment could not get any more somber, upon picturing the scene, I couldn't help but think: How very Harry it was to drop dead in the middle of a meal.

The next morning after a fitful night's sleep, I phoned Finkelman and got his machine.

"This is Coco Harding. I *must* see you today. It's an emergency."

Finkelman picked up.

"This is Dr. Irwin Finkelman."

"I have some horrible news: Harry Troutman is dead."

A pregnant pause followed by two "I sees." "Can you be in my office at two fifteen tomorrow?"

He then phoned the Seaport pharmacy and loaded me up on Valium to get me over the hump of bereavement.

40

"For three days after death, hair and fingernails
continue to grow, but phone calls taper off."
—Johnny Carson

"That's All, Folks!"

Frank E. Campbell Funeral Chapel at 81st Street and Madison Avenue has had the privilege of serving many heads of state, United Nations ambassadors, dignitaries, royalty of many nations, members of the entertainment world . . . and this morning, Dr. Harry Troutman was being laid to rest.

The soft lighting, furniture, tapestries, and art objects lent themselves to a serene atmosphere of peace and calm. On this particular Tuesday, the chapel was bustling with throngs of people whose lives had all been touched socially or professionally by Harry. Devoted patients, most of them women, all taut and tightened, descended upon Campbell's en masse, paraded down the aisle, and filled the pews. Members of La Chaîne des Rôtisseurs and restaurateurs from New York's finest gathered to pay their respects, knowing that they had lost one of their best. A few who had personal relationships with Harry had their own stories to tell.

"Now, here was a gentleman who knew his wines. A true gourmet who wasn't afraid to order white with meat and red with fish."

"A man of distinction," said another, "who put his trust in the hands of the chef to make the decisions—who cleaned his plate with gusto. He will be missed."

"I remember the night we ran out of frogs' legs," a chef from one of New York's finest spots reminisced. "Did he complain? No. 'Another frog's life saved' is what he said. The man had a sense of humor, bar none."

"Dr. Troutman was one of my most faithful patrons." Sirio Maccioni of Le Cirque was visibly anguished.

Naturally, the New York restaurant owners grieved . . . their incomes would be decreasing significantly in the coming year.

Numbed out on the Valium that Finkelman had prescribed, I hung on Parker's arm as he escorted me to a pew near the front. It was all happening so fast that my mind was still a blur.

Éclaire, ever the queen of protocol, had ordered the freshest and most exquisite flowers, adding more of a touch of gaiety than sadness to the moment. Floral fragrances filled the air and the room was ablaze in color. Mascara dripped down countless faces of women appropriately dressed in their funeral attire or, as Harry would have said, "dressed to kill." But Harry was gone and with him a love affair so intense and heartbreaking, I wasn't sure I would be able to stand its end.

Bridgette spied us and waved. She had obviously forgiven Harry for his last surgical "misadventure" with her. She was dressed in a flowery print dress so out of place it was laughable. The mourners stared.

"Let them mock me. I refuse to wear black," she said, as she shimmied her way across the pew and took a seat next to me. "Black is so damn gloomy and grave . . . so depressing."

A hush fell upon the room. Éclaire entered with Muffin clinging to her arm—Muffin, who appeared heavy with grief and an abundance of weight, was wearing a black spandex all-occasion dress. Éclaire, in a gorgeous Chanel suit, her face veiled, entered the front row pew and stared straight ahead, the epitome of grace and dignity.

"Daddy, Daddy," Muffin wailed as she passed the casket. Éclaire pinched her daughter on the arm and under her breath could be heard whispering, "Muffin, darling, please, decorum above despondency." Emily Post would have beamed.

The eulogies were magnificent, each one a personal tribute to Harry. A colleague of Harry's spoke eloquently: "Let us remember a man who made an impression on us all . . . a man who changed the face . . . uh . . . faces of society and beautified our landscape." Upon hearing that, Bridgette lowered her eyes to her chest and smiled down on her breasts. Truer words were never spoken.

A bouquet of flowers ran the entire length of the cherrywood casket. Inside lay Harry in his final resting place. I stared long and hard, expecting that at any moment, he would push open the lid, shouting "That's all, folks!" and rise like Vesuvius to invite us all to lunch.

Sadly, that was not going to happen. After tearful hugs and condolences, and a long drive out to the cemetery, we were back in Bronxville, where only last weekend, jollity reigned. Now, Éclaire sat in her sunroom, the grieving widow surrounded by her entourage, waiting on her hand and foot.

Alice wouldn't leave her side and assumed the role of the protective friend, making sure Éclaire stayed nourished and hydrated.

"Darling, some Pellegrino, perhaps? Sweetheart, just try to eat a little something . . . an egg, perhaps? Some chopped liver?" Alice pleaded.

"I couldn't possibly eat a thing," Éclaire said, "maybe just a teensy-weensy glass of wine to take the edge off the pain. Harry has a nice Cloudy Bay sauvignon blanc in the wine cellar. We purchased a case on our last trip to New Zealand and now he won't be drinking any of it."

This set her off on another crying jag as Alice clucked over her and brought her another box of tissues. "There, there, angel, Harry is watching over you."

"I'll take it from here," Parker told Alice. "Éclaire, you're not alone, dear. Our job is to make sure your every need is met."

I'll just bet we all will, I thought. Now that Harry was gone, Parker quickly moved into his new role as caregiver to the poor and helpless Éclaire—one he obviously enjoyed playing to the hilt.

"Night or day, we'll be available, dear." Parker held her delicate little hand on which a four-carat ruby ring sparkled like a neon light. "And Coco will be at your every beck and call, too. We're just a phone call away. All you need to do is whistle." Lauren Bacall could not have said it better.

I slipped into the bathroom. Another hour of this and I would need a Valium drip. Damn it, Harry, I thought, how the hell could you let this happen . . . over a fucking bagel, for God's sake? How could you leave me like this? And then my mind raced. Where the hell was Éclaire anyway? Why wasn't she around to save him? One good Heimlich in the ribs and Harry might still be with us.

We stayed with Éclaire long into the night, after the last person left.

"You two must be exhausted," Éclaire finally said, relieving us of our duties. "Alice will be staying over, so no need to fuss over me. You can come back tomorrow."

"Only if you promise to call us if you feel even the slightest bit unable to cope," Parker said.

"You know I will. It's so comforting to have the love of dear friends at a time like this."

"Be strong, Éclaire," Parker hit her with a final platitude. "Harry would have wanted it."

Upon arrival home, a letter was waiting:

Dear Suspect,

The dirty deed is done. Will the guilty party please step forward.

Jacques Cuze

Early the next afternoon, after Parker insisted I check in with Éclaire to make sure she was in a holding pattern, I drove into the city to see Finkelman. I had hardly slept a wink, but felt enough in control to drive. Finkelman was in pacing mode when I arrived.

"As I predicted," he said, his squinty little eyes pointed at me. "I told you someone was going to die."

"You said someone was going to get killed," I reminded him. "This was an accident."

"Maybe yes, maybe no," Finkelman speculated. "I tend to think murder might be the more appropriate word."

Hercule Poirot had sprung to life. I played along.

"All right, then, whom might the murderer be?"

"Ah, the big question we all want answered."

"So, you're saying that Harry's death wasn't an accident?"

"I'm saying there is more here than meets the eye."

"The man choked to death," I said.

"Have you asked yourself why?"

"He ate too quickly?"

"Come, come my dear, what were the telltale signs?"

"Éclaire said that when she joined Harry for breakfast, his face looked red, most likely from too much sun, and that his lips were engorged—blown up twice their size, she told us."

"Don't you find that strange?"

"A bad sunburn can do that," I said.

"I find it all very interesting." Finkelman went off into his reverie. "It was before noon. The morning sun on Sunday last was hardly strong enough to burn one's skin, in so short a time. If I recall, it began turning cloudy by eleven o'clock and the temperature was only in the high seventies. I'm afraid, Coco, that we have more on our hands than a simple accident."

"Are you saying that Harry's death was orchestrated?"

"Perhaps it was."

"Who would want him dead? Harry was adored by all."

"So it seems. But, I have reason to believe there were those who did not wish him well."

"How would you even know that? You never met Harry or anyone else who knew him, for that matter."

"To quote the remarkable Monsieur Poirot: There is nothing so dangerous for anyone who has something to hide as conversation."

"What does that mean?"

"Speech is the deadliest of revealers," he quoted again, "and crime is terribly revealing."

"You're starting to scare me," I said.

"Acute fear always produces the truth, Coco."

"Are you quoting Poirot again?"

"I am," Finkelman said, "but instead of busying ourselves with the nuances of Harry's death, let us address your grief. Tell me, how are you holding up?"

I spoke longingly of Harry and cried my way through the remainder of my session, and to show just how compassionate Finkelman could be, he didn't charge me for the additional time.

~

The next few days, Éclaire and Muffin received relatives and friends in Bronxville. Rooms burst with sympathetic mourners, some of whom sat by Éclaire's side and regaled her with their personal recollections of Harry. While some muffled their pain in recounting humorous stories, Muffin buried hers in food. Intermittently, Éclaire took her daughter aside and told her, "Daddy would not like this one bit, Muffin. Put down that Danish pastry and eat some fruit, instead."

Alice scurried back and forth making sure everything was running smoothly, checking on Éclaire at regular intervals. It was only after the week was over that a new turn of events occurred.

After Éclaire had called 911, the EMS had arrived within minutes. CPR proved useless and Harry was pronounced dead on the scene and brought to the morgue. Éclaire, questioned briefly and heavily sedated, was brought home to mourn, followed by a visit a few days later and a string of questions from the investigator on the case, Jonas Farb, sent over by the medical examiner who had performed an autopsy on Harry's remains. The following Friday afternoon, Detective Farb sat in Éclaire's living room and pulled out a spiral notebook.

"Mrs. Troutman, as you know, a forensic examination was conducted following the death of your late husband."

"Yes, much to my disapproval." Éclaire, Alice at her side, stood resolute and strong.

"The nature of Dr. Troutman's demise makes it necessary to investigate further."

"Oh?" Éclaire dabbed her eyes with a hankie.

"The findings are suspicious, to say the least. In cases such as these . . ."

"What cases?" Éclaire interrupted, defensively.

"Cases where the details of the deceased's passing do not coincide with the evidence at hand."

"What evidence?"

"I'll get right to the point, Mrs. Troutman. It seems that while Dr. Troutman did die of asphyxiation, he sustained a severe allergic reaction prior to eating the bagel in question."

"I don't know what you mean," Éclaire said. "What kind of allergic reaction?"

"The medical examiner believes that due to the outward appearance of Dr. Troutman at the time of his death, that he ingested another substance that caused an anaphylactic shock reaction."

"Really?" Éclaire shifted in her chair.

"His lips were enlarged several times their normal size, he had a rash over most of his body, and the entrance to his throat was blocked. It is clear that he had some kind of allergic reaction to something he had eaten."

Éclaire cocked her head to the side and blinked five times in succession. "I can't imagine what."

"What we will need to do, Mrs. Troutman," Detective Farb said, "is to carry on a thorough and detailed investigation with all parties who were on intimate terms with the late Dr. Troutman."

"Intimate?" Éclaire asked.

"The people who knew him best: his family, friends, social acquaintances. I would like a list of each person who was with Dr. Troutman in the days before this tragic event occurred, along with others who played an active role in his life. Only then can we piece together the puzzling circumstances surrounding his death. I'd like to begin with you, Mrs. Troutman, and then ask your friend a few questions."

Alice winced. "Me? I don't know a thing. I wasn't even here when this happened."

"Mrs. Troutman, I understand from your housekeeper that it was your friend who picked up the food at Zabar's the morning of the party."

"Yes, that's true," Alice said. "I was purchasing some food, and since we were coming to the Troutmans' on Saturday night, Éclaire asked me to bring along some brunch items, too."

"What sort of items?"

"The usual: cheeses, fish spreads, cream cheese, pickled herring, smoked salmon, and, of course, the bagels."

"To your knowledge, Mrs. Troutman, was your husband allergic to any specific foods?"

"Well, he never touched shellfish," Éclaire said. "I never had any in the house."

"When Dr. Troutman's stomach was pumped, there was evidence of shellfish in his system, shrimp to be exact."

"How is that even possible?"

"What about you?" Detective Farb turned to Alice. "What did your purchases include?"

Alice went through the list.

"Do you or your husband have any food allergies?"

"No, we eat everything."

"Shellfish included?"

"Especially shellfish. My husband specifically told me to buy some lobster salad."

"What about shrimp?"

"I think I may have picked up some shrimp spread, too."

Éclaire looked at Alice. "Oh my God, there was a pink spread that morning. You don't think you might have given us the shrimp spread by mistake, do you?"

Alice became noticeably distressed. "Sunday morning, when I was preparing breakfast, for my husband and me, I wondered what happened to the shrimp spread. I figured that Zabar's had forgotten to include it in the order."

"You don't think that maybe they put it in the wrong bag?" Éclaire asked.

"I don't know."

"Who set your brunch table, Mrs. Troutman?" Detective Farb asked.

"Well, I did, but I figured the pink spread was laced with lox, not shrimp. They both look the same."

"So, it's entirely possible that your husband ate the spread thinking it was lox, not shrimp."

"Anything is possible," Éclaire said, becoming agitated. "I . . . I . . . just can't believe this could happen."

She then lowered her head in her hands and began sobbing.

"Oh my God, my God . . . my precious Harry."

"That will be all for now, Mrs. Troutman. I apologize for having to put you through this difficult round of questioning, but I will need to pursue this further. After you collect yourself, may I trouble you to prepare that list, with phone numbers included, of persons whom we can contact regarding this matter?"

"Yes, yes," Éclaire spoke through her tears. "I will go through my husband's address book and give you any phone numbers you wish."

Farb was not entirely satisfied and didn't want to close the case . . . at least, not yet. The first on the list to be questioned were Parker and me. Detective Farb made a trip to Seaport on the following Monday. Sitting on our back deck, I offered him an iced drink, which he declined.

"Mr. and Mrs. Harding, you have been friends of the Troutmans for several years?"

"Exactly two," Parker said. "My wife, a writer, often met with Dr. Troutman regarding articles she was writing."

"So Dr. Troutman was your mentor?"

"Yes," I said. "Harry was very knowledgeable in the food area. I met him and his wife at a Chaîne event a few years ago and all of us soon became friends. Harry and I had a working relationship aside from our friendship."

"And his wife approved?"

"Of course. Éclaire Troutman even encouraged it."

"That seems very noble. How about you, Mr. Harding. Were you as close to the Troutmans as your wife?"

"I certainly was. We enjoyed their company and often spent time at their Hamptons home, as well as dining together whenever possible. The Troutmans are very hospitable people."

I was becoming intrigued as I listened to Detective Farb ask all the right questions. It was actually fun watching Parker squirm through an air of guilt that seemed to hang heavily over him.

"How well did you know Mrs. Troutman?" Farb asked Parker.

"My wife and I both know Éclaire very well. Coco and Éclaire are good friends, often spending time together lunching and shopping, the usual things women like to do."

"Did Mrs. Troutman ever confide any personal concerns she might have had regarding her husband?"

"No," I lied through my teeth, "she held Dr. Troutman in the highest esteem and was always extolling his virtues, both as a physician and a husband."

Parker seemed relieved and nodded approvingly.

The interrogation process went on for another half hour until the detective seemed satisfied.

"Thanks," Farb said. "No more questioning . . . for today."

We watched him drive away in his '98 Chevy Cavalier.

"Well, that's over," Parker said. "We're in the clear."

"Wishful thinking," I said.

"How the hell can they pin anything on us? We weren't even around at the time of Harry's death and anyway, this was obviously a terrible accident on Harry's part. The guy had an allergic reaction, gasped for breath, choked on a bagel, and . . . sayonara."

"You've tied it up into one neat little package, haven't you?"

"Coco, it sounds crazy, but it's the truth. This isn't a crime. It's a culinary mishap."

~

Farb continued to interrogate the suspects, including Bridgette. After leaving us, he drove to her home in Greenwich.

Bridgette was sipping a gin and tonic out by her pool and offered one to Farb.

"Sorry, no drinking on the job, but it does look tempting." Instead, Bridgette whipped up a lemonade and charmed the pants off him before the questioning had even begun.

"Tell me your affiliation with the late Dr. Troutman," Farb asked.

"Open your eyes and take a look," Bridgette said, thrusting her chest in Farb's face.

"So," he stared at her breasts, "you, uh . . . had . . . er . . . a professional relationship with the doctor?"

"You can say that. But if I had known he was going to kick the bucket, so to speak, I would have had a facelift while I still had the chance."

"And socially?"

"Yes, the Troutmans are good friends of my brother, Parker, and his wife, Coco. I've attended several of their dinner parties. That's where I first met Harry. But those damn letters, that's the part I can't figure out."

"Oh?"

"Somebody knew all along that Harry was going to die. I just can't figure out who it was, though I have my suspicions. I do know that my sister-in-law has been seeing a shrink."

"And?"

"She probably tells him everything."

"Are you suggesting that Mrs. Harding is connected with Harry's murder in some way?"

"I never said that. Anyone could have killed Harry."

"So you don't believe that Dr. Troutman's death was an accident?"

Bridgette walked up to the detective and looked him straight in the eye, her boobs brushing his chest.

"Detective, we both know that there are no such things as accidents."

She refilled her glass with gin and clicked it against his glass of lemonade.

"All's fair in love and death," she toasted.

Farb stayed with Bridgette for another hour, until she was so looped that she no longer made any sense.

41

"There comes a time in every woman's life
where the only thing that helps is a glass
of champagne."
—Bette Davis, *Old Acquaintance*

Partners in Crime

It was now two weeks after Harry's death and his name was still buzzing at all the top dining spots in Manhattan. Women who were scheduled for surgery were in a quandary as to whom they could now turn to for their face and body restoration. The office phone was ringing off the hook and Harry's receptionist, Sabrina, had to tell all who called that they would need to see another plastic surgeon, and recommended a few doctors. Parker and I paid frequent visits to see Éclaire, until we felt she could manage on her own. Éclaire played her role as the grieving widow with style. During the mourning period, she had managed to sneak out of the house and squeeze in a full body massage, manicure, pedicure, and haircut, and was looking better than ever.

One afternoon, Alice dragged her over to the Pierre Hotel for lunch and ordered a bottle of Cristal champagne. Occasionally, a random passerby who knew her stopped by the table to offer condolences.

"It's beginning to get tiresome," Éclaire confided to Alice.

"The price you pay for being married to a famous husband."

"That's past tense, dear. Remember, I'm a widow now."

"A black widow," Alice said.

"No, darling." Éclaire looked across the table. "The Merry Widow."

"So, now what?"

"Time will tell."

"Has the good detective returned?"

"Only once, but he has nothing to go on."

"What about Parker?" Alice asked, acknowledging out loud what she had known all along.

"He's being my constant watchdog, calling me night and day. He's starting to get on my nerves."

"So, the bloom is off the pee-pee? No more wild and crazy sexual escapades?"

"Please, sweetie," Éclaire nibbled at the corner of a roll, "I'm a woman in mourning."

"Parker can be pretty insistent," Alice reminded her.

"He's becoming a bore. The last time we were together, I was on the verge of an orgasm and his sexual organ deflated right there in the middle of my screaming 'make me come.'"

"I've always said, when it's no longer illicit, the prick will start to wilt."

"I'm still not sure Detective Farb isn't on to us."

"All I did was buy some shellfish, for God's sake," Alice said.

"Yeah, and I just happened to serve it to Harry."

"You didn't force him to eat it, did you?"

"No, but I could be accused of not practicing safe fish."

"It's simply a case of mistaken identity," Alice said. "What you thought was lox was shrimp. What would a judge give you for that?"

"Fifty years to life?" Éclaire said.

"Look, babe," Alice leaned in, "we planned this together and it went off without a hitch. It's a fait accompli. Harry and Coco had their last fuck that Saturday night. I saw them going at it when I peeked through your storage room window."

"At our party? That slut."

"You should talk. You and Parker haven't exactly been little vestal virgins. Remember, doll, the world is your candy store . . . and keep in mind, you're also a very rich woman. Sit back and enjoy the ride."

She picked up her glass of champagne and clinked it against Éclaire's.

"Here's to the two hottest bitches in New York," she said.

Jonas Farb was not happy. Something was sticking in his craw. All the people he cross-examined seemed innocent enough and none were with Harry at the time of his death, except Éclaire. And she had not discovered the body until forty-five minutes after the fact. But it just didn't add up.

The final round of questioning was with Hedy. She and Farb sat in Parker's study, the large oak-paneled French doors tightly shut.

Hedy was reserved, but forthcoming. "I've been with the Hardings for many years," she spoke admiringly. "They have been very good to me."

"Do they seem compatible?" Farb asked.

"Certainly. Hardly a cross word between them. Mr. Harding is a hard worker—a man who knows the value of a dollar, but you can see for yourself that he and Mrs. Harding enjoy a lovely lifestyle and make sure that I am well taken care of. They are a pleasure to work for." Then Hedy turned reflective.

"Is there something more you would like to say?" Farb asked.

"Well, there is just one thing and I hope I am not speaking out of turn, but a while ago, when I was preparing the Hardings' clothes for dry cleaning, I found something inside Mr. Harding's jacket pocket."

"What was that?" Farb had his pencil poised.

"A piece of underwear," Hedy blushed, "belonging to a woman."

"Can you describe it?"

"A very skimpy pair of . . ." she moved her chair closer to Farb and whispered, "red panties."

"Had you ever seen these before?"

"Never. They were unfamiliar. And . . . I'm not certain if they belonged to Mrs. Harding."

"As far as you know, has Mr. Harding been faithful to his wife?"

Hedy was abashed. "Mr. Harding is an honorable man. He reveres his wife. He has never indulged in carnal indecencies. Of that you can be sure."

"I know this is difficult for you, and I apologize, but if Mr. Harding is such an honorable man, why do you think a pair of red panties was in his jacket pocket?"

"I'm afraid you will have to take that matter up with Mr. Harding," Hedy said. "And when you do, I would appreciate it if you wouldn't mention this conversation. My position could be in jeopardy."

"I understand," Farb said. "This is strictly between us. What did you do with the panties after you found them?"

"I removed them from the jacket pocket and hid them in my suitcase."

"Why did you do that?"

"I felt they might be incriminating, if Mrs. Harding discovered them."

"Then you *were* suspicious?"

"No, I was protective," Hedy snapped back.

"Do you still have them?"

"I do."

"I would like to have them."

"Why?"

"As proof."

"As proof of what?" Hedy was now perspiring. "I'm sure there is a reasonable explanation to all of this. I don't want to get Mr. Harding in trouble."

"The panties, please," Farb gently demanded.

"I'll run upstairs and get them."

"Thanks. You have been most helpful."

But Parker was not as cooperative when he was later questioned again.

"How the hell do I know how a pair of lady's panties got inside my jacket pocket? Maybe my wife put them there."

"Does your wife own red panties?"

"I don't know. She might. I don't make it a practice of checking my wife's underwear."

"So this is a total mystery to you."

"Of course, and frankly I'm offended by these questions."

"Mr. Harding," Detective Farb stared at him, "are you having an affair?"

"Now I've heard everything. No, I am not having an affair."

"Are you prepared to take a polygraph test, Mr. Harding?"

"What is this? You come into my home and accuse me of inappropriate behavior. How dare you."

"This is a murder investigation, Mr. Harding."

"Who told you about the panties?"

"That is irrelevant, sir. *Who* told me is not your concern. *Why* they appeared is more to the point."

"I—I have had just about enough for this morning," Parker said. "I want to call my attorney."

"That's probably a good idea," Farb said.

Farb headed back to the Eighth Avenue precinct where his partner, Frankie Michelli, asked, "So, you got anything?"

"Not sure yet. There's one more party I still need to contact."

"Who's that?"

"The shrink. He might know something."

"Shrinks don't talk," Michelli said.

"This one might."

"Based on what?"

"It's been a rough day," Farb said. "Let's go grab a beer. I'll tell you all about it over at McHale's."

~

Bridgette, in her semi-inebriated stupor, had passed on information about Finkelman and how I had been seeing him for years. She was even helpful enough to provide his full name, which Parker had given her when she said she might be interested in seeing a shrink. Farb's interest was immediately piqued. He called Finkelman the next day and made an appointment to see him.

When he arrived at his office, Finkelman was dressed to the teeth, looking very Poirot in a three-piece suit and a large pocket watch dangling off his waistcoat. He had chosen a bow tie of emerald green and when Farb looked down at Finkelman's feet, he could see his own reflection in the patent leather. Finkelman was noticeably anxious, but greeted Farb in a friendly manner and offered him a chair.

"Is this where you conduct your sessions, Doctor?" Farb asked.

"Yes, most of them sit right there where you are sitting, except for those who are in analysis and use the couch."

"How long has Mrs. Harding been a patient of yours?" Farb got right to the point.

"I have been treating Mrs. Harding for about two years. She had come to me years ago and then returned for some additional therapy."

"Was there a specific reason for her return?"

Finkelman began picking at his cuticles. "Quite often, a patient will reenter treatment when specific issues have resurfaced and need to be addressed."

"And Mrs. Harding? Did she have specific issues?"

Finkelman cupped his hands together and circled his thumbs, nervously. "As with you, Detective, I am unable to offer a detailed analysis of my patients' affairs. It is privileged information, which I am not at liberty to divulge."

"Doctor, I am here to investigate a matter that might involve Mrs. Harding. Surely, you can offer some insight as to the mental health of your patient."

"Mrs. Harding is of sound mind, Detective. Like all of us, she is grappling with conflicting issues in her life."

"Such as?"

"The daily ambivalences all of us face."

"To your knowledge, Doctor, was Mrs. Harding involved with any other man besides her husband?"

"That, Detective, is a perfect example of client privilege, which I cannot, under the laws laid down by the Hippocratic Oath, be asked to reveal."

"Doctor, it is my belief that the death of Dr. Harry Troutman might be tied up in his relationship with your patient."

Finkelman's "I sees" had reached into the double digits.

"Your cooperation would be most appreciated . . . no . . . most essential, in helping to put closure on this crime."

"Was Dr. Troutman's death the result of foul play, Detective?"

"One might say so. Withholding anything that could move us ahead in this investigation could prove to be detrimental. What I am saying, Doctor, is that I can issue you a court order demanding that you share with me what you know about Dr. Troutman's demise."

Finkelman was more intrigued than frightened. As Farb continued, Finkelman slipped into his Hercule Poirot role, cleared his throat, and sat back in his chair. Then he reached inside his desk drawer and pulled out an envelope.

"I think I may have some tangible evidence that might interest you, Detective."

As the late autumn afternoon sun streamed into the office, the two of them sat long into the early evening. At 6:30, Farb rose from the chair and shook Finkelman's clammy hand.

"You have been of great help to me, Doctor. This has been a most enlightening visit, I thank you for your cooperation. You have made a very wise decision."

Finkelman escorted Farb to the elevator.

The doors opened and Farb entered the small cubicle. He pushed the lobby button and was delivered to the first floor, leaving Finkelman standing in the hallway. As Farb descended, Finkelman took out his handkerchief and wiped his brow. "*Mon Dieu,*" he said aloud. "*Mon Dieu.* What have I done?"

PART FIVE

Just Desserts

(Anti-Climax)

42

"The bagel is an unsweetened doughnut
with rigor mortis."
—Beatrice and Ira Freeman

The Last Burp

Parker hired the best attorney in Manhattan, Elias Stark, who, for an obscene amount of money, assured him that there was no jury that would ever convict him on any count, including conspiracy to commit a crime. After careful training with a polygraph expert who taught him the ropes, he aced the test. In the end, it was thrown out of court since there was no evidence that it was even reliable.

"Polygraph tests are constructed only as a ruse to intimidate the suspect," Stark assured him.

"I may have been sleeping with Éclaire," Parker told Stark, "but it was really to get back at my wife."

"So you knew Coco was having an affair with Harry?"

"The entire time. So did Éclaire. We commiserated together and used recreational sex as a way of coping. Stupid, but true. I always loved Coco, but Éclaire had it in for Harry. On numerous occasions, she wished him dead."

"I guess her wish came true," Stark said.

"I wasn't the first guy she slept with, either. She once took up with one of Harry's male nurses."

"How do you know that?"

"She told me . . . bragged about it, actually. No, I was just one in a long line of other men, including a couple of maître d's. No wonder the Troutmans always got seated quickly."

"Do yourself a favor," Stark advised. "Stay away from that Troutman woman. She's nothing but bad news."

Stark was right. Unbeknownst to Parker, Éclaire had taken up with her personal trainer, Alberto from Brazil, who not only tightened her pecs and abs, but erased any traces of gloom and doom with his fabulous bedroom techniques.

Parker sat across the desk from his attorney, his fingers crossed and resting on his chin. "I hear you," he said.

Epilogue

"Any moment before the end might be
the most important one."
—Hercule Poirot (Agatha Christie)

On a late weekday afternoon, I sat in Dr. Caroline Dent's office—my new therapist, whom I began seeing a month following Harry's death. I felt I needed some help, a person who could transport me back to where I could look at myself in a mirror and see only me, not me and Harry.

Harry left an indelible imprint on my heart that I needed, not to erase, but to find room for, like a welcomed guest who would remain quietly there, minding his own business and not intruding on my emotions.

Dr. Dent's office was attached to her house. An entire wing overlooking the water was devoted to souls like me who needed, as Annie would say, "a little fine-tuning." I had now traded a Central Park West view for the Long Island Sound. It was my first session where I was asked to recap the events of the past months.

Dr. Dent had been highly recommended by some of Seaport's most neurotic. She greeted me warmly and offered me a chair. Dressed in a smart tweed suit, she appeared to be in her mid-forties. She was thin, well-coiffed with auburn hair that barely touched her shoulders. She had a refined air and a brightness about her that endeared her to me straightaway. A whiff of Clinique's fragrance, Happy, wafted past me as she walked over to her chair.

"You indicated on the phone that you've been through an ordeal," she offered the gift of a sentence.

"It's not that Parker and I weren't happy," I said, breaking the first awkward silence, "but, Harry was just too damn irresistible."

"You loved Harry?"

"Passionately."

"And, with that kind of love often comes madness." Dr. Dent's voice was calm, her demeanor relaxed.

"But it's not that I didn't learn my lesson," I sounded almost apologetic.

"Hopefully, we all learn something from our actions. So what was your lesson?"

"Never to eat another bagel for as long as I live," I said, half smiling.

"But seriously?" Dr. Dent countered.

"Seriously?" I looked up at her. "Although, I must admit, it was the ride of my life, the trip alone could kill you."

"But Coco, I see you are still very much alive. Let's take a trip back into the past. What about the others? Please, fill me in."

"Oh, yes, the others . . . we can't forget them."

"Let's begin, then."

"I guess I'll start with the wicked witch of the family: my sister-in-law, Bridgette."

"She sounds difficult."

"That's an understatement. From the day I met Parker, she tried making our life a living hell. But the good news is, she eventually sold her Greenwich house, moved to Rhode Island, and married Willy Fitz, but he died soon thereafter."

"What happened?"

"He was on a sailing trip in the Mediterranean when a falling mast clobbered him on the head, knocked him overboard, and he drowned."

"Really?" Dent offered a typical shrinky retort.

"May I call you Caroline?" I asked.

"If that makes you more comfortable, of course."

"Bridgette was so high on martinis that she had fallen asleep on the starboard deck. When she woke up, she couldn't find Willy. Neither could the crew, who were smashed on piña coladas. Bridgette inherited half of the Fitz estate. She moved to a condo on Fisher Island, Florida, and spends her time having plastic surgery and traveling. The rich bitch couldn't have planned it better. And speaking of bitches, let me tell you about Alice and her trophy beau, Charlie."

"I want to know everything, Coco. All the facts are crucial to your mental health."

At least, I mused, I have a shrink who doesn't lapse into a barrage of Finkelman-esque "I sees."

"Alice was a patient of Finkelman's for more than twenty years. He treated her for chronic post-traumatic stress syndrome from a childhood event she never could remember."

"How did you find out about that?"

"Éclaire told me that Alice was a basket case. She said she was seeing a shrink, but who knew it was Finkelman? From the day I saw Alice coming out of his office, I should have known that something funny was going on."

"Funny?"

"Creepy, actually. At first, I put it all aside and took her sighting as a coincidence, but I instinctively knew that Alice couldn't be trusted."

"Ah, instinct, still one of the best tools we have."

"But Alice and Charlie are doing just fine," I resumed. "They jetset around the world buying art. And Charlie has become one of the leading mature male models for *GQ*. Alice designs her vegetable jewelry. Last I heard, she was commissioned by the princess of Tasmania to create a tiara made of diamond- and sapphire-studded rutabagas."

"Tell me more about Alice." The doctor picked up her notebook.

"Alice is one shrewd cookie. She obviously told Finkelman everything she knew about our alleged affair."

"Alleged?" Caroline asked.

"Okay, our hot and torrid affair."

"How did Alice and Éclaire know about your affair with Harry?"

"They knew about us the whole time. After all, Harry was flaunting our affair under Éclaire's nose. We just figured she was oblivious, when the reality was, she couldn't have cared less, especially since she was sleeping with *my* husband."

"While you were sleeping with *hers*," Caroline finished the sentence.

I dismissed the doctor's remark.

"Then, to top it off, Alice's psychic confirmed her suspicions."

Caroline smiled. "The quick-fix route, eh?"

"It's evident that Alice plotted Harry's death along with Éclaire. They were a real pair. But they were never prosecuted." I took a sip of the latte I had brought along as a crutch, something to hold on to when words failed.

"It gets even better," I continued, pulling my chair in closer to Dr. Dent's. "Let me tell you about Éclaire."

"Please do." Caroline removed her glasses, revealing a pair of soft gray eyes that matched her cashmere sweater perfectly.

"You might not believe what I'm going to say."

"Trust me, I've heard everything," Caroline assured me.

"When Éclaire was brought down to the precinct for questioning regarding Harry's death, she fainted during her polygraph test and was rushed to the hospital. She once told me that she suffered from a nervous disorder. She milked that for all it was worth. Soon after, she quickly sold her Bronxville home and moved to East Hampton with her daughter, Muffin."

"Muffin? Is that her real name?"

"It's Melissa, but Éclaire and Harry gave her that nickname

early on. Little did they know she'd grow up having a weight problem. The name fits her to a T."

"Please continue."

"After her affair with Parker, Éclaire had a brief love affair with her personal trainer, Alberto. But then Éclaire met another man she began seeing. I won't tell you about that yet. I'm saving the best for last. I don't want to shock you completely."

"I don't shock easily," Caroline corrected.

"I need to go in order. First, there's the matter of the red thong."

"Thong?"

"The evidence that really got Finkelman going."

"Whose thong was it?" Caroline zeroed in.

"Éclaire's, but she never told anyone. She and Parker were going at it one afternoon on the sixteenth hole at Parker's club in Great Neck, when she surreptitiously hid the thong in his golf bag."

Dr. Dent could not scribble fast enough.

"I know all this because Parker finally confessed."

Dr. Dent uttered an audible sigh.

"Since Harry's death, Éclaire has given up on plastic surgery. I heard from someone who knows her, she is slowly beginning to lose her looks. She always did have an ongoing battle with cellulite. By now, she's probably tossed out all her bikinis." I chuckled. "I understand that she takes pottery classes and even tried getting her real estate license, but flunked the test, twice. She still goes to the city for shopping sprees and her hair appointment with Serge. My friend, Annie, bumped into her at Saks. Éclaire told her that she and Alice lunch regularly, at all the best Manhattan restaurants, I assume, where Éclaire probably still gets the best table and never has to wait. She told Annie she never plans to shop at Zabar's again."

"You sound angry, Coco. Or, do I detect slight jealousy?"

"Of whom?"

"I don't know. Something to explore."

"Well, there was Harry's nurse, Krystle."

"What about her?"

"Krystle Kowalski was Harry's right-hand gal. Occasionally, I wondered about her and Harry. But as it turns out, she was suspicious of Éclaire all along. And she feared for my life, too."

"So she knew about your affair?"

"She knew that Harry and I were close and she needed to warn me. I received a threatening phone call."

"Call?"

"An anonymous caller, with the warning, 'Don't risk it.' Krystle later told me she had persuaded her husband, Joe, to place that call to me."

"Sounds like she was looking out for you."

"Yes, Krystle is a good woman. I grew to like her. After Harry died, she and Joe moved to Honolulu, where Krystle plans to give hula lessons and make leis, while Joe hopes to run a luau catering company. Parker and I have an open invitation to visit them anytime."

Then Caroline threw me a whopper. "Do you think Harry was faithful to you?"

"Yes, except at first, as I said, I was a bit leery of Krystle. She was behind-the-scenes, making sure the office ran smoothly . . . and making sure Harry ran smoothly, too. And she's a real beauty. I admit, I did feel uneasy at times."

"So you didn't trust Harry completely?"

"Not always. Sometimes, I was suspicious even though I knew he loved me. Harry swore he had nothing to do, sexually, with Krystle, even though once, at a Halloween party, she came up and kissed him. But Harry said it was an accident. He was dressed up in a tiger costume when Krystle laid one on him. When she discovered it was Harry, she was so upset, she went to confession the next day."

I inched closer. "I've been having some weird dreams, lately."

"Please, enlighten me. Dreams can be most revealing."

"A few nights ago, I dreamed about our housekeeper, Hedy."

"Can you elaborate?"

"It was all very vague. But, I woke up feeling anxious. Hedy has seemed quite strange these past few weeks, as though she knows something."

"Perhaps she does."

"We'll never know for sure. But, she was affected by the entire traumatic event. Parker and I sent her on a two-week vacation to Aruba to gain her composure. But . . . there's a happy ending here: Our gardener, Emilio, joined her on the trip and proposed marriage to Hedy under a bleeding orange tree. They married last Saturday at a small private ceremony at our club here in Seaport. Parker gave her away and I was the matron of honor. Later, Hedy confessed that she wore a red thong under her bridal dress. Makes one wonder."

"Sounds like Hedy has a sense of humor," Caroline said, smiling.

"Hedy is a constant ray of sunshine in our lives. We couldn't live without her."

"Almost like a surrogate parent?"

I shot Dr. Dent a look. "In a way. She does keep our household together."

"Coco, what transpired in your treatment with Dr. Irwin Finkelman?"

I sat back, squirming slightly.

"Dr. Finkelman, now there was a character. He was on to all of us from the start. Finkelman knew everything, but tried keeping his cool, which, if you knew him, was not an easy task. He fancied himself to be a sleuth. I can't tell you the countless sessions we had where he took on the persona of Hercule Poirot. He was a master game-player, and the one who sent the Jacques Cuze letters that caused all the commotion."

"Jacques Cuze?"

"The mysterious spy who threatened us at every turn."

"Who received the letters?"

"Parker and me, Bridgette, and, of course, Harry and Éclaire. We're the ones in the lineup."

"So Dr. Finkelman was really Jacques Cuze?" the doctor asked.

"The one and only. He admitted he got the idea of the letters from Agatha Christie's *Ten Little Indians.* Later, he handed over all the letters to Detective Farb and pleaded temporary insanity. He was charged with criminal mischief and did six months of community service, treating neurotic menopausal women for anxiety disorders."

Caroline looked askance.

"Word has it that he goes to Fire Island every August, writes mystery novels, and sunbathes in the nude. Knowing him, he probably had a mini-breakdown and is on Zoloft for life. My guess is he still wears bow ties. Detective Farb told Parker all about Finkelman."

"Detective Farb?"

"Now we're getting to the juicy part. And, Caroline, I hope you're ready for this."

"I'm all ears."

"Detective Jonas Farb could have thrown the book at Alice and Éclaire, but he was governed by lust. He let both of them get away with murder."

"Lust?" Caroline perked up, her pen poised.

"I'm getting to that. Farb divorced his wife of thirty years, turned in his badge, and is living blissfully in sin in East Hampton with Éclaire and Muffin."

"Please, Coco, continue."

"I heard that Farb and Éclaire joined a swinging couples group and took up Greek folk dancing. They recently won a ten-day cruise to the Greek Islands. When Farb was out fishing one afternoon, Éclaire had a quickie with a waiter named Nick."

"You know all this for a fact?"

"Hercule Poirot told me," I giggled uncomfortably.

"So you can't be sure."

"My best friend, Annie, and her husband, Saul, sailed on the same ship with Éclaire and Farb. It was one of those bizarre coincidences."

"Coincidence again?" Dent mused.

"Annie observed them the entire time and she was never even noticed."

"Tell me more about Annie."

At that moment, I noticed a glass bowl filled with bite-size chocolates on Caroline's table. We laughed in unison.

"Annie helps to keep me sane. She's the Tiffany of women, as my mother, Yvonne, would say."

"Your mother sounds like an interesting woman."

"You have no idea."

"Hopefully, I will." Caroline didn't miss a beat.

"Annie is my one connection to Harry. We meet regularly at A Scone's Throw and reminisce."

"Is that painful?"

"Actually, it's cathartic. I have no one else to talk to about Harry."

I grabbed a tissue from the box, and suddenly broke down.

"I miss Harry terribly," I sobbed. "Life's just not as exciting without him. But I never meant to hurt anyone, especially not Parker."

"Talk about that," Caroline offered a psychiatric shoulder.

"Parker and I have a good life. The sex stinks, but I think we both have a newfound respect for our marriage."

"Which is . . . ?"

"We love each other and want to make our marriage work."

"So, you don't foresee any more affairs in your future?"

"Of course not. Harry was a one-shot deal," I laughed through my tears. "Parker is a good man."

"In what way?"

"He accepts me for who I am. How many women can say *that* about their husbands?"

"You mean, he knows that you aren't perfect?" Her words stunned me for the moment.

"Keep going, Coco."

"Sure, Parker can be a big bore, but you know what? Everyone and everything gets boring after a while . . . unless you find ways to keep it alive. That's the trick."

"Keep what alive?"

"Life," I said.

"Tell me about your life, Coco."

"Well, I'm thinking of starting a novel, and, of course, I'm still grinding out those columns each week for the *Gazette*."

"I read them," Caroline interjected.

"Oh? Really?"

"Yes, they're funny and occasionally poignant. You seem to wrap a layer of humor around your feelings, perhaps to buffer other emotions."

"That's what I get paid for. Humor is what motivates me."

Caroline shot me another zinger. "Were you ever considered a suspect in Harry's death?"

"Yes, of course, along with everyone else. I told my attorney, Delia Champlin, I was in love with Harry, but a crime of passion was hardly my MO. Her meticulous, legal fine-tooth combing cost us a bundle, but then I was no longer a suspect and the case was dropped. It was pretty hairy for a while."

"You must be relieved."

"Yes, I couldn't quite picture myself in the slammer. I would never have been able to handle it as graciously as Martha Stewart did. I mean, what would I do, stencil the cells?"

"There's that humor again," Caroline broke in.

"Life is beginning to get back to normal. Parker plays a lot of golf and runs back and forth between his two country clubs. But I can tell you this: He has definitely developed an irrational fear of women's panties."

Dr. Dent laughed.

"Coco, before we stop for today, how do you see yourself at this moment in time?"

The sun was starting to set over the Sound as I sat back and reflected.

"I feel I'm always on the verge of something, but I'm not quite sure what. I can't seem to get a grip on it all."

"We have some work to do, but this is enough for today."

"It's over . . . already?"

"It never *is* quite over, is it?" Dr. Caroline Dent said, rising from her chair and leading me toward the door.

Read on for a preview of the latest novel
from Judith Marks-White

OUTRAGEOUSLY BLONDE

Coming soon from Ballantine Books

PART ONE

Marilyn Posner Reminisces

"The difference between my day-to-day blonde life and the day-to-day brunette life is not extreme. It is manifested in a gentle rise of the tidewaters of public friendliness . . ."

—Natalia Ilyin (a "bottle blonde") in *Rapunzel's Daughters* by Rose Weitz

Prologue

Deep inside me lurked a long, leggy blonde trying to escape. She was the image I created for myself—the look I loved. Sadly, nobody knew she was in there but me . . . until recently when everything changed and my blonde obsession became a reality.

Looking back, the role models I latched onto throughout my youth were the great blonde Bombshells of all time: Jean Harlow, Jayne Mansfield, Lana Turner, and of course, Marilyn Monroe, the only Marilyn I knew who defied the norm. She was the grande dame of them all, the starlet of the golden age of film who knew how to snag a man whether it be a famous baseball player or the president of the United States.

Early on, I observed men: my father, my cousin Josh, even my uncle Charlie, the letch of the century, all of whom had a thing for blondes. And why not? Blondes look pure and innocent. Men want to come to their rescue even when they aren't in danger. Blondes look wholesome. They don't need makeup, and most important, as the saying goes, blondes have more fun. I wanted to have fun, too, but my hair was frizzy and wild—follicly challenged if you will—and while it did attract a lot of attention, it was the smooth, sleek, blonde-haired beauties who tickled men's fancies.

As for the bad rap blondes have been handed about being dumb, the pros outweigh the cons. A friend of mine is married to a blonde named Pru. He thinks she personifies brains and beauty. I don't agree. I once asked Pru a question that I didn't think was too difficult:

"Do you know what time it is?"

"Yes, I do," she said. Then she smiled and walked away. I rest my case.

That aside, I still think blondes have it made.

Amelia, my roommate at Vassar, a natural wheat-haired blonde from Louisville, Kentucky, set her alarm for eight A.M. to make an eight ten class. She splashed cold water over her face, dressed quickly, and was out the door. I arose at seven thirty to make a nine fifteen philosophy class. I needed time to prepare. It was unfair to shock my professor so early in the morning by appearing unkempt and pale as a ghost. Professor Harlan Gould, an intelligent though somewhat somber man, held a deep appreciation for Aristotle and Spinoza, and an even greater appreciation for the female form and face. I arrived in class, well-coiffed with makeup in place, and took a seat in the front row, looking relatively put-together. Next to me sat a girl from the midwest, still in her flannel pajamas, taking notes, yawning, and looking adorably blonde. I ended up with an A in the course. She ended up with Professor Gould, who fell in love at first sight. She says she owes it all to fate. I think she owes it to being a babe.

My friend Jack insists that blondes don't do it for him. Says Jack: "I prefer the sultry, mysterious look of brunettes. Brunettes exude sensuality. Blondes are bland. Blondes are boring."

So, why is it I once saw Jack trip over a curb on Madison and 75th when a tall, lanky blonde exited the Whitney Museum?

No man ever fell off a curb for me except my husband, Maxwell, who, when I upset a bag of groceries, tripped on a Spanish onion. If I were blonde, that never would have happened. Blondes aren't klutzy. Blondes are cool. My blonde friend Cindy lost a contact lens and everyone in the immediate vicinity rallied round. When I dropped my car key, the only one who gave a damn was some mutt, who licked my face while I was crawling around in the grass. It was enough to make me want to "dye."

Furthermore, blondes fit in anywhere. They blend in with the scenery and match the décor. Stick a blonde in a room and she'll enhance a color scheme just like a golden retriever. I once saw a blonde whiz by in a red convertible. She looked fantastic. When

I'm in any open-air vehicle, my hair flies wildly askew. Blondes never look askew. They look marvelously windblown.

I want to be a blonde because gentlemen prefer them. A willowy blonde hanging on a man's arm is a nice accessory. The last time I clung to a man's arm was when I sprained my ankle. A cop found me stretched out on the sidewalk and brought me to the Lenox Hill emergency room where I waited an hour and a half. A buxom blonde with a bloody nose came in after me. She was seen at once. Do nose bleeds take precedence over ankles, or is it that blondes are considered medical emergencies?

Back in high school, I had a crush on the neighborhood boy, Harry Wexler. It was mutual. We spoke on the phone nightly. We studied together and made out on the couch in my den. We went to the movies, took long walks, and hung out. When it came time for the junior prom, he didn't ask me. He invited Autumn Simpson who lived around the corner. Who else but a golden blonde could ever get away with being named Autumn? Even at fourteen she was well developed. She had straight teeth that never required braces, long hair that curled just right at the ends, and legs that never quit.

"Autumn has a peaches-and-cream complexion," my mother liked to remind me. "If you stop eating sweets, Marilyn darling, you can look like peaches and cream, too."

Is it any wonder that my least favorite fruit is the peach?

Autumn moved through her adolescence with an air of confidence and a sense of intrigue. She was an idol to one such as I, a mere Marilyn, who bit her nails and had hair that took up a lot of space. I was born at a time when the name Marilyn was popular. It conjured up the snot-nosed girl next door, the infuriating brat caught passing notes in class, or gobbling down bags of popcorn at Saturday-afternoon movies. The Marilyns I knew had glaring flaws: buck teeth covered with metal braces, an overabundance of freckles, and a proclivity toward chubbiness. Marilyns had blemishes and never went anywhere without their Clearasil. My braces had tiny rubber bands I loved to snap. Even worse: I giggled. Many were the afternoons when I could be found in the school corridor having been removed from the classroom because I simply could not control myself.

"Marilyn, when you can pull it together and collect yourself, you may rejoin the class," my teacher, Miss Theodora Remington, admonished, as she escorted me to the door and relegated me to the cold, hard wooden bench in the hall where I was asked to contemplate my behavior.

There I sat, staring down at the long hallway, feeling misunderstood and trying to "collect myself" while the bevy of blonde beauties in my class could do anything and never got into trouble. By the end of the hour, I had learned nothing. I was, after all, a Marilyn and "pulling it together" was not part of my MO.

My mother anticipated minor disasters. She programmed me to "be careful" lest some misfortune befall me when I wasn't looking. Autumn's mother, Mrs. Simpson, never worried. She didn't spend hours talking about "reaching potential." Autumn had already reached her potential by the very fact of being blonde, while I, the clumsy brunette, was still tripping over myself. Believing I could change my persona, for a while I spelled my name "Merry-Lynn." It didn't work.

It was always Autumn, never Marilyn, who made the cheerleading team, who had three boyfriends simultaneously, and who could devour an entire bag of Oreos without gaining an ounce or having to pop a zit. I had fittings with orthodontists. Autumn had fittings with dressmakers. I went on diets. Autumn went on vacations. One fact was certain: I was never going to amount to anything unless I shed my Marilyn image, starting with my hair.

One afternoon, during my senior year of high school, I decided to go blonde. I grabbed the bottle of Peroxide that had been stored in our medicine chest since the Eisenhower administration. I coated one, long streak with the solution, resulting in a hideous yellow-orange color that ran along the entire length of my head. I looked like a skunk on a bad hair day. My mother had a fit and dragged me to her hairdresser who remedied the situation. By the end of the day, I was back to my old mousy-brown self, knowing in my heart that I was never going to make it in the world without taking drastic measures.

What finally convinced me that blondes have it made happened years later when my manicurist, Ginger, the dirtiest blonde I ever met, told me a story.

"I was speeding," she said, "my hair blowing out the top of my Mazda Miata, when a cop stopped me. I had to think fast."

Ginger put down her emery board and leaned in toward me.

"I looked him straight in the eyes, strategically placing a blonde wisp of hair over my cheek for that sultry look. 'Officer,' I said, batting my baby blues, 'the wind blew my hair out of control. I couldn't see the speedometer.' He stood there sizing up the situation and saying nothing. Then, he reached for his pad and issued me a ticket. But . . . that's not all."

I hung on Ginger's every word.

"A week later, he looked me up and asked me out on a date. Six months later we were married. It'll be fifteen years this June."

I sat back, watching Ginger apply a second coat of polish to my perfectly manicured nails, before asking her the big question: "Do blondes have more fun?"

"What do *you* think?" Ginger snapped her gum, giving a shake of her blonde mane. "Look at me: Am I fabulous or what?"

1

The Bombshell

"Weren't you a blonde when I came in?"
—James Bond, *Diamonds Are Forever*

A blonde does not simply become a blonde. It's in her all along.

"It's a mystique," my husband, Maxwell, said when I asked him why blondes were so appealing, "an irresistible, undeniable force that makes men's eyes go pop and their heads turn in their direction."

Perhaps I should have seen the clues right there. But I was too busy living what I thought was the perfect life. I didn't notice when excitement took a nosedive into the comfortable and predictable—when our sexual sessions were sandwiched between the layers of days that made up our marriage. For me, it all seemed to fit neatly together as long as I was willing to overlook the fact that boredom was starting to seep in between the cracks.

Back then, I was still very much a brunette with curly, shoulder-length hair that every summer blossomed into a puffy mane, similar to the full hydrangeas flanking the path leading up to our Tudor house. Here in Sunnyville, the landscape was punctuated with blondes of all types and shades—maintenance-free blondes, who required little upkeep. They merely awakened to a new day and finger-combed their hair, which was styled by Mark the Magnificent. Then they jumped into their shabby-chic workout clothes, ready for whatever lay ahead.

When I grew up in Teaneck, New Jersey, brunettes ruled. There was hardly a blonde in the bunch except for Mindy Solansky, my best friend Janie's mother, who was a natural blonde . . . or so I believed until one afternoon when I was over at Janie's house and the truth was revealed. We were sitting at Mrs. Solansky's vanity mirror applying lipstick when, suddenly and without warning, Mrs. Solansky emerged from her shower and I caught a glimpse of her black bush peering out at me from beneath a giant white bath towel. I went home, all excited to tell my mother.

"Mrs. Solansky isn't a real blonde," I said.

"How do you know that?" my mother asked, wiping perspiration off her forehead and sliding a tray of cookie dough into the oven.

"I saw her pubic hair."

My mother stopped short. "Why were you looking at Mrs. Solansky's pubic hair?"

"Because it was there," I said. "I didn't mean to look, but Mrs. Solansky had just taken a shower and I snuck a peek when her towel came undone."

After that, my mother suggested that Janie Solansky come to my house instead of my going to hers. But, natural blonde or not, I still held Mindy Solansky in high esteem for a myriad of reasons that my mother would never understand. She spoke and dressed differently, and she was the only divorced woman in our neighborhood. Her long, blonde hair cascaded down her back while the rest of our moms were carefully cropped brunettes, not "Bombshells" like Mrs. Solansky—a term my father used to describe her.

Mindy "The Bombshell" Solansky always dressed up. Unlike my mother, an interior decorator who spent most of her evenings shuffling through *House & Garden* magazines or making pot roasts, I could not recall Mrs. Solansky ever wearing an apron.

What I do remember was her array of cashmere sweater sets, toreador pants, and a string of cultured pearls. Her nails were polished with Revlon's Fire and Ice and she had red lipstick to match. She always looked perfectly put-together.

She had her own way of raising a daughter, which was alien to the way I was brought up. Janie was one of those girls who kept her Days of the Week underpants folded in neat little piles starting with Monday and ending with Sunday. Janie once wore a Wednesday on a Friday and Mindy went ballistic. "Darling," she said, "you need to stay consistent." In the Solansky household, matters of underwear were of vital importance.

I envied Janie, who made monthly visits to a dermatologist in Manhattan, a half hour from Teaneck. I thought it was exciting to go into the city and see a doctor who gave her expensive salves for her face. Yet, despite all her dermatology visits, Janie still had the worst case of acne of any girl in our class. After each of her doctor's appointments, Janie and Mindy had lunch at Hick's and ended up at Saks where, on her eleventh birthday, Janie was treated to her first pair of nylon stockings.

My mother's treatment was simpler: "Don't squeeze your pimples," she hollered.

Mindy Solansky never raised her voice or admonished Janie publicly. Even then I knew that was because Bombshells were soft-spoken and genteel. They could get their points across without histrionics. Mindy did, however, make Janie wear white muslin gloves to bed so her hands wouldn't touch her face.

Janie and Mindy were a real team. They even dieted together. While I wolfed down bacon and turkey club sandwiches with Hellmann's real mayonnaise, Janie grew thin eating cottage cheese on a bed of lettuce with a maraschino cherry on the top.

I aspired to be exactly like Mindy Solansky. I watched her carefully, trying to pick up tips on how to be a Bombshell. My mother had common sense. Mindy Solansky had pizzazz. My mother arranged furniture and smelled of Lemon Pledge. Mindy the Bombshell smelled of Shalimar and spoke in a breathless whisper. I practiced talking like Mrs. Solansky, too.

On those occasions when I was allowed back at Janie's house, I snuck off to Mindy's room and sprayed a little Shalimar on my wrists and painted my stubby fingernails with Fire and Ice, which my mother made me remove as soon as I came home. Life at the Solanskys' always seemed magical and forbidden.

Wednesday afternoons, Mindy Solansky drove into the city for matinees with her friends. On those days, Janie and I would go to her house where the maid served us lemonade and vanilla wafers. Then, we would retreat to the Bombshell's bedroom where all sorts of marvelous adventures awaited. Mindy Solansky had the largest bedroom I had ever seen, her four-poster bed was fit for a queen. The comforter matched the draperies, which matched the cushions, which matched the dust ruffles, which matched the wallpaper. Matching was important to Mindy Solansky.

"Never wear navy socks with white shoes," she once told me when I was sitting in their dining room having lunch. At the Solansky house, one never ate in the kitchen. One dined formally in their dining room, whether it be a steak or tuna fish sandwiches.

"They're only sneakers," I said.

"Even so," the Bombshell replied. "If you're going to wear white sneakers, you must wear white socks. Remember that."

I told my mother what Mindy Solansky had said.

Despite the fact that color coordination meant everything to my mother, and though she was the swatch queen of Teaneck, who had built her reputation on "you-can't-go-wrong-with-black," when it came to Mindy Solansky and her opinion on socks, my mother and Mindy parted company.

"Don't hand me that," my mother said. "You'll wear whatever socks are in your drawer, whether they match or not."

There was no denying that Elaine Schmerzler, my mother, and Mindy Solansky, my idol, were never destined to be best friends.

I knew that my mother was smarter than Janie's, yet it was Mindy Solansky who became my role model for everything . . . especially men. One particular Saturday night during a sleepover at Janie's, a dark, swarthy, and handsome man with a greased pompadour rising high above his hairline arrived to take Mindy Solansky on a date. While he waited in the living room, sipping Harvey's Bristol Cream, Mindy the Bombshell was upstairs dressing to kill. Janie and I watched from the foyer as she appeared on the landing in a burgundy brocaded jacket, a long velvet skirt, and a blouse with a plunging neckline. Her blonde hair was piled high on her head, and swirled into a French twist, secured by a rhinestone comb. She wore deep, crimson lipstick, making her ivory skin translucent and her aura seductive. Mindy Solansky was a real knockout.

I kept that picture of Mrs. Solansky in my mind for years. I grew up believing that if I played my cards right, and followed The Bombshell's beauty regimen, I could grow up having porcelain skin and handsome men in my life. I would be fascinating and mysterious and have a je ne sais quoi quality like hers.

"Mrs. Solansky goes out with men who look like movie stars," I told my parents over dinner.

My father cocked back his head and laughed, while my mother threw another drumstick on his plate.

"Mindy Solansky is a real babe," my father said, "a Bombshell all the way."

My mother shot him a look, then snuck off to reapply her lipstick and run a comb through her hair, so maybe, if she tried hard, she could be a babe, too.

In a nutshell, Janie's mother—my inspiration—personified all that was blonde and beautiful. Yes, Mindy *was* a real babe, while most of us had mothers who were simply . . . moms.

The last time I saw Janie and her mother was ten years later when I had moved out of my parents' house, and bumped into them purely by accident at the Chanel counter in Saks. Janie looked terrific. Her skin had cleared up nicely. She married a dermatologist from Philadelphia and had three kids. She spoke in a breathless whisper. Mindy Solansky, pushing seventy, never remarried. Rumor was she didn't want to share her wealth with anyone. Her once ivory skin, now leathery, had been baked too long in the Boca Raton sun where she resided for many years. Janie took me aside and told me that her mother was still going strong, and was on her third facelift. Mindy was wearing a baby blue cashmere sweater set and her string of pearls. She wore too much blush and her false eyelashes were caked in mascara. Her platinum blonde hair made her look like a fading vaudeville glamour girl of the '30s. But, all I could think of was that afternoon at Janie's house when Mindy's black bush was unveiled.

The three of us stood there eyeing one another up and down as we filled in the blank spaces of our respective lives. Then Mindy Solansky looked down at my feet.

"You should never wear patent leather shoes until after Memorial Day," she said.

If my mother had been there, she would have told Mindy "the Bombshell" Solansky to drop dead.

As I moved past my adolescence into an uncertain future, Mindy Solansky's legacy remained. More than anyone else she was my measuring rod for all I aspired to become. Despite my fancy education and my marriage to Maxwell E. Posner (the "E" for egomaniac), one of the most eligible bachelors in Manhattan, more than all the "be careful"s my mother flung at me daily, the mental image of Mindy Solansky descending the stairs in all her blonde glory was frozen in time. I had learned from the best. Mindy, by her very presence, had shown me there was more to life than being a brunette, and that eventually the outrageous blonde inside me would emerge. I could be a Bombshell, too. All I needed was time.

PHOTO: © MARK MEYERS

JUDITH MARKS-WHITE joined the staff of *Westport News* in Westport, Connecticut, in 1985, penning a humorous/reflective column about life, love, and family in the United States. She also worked for Time Inc. and has taught writing in Connecticut for many years. She has received numerous writing awards from The New England Press Association, The National Federation of Press Women, The Connecticut Press Club, and Matrix: Women in Communications. She is a member of the National Society of Newspaper Columnists and the National Association of American Pen Women. She has contributed to many anthologies including *Chicken Soup for the Mother and Daughter Soul*, *Chicken Soup for the Father and Daughter Soul*, *I Killed June Cleaver*, *Pandemonium: or Life with Kids*, and numerous publications on a variety of humor. She lectures frequently to wide audiences on The Writing and Marketing of Humor and other related topics. In March 2003, she was honored as one of the Ruth Steinkraus-Cohen Outstanding Women in Connecticut, celebrating her achievement and dedication to public service through the art of column writing. *Seducing Harry: An Epicurean Affair* is her first novel. She lives in Westport, Connecticut, with her husband, Mark (who, she would like to clarify, is not the model for either Harry or Parker). She is working on her second novel. Visit her website: www.judithmarks-white.com